THE RULES

PROJECT PAPER DOLL

STACEY KADE

HYPERION
NEW YORK

First Disney Hyperion paperback edition, 2014

1 3 5 7 9 10 8 6 4 2

V475-2873-0-14015

Printed in the United States of America

Library of Congress Catalog-in-Publication for Hardcover: 2012023957

ISBN 978-1-4231-5379-5

Visit www.hyperionteens.com

To Susan, my sister and my best friend. You've always been there for me (well . . . after you were born. Not much you could do about the twelve years and 361 days before that, I suppose). Thank you. I love you, and I'm thankful every day that you are part of my life.

PROLOGUE

Ariane Tucker

I HAVE A DEAD GIRL'S NAME. TECHNICALLY, I SUPPOSE I have a dead girl's life. Either way, I've had them both now longer than she did, so I guess they're mine.

The original—or maybe the real—Ariane Tucker lay dying in a hospital bed five hundred miles away even as I first tasted fresh air, saw the sky, or experienced the world outside the small white room where I'd lived for as long as I could remember.

I try not to think about that because, as horrible as it may sound, I'm grateful to Ariane for her death. I owe her my freedom.

If she'd been a happy, healthy child, I don't think her father—now my father—would have done what he did. Plucked me out of the darkness and saved me when the walls were shaking and the air was full of smoke.

But that Ariane Tucker was fully human.

I'm not.

So there are Rules that come along with my being Ariane. They're simple but essential for my safety and my father's:

1. Never trust anyone.
2. Remember they are *always* searching.
3. Don't get involved.
4. Keep your head down.
5. Don't fall in love.

I followed these Rules faithfully for ten years, once I was old enough to understand what they meant. The trouble with rules, though, is that you'll always be tempted to break one—for the right reasons, due to unavoidable circumstances, because it feels as if there's no other choice. And once you break one, the rest seem like so much broken glass. The damage is already done.

CHAPTER 1

Ariane Tucker

ESTABLISHING A ROUTINE IS ESSENTIAL FOR HIDING IN plain sight. Full-blooded humans are very habitual, as it turns out. They eat the same thing for breakfast for weeks on end, park in the same spaces, and buy the same brand of toothpaste. The best way to blend in was to follow suit. To create my own patterns and follow them without exception. Of course, in my case it was an artificial construction, not the result of naturally occurring preferences or, let's face it, a severe lack of imagination.

But *they* didn't know that.

So, Tuesday morning, first day of my junior year: Tuesday equals cornflakes. Morning, particularly on the first day of school, equals conversation with my father.

In the beginning, these father/pseudo-daughter talks were in preparation for my life outside: to discuss the challenges I would face throughout the day, the exercises I needed to practice, and the plans my father had made to further my assimilation. He worked nights, so morning was the only time available and, conveniently, the only part of the day where I hadn't screwed up yet.

These days, though, our morning conversations were more often just catch-up, with a little, "Hey, remember you're not like everybody else." Like I needed *that* reminder.

But today was different, and it shouldn't have been. It didn't start out that way.

The kitchen TV, positioned on the counter by the sink for optimal viewing, was tuned in to Fox News. The shrill voices of the morning-show hosts debating the latest conspiracy polluted the air with noise, fear, and chaos. As usual.

"Really?" I asked my father, who was already sitting at the table with his bowl of cornflakes.

He grunted noncommittally, his gaze glued to the crawl on the bottom of the screen. He'd been obsessed with the news lately, particularly anything to do with a senate hearing committee investigating the misappropriation of funds within the Department of Defense. Once a military man, always a military man, I guess.

I took my seat next to him with a sigh. It wasn't that the TV people—who must have received vocal training to hit that perfect blend of righteous outrage and near panic—were wrong, exactly. Their government *was* keeping secrets. I was living proof of that. They were just worried about all the wrong things. All the time. It was frustrating to watch, honestly.

"You know," I said, "studies have shown that watching this stuff makes you ten percent more paranoid and seventy-eight percent more likely to buy an old missile silo and convert it into a personal bunker for postapocalyptic living."

That caught my father's attention. He gave me a sour look, telling me exactly what he thought of my made-up statistics. "It wouldn't kill you to be more politically aware," he said, pointing his spoon at me.

I reached for the cornflakes. "A lot of things won't kill me," I said. In fact, that list was much longer for me than for a full-blooded human. "But that's not much of a recommendation, is it?" I poured cereal into my bowl and held up one of the flakes. " 'Taste this. You'll survive it!' Coming soon to cereal boxes and commercials everywhere."

He rolled his eyes. "Funny."

I grinned. "I can be. Occasionally."

"Less often than you think, kiddo." But he was smiling with a fondness that still took me by surprise. "So," he said, hitting the mute button on the remote, "first day of school again. Do you have everything you need to—"

His cell phone trilled, a soft but intrusive sound that startled both of us. He didn't often get work calls at home.

He plucked the phone off his belt and squinted at the screen, holding it out at arm's length so he could read it. He'd forgotten his reading glasses again.

I kept eating, waiting for him to declare it a wrong number or to roll his eyes and mutter something about Kagan being an idiot. I had no idea who Kagan was, but apparently, according to my father, he achieved Olympic standards of idiocy on a regular basis.

Instead, I watched as the color drained from my father's face.

Fear turned my mouth to sand, the bits of cornflake now unswallowable little rocks. "What's wrong?"

My father shoved back from the table, the phone in his hand. "Stay here," he ordered, and headed toward his den. A moment later I heard the door snap shut.

I put down my spoon with a shaky hand. Other children had nightmares about clowns, monsters, and—in my friend Jenna's case—the Hamburger Helper hand from the commercials. I often dreamed about big black vans pulling soundlessly into our driveway and faceless men snatching me from my bed before I could scream.

I got up and spat my cereal into the sink and rinsed my mouth out with water. My head was spinning with horrible scenarios, each worse than the last, a veritable catalog of everything that could be wrong.

I could have tried to listen in on the conversation—not my father's words, but his thoughts. But that ability—like much of me—didn't function nearly as efficiently as intended. And on top of that, my father was not easy to read. I could get virtually nothing from him unless he wanted me to, thanks to the intensive mental training he'd undergone during his years of service.

Still, there was one thing I knew for sure: if they were coming, it was already too late for me. I'd have time only to hide, not escape, and that would do no good.

In theory, I should have had nothing to fear. A dozen soldiers or "retrieval specialists" were supposed to be a minor obstacle for someone like me. But I wasn't quite up to spec in that regard. At least not anymore.

My heart fluttered unevenly in my chest, reminding me

that, no matter how much I sometimes hated it, I was part human. Weak.

I sat back down and picked up my spoon, examining my upside-down reflection in the bowl of it. Had someone recognized me?

I look human enough to "pass," of course. All part of the design. Don't want people freaking out about an alien spy/assassin; that might lower the odds of my being able to walk up to someone and pick their brain for information, or, you know, kill them.

But passing wasn't quite the same as blending in. That, I had to work at.

I reviewed the alterations to my appearance in the distorted view, reassuring myself that my camouflage was still intact.

Lowlights in my too-light hair brought it closer to the human range of color. But the texture was still off—heavy and soft, but it caught on fingertips like the raw silk shirt Jenna had appropriated from her mom's closet last year—and it grew out with strange bends and kinks in it, which I hated. So I kept it pulled up in a ponytail or in a messy knot that hopefully looked deliberately, artistically disarrayed instead of barely controlled.

Colored lenses made my eyes a murky but human blue, disguising the unnatural darkness of my irises—they were virtually indistinguishable from my pupils.

My skin was slightly too pale, verging on a silvery gray in some lights, but there was nothing I could do about that. It wasn't enough to be noticeable, really, unless I stood next to someone who'd fake-baked to a Cheeto orange . . . or if you knew what you were looking for.

And there were people who did. Far too many of them.

Was that what the phone call was about? I swallowed, my throat suddenly painfully dry.

My only saving grace so far was that their attention had been focused on locations far from their own backyard. I lived less than ten miles from GenTex Labs, home to Project Paper Doll and site of my very own personal hell.

My father returned to the kitchen suddenly, catching me by surprise. I slapped my spoon in place, producing a louder than expected crack, and we both flinched.

"Is everything okay?" I asked.

He nodded wearily, but I could tell he was distracted. He didn't sit down, just leaned forward with his hands braced on the table as if he needed the support.

A pulse of fear sent me to my feet, and my chair tipped over backward. "Do you need your pills? I have them right here on the windowsill." My father was not young. He was still in good shape—thanks, he said, to the regimented training he'd picked up from being Special Forces in his twenties—but he would be fifty-six this year. He'd gone completely gray in the years I'd known him, and while his gaze was as sharp as ever, lately he'd taken to moving as if he carried a heavy weight on his shoulders. Last year, I'd ignored every lesson he'd ever taught me and called 911 when I found him collapsed on the floor in the hall, gasping for air. It turned out to be a panic attack, brought on by stress. He also had spectacularly high blood pressure, another sign that his body was not handling the demands of his life very well. Wonder why.

I started toward him, but he waved me off. "I'm fine. I

already took my meds this morning. Go on to school. You don't want to be late."

No, because that would be a violation of Rule #4: *Keep your head down.* When my father had first given me that rule I'd taken it literally, which hadn't helped matters. A second grader walking around with her head ducked down below her shoulders wasn't exactly normal looking. Hey, you try living in a secret underground lab for the first six years of your life and see if your understanding of the metaphorical isn't a little shaky.

The point is, people notice you when you are late. But they also notice when you are early.

I felt a fresh rush of frustration at walking this so-fine-as-to-be-almost-invisible line. GTX didn't own me, not anymore. But they still controlled my life, down to the smallest details. And sometimes that was the worst part.

I could never have anyone at the house or go over to anyone else's. I had to keep to myself, but not so much that they would worry about my being socially dysfunctional and force me into counseling. I lived with the constant fear of standing out in some way, even if it was for something good. I would be a B student forever even though I'd surpassed the high-school-level curriculum years ago. B's were the perfect nondescript grade, not low enough to attract teacher intervention, and not high enough to rate nomination for the honor society.

I hadn't even been able to go with my father when the ambulance took him to the hospital last year. GTX often lends out their specialists, and one of the doctors might have recognized me.

That was my life. And it would be for the next two interminable years, until I could escape under the cover of all the other graduating seniors.

Once I was gone from Wingate I'd be free. Well, freer, I suppose. I'd never be able to relax completely, never be able to just exist without thinking hard about who or what I was supposed to be. But living farther away from GTX—and the omnipresent sense of danger—would help, at least a little.

I pushed my chair up into place, but I didn't leave right away. I had to know. "Are they on to us?" I asked, forcing the words past a sudden lump in my throat. My father still worked for GTX—he had to. Quitting after their prized possession up and disappeared would have looked suspicious. As far as anyone there knew, I was the daughter he'd gained full custody of after the death of his ex-wife in Ohio. And his staying at GTX did provide at least one major advantage: he had sources throughout the company who were usually able to tell him what was in the offing well in advance.

He looked up, startled. "No, Ariane. No. It's nothing like that. Just something I need to handle."

I nodded stiffly. I would die before I'd let GTX take me or punish my father for helping me.

"You don't have to worry." He reached out and touched my shoulder carefully, gingerly.

I forced myself not to flinch away. Sometimes I wasn't so good with being touched. It was yet another way in which I could be caught. Most people didn't avoid a casual touch as if it might cause them to burst into flame. Then again, most people hadn't spent years being poked, prodded, and broken (deliberately) for the sake of scientific advancement.

"Okay." I tried to smile, wishing my father looked more certain or less gray—that was my territory—and pulled away as soon as I could, my heart thundering away on the slow-to-fade rush of adrenaline.

Sometimes I could almost forget. Those days in the lab seemed so far away, a nightmare with a little too much detail. Other times . . . well, let's just say today was going to be one of *those* days.

"Ari!"

The shout came from above me in the crowded and noisy gym, loud enough to make me jump. Twitchy was my middle name today.

Actually, I don't know if I have a middle name, come to think of it. I've never seen the birth certificate that is, theoretically, mine.

I watched the crowd as heads turned, some toward the shouter but most of them toward me. It felt like a spotlight was shining down on me here on the floor.

I winced. *Thanks, Jenna.* I found her bright and eager face in the second set of bleachers, about six rows up. She was waving furiously as if I hadn't heard her—as if half the school hadn't heard her. It wasn't her fault, though. That was just Jenna. Enthusiasm turned up to eleven. I envied her that. If relentless optimism and determined cheerfulness were actually requirements for the cheerleading squad at Ashe (instead of heavy eyeliner and rumored sluttiness), then Jenna would have been captain. Maybe even a squad unto herself.

I headed deeper into the gym and then picked my way up the bleachers toward her—stepping around legs stretched out into the aisle, backpacks tossed carelessly in the way. With every step I felt people watching. Most of the school was here this morning—forced containment before the first bell to keep us "out of mischief." Uh-huh. As if there weren't plenty of time for that later in the day. It seemed to me that the teachers didn't want to give up their valuable gossiping-over-coffee time to monitor the halls before school.

No matter what my father said, it might have been worth the risk of being late to avoid this cattle call. A thousand minds in one place, buzzing with the anxiety, excitement, and sheer terror of the first day of school, made my head hurt. All the practice in the world couldn't block the tsunami of thoughts and emotions.

But as long as I kept myself from focusing on it—harder than you'd think—it was just a distant and vaguely annoying hum in the back of my brain. Like a radio tuned to hundreds of stations all at once.

"You're here!" Jenna squealed as I reached her row. She stood up and leaned over three people I didn't recognize to squeeze me in a hug that was just short of painful.

I'd been expecting it—the hug was Jenna's handshake—so it wasn't too bad. She knew I wasn't, in her words, "touchy-feely," but that seemed only to act as incentive for her to break me into it. Which had, more or less, worked. I trusted Jenna enough that I could quell my usual panic at someone being in my personal space. It wasn't like she was going to spring a surprise syringe on me, unlike various lab techs over the years. And sometimes that casual affection was nice. A reminder that I was real, that someone could see me, even if it was a false version of "me."

Besides, attempting to pull free would just hurt her feelings and possibly land me with a cracked rib or two. Not an exaggeration. My bones are fragile. Part of that whole space-faring-race thing. No gravity, less bone density or something.

I patted Jenna's back awkwardly, which met her requirements for a response most of the time, and she released me.

"I have the best news," she said, her eyes sparkling. She turned to the strangers, who were watching all of this like a reality show playing out in front of them. "Do you mind moving down for my friend here?" she asked without a hint of sarcasm.

The three of them, two girls and a boy—freshmen probably, judging from how young they looked and the overwhelmed and slightly terrified expressions on their faces—squished together to make room for me.

Jenna sat and pulled me down next to her. "Why didn't you answer my texts?"

Because answering would have led only to more texts and the demand for me to come over eventually. Jenna's house was classified as strictly forbidden.

"My dad. You know that," I said, using the too-familiar term that I never applied to him in person. Well, I had once. It had just slipped out over breakfast one morning about a year after I'd been living with him. *Can I have more toast, Dad?*

I hadn't intentionally been testing my boundaries with

him (for once), but I'd found one nonetheless. He'd winced like it physically hurt him to hear the word.

He'd recovered quickly, handing over the plate and asking me if I wanted more peanut butter, as if nothing was wrong. But it was too late. I'd seen his reaction, and I knew what it meant. I might have his daughter's name, but I would never be her.

So I called him Father, when I had to call him anything, and that seemed to be okay with him. But every time I thought or said that, it reminded me of the moment with the toast. Reminded me that even though he loved me and had risked his life for me, I would never be quite enough.

"Summer is family time," I said to Jenna, reciting the excuse my father had given me to use when Jenna first started asking to me to come over—the summer after our freshman year.

Jenna rolled her eyes. "God, he is so strict." She impatiently brushed her blond hair away from her too-pink cheeks. "Which means you spent another summer in virtual reality."

My face grew hot. I looked around for anyone who might have been listening. Last year, I had, in a moment of weakness, confessed a secret to Jenna. Not the big one, of course. But still one I'd rather not have spread around.

She nudged me with her elbow gently. "And how is life in Dreamville? Perfectly perfect, as usual?" she asked, with a grin.

I cleared my throat. "It's fine," I said, resisting the urge to shush her. Not that this secret was anything bad, just embarrassing. "What's going on with you? What's your big news?" I asked quickly, hoping she'd take the bait and change the subject. For Jenna, most of the fun came from sharing. And it could be just about anything—a sale on lip gloss with glitter, a new guy in school, or a diet that she was convinced would help her lose five pounds, the last obstacle to popularity, in her mind.

She brightened immediately. "So, last week, I'm coming home from dropping off Bradley at the pool, right?"

Bradley was Jenna's younger brother. I nodded.

"And you'll never guess who I bumped into at the mailbox." She bounced excitedly in her seat.

A very bad feeling started in my stomach.

"Rachel Jacobs!" she crowed, squeezing my forearm in excitement. This time, I practically heard my bones creaking and had to pull away.

"Carpal tunnel," I managed weakly, in answer to her frown. But my mind was spinning too quickly for words. Rachel Jacobs? Rachel was behind this too-happy glow of Jenna's? This story could not end well.

Jenna's goal since moving to Wingate our freshman year had been to break through her middle-of-the-road status—not popular, not unpopular—and become one of the revered ones, a member of Rachel's inner circle. At her old school, she'd told me, she'd been too shy, too sensitive, too easily dissuaded from getting what she wanted. But she was determined to change all of that here at Ashe.

That alone might have made it impossible for us to be friends, except Jenna wasn't having a lot of luck with her mission. She wasn't an athlete. She was cute but not heart-stoppingly beautiful. Her family was rich—her mom's an orthodontist and her dad's a senior partner at some big law firm in Milwaukee—but they didn't shower her with cash and ridiculous leniency. Her curfew was earlier than mine on weeknights, believe it or not.

But more important, she wanted it too badly. That was an automatic disqualification, as far as I could tell.

Plus, Rachel Jacobs was evil. Well, not evil as in demonic-possession or hell-spawn-wandering-the-earth evil; though occasionally she made me wonder. No, just plain old enjoy-the-pain-you-bring-other-people-because-it-makes-you-feel-better-about-yourself evil. And she came by it honestly: her grandfather, Arthur, was the head of GTX. The CEO, in fact, and the man responsible for my very existence. If you think that should make me grateful to him, let me remind you that existing is not the same as living. And in the six years I'd *existed* at GTX, he'd done enough to make me regret even that.

I'd done my best to steer Jenna away from Rachel whenever possible. But they were neighbors, and there was nothing I could do about that. It was the primary reason why Jenna's house was off-limits for me.

The real trouble was, Jenna had no survival skills. As much as I cared about her—she was probably the only human besides my father that I would fight to protect—she was a little like a brain-damaged rabbit that kept hopping too near the snake, convinced that they could be BFFs if they took the time to get to know each other. She really thought that friendliness would win out over everything else.

"We've been hanging out every day since," Jenna said triumphantly.

I stared at her, baffled. That made absolutely no sense. Jenna wanted to be Rachel's friend so bad that it gave Rachel a perverse pleasure in denying her the opportunity. I'd watched it play out in front of me last year. And Rachel hadn't even attempted to justify it in her thoughts. (In spite of my thought-reading limitations, I could almost always hear Rachel, except in the most crowded of rooms. She was a loud thinker, operating at a higher decibel than most everyone else. As though even her thoughts suffered from too much self-importance, wanting to be proclamations instead of random scatterings in her brain.)

"Really?" I asked, trying not to sound too skeptical. "Did she say—"

The bell rang, and suddenly the crowd moved as one, a lumbering giant made up of a thousand tiny parts. Thoughts and emotions reached a fevered pitch and spiked through my brain like an ice pick to the skull.

Jenna picked her way down the bleacher stairs, talking to me the whole time; but between the noise echoing in the gym and the chaos inside my head, I missed most of what she was saying.

". . . at the pool because Cami and Cassi were in Paris . . ."

Okay, that could be one piece of the puzzle. Rachel was probably insecure enough to require an adoring audience at all times. With the twins gone, she might have been forced to desperate measures.

". . . and Zane was there!" Jenna reached the floor and turned to face me, her hands clutched over her heart as if it might bump right out of her chest, cartoon-style. (FYI, cartoons are terrifying when your grasp on how the real world works is tenuous, at best. I had nightmares about Wile E. Coyote and safes falling from the sky for weeks after first watching that show.)

"We talked," she said dreamily. "It was amazing."

I resisted the urge to roll my eyes. Zane Bradshaw. Thanks to Jenna's crush, I could recite every known fact about him. Lacrosse player, son of the Wingate Police Chief, favorer of nineties rock and those preppy button-down shirts. He was good-looking and almost freakishly tall, but built with enough muscle to keep from appearing strange. He was everything I would have found attractive—tall, broad shoulders, dark hair, and blue-gray eyes. (What can I say? I have a type. In the lab, as part of my "cultural training," I'd seen the original Superman movies from the seventies and early eighties, and they'd made a huge impression on me. At the time I'd wanted Superman to rescue me. But then when I got older and watched the newer versions, with Brandon Routh and Tom Welling, I may have, um, slightly altered that fantasy.)

But Zane Bradshaw—resemblance to my all-time crush aside—was one of the mindless flock. He followed Rachel Jacobs around, participating in all her mean reindeer games like he was missing the portion of his brain that allowed for independent thought. The only exception had been last year in Algebra II when he'd noticed I was using pen on my homework and thought it was strange. That had been a mistake on my part. I hadn't thought about the math being difficult for other people, which meant it probably should have been difficult for me, too. Hiding in plain sight means questioning every choice I make, thinking it through twenty different ways—all without looking like that's what I'm doing—and sometimes I screw up.

Fortunately, Zane didn't strike me as interested in much other than himself.

Jenna looped her arm through mine, more gently this time, as we waited for the crowd to move forward. "It was a good conversation, you know, and with it being Bonfire Week . . ." She bounced up on her toes in excitement.

Ugh. Bonfire Week. Ashe High had a stupid tradition that was supposed to help make freshmen feel welcome and rev everyone up for the coming year. They called it Bonfire Week even though it was only four days and the bonfire was the last night. There'd be an activities fair/carnival thing tomorrow night in the gym; a varsity vs. junior varsity exhibition football game on Thursday, where the cheerleaders, poms, and band would show off everything they'd learned in their various summer camps; and on Friday there'd be a bonfire, followed by a dance in the gym, which only the freshmen actually attended. Everyone else with a shred of social standing would be going to the unofficial bonfire party. Or so I'd heard. I'd never gone to any of it. Too risky. I didn't need that kind of exposure. The entire freaking town showed up for parts of it, and the parade on Saturday morning was sponsored by GTX. Uh, no.

"So, I think Zane might invite me to go with him. Not as his date, but just, you know, to hang out. Maybe. I don't know. What do you think?" Jenna looked at me, her face hopeful.

Oh. I scrambled to find an answer that would not completely crush her and yet be semi-truthful. Rumors had circulated for the last year or so that Rachel and Zane had hooked up, off and on, unofficially. *Scandalicious*, as Jenna would say. If those rumors were accurate, it seemed unlikely that Rachel would allow anyone to interfere with that; but if she truly was being friendly to Jenna . . .

"Anything is possible," I said finally, feeling the lameness of my response. *Possible* was definitely not the same as *probable.*

But Jenna didn't seem to notice. She brightened and gave my arm a painful squeeze. "I knew it." She let out a squeal, and I winced.

Then she took a deep breath. "Okay, so with all these new developments, I know you're probably worried about what's going to happen with you and me this year," she said as we walked through the gym doors and into the front hall.

Actually, no. I hadn't yet gotten past my confusion about Rachel's new inconsistent behavior to think about anything like that.

"But I want you to know, I don't abandon my friends. I'm not like that."

And she wasn't. If she, by some chance, ended up on the periphery of Rachel's circle—Rachel might very well have recognized the wisdom of keeping a follower who would eat shredded glass to keep her happy—then Jenna would drag me kicking and screaming with her.

Terrific. Then I'd be the one leaving Jenna. I really didn't want to have to do that. We'd only become friends because Jenna kind of hadn't given me a choice, sensing in me the same kind of loneliness that she'd felt as the new girl. But now it was more than that. I would miss her.

Jenna continued chattering away as we climbed the steps, but it wasn't until we reached the second-floor hallway that I started picking up on something strange in the air, a vibe I couldn't place. It was a strong thread of excitement, anticipation, and dread—but from more than one person and loud enough to catch my attention, which was unusual.

I kept nodding at Jenna and tried to hone in on what I was sensing.

Hearing thoughts is never like what you see on television or read in books. People don't walk around thinking in complete sentences, let alone entire paragraphs of exposition.

If GTX's experiment had continued after me, there would have been whole teams of people like me—all of us able to communicate silently with one another as we spied on the enemy or moved in for a kill.

But with untrained human minds, it was a mess. Everybody shouting scattered words and phrases at the top of their lungs, essentially. And sometimes I only got pictures or feelings. It was hard to tell what was going on in someone's head—on the rare occasions when I wanted to—especially when there were lots of people around, jostling and shoving, their minds as jumbled and out of sorts as their bodies.

. . . not me. Thank God.

. . . just so mean . . .

. . . makes me look fat. I know it.

This is going to be awesome!

If Mrs. McCafferty puts me in the front row again, I'm going to . . .

"Don't you think?" Jenna asked, nudging me.

"Uh-huh," I said, distracted. I wasn't getting enough to piece it together. We were on the move, and so was everyone else, which made it impossible to isolate one mind. The best I could determine was that the people buzzing about whatever was going on were coming from the opposite direction. The people around us, slowly moving upstream in the hall, were still caught up in their mundane worries about homeroom and what they were wearing.

Jenna laughed. "You spaced on me again, didn't you?"

I grimaced. "Sorry. Just thinking things through." Normally I would have let it go. The last time I'd sensed so many minds in an uproar, the cafeteria had been serving french fries on a Tater Tot day. Who cares?

But this . . . this was different. It felt more personal, and I didn't know why.

"Zane!" Jenna chirped, and bolted ahead of me.

Bradshaw was leaning against a wall, head and shoulders above everyone else, right at the intersection by our lockers.

A quick flash of weary patience crossed his face when he saw Jenna, but he hid it quickly enough that she didn't catch it, thankfully. He greeted her civilly enough, and paid attention to whatever she was describing with great animation—lots of big hand motions, exaggerated expressions, and giggling.

Oh God, Jenna . . . No matter what had happened over the last week, one thing I could guarantee had not occurred was Zane Bradshaw developing a sudden interest in a girl he'd never acknowledged as alive before.

I cringed in expectation of some humiliating putdown, but Zane just smiled down at Jenna with that same mildly exasperated benevolence humans usually reserve for adorable puppies trying to chew their shoelaces.

We shouldn't have done it.

The clarity of that single thought and the punch of accompanying shame from Zane blasted through the rest of the noise.

That's when I got one image from Zane Bradshaw's head loud and clear, no distortion.

A locker smeared with some kind of white paste, the words "Pain In My Ass" scrawled in flowing cursive at the top, flattened tubes of Preparation H dangling from the ventilation slats where the contents had been squeezed inside . . . and Rachel's smiling face.

Oh no. I knew her friendship with Jenna was too good to be true. Rachel had simply traded in the immediate pleasure of crushing Jenna for something a little more long-term and hateful.

"Jenna!" I shoved through people to get to her, ignoring the verbal and mental protests as my elbows connected with unprotected sides. "Jenna!"

"What?" She looked around at me, startled. Her cheeks were pink, and her eyes were sparkling.

"We need to go . . . uh . . ." I fumbled to find words, trying to push past my desire to grab her arm and haul her away without explanation. Without meaning to, I glanced up at Zane, who looked away. *Coward.* All he would have had to do was lead her off or ask her to go with him anywhere, and she wouldn't have thought twice about it. She wouldn't have thought *once* about it.

"I need juice," I blurted. Jenna was always on me about

what I ate, or didn't eat. To say that I had food issues would be putting it mildly. Fortunately, that helped me blend right in with about every other girl at Ashe. "The nurse's office. I forgot to eat breakfast again, and now I'm feeling kind of out of it, like I'm going to faint. . . ." I kept babbling until Jenna nodded, her forehead crinkled with concern.

"I think I've got breakfast bars in my bag. Let me drop off my stuff and dig them out. Stay here with Zane."

Before I could stop her, she darted around Zane and the corner to her locker.

Crap, crap, CRAP.

I followed her, praying that the crowd of spectators would be too large for her to see her locker before I could get to her again.

But as always happens in situations like this—people parted like a set of automatic doors on her approach.

I saw it at the same time she did. She froze midstep, her shoulders stiff and her head cocked to one side, as if she wasn't sure of what she was seeing.

The wisest thing for me to do would have been to walk away. Pretend I didn't see it. I couldn't afford to get involved, not with so many people watching. They'd notice. They'd talk. Both were too dangerous to contemplate, especially after I'd spent years cultivating a status just this side of invisible.

Jenna's shoulders started to shake.

I couldn't just stand there and watch her fall apart.

I rushed to her side. "Listen to me," I said in a hurried whisper. "We are going to walk right past like we don't even see it. We're going straight to the bathroom and—this is the important part—you cannot cry until you're inside."

She didn't respond.

I gave her arm a shake. "Do you hear me?"

Jenna nodded, her head moving a fraction of an inch, but I could hear her breathing getting choked, the way it did every time she called me after watching *The Notebook*.

"If you cry in front of everyone, they win. Get it?"

"But why do they want to—" Her breath caught on a barely repressed sob.

"Doesn't matter. Let's just go." An unfamiliar pressure was building inside me. I was not going to let Rachel win this one.

With my hand on her arm, I pulled Jenna toward the bathroom, and thankfully, people moved out of our way.

"Oh my God, Jenna what happened to your locker?" Rachel asked as we passed by.

Jenna stiffened.

"Ignore her," I whispered.

Rachel sighed loudly.

A glance over my shoulder showed Rachel starting to follow us with an annoyed look. Yeah, being forced to walk somewhere to torture someone is *such* a hassle.

Before I could think it through, I shoved Jenna ahead of me toward the bathroom and moved to block Rachel's path.

My heart was pounding so hard it made my whole body shake. "You are going to go away now," I said quietly; but in the sudden silence surrounding us, I suspected that almost everyone heard me, even Zane in the distance. Evidently, he'd decided it would be worth it to watch the show.

Rachel laughed. "Excuse me, who are you again?"

I ignored her. "All of you," I said, directing my gaze toward Rachel's crowd—the twins and a bunch of Zane's buddies—a few feet behind her.

She faced off with me, the pointed tips of her stilettos (who wears shoes like that on the first day of school but Rachel Jacobs) almost touching my battered imitation Chucks.

"I think you need to mind your own business," she said.

Rachel was pretty. She was taller than me with long black shiny hair that looked expensive and high maintenance. She didn't resemble her grandfather at all except in the expression on her face. Hard eyes, mouth smiling but not really. It screamed, *You are nothing, and I can do whatever I want.*

Suddenly I was little and stuck in that lab again with no way out, and Dr. Jacobs was telling me that it was fine if I didn't want to cooperate. As long as I didn't mind being alone in the dark for a few days. After all, he couldn't pay his team to be here if I was going to waste their time.

Overhead, the lights flickered, and I couldn't stop it. Worse, I wasn't sure I wanted to. Echoing pops sounded as the lightbulbs exploded, and glass rained down.

People started screaming and running, Jenna's misery forgotten in their desire to protect themselves. One of Rachel's devotees, Trey, I think his name was, rushed up to pull Rachel under his arm and hustle her away.

Ah yes, I was striking terror in the hearts of humans everywhere. My planet-invading parents would have been so proud.

My Earth-based father? Way, way less so.

CHAPTER 2

Zane Bradshaw

"I MEAN, WHO DOES SHE THINK SHE IS?" RACHEL SAID with a loud huff.

Twelve hours later and she was *still* bitching about the thing with Ariane Tucker and Jenna Mayborne this morning.

I shook my head. As usual, when Rachel didn't get what she wanted, she had to make life miserable for *everyone*.

I was stretched out on two wooden benches on Rachel's enormous back deck, my eyes closed and my feet hanging off the end—one of the many disadvantages of life at six foot four. But it wasn't uncomfortable enough for me to move yet. I held a cold beer, my third, on my stomach. Condensation rolled down the bottle past my fingers to create a damp and chilly place on my shirt.

A few feet away, Rachel and the twins, her nearest and dearest cronies, moaned about Ariane over the slosh and splash of the hot tub.

"Rachel, she's only been in our class for forever." Cami

Andrews punctuated her disbelief with a slap of water. "She moved here from, like, Ohio. Her mom died and she came to live with her dad." She paused. "And she was really sick a long time ago or something, but she got better." I could hear the frown in her voice as she tried to remember the details.

Cassi seemed to be humming "The Star-Spangled Banner" under her breath, for no apparent reason.

"I *know* who she is," Rachel said, sounding further irritated. "I've heard her name before. It's just like, suddenly she comes out of nowhere and she's, what, Miss Morally Righteous, Defender of the Annoying? What business is it of hers, anyway?"

In theory, it had been none of Ariane's business at all, which made it all the more awesome. Not that I could say that aloud.

But the truth was, most people wouldn't stand up against Rachel even if she was torturing them directly. And quiet, sit-in-the-back-of-class Ariane had come to Jenna's defense, shocking the hell out of me and everyone else. The good timing of the unexpected special effects—apparently a transformer had blown a couple blocks away, which made the lights pop—hadn't hurt either, adding a whole *Carrie*-esque feel to the moment.

Ariane hadn't flinched, even with Rachel in full-confrontation mode and breathing fire. I never knew she had it in her—an unhesitating lack of fear. I admired the hell out of that.

"She's in my gym class," Cassi offered in her breathy voice. She and Cami had seemingly formed a pact early in life that Cami would be the smart one, relatively speaking, and Cassi would be the pretty one. This despite the fact that they were *identical* twins. Regardless, they each played their role to the hilt. "But she never participates," she added, sounding confused. "She sits on the bleachers. Or on the grass. But only when we're, you know, outside."

See what I mean?

"She was in my Advanced Comp class. I think," Cami said.

"What are we talking about?" Trey had evidently abandoned Matty and Jonas in the pool. His feet made splatting sounds on the deck as he approached.

"That *girl*," Rachel said, with a pout in her voice.

Oh God, not this again. I could predict how this was going to go. Rachel would be all needy and "love me, love me," Trey would swoop in and try to save the day, and then Rachel would find some way to bitch-slap him back to the last century. That's the trouble with having the same friends your whole life—you know what they're going to do before they do it. Various people on the fringes of our circle flowed in and out, depending on Rachel's mood, but at the core, it was always Trey and me and Rachel and the twins. Since that first day of kindergarten, when Rachel had picked our table to sit at and scored us all an extra cookie at snack time by telling us to hide the first ones we'd gotten.

"Babe, you're not still upset about her, are you?" A louder splash and a shriek from either Cami or Cassi meant Trey had joined them in the tub.

And here we go . . .

I opened my eyes and squinted in their direction long

enough to see Trey slipping his arm over Rachel's shoulders. I'd give that about three minutes.

"I've never even seen that girl before," he said, baffled. "She must be new, right?"

Dude. Trey. I sighed. He never saw anyone but Rachel. Especially not someone like Ariane Tucker, who looked as if she practiced being invisible. To be fair, I'd never paid much attention to her either, until last year when I sat behind her in Algebra II. Then, I don't know . . . no matter what my old man says, his eye for detail must have rubbed off on me. Something about Ariane was off in some vague, indefinable way. No one would probably describe her as pretty, but there was something about her that drew me in. Maybe *attractive* was a better word, in that I couldn't define what caught my eye, but it was impossible to look away once I noticed her. Most people didn't seem to notice her at all, which seemed more than fine with her. Another oddity.

I'd gathered pieces of the puzzle that was Ariane Tucker here and there—like how she always did her homework in ink. INK. Who does their math with a pen?—but never enough for them to add up to anything.

Today's events only gave me more mismatched details to work with, building my interest.

"Something you want to add, Zane?" Rachel's voice cut through the too-hot August air, bringing a chill with it.

"She always missed two questions." I wasn't sure why I spoke up. I knew better than to engage in Rachel's games. Blame it on the beer buzz or exhaustion from surviving the summer with my dad constantly on my case. I'd thought life would be better with Quinn—my perfect older brother—staying at college this summer to work. Less opportunity for direct comparison, and therefore less falling short on my part. But if anything, my dad was worse than ever.

I'd been living for the start of school until Rachel had to go and make things complicated this morning with her "joke." I was so tired of all this "we're better than everyone else" bullshit. I couldn't believe I'd once found it funny.

"What did you say?" Rachel demanded.

I stared up at the designer Japanese lanterns hanging above my head. "I sat behind Ariane in math last year. She always used pen, and she missed two questions on every test, quiz, assignment, everything." She was so much shorter than me, it had been easy to see over her shoulder when Mr. Scaliari handed back our stuff. I'd started paying attention when I noticed the ink thing.

"The same two questions?" Cami asked, frowning.

"No, different ones every time, but always two," I said. Which meant sometimes she got a 98 out of 100 and other times, when it was a three-question quiz, she completely failed.

Also, she smelled like lemons, but the real kind, not the fake dishwashing-soap stuff. I was pretty sure her hair was lighter than she wanted people to think—the dark streaks were dyed. It was possible there was trouble at home—she'd had splinted fingers four times last year. And I thought she might have a tattoo. The collar of her shirt had slipped back one day on her thin shoulders, and I'd seen the edge of one of those big square bandages. The kind my mom had used on my knees for those massive skateboarding wipeouts in my earlier days. Then, once I'd noticed that and knew to look for it, I saw the faint outline of a rectangle underneath her shirt in the same place every day. It couldn't have been an injury, not for that long. My next best guess was a tattoo, one she was ashamed of. It happened—an exercise in poor drunken judgment, usually on spring break. Marcos Pyter, one of the middies on our lacrosse team, put his ex-girlfriend's name on his arm *after* she was already his ex.

But quiet, obedient, possibly abused Ariane Tucker with an embarrassing tat? I couldn't make that fit. Then again, I couldn't make today's events square with what I knew of her either. And unlike Rachel, I was kind of fascinated.

"Whatever," Rachel said impatiently. "So she deliberately misses questions because she doesn't want anyone to know she's a brain or something. Who cares?"

A girl who took on Rachel Jacobs in front of a crowd didn't strike me as the type to worry about people thinking she was too smart.

"The point is, she shouldn't have gotten involved," Rachel continued. "It had nothing to do with her."

Trey rubbed her shoulders. "It doesn't matter, babe, does it? It's over. Mayborne got the message."

I groaned and shut my eyes, bored already with the inevitable fallout. Trey was a good guy, but he seemed doomed to repeat the same Rachel-related lessons over and over again.

"Trey! No!" she said. "She humiliated me in front of *everyone*. I can't let that go."

I could have pointed out that Ariane had been far from humiliating anyone. She'd just stood up for Jenna and refused to knuckle under—which, in Rachel's mind, was probably the equivalent of forcing her to lick someone's shoes.

Rachel didn't handle disappointment well. She hadn't had a lot of experience with it. Her parents were always gone, leaving extra money in her account and Rachel to her own devices most of the time. Her father traveled for GTX, and her mother was either with him or at a "spa" somewhere. Her grandfather, Dr. Jacobs, adored her. He showered her with expensive gifts—clothes, a car, vacations to any sunny island she wanted. (I'd once seen Rachel end one of these poolside kickbacks to take his call. He was always caught up at work, and I suspected she valued the rare moments of his attention more than anything he ever sent to the house in a big red bow; not that she'd admit it.)

Despite (or maybe because of) all of this, Rachel was extremely generous with those she deemed worthy. Trey, Cami, Cassi, and I had an open invitation to her house and everything that she owned, which was saying quite a bit. She treated us like family in place of her blood relatives.

But she expected blood loyalty in return.

The water sloshed loudly. "Jonas!" Rachel called in the direction of the pool. "Come here, I need you."

"Babe," Trey protested. "I'm right here—"

"Shut up. It's not about that." Rachel's voice had taken on a greedy intensity that I knew all too well.

I didn't like where this was going. Jonas tended to act first and think later, if at all. In Cub Scouts, on an overnight camping trip in fourth grade, he'd been showing off his supposed knowledge of karate *inside* the tent and snapped the main plastic support pole, collapsing the tent around us. In the rain.

I opened my eyes again.

Jonas jogged over from the pool. "What's up?" He raked a hand through his hair and flicked the water on Cassi to make her shriek.

Rachel rested her chin on her folded arms at the edge of the hot tub. "I want you to ask that Ariane girl to Bonfire Week."

Oh, not good. Rachel was scheming, and that never ended well for anyone but her.

Jonas's face fell comically. "Are you kidding?"

Rachel raised her eyebrows in response.

Jonas stepped back, shaking his head. "Oh, come on, Rachel," he pleaded. "I'm this close to sealing the deal with Lainey Pryce."

"Lainey Pryce will sleep with anyone," Cami said with distaste.

"Not since she went to church camp in June and became a born-again virgin." Jonas grinned. "Challenge accepted."

Yeah, these were my friends.

"So sleep with this one instead." Rachel waved a hand dismissively. "You want a challenge, she barely talks to anyone."

"Because she's a freak. I have a reputation, you know." But I could hear him wavering, tempted by the idea of trying his superpowers of seduction against Ariane. Jonas was all about the challenge and not so much dealing with the aftermath.

I sat up. "I'll do it." The words were out of my mouth

before I could stop them. What the hell was I saying? I didn't need this kind of trouble. I had more than enough already.

"What?"

I wasn't even sure who'd asked the question: Rachel, Trey, Cami, Cassi, and Jonas were all staring at me.

I shrugged. "I said I'll do it. I'll ask her to Bonfire Week."

Jonas exhaled loudly in relief. "Thanks, dude. You saved my life." He turned and headed back to the pool, shouting at Matty about a cannonball contest.

"You hate Bonfire Week," Trey said.

"I doubt Ariane's much of a fan either." I had trouble picturing her face painted in the school colors. "So we'll have that in common."

Rachel narrowed her eyes at me. "Why?"

"Why, what?" I stalled for time, knowing what was coming.

"Why are you suddenly Mr. Social when it comes to Ariane Tucker?"

"Rachel," Trey muttered in careful warning.

"No, for the last year he's been basically ignoring us. I think we have a right to know what has triggered his sudden return."

And there it was . . .

Rachel *would* bring that up. I already lived with the pitying looks and the whispers, though they'd faded somewhat over the last few months finally. Was it necessary to keep reminding everyone what had happened?

"You want someone to ask her out," I said. "And I've spoken to her a few times." A slight exaggeration. Unless you count learning that 2.333333 was not the answer to number 10 in the homework. And she'd barely glanced in my direction during that exchange. Still, I couldn't stand the thought of Rachel siccing someone else on her. What Ariane had done today took a lot of guts. She didn't deserve to be demolished by whatever Rachel had planned, and Jonas wouldn't give a damn. But I could try to stop it from getting out of hand.

I was tired of these games Rachel played, but it was too late to strike out on my own. I only had two years left here. It wasn't worth the effort. Not to mention, being friends with a member of the illustrious Jacobs family was pretty much the only thing I'd managed not to screw up, in my father's opinion.

Rachel cocked her head to one side, giving me a considering look. Then she stood up in the hot tub and stepped out. The ends of her dark hair were wet, and goose bumps covered the skin that was not covered by her red bikini.

I braced myself, expecting her to begin firing off questions, her suspicions aroused.

But instead she leaned down, smelling of chlorine and that heavy musky perfume she favored, and said, "Welcome back, Zaney." Then she brushed her mouth over mine, which shocked the hell out of me.

She strolled off toward the house, leaving me to deal with Trey, who was glaring at me like he wanted to set me on fire.

Great.

That was Rachel for you—always looking for the two-for-one when it came to causing chaos.

CHAPTER 3

Ariane

MY FATHER WAITED UNTIL MY SECOND BITE OF BREAKFAST on Wednesday (four scrambled eggs for my higher protein needs) for the ambush.

He slid a newspaper across the table. "Were you planning on telling me about this?" he asked, leaning forward in his chair.

The edge in his voice took me aback, as did the faint smell of alcohol on his breath. It wasn't really morning for him, as he'd yet to go to bed, but still. I hadn't seen him drink—at all—since the first few months of my life Outside, when he was mourning the loss of his daughter. I'd only been living with him for a couple weeks when he received word that she'd died. Back then, I would slip out of my room—which I wasn't supposed to do—and find him in the living room drinking scotch and staring at photos of his Ariane, which he normally kept hidden in the basement. He had not expected her to recover; I'd known that much when he'd given me her name. But that knowledge had not helped him in any way. If anything, it had only made his grief worse. He'd gone through a period where he always had a bottle in hand. But that was a long time ago.

So I knew even before looking at the newspaper, something was very wrong.

The article was in the middle of the paper and tucked beneath a gigantic ad for the local tire store, Rubber Mike's. I didn't read the whole thing; didn't have to.

Lights Out at Ashe High

An unexplained power surge yesterday morning shattered lightbulbs in an upper hallway of Ashe High School, raining glass shards down upon students. . . .

Crap. I sucked in a breath and choked on my eggs.

I'd stayed up late last night to watch the news and run a few Internet searches—not too many, in case GTX was monitoring—to see if the incident had caught media attention. But what wasn't big enough for TV or showy enough for the Internet (had to leave room for imploding celebrities and cute cats stuck in boxes) was just right for the Wingate local paper.

God, why did yesterday have to be the one day free of the small-town idiocy that normally dominated the paper, the day that someone *hadn't* stolen an entire neighborhood's worth of garden gnomes and arranged them in various sexual positions on the front lawn of the Methodist church?

(Actually, I'd found that pretty funny at the time. You can't get better examples of hypocrisy than people confronted with blatant—albeit gnomish—displays of sexuality. They get red-faced and blustery all the while intensely wishing they could get their significant other to try what the red gnome was doing to the blue garden fairy. You can't hide thoughts like that from me, people, not without a lot of training and practice. Genius advancement or design flaw, take your pick.)

Coughing, I spit the eggs into my napkin. "How bad is it?"

"Bad enough." My father looked grim and tired, but he wasn't shoving me toward the back door with an urgent whisper to flee, so I wasn't, it seemed, in immediate danger of being recaptured. I relaxed a fraction.

"Were you going to tell me?" he asked again, tapping his finger against the paper. He looked every inch the imposing head of security that he was. He was still wearing his uniform, and his shirt bore the impressions of his shoulder harness, though it and his gun were probably already locked in the safe in his bedroom. His jacket, emblazoned with the GTX logo, hung from the back of his chair. Normally he would have put it out of sight already, knowing how much I hated it.

(At some point in my very early life at GTX, maybe right after I was born, they'd marked me like livestock. My right shoulder blade held a tattoo of the GTX logo, a big stylized G, and my project designation, GTX-F-107, just beneath it in crude lettering. I wore a bandage over it to keep anyone from seeing it, but I still had to look at it in the mirror every day when I applied a new bandage. And the sight never failed to make me feel sick and so very angry.)

"I can't protect you if you're going to hide things from me," he added with a deep frown.

The censure in his voice made my stomach ache. I hated disappointing him, this man who'd risked everything for me. "I wasn't hiding it." I swallowed hard, avoiding his gaze. "It was just . . . nothing."

He didn't say anything, but his dark expression told me how "nothing" he thought it was.

"It was over as soon as it started," I added quickly. Like every other similar incident since my departure from GTX, though admittedly it had been almost a year since the last one (in which I might have turned a page in my English lit book without touching it) and this one was slightly higher profile. "Mr. Kohler made an announcement about it being a bad transformer, and no one thought anything about it."

"Were you in control?" my father asked.

I hesitated and then said, "No." Just like always, the barrier in my mind—the one that cut me off from the most powerful of my abilities—had fallen and then gone back up with no direction from me.

"Are you sure?" he persisted. Clearly we'd reached the interrogation portion of this conversation.

Yes, I'm sure, because if I'd had my way, there would have been a Rachel Jacobs–shaped hole in the wall instead of just a few broken lights. Not a good answer. "Pretty sure," I said instead. "And I tried again when I was alone, a few minutes later. No luck."

Technically, I hadn't been alone. Not completely. Jenna, the sole other occupant of the bathroom, had been in the handicap stall, sobbing too hard to let me in. The metal latch on a stall door is as simple a mechanism as they come. But with every bit of focus I could summon, to the point of making my head throb with the effort, I hadn't been able to make that little metal bar rise up and drop away.

Eventually I'd given up and simply knocked. Some super-secret weapon I am. Behold my ability to knock. Sometimes I wondered why GTX would even want me in my current condition. The mental wall that my six-year-old self had erected around my telekinesis as a self-protective measure was incredibly effective. No matter how hard I tried, I couldn't *make* that wall drop. I could still hear people's thoughts and sense their emotions—those functions remained intact. But everything else? Gone.

The ability to manipulate objects without touching them—throw, bend, deflect, speed up, slow down, summon from across the room, all of that—had once been as easy and simple for me as breathing. It hadn't seemed magical or special, any more than a human would have been astounded by their brain translating electrical impulses into sight. It was just something I could do. A seeing person among the blind.

Toward the end of my stay in the lab I'd progressed beyond controlling inanimate objects and moved on to bigger and better things. With enough concentration I'd been able to target specific muscles within the body, stop them from moving. I was that good . . . or bad, depending on how you wanted to look at it. I could keep the muscles in your legs from working, and hold you quiet and still while I did whatever I'd been commanded to do.

I'm not sure anyone should ever have that kind of power.

And now I didn't. Not in a readily accessible or controlled manner, anyway.

My father leaned back in his chair with a sigh. "You created the block, you should be able to bring it down," he reminded me for the millionth time.

"I know," I said tightly. But knowing that didn't seem to make a difference.

After what had happened in the lab all those years ago, after what I'd done . . . it was as if that part of me had been lopped off or shut away behind an impenetrable wall. My father told me it wasn't uncommon for human children to block memories of a traumatic event. He suspected my sudden inability to access that part of myself was a more severe form of this same phenomenon.

He thought that with time, patience, and practice, what I'd lost would return to me. But it had been ten years of all three now with little or—let's face it—no progress. Except, apparently, when Rachel Jacobs was on a rampage.

On rare occasions, like yesterday, the block would sort of thin out for a few seconds, and my telekinesis would break through, like a buried memory floating to the surface. Usually with disastrous results, because I wasn't in control of the flood of power. And then, before I could even *try* to get control, the block would close me out again.

Honestly, most days I didn't care that my ability was gone. I wasn't really sure I wanted it back—it had only brought me fear and pain. But I couldn't tell my father that.

"You need to start practicing again." He scrubbed his face with his hands. He probably hadn't slept since sometime yesterday; exhaustion was catching up to him. "If the block is finally starting to disappear and you don't have control, those bursts of wild power are going to lead GTX right to us." He looked at me, worried. "You'd be completely defenseless."

In spite of my reservations about getting my ability back, I knew he was right. But *more* practice?

Something between a bitter laugh and a scream of frustration lodged in my chest with an ache. The truth was, "practice" was a joke. For years I'd spent several hours a day after school trying to move a red foam ball into a plastic blue cup without touching either one. It was pointless. I'd stared at those objects for so long it felt as though the afterimages were permanently burned into the backs of my eyes. And the only time that stupid ball ever moved was when I accidentally jostled the table with my knee.

How was I supposed to regain control over a power I couldn't even access with any degree of regularity? I'd given up trying about six months ago.

"Practice won't help." I rubbed at the ache beneath my breastbone. "It hasn't helped."

"We have to do something," he said. "We're running out of time."

I froze.

"One of my sources at GTX says they're ramping up the search for you. With the changeover in the administration, new people are in key positions, and the hearing committee on DOD spending is making everyone jumpy. Someone's going to be checking to see where all the government funds went for this research, and GTX will want to have something to show for the project," he said. The "project" meaning me.

I shivered. That explained the phone call yesterday morning and why he'd been following the news about the hearing committee intently. "How close are they?" I asked, my throat suddenly tight with fear.

My father closed his eyes. "I don't know."

He looked tired—the skin sagging around his eyes—and so much older. As if twenty years had passed instead of ten since the night at GTX when he'd first acknowledged my existence with a discreet wave. He was the only human ever to treat me as a *person* and mean it. For the first six years of my life, give or take, I'd thought my name was Wannoseven. It was only after I escaped—with Mark Tucker's help—that I learned Wannoseven wasn't a name at all but a numerical designation. 107. Pathetic. I'd answered to a number, one Jacobs and the others had assigned me.

My first few years in the lab weren't bad. Actually, they were awful, but that's only based on the knowledge I have now, thanks to ten years of living Outside. At the time, the lab was my home, and while I certainly hated parts of it (the constant testing—no kid likes to get shots or have her blood drawn; and let me tell you, electrodes inserted at the back of your head aren't much fun either), I didn't know any different. It wasn't that I thought other children were undergoing similar experiences in their own homes; it was more that I'd never met another child. I knew they existed—I'd seen them in my cultural training sessions, but I'd also seen talking dogs (Scooby-Doo), a man who rode a brontosaurus at work (Fred Flintstone), and countless women who woke up from long hospital stays to discover they were someone else entirely (soap operas).

Consequently, my views of the "real" world were initially a little jumbled. I could find Earth in the solar system, identify the various countries on the planet, and pinpoint our location in Wingate. I could even tell you something about all of those things in any one of the five different languages I'd been taught (English, Chinese, Spanish, German, and Arabic).

But none of it *meant* anything to me. I'd lived inside the same four white walls every day. The world of Little Red Riding Hood described in the book of fairy tales I'd memorized was as real to me as any map of Earth. Knowledge without context. That was my problem.

It led to an obsession with Outside. That was how I'd thought of it then, a vast location that was as mysterious, exciting, and frightening as anything I could imagine. The logical part of my brain knew there were states and cities and countries and oceans. But the other part of me, the bit that was both fascinated and horrified when the wolf ate Grandma and *she survived*, thought of it as a wild and unruly place where anything was possible. And I wanted to experience it. I wanted to feel the grass beneath my feet, to see if it could really grow taller than I was. (I'd seen only part of *Honey, I Shrunk the Kids* and misunderstood what was happening in the back half of the story.)

I wanted to see where Dr. Jacobs and all the lab techs (save one or two on the night shift) went when I slept. I think I somehow had the idea that they were all getting together and doing something fun without me.

I wanted to see the sun, feel the warmth against my skin. (You have no idea how often you all talk and think about the weather: what it is, what it will be tomorrow, what it should be.)

Dr. Jacobs, who I thought of as my ally, my friend, at that point (*he* wasn't the one holding me down to stick me with needles or taking away my dessert when I bit someone), kept promising me that I would go Outside one day, but for now I was special and they were keeping me safe. And I believed him.

I know, I know. But I think he believed it too. Or at least I never picked up any thoughts from him that indicated he was lying.

No, that I got from Leo.

The lab techs didn't wear name tags or have their names embroidered on their white coats, the way Dr. Jacobs did. But when you can hear thoughts, even as sporadically as I could, it's not hard to pick up names and make the connections.

Leo was the short but strong tech they always sent in on bone-marrow days. Having your bone marrow taken is extremely painful, so whenever I saw Leo coming, I knew what was in store. And I did everything I could to stop it, which was more than your average human child of three or four.

One of my most vivid memories—one of those pivotal moments that divided my existence into Before and After—is of Leo leaning over me in the corner of my room, where he'd trapped me. His mouth was bleeding. The sharp edge of a book had split his lip.

He caught my wrists together in a single thick fist, grinding them together until I cried out. "They're never going to let you go," he whispered, his teeth stained a horrible pink. "They're going to keep you in a jar just like all the other freaks."

I felt the truth in his words, along with the hate and fear bubbling out from him like his foul breath. *Alien. Freak. Fucking Martian.*

I knew those words, knew what they meant—the Great Gazoo on *The Flintstones* was an alien—but I'd never heard them applied to me before.

It didn't make sense. But it also spoke to some distant feeling I'd felt flitting around inside me—that I was different from everyone else. Not special, as Dr. Jacobs had said, but different. Even as sheltered as I was then, I'd grasped the nuances between the two: special was good, revered even; different was not.

If Leo was trying to shock me into compliance, it worked. I froze, his words banging around in my head like noise I couldn't shut off, and he hauled me out of the corner without a fight.

That had been the last time I'd seen Leo. The techs weren't supposed to interact with me, except as required by their tasks. ("Stand up." "Sit down." "Does that hurt?") I'd heard Dr. Jacobs warning them about "unnecessary conversation" before. Looking back on it now, I suspect he was probably trying to limit any outside influences beyond what he approved and introduced.

But getting rid of Leo was too little, too late. The damage was done. After that, I *knew* I was different, even if I didn't exactly understand how, and that Dr. Jacobs might not be the friend he wanted me to think he was.

That was the first time I remember feeling trapped. Not just in the room, but by my inability to do something about the knowledge I'd acquired. I'd changed—my mind had cracked open just that tiniest bit to the reality around me—but nothing else had.

It would be years before I'd have a chance to act on the information, but the seed had been planted and it would grow, reaching up for the sun I hadn't yet seen.

I couldn't go back to that room now, to that existence. The thought of it made me feel like I couldn't breathe.

"We should leave, just go. Right now," I insisted, pushing my chair back from the table. My father had heard from his GTX sources that families who moved away from Wingate were subject to intense scrutiny, especially if they had children of an appropriate age (as in ones who could be GTX's missing experiment in disguise). We had never wanted to take that risk—not when hiding in plain view was still a good—if not, the best—option. But now, if they were closing in on us, what did it matter?

"It's too late." My father opened his eyes and gave me a weary smile. "If anyone is keeping an eye on us here, they'll be expecting us to spook. We might confirm something they've barely had time to consider as a possibility."

And running when they already had us in their sights and I wasn't able to defend myself—or him—would prove pointless. A lame mouse trying to outrun a cat in a closed maze. They'd get us in the end. I wouldn't be able to stop them.

A fresh burst of hate for Dr. Jacobs bloomed inside me. If he hadn't tried to force me into obedience, I wouldn't be this broken. I'd still be a freak, but a fully functioning one, at least.

"Maybe we're going about this wrong," my father said, with a thoughtful frown. "What happened yesterday? What was the trigger? If we can replicate the situation, maybe we can use that to figure out how to keep the barrier down and get you back in control."

He was probably thinking about things like my mood or the actual environment—lighting, sounds, smells, etc. He'd hypothesized something similar before, during the year we experimented with hypnosis. Turns out I'm not particularly susceptible. Not altogether surprising if you consider how unwilling I might be, even on a subconscious level, to let someone mess with my head.

I hesitated before responding, mainly because I knew he would not like the answer. *I* didn't even like the answer.

"Ariane." He leaned forward, elbows on the table. *I shouldn't have to ask twice* was evident in his tone.

I took a deep breath and explained what had happened, as clinically and unemotionally as possible. Except for the part where I'd lost it a little when confronted by Rachel. Couldn't de-emotionalize that.

When I finished, my father was furious. "Do you have any idea how dangerous that was? What if someone had taken video of you with their phone? It would be all over the Internet and then where would you be?"

I grimaced. Locked up again at GTX, no doubt. They had teams searching for any sign of me, and a video of what happened yesterday—small, pale girl in the midst of a mysterious explosion—would be more than enough to catch their attention.

"And we've been over this before." He pointed an accusing finger at me. "You're supposed to stay away from the Jacobs girl. You know better than that. She causes problems for you."

I shifted uncomfortably. He was right. *Avoid Rachel Jacobs* had been an unofficial Rule since third grade.

Rachel had been mocking Kyla Portnoy for her four-color box of generic crayons, and, infuriated, I'd accidentally turned Rachel's box of 120 Glitter Crayolas into a colorful mound of wax confetti. It was another instance in which the barrier in my head had temporarily vanished and my out-of-control ability had resurfaced.

Fortunately, the crayons had been in Rachel's desk at the time, so other than a muffled thump, no one had noticed a thing until she went to take them out. And discovered that poor Kyla Portnoy now had more crayons than she did. She threw a huge fit, kicking and screaming and threatening retribution. It had been, simply put, awesome, even if I hadn't done it intentionally. I'd told my father about the incident, though, and received the first and only addendum to the Rules.

And I did try to steer clear of Rachel, but yesterday had been an unavoidable exception. "She was hurting Jenna," I protested. "Being deliberately cruel." Which, as my father well knew, was a kind of hot-button issue for me. The powerful lording it over the powerless. I couldn't stand to see it, knowing how it felt to be so helpless at someone else's hands.

He sighed heavily, some of the anger draining out of him. "Jenna is a prop. Part of your cover," he said slowly and with great emphasis, as if he could drill the words into my brain. "She doesn't know the real you, and if she did, I can assure you, she wouldn't be nearly so quick to defend you in the same, or worse, situation."

I winced. The emotional side of me wanted to argue that he was wrong, but I knew that he wasn't.

"You're not normal, not one of them. You can't forget that."

Fury swelled in me. Like I could forget. Like I wanted to. To be clear, I don't wish to be *more* human. After all the thoughts I've heard rattling around in your skulls? No thanks. But to have a taste of the ease with which most of you coast through life? Never having to worry about anything other than being yourself? Must be nice.

My father got up to scoop more eggs onto my plate. Some of what I was thinking must have shown on my face. "What I mean is," he said in a gentler tone, "you can't get caught up in petty games and manipulations. You have to be above it all."

Don't get involved. Keep your head down. "So in other words, Rachel Jacobs and her clot of humanity do whatever they want, and I have to be the better so-called 'person,'" I muttered.

"They have the privilege of being the primary species on the planet." He returned the skillet to the stove top with a clatter. "Hey, look at me."

I turned in my chair.

His face was lined with tension. "We can't afford any more mistakes."

"I know."

"So do what you got to do, kid."

I nodded reluctantly. I had to be above it all. If I let Rachel get to me, if I slipped too often, it wouldn't be about letting her win anymore. That would be the least of my problems, especially if my father was right about the increased efforts to find me.

He patted me gingerly on the shoulder. "I'll check with my sources and see what they can find out about the new search. You keep working on your control."

Or lack thereof, but he was too kind to say it. The fact was, at this point, after so many years and so many different attempts at bringing down the wall in my head, I was fairly certain it was hopeless. Unless we could convince Rachel Jacobs to move in. Ha-ha.

"Finish your eggs," he added. "You need the protein. Don't make me nag you." He gave me a fond but sad smile.

My father, ever watchful, waited until I picked up my fork, though my stomach roiled at the thought of food, especially cold eggs tainted by the fear and momentary panic of this morning. I wasn't sure how I'd ever eat again, never mind enjoying what had once been my favorite meal.

Guess I'd have to fake it. Just like everything else.

CHAPTER 4

Zane

So it turns out that late-night flashes of brilliance often look a little less brilliant in the bright light of morning.

Ariane Tucker. I was supposed to ask Ariane Tucker to Bonfire Week today.

I squinted at the sunlight pouring into my bedroom and pulled the covers over my head.

Seriously not one of my better ideas. First, it involved Bonfire Week, which was always a pain. It was supposed to be about school spirit in general, but usually turned into a weeklong celebration of the only "worthy" sport: football. And frankly, I got enough of that crap at home. Second, Rachel no doubt had a larger game plan of humiliation in mind, even if I didn't know what it was yet. And third, I barely knew this girl. Based on the hate-filled glares she'd sent at me yesterday during the whole Jenna debacle, I wasn't entirely convinced of my ability to talk her into anything.

Maybe I should have just let Jonas do his best. Ariane probably wouldn't have fallen for it anyway. And even if she had, why did it matter to me?

I had no idea. But I was stuck now.

I groaned and forced myself out of bed and into the shower, my head throbbing. It seems that drinking five beers shortly before bed also sucks first thing in the morning.

Fifteen minutes later I stumbled into our kitchen, my hair wet and my clothes sticking to my skin. I'd been doing pretty well to make it through the shower at all. The effort of drying off might have pushed me too close to the line, transforming the possibility of puking to reality.

"Late on your second day. That's a good start," my dad said from his position behind the island, where, coffee cup in hand, he was flipping through the newspaper. Probably looking for mentions of himself or his "team." My dad was one of those people where nothing existed or counted as important unless someone else was talking about it.

I ignored him, making my way over to the bread box. But when I lifted up the lid, I found only the empty blue-and-white plastic bag. I'd have to get to the store this week sometime.

Stomach churning, I dug to the bottom of the bag and found the dried-out heel. Gross. But I chucked it into the toaster anyway. I needed something in my gut, and after last night's events, I was betting I wouldn't be able to talk Trey into stopping for a greasy breakfast. In fact, I probably should have been worried about whether he'd show up to give me a ride at all, but that felt like too much work. If he didn't show, I'd have to ask my dad for a ride, and that was not happening.

I braced my hands against the cabinet by my head and closed my eyes, resisting the urge to lay my face against the cool, smooth wood. The room spun if I moved too quickly.

My dad snorted. "If you're going to run with the big dogs, Zane, you've got to be able to keep up."

Like Quinn. He didn't say it, but I knew that's what he was thinking. My older brother's high-ranking position among the Ashe High elite had been a foregone conclusion; that they'd accepted me as well (albeit with far less fanfare) had come as a genuine surprise to my dad. Consequently, he seemed to view it as a privilege that might be revoked at any time, if I proved myself less than worthy. And that would be a darker stain on the family name than if I'd never been "in" in the first place.

Quinn had never had to worry about any of this, of course. He was perfect at everything, just like my dad. He'd have partied last night, woken up for a five-mile jog at dawn, finished a report on his summer reading, and gulped down some kind of disgusting and healthy smoothie consisting of raw eggs and wheatgrass, with no ill effects. Unlike me, where the mere thought of raw anything . . . My stomach turned over on itself, and I shuddered, trying to think of something else.

I silently begged the toaster to hurry up so I could take my mangled breakfast to the porch and wait for Trey, who would, please God, show up. I could tell it was going to be one of those mornings with my dad, where he wouldn't leave off.

"Did you get dressed in the dark?" he asked a second later.

See? Though, in this instance, his assumption was partially

correct; I'd had my eyes half closed against the too-bright sun.

". . . at the Salvation Army?"

Son of a bitch. He was in a mood this morning. I was wearing . . . something. I was fairly certain it even matched. I had a vague recollection of a blue T-shirt and then something with a collar—maybe one of Quinn's stretched-out button-downs that had made its way to my drawer when it wasn't tight enough for him anymore. I don't know how he could stand to have something pressed against him like that, pulling at his neck. And I was pretty sure I'd grabbed my favorite jeans from the floor, the ones with the ragged hems that made my dad crazy. That would probably explain the Salvation Army comment.

But what the hell, dude. My clothes were *my* clothes—well, except for Quinn's hand-me-downs—and how I looked was *my* business.

I knew better than to engage, but my head hurt, the toaster was giving off a disgusting smell of burned crumbs and hot metal without relinquishing my toast, and my dad was pissing me off.

I turned my head carefully in his direction and cracked my eyelids open. "What about you, Dad? Is there a parade stand somewhere missing you?" He was wearing his formal dress uniform—white Oxford shirt and dark blue tie under a jacket with gold braid on the sleeves, patches on the shoulders, and all manner of shiny (oh, too shiny today) buttons, collar brass, lapel pins, and badge. His hat, with more gold braid and another shiny badge, lay on the island next to his paper.

Wait, was it a Wednesday? I had to think about it for a second. Yeah. It was. That explained both his mood and his uniform choice. On the third Wednesday of every month he had meetings over at GTX. In theory, these meetings were with the GTX Community Outreach department, giving updates on the anti-drug program GTX sponsored for the elementary school, or presenting the need for more bulletproof vests or new computers in the squad cars. But I think my dad probably saw it as a foot in the door. Except he'd been attending these meetings for a few years now, and, as far as I knew, he'd never managed to wedge additional body parts through.

My dad glared at me. "You think you're so smart." He set his coffee mug down with a sharp crack that reverberated through my head. "But people are judging you based on how you look, whether you like it or not. And if you want to be taken seriously, you have to dress the part."

I rolled my eyes, though it kind of hurt. My dad was forever trying to get in good with GTX—they were the only game in town when it came to power, money, and influence—and it irritated him to no end that they had their own expensive and well-trained security force, experts who avoided interacting with him and his guys except when absolutely necessary.

It was a snub of the first order, to my dad's way of thinking, as good as declaring to the world that GTX thought the Wingate police were local yokels, barely able to handle cow tipping, mailboxes on fire, and old Mrs. McCarty shoplifting candy bars again. But my dad was Jay Bradshaw, hometown favorite, football hero of legend, man who'd pulled himself up from a trailer park existence to be the bright shining star of this craphole town.

Wingate threw him a parade when he left for college, and then again when he came back to work for the police. Not a joke.

Everyone worshipped him, except the folks over at GTX.

I'd spent years listening to my dad bitch about their head security guy, Mark Tucker, cockblocking him. Whenever GTX had a problem, whether it was the stolen research project from ten years ago that my dad *still* complained about, or protestors setting up in front of the gates, Mr. Tucker always told my dad they preferred to "handle it internally." And my dad was stuck—he couldn't do anything unless GTX called him in or there was reasonable proof of a threat to Wingate.

Sometimes I thought his only goal in life was to beat Tucker and get in those doors on a call to serve and protect.

Huh. Tucker. My alcohol-addled brain was slow in making the connection. I wondered if Mark Tucker was any relation to Ariane. That seemed like something I should know, a fact that someone had probably mentioned at one point or another, but I couldn't remember for sure. At least not without concentrating on it more, which wasn't a good idea at the moment, with my dad about to vent steam from his ears.

He crumpled up the newspaper and swept it to the floor before stalking over to get into my face. "You think you can do anything you want and it doesn't reflect on me, on this family?"

His coffee breath wafted over me, and I struggled not to wince.

"This is it, Zane. You're a junior now. Time to stop screwing around and get serious."

Like I hadn't heard that a thousand times already in the last three months. But a thousand and one, that was the key, clearly. "Thanks, Dad," I muttered.

"You're an arrogant little shit," he spat.

"Because of what I'm wearing?" I asked incredulously. There was only so much damage wearing faded and worn-out clothes could do to a reputation, right?

"You have a piss-poor attitude, and it's going to catch up with you." He jabbed a thick finger in my chest. "I swear to God, your brother was nothing like this. Why can't you be more like him?"

And there it is. The million dollar question of genetics, environment, and disappointed parental expectations: *Zane, why aren't you Quinn, just younger? Then we could have enjoyed Quinn-ness for that much longer.*

"Quinn gets it," my dad said with great satisfaction, as if that should wound me. "He knows what it means to play ball."

"Yeah, well, Quinn's also kind of a douche bag," I muttered. Which was true. He was just like my dad, king of a small hill, and determined to have everyone know about it.

I didn't blame Quinn for basking in my dad's approval and making the most of it; hell, I'd have done the same. The man was not easy to please. I'd spent years trying to get even the faintest bit of that light to shine in my direction. It would have been nice if Quinn had at least acknowledged, even just between the two of us, that we weren't exactly on a level playing field; but that wasn't him.

To be fair, though, my big brother could have used his

advantage and spent his time torturing me pretty much without consequence. Instead, he'd basically ignored me, as if being inadequate might be contagious. Sometimes I wasn't sure if that wasn't worse.

My dad's eyes bulged in a way that I hadn't seen since he was my PeeWee football coach and crazed by my complete lack of talent for the game. "What did you say about Quinn?"

"Nothing." This conversation—if you could call it that—was definitely reaching an end. I reached over and yanked up the lever on the toaster just as Trey leaned on the horn outside, loud and long. Thank God.

I snagged my half-scorched, half-stale bread from the toaster and spun away from my dad. "Gotta go," I said as I headed for the back door. *It's been fun*, I wanted to add, but I knew there was only so far I could push him before he snapped and decided to "teach" me something. My dad was of the "tough lessons need a tough teacher" school of thought. We had a few dents in the living room drywall in the shape of my head to prove it. I was taller than him now—another thing I suspected he hated—but he was broader than me and in good shape. (He'd kept up with the workout schedule he and Quinn had created together, with the weights in the garage.) Not a man to push without expecting to get pushed back. Hard.

Not a man for letting someone else have the last word, either.

As I shoved open the screen door, he fired off his final volley. I was expecting it; most of our fights ended in the same way with the same words, or similar ones. But that didn't mean they hurt any less when they came. "You're just like your mother," he said, his voice thick with such barely repressed disgust I wondered why he bothered.

I was too much McDonough and not enough Bradshaw. I'd been hearing that since I was old enough to understand the words. I resembled my mom's side of the family—the height, dark hair color, blue eyes, and the genetic lack of a stick up my ass.

According to my dad, the McDonoughs were trailer-park trash—all of them criminals or lazy, lacking in ambition and good sense. Of course, that hadn't stopped my dad, hometown hero returned, from hooking up with my mom, even as he was "officially" dating the mayor's daughter.

When my mom got pregnant, they had to get married. No choice in that. Not in Wingate. The town might turn a blind eye to slumming, but leaving Mom behind in a "family way"? Bad idea, particularly for someone with my dad's reputation and ambitions.

That, at least, explained Quinn. I had to presume, then, based on the sheer level of frustration he seemed to have at my mere existence, that I had been another even less-welcome accident. That he wished I'd never been born.

I'd said as much to my mom one day when I was eleven and I'd come into the house bleeding and humiliated (and even worse, fighting off tears) after a particularly rough game of "touch" football with my dad and Quinn.

She was quiet, focused on spraying Bactine on my scraped-up elbows. "Your dad grew up in a trailer the next row over from mine. Did you know that?"

I stared at her. Grandma and Grandpa Bradshaw lived a

few blocks away in a small, neat house, where the furniture was still in late-nineties mint condition beneath the plastic protective covers. At least they did now. But that explained why some of the things they did—like letting their lawn grow too long because they didn't want to pay someone to mow it, or fishing pop cans out of the neighbors' recycling bins to turn them in for money—drove Dad vein-popping insane.

"He's not a bad person," my mom said in that same calm, even voice. "He just doesn't know how to be okay with who he is, where he's from. And sometimes we remind him of everything he's trying to forget." Her mouth tightened in a hard line before her entire expression collapsed and she started to cry.

She stopped herself quickly, wiping her eyes and returning to bandaging my wounds like nothing had happened. "But we've got each other. So we're okay, right?" she'd asked me in a determinedly cheerful voice.

I'd nodded quickly and repeatedly, catching a glimpse of my scared face in the bathroom mirror. There's nothing worse than seeing your mom fall apart. Particularly someone like my mom, who had always seemed impervious to everything my dad threw in her direction.

Seemed being the key word there, as appearances apparently turned out to have no bearing on reality.

You're just like your mother. Standing there in the back door, just a foot away from escape, I pictured my dad's words as arrows, striking a target on my back. Bull's-eye, every one of them. I shrugged involuntarily against the imagined sensation of them lodging right below my shoulder blades.

"Not enough like her," I mumbled. Because, after all, *I* was still here.

I let the door slam shut after me.

Trey lifted his head up from the steering wheel and squinted at me when I got in on the passenger side. "Dude, you look like hammered shit."

Juggling my so-called toast, I chucked my backpack into the backseat and pulled my seat belt on. "I always forget—is hammered shit better or worse than non-hammered shit?"

"Funny," he said through a yawn.

"And you're one to talk." I frowned. Trey looked bleary-eyed and half awake, and he hadn't even been drinking last night.

His jaw dropped in another bone-cracking yawn. "Didn't get much sleep."

I wondered if that was my fault. But he'd come to pick me up anyway, which I appreciated, especially after the scene with my dad. Nothing like being able to storm out and go somewhere instead of having to crawl back inside in humiliation.

Trey straightened up and shook his head rapidly, as though the vigorous motion would help him wake up. "Your dad giving you a hard time again?" He nodded toward my house, and I looked up in time to see my dad glaring at me from the doorway before he slammed the door with such force it rattled the car windows.

That was one of the benefits of having the same friends for eleven years. They knew all your crap and you didn't have to explain it.

"Yeah." I took a tentative bite of the toast. It was gross, stale-on-the-verge-of-moldy, *and* charred. But better than nothing.

"Sucks." Trey put the car in reverse and looked over his shoulder to back out of the driveway. "Dude needs to get over it."

"Yeah. Right." Not in my lifetime.

I waited until Trey reached the street to speak again. We didn't usually talk much in the car—neither of us are morning people—but it was eating at me and I had to know.

"I wasn't sure you'd show this morning. Thought you might still be pissed." I'd tried to explain to him last night that the kiss hadn't meant anything. Rachel was messing with us, her way of entertaining herself.

But he'd waved me off and remained sulking in the shallow end of the pool. I'd had to get a ride home with Cami and Cassi, which was its own form of torture. I'd never been alone with the two of them before, and though they were, theoretically, genetically identical, you've never seen two people argue so much. Whether this song sucks or not, if it's too hot or cold, whose perfume smells better, pink versus red. I didn't even understand that last one. And they wanted my opinion to settle every single debate. (For the record, I think I came down on the side of pink.) I'd always thought Rachel hung out with them because they told her what she wanted to hear. Now I wondered if they needed her—in a referee capacity—far more than she needed them.

Trey shrugged. "It's cool."

I looked at him, surprised and relieved. I relaxed in my seat—as best as I could with the dash digging into my knees—feeling some of the weight on my shoulders roll away. One less thing to worry about.

"Rachel explained it," he added.

I stiffened. Yeah, I bet she did.

As if confirming my suspicion, he hesitated and then said, "She was happy to see you having fun again. But you know you don't have anything to prove to us or anybody else."

Damn it, Rachel. "It isn't about that," I said tightly. *Poor Zane misses his mommy. Boo-hoo.* It was about so much more than that. But people only cared about the surface.

"Whatever, man," he said. "I just mean I'm here if you want to talk about it."

What was there to talk about? If my life sucked, what was the point of hashing it out with everyone, asking them to feel sorry for me? It wouldn't change anything.

"No one knows what's going on with you," he added. "And you're different since your mom—"

"Don't." I glared at him, and he clamped his mouth shut, which was wise. I couldn't believe he was going there. Or rather, that Rachel had more or less pushed him to it. I could picture it, her eyes all faux-sincere, talking about poor Zane. *You know, his mom abandoned him. She stuck around for Quinn, but not for him. . . .*

Son of a bitch. I could feel the burning mix of humiliation and rage rising up inside me. People talking about me behind my back in the guise of pretending to care or wanting to help—was that ever going to go away?

"Just trying to look out for you, man," he muttered.

Yeah, but he was one of the few. Everyone else was just

in it for the entertainment value, something to add a little interest to an otherwise boring day. And I didn't want to talk about it, even with Trey.

Rachel was waiting in the parking lot next to her car when we pulled in. She was all smiles, waving at Trey as though she hadn't demolished him only last night. He sprang out of the car, barely taking the time to put it in park first.

"Baby," she cooed, throwing her arms around him.

Dude. He should rip his heart out of his chest and toss it on the ground. Save her the time and effort.

I grabbed my backpack, got out, and slammed the door.

Rachel pulled away from Trey. "Zane," she said in greeting. She patted Trey's shoulder. "I hope Trey explained everything from last night." She was smiling, but I could see the calculating going on beneath the surface and maybe more than a little anger. She wasn't happy she'd had to work so hard to win Trey back to her side. *Good.*

I nodded, not trusting myself to say anything.

"So you're still on board with our little plan?" she asked.

"Asking Ariane Tucker to Bonfire Week and then what? Pouring pig's blood in her locker?" There had to be a catch here somewhere, I knew it.

Rachel gave me a disgusted look, probably at the idea that she'd repeat a trick so close to the one she'd pulled yesterday with Jenna. "No. It's like we talked about. Take her to Bonfire Week."

"Except for the party at your house," I said. There was no way Ariane rated highly enough on the social scale to receive that invite.

Rachel's eyes sparkled. "No, *especially* the party at my house."

Uh-oh. "And then what?" I demanded.

She lifted her shoulders and gave me a wicked smile. "Nothing. Not our fault if she falls for your charms and you suddenly and publicly change your mind and dump her . . . loudly."

I sighed. Rachel couldn't guarantee a good party without a show, and humiliation was her specialty. I'd been into it once. Feeling better by making other people feel worse. But after living with my dad constantly on my back for the last year or so, I'd lost my taste for it.

But if I refused now, she'd probably send Jonas, who wouldn't hesitate to follow through. And then it would become all about me, poor messed-up Zane. What happened to him after last year? He's no fun anymore. Blah, blah, blah. All the whispers and looks of fake concern that I hated.

Saying yes, though, would mean Rachel had me under her thumb, like Trey. My dad was already attempting to run my life; I didn't need someone else telling me what to do.

A fierce wave of white-hot fury flooded up through my chest. I was trapped. Son of a bitch. I would *not* be backed into this corner.

"Hello? Zane? You in there?" Rachel waved a hand in front of my face and then exchanged a faux-concerned look with Trey, playing her role to perfection.

Unless . . . In a quick flash, the all-too-familiar pieces of the scheme—Rachel, a plan, a victim, Ariane Tucker, humiliation—fell together in a slightly different order; one I was willing to bet Rachel had never considered.

Maybe Rachel should get a taste of her scheming world from a slightly different angle. Nothing too dramatic—I wasn't an idiot. Just something to make her think twice. I might not be able to get my dad off my back, but Rachel was a different story.

I smiled grimly. "Sure," I said. "I'm in."

Trey nodded in happy approval. Rachel squealed and threw herself into Trey's arms and then promptly winked at me—long, slow, and seductive—over his shoulder.

I resisted the urge to roll my eyes. Yeah, fine. If Rachel wanted a game, she'd get one. All I had to do was convince Ariane Tucker to play.

CHAPTER 5

Ariane

IN THE LAB, SOMEONE WAS ALWAYS WATCHING. I WAS never alone. One wall of my room was glass—it could go from opaque to translucent with the press of a button. And it did, often. Sometimes in the middle of the night when I was sleeping (with the lights on to see how I'd handle sleep deprivation). Or when I was eating (my initial response to ice cream was to spit it out—it was too cold for my teeth) or watching the screen embedded in the opposite wall, which played military training videos and a carefully selected mix of modern American programming to teach me the cultural shorthand humans use in daily interactions.

I grew to expect the disappearance of that "wall" at any second. The area on the other side of the glass—filled with monitors and computers—always had people tracking my movements, measuring every change in my pulse or respiration or brain waves. They also had cameras that recorded what I did when I thought no one was watching. That worked only until I was old enough to figure out that they shouldn't have been able to interrogate me about something I'd done when the "wall" was up unless they had some other way of watching. (For prize-winning scientists, foremost in their field, they weren't very smart. Once I knew that any illusion of privacy I had was just that—an illusion—I took to hiding under my cot, with the sheet hanging over the edge to block their view, when I needed a moment alone.)

In short, I was used to the feeling of people watching me—that was my normal. In fact, the first night I spent in my father's house I made him leave my door open. The idea of privacy, as thrilling as it was, was terrifying in its newness. I'd never been alone before.

And it took me weeks to get used to the idea. I became the most paranoid grade-schooler in existence. I could never quite shake the feeling that I was being watched, that GTX was seconds away from swooping in and taking me away. The world seemed huge (and so very loud), and every person in it was staring at me.

If it hadn't been for my father and his Rules, I might have cracked, suffered a complete mental break, and ended up living under the bed in my new room with a hat constructed from aluminum foil (which, I can tell you, doesn't work. I could still hear you all thinking, even with a double layer).

But he taught me that humans noticed what was different, what stood out. And screaming every time a stranger tried to talk to me . . . well, that was definitely different. (My father would explain my unusual behavior to concerned strangers as trauma from spending so many years in and out of hospitals and then losing "my" mother and moving to a new place.)

My objective became to blend in, to become invisible. It was a game to me, fooling everyone and protecting myself. I made mistakes occasionally (hey, when your education about the real world consists mainly of what you see on television, you'd probably think a whole lot of crazy things are possible, too. Including that, it would appear, the vast majority of children in the United States don't know who their biological father is, based on daytime talk shows). But I caught on fairly quickly—desperation is a powerful motivator.

I still suffer occasional spikes in paranoia when someone holds eye contact with me for a split second too long, or when the same car passes our house twice within a few minutes. Lost pizza delivery guys are the bane of my existence.

Or when I walk into school and everyone is staring at me. . . .

It took me a few seconds to notice, as focused as I was on tuning out the massive wave of thoughts and emotions. The main hall was jammed with people, everyone flooding in from the gym to their lockers before first period. I'd avoided the morning cattle call by leaving my house eight minutes later than usual.

Jenna had received special permission to go to her locker early to continue the clean-up efforts that the janitorial staff had started yesterday. Apparently, hemorrhoid cream doesn't come off so easily.

She'd called me last night in tears, pleading with me to

meet her at her locker, for moral support. How could I say no? It didn't seem inherently risky, and I had to go that way to get to my own locker anyway. No big deal.

But I hadn't gotten more than fifteen feet inside the main doors before I heard my name being whispered several times in quick succession, and then a surprising lull in conversation, which was usually only prompted by the arrival of the principal or the start of an argument that everyone wanted to hear.

I looked up and found dozens of faces—all blurring together in an unrecognizable mass—turned toward me in a way I hadn't seen outside of my nightmares.

I might have panicked, thinking they were finally on to me, except no one was running away. No one was screaming.

If anything, they were edging slightly closer, as if they wanted to get a closer look at some kind of spectacle or celebrity.

I dropped my guard and listened, trying to pull relevant thoughts from the muddle of excitement and noise.

. . . what her locker is going to look like?

That's her.

. . . told Rachel Jacobs off.

I would NOT want to be her.

She is so dead. . . .

Great. Word had spread about my little confrontation with Rachel yesterday, and now everyone wanted to stare at the girl who'd dared to go up against her. Even though I hadn't been the one doing the provoking at all.

Whatever.

I fought my way through to the stairs and up to Jenna's

locker, ignoring the stares and whispers on the way.

The area by Jenna's locker had a crowd around it again, thinner than yesterday but more than enough. And they were all here for the same reason—to gawk at Jenna and the misfortune they were grateful had landed on her head instead of theirs.

Vultures. She didn't deserve it. She hadn't done anything wrong. A flicker of fury at Rachel rose up in me. One day she'd get what she deserved even if I couldn't be the one to bring it down on her.

Through a gap in the crowd I could see Jenna standing at her locker, her shoulders slumped, radiating misery. She had her back to the people watching, and her movements were wooden and awkward as she bent down to pick up another industrial brown paper towel from the stack at her feet and wipe it in hopeless circles on the inside of her locker door. Even from where I was I could see she was only smearing the hemorrhoid cream around, making it worse.

Where are you, Ariane? Hurry up! Jenna's pleading thoughts pierced through the noise as if she'd shouted.

I started toward her, determined to shove my way through the gawkers (and maybe crunch a few toes and knock a few ribs in the process), but then the memory of my father's voice rang out in my head.

We can't afford any more mistakes.

I stopped. If I pushed my way in to pull Jenna out, that would only set off another round of speculation and attention. It might even draw Rachel back to me. I couldn't do that, couldn't take the chance.

I'd broken Rule #3 by getting involved, but I could

avoid the possibility of making things worse, by following Rule #4 and keeping my head down.

Except for Jenna . . . It would definitely be worse for Jenna. Her mental chanting of my name, like some kind of prayer, continued, a low-level buzz in my consciousness.

I hesitated, shifting my feet, as people flowed around my middle-of-the-hall position with irritated sighs and muttered swear words.

Jenna would be so hurt if I left her here to fend for herself. And she would cry. I hated it when she cried. It made me feel all panicky and unsure of what to do. Sometimes it even made my nose and eyes sting in sympathetic response. And I don't cry. Or at least I haven't in years.

But my father was right. As much as I cared about Jenna, there were larger issues at stake. I couldn't place protecting her emotions above my father's safety, and mine as well.

A fresh surge of hatred for the Rules and their necessity rose up inside me. *God damn GTX.* And I meant it in the literal sense, the way so rarely used by full-blooded humans these days. I wanted an all-powerful, supernatural force to come along and sweep away any hint that GTX had ever existed, leaving behind nothing but a burning hole in the ground. (Yes, the Bible—along with the Koran and the Torah—had been among my cultural studies. And no, I wasn't sure what I believed, but that didn't stop me from wanting what I wanted.)

With a sick feeling in my stomach, despising myself almost as much as I did GTX, I turned away from Jenna's locker and hurried across the hall, down to my own. I'd text her during first period, make sure she was okay, and then create some kind of reasonable lie for my absence.

That was, in fact, my life. A whole series of reasonable lies. What was one freaking more? Staying invisible, under the protective cloak of half-truths and out-and-out fantasy was the best thing—the only thing—I could do for myself and my father, even though it made me want to scream.

"Hey! Wait!"

I ignored the shouting behind me; it couldn't be for me. The only person who might shout for me was Jenna, and this was a guy's voice.

"Ariane!"

I froze, then looked over my shoulder to see Zane Bradshaw barreling toward me, everyone scattering out of his way, frightened villagers running from a fairy-tale giant.

I turned away quickly, my face burning. Having one of the most popular guys in school shouting your name in a crowded hallway was only slightly less noticeable than, say, taking out a billboard next to the interstate with your picture on it. And the words "LOOK AT ME."

God, I hoped Jenna hadn't heard him. I winced at the thought. What did Zane Bradshaw want with me anyway? It couldn't be anything good.

I resisted the urge to squeeze myself into an open locker and, instead, resumed walking, moving as quickly as I could without encouraging more stares. Maybe if I got far enough away he'd give up and forget about me. Today was not the day for this. In fact, *never* would be the day for this, as far as I was concerned.

But oh no, I couldn't get that lucky.

Within a few seconds he'd caught up with me, looming

over me like a tall annoying tree. His legs were so much longer than mine, he'd covered the same distance in half the time.

Stupid tree legs.

"I need to talk to you," he said, breathless at my side, as if he'd run up the stairs and down the hall to find me. His handsome face was flushed, he hadn't shaved, and there were big dark circles under his eyes. I could smell soap on him, as if he'd just stepped out of the shower, and his dark hair was damp.

Something was definitely up. He was almost vibrating with a sense of urgency, and I got the feeling of impending doom hanging in the air. Then again, generally speaking, I wouldn't ever have a *good* feeling about Zane Bradshaw tracking me down to "talk." That was so far from the norm, the world might as well have turned upside down.

"What do you want?" I asked, my voice tight, barely above a whisper. I could feel people watching him, and therefore me.

He held his hands up as if declaring he was weapon-free. "Just to talk, that's all," he said in what felt like an excruciatingly loud voice. Then he seemed to realize how many people were watching. "In private," he added.

I stared at him. What he could possibly want to talk about? We had no classes together this year, and obviously we didn't run in the same social circles. Because I was allergic to bitch. Not that Rachel Jacobs would have had me as a friend even if I'd wanted her to, but I liked to remember that it was my choice, too.

Out of the corner of my eye I caught more people turning

in our direction, curious about who Zane Bradshaw wanted to talk (loudly) to.

Great. So much for staying invisible. Still, there was a simple solution.

"No," I said flatly, and turned away.

My father always said never offer a choice if there's only one right answer.

CHAPTER 6

Zane

I'VE NEVER SEEN ANYONE SO RESISTANT TO THE IDEA OF a simple conversation. The girl who had gone toe-to-toe with Rachel looked as if she'd rather crawl across a bed of nails than talk to me. And that was before she darted away down a side hall.

Damn it.

I took off after her. "Ariane . . . wait."

She didn't slow or stop, just kept moving at a pace that I could barely keep up with, which was saying something, considering how short she is. This close to her, I realized the top of her head—with all her strange hair pulled up and sort of contained—wouldn't even reach my shoulder.

Jesus. She was miniature. Okay, probably not, but it seemed like it when there was almost a foot-and-a-half difference in our heights.

The realization sparked a surprising wave of disgust for whoever had caused all her broken fingers last year. I didn't believe anyone was *that* clumsy naturally.

It occurred to me, belatedly, that she might be afraid of me. After all, she didn't really know me. Not any more than I knew her. And I was big and she was small—I knew how that dynamic could work.

I slowed a step, giving her room to breathe. "Hey, I just need a minute," I called to her.

"Go away. Please," she said, so quietly I barely heard her over the chaos of last-minute phone calls, lockers slamming, and some announcement over the loudspeaker that no one was paying any attention to. The warning bell was going to ring soon, and we were running out of hallway. If she was planning on taking the back stairs to make a getaway, I was out of luck. I wouldn't have time to chase her down, explain what was going on, and get upstairs again in time for class.

I swallowed a surge of frustration. I hadn't had to work this hard to get a girl to talk to me since eighth grade, when I was still just "Quinn Bradshaw's little brother." "Look," I said, "if you'll hear me out, I think—"

Ariane spun around to face me, and her heavy backpack, loose on one shoulder, swung with the motion. I was surprised the weight of it didn't pull her over backward. "I realize someone saying no to you is probably a new experience," she said, her voice quiet but sharp, "so let me help you with it. It's the opposite of yes. It means I don't want to talk to you for a minute, thirty seconds, or any other standard or nonstandard measure of time. Got it?"

I gaped at her. She wasn't afraid; she was angry. At me. And the injustice of that stung deeply, especially after the morning I'd had. She didn't know me. She didn't know what my life was like. "What is your problem?" I demanded. "I haven't done anything to—"

"No, you're right." She smiled without humor. "You didn't do *anything*."

Her tone and the accusation in her gaze made it clear she was referring to the incident with Jenna.

I sighed. "That was . . . not my idea. And it's complicated."

"I'm sure it is, Zane," she said blandly, leaving no doubt that she believed it was anything but. "Good luck with that." She walked away.

"It's about yesterday," I called after her, a last-ditch attempt. She had to know that Rachel wasn't going to let that go, right? She had to be expecting some kind of retribution.

She went perfectly still, and a freshman with his nose buried in an unreasonably thick binder nearly knocked into her.

"What about yesterday?" she asked warily.

I caught up to her in a couple of steps. "Come on." I tipped my head toward a closed classroom door. It obviously wasn't in use this hour; otherwise it would have been open. That meant it was probably locked as well. But standing in front of it would get us out of the flow of traffic.

"Don't." Ariane preemptively shifted away from me as if I was going to try to drag her.

Holy shit. Someone had done a number on her.

I held my hands up. "Wasn't going to."

"Sorry." She looked around, weighing her options, and then followed me over to the door, moving as if every step cost her. "I can't be late to class. What do you want?"

"I need your help."

She looked up at me, surprised, and met my gaze directly for the first time. "What?"

Contact lenses, I realized. She was wearing contacts. I could see the edges of them around the unnaturally dark blue of her irises. Which probably meant that her eyes weren't blue at all, but some darker color, altered by the tinted lenses.

Weird. I frowned.

The vanity of colored contacts did not jibe with what I knew of her. She didn't seem like Rachel or the twins, obsessed with clothes and expensive haircuts and makeup. She wore jeans and T-shirts mostly, and her hair was always in that half-controlled messy ponytail/bun thing. Once again, she seemed less a whole person and more a conglomeration of parts that didn't make sense.

Ariane glanced away abruptly, pink rising in her pale cheeks.

I'd been staring. And now it was my turn to apologize. "Sorry." I hesitated, not sure how to approach all of this. "It's Rachel."

She stiffened.

I hurried to explain. "What you did yesterday, Rachel's got it into her head that you were deliberately trying to humiliate her and—"

"It's your job as a henchman to warn me off, maybe scare me or manipulate me into doing something she wants," she said flatly.

"No. God. No," I said, shocked. We weren't the freaking Mafia. Though it occurred to me that Ariane wasn't far from the truth. Rachel was never that direct about it, but her "pranks" had the same effect as a threat: *Do what I want, be who I say you should be . . . or else.* And I'd taken part in how many of those over the years? I felt sick.

Ariane raised her pale eyebrows in question.

"Okay, yes, sort of," I admitted with a grimace. "But it's not what you think . . . not really. I'm not going to go through with it or anything. . . ." I fumbled for the words, trying to find a way to explain this that didn't make me sound like the world's biggest asshole. I didn't have Quinn's gift for spinning awkward truths into silky smooth half-lies everyone was happy to swallow. He was a born politician, but normally I wasn't this bad. Something about the way Ariane stood there, cool and distant, impassively watching me bumble along . . . it made me feel exposed, a lower life-form trapped under her microscope.

"Rachel wants me to ask you to Bonfire Week." The words came out in a rush. There.

Looking more tired than surprised, she closed her eyes for a long second—her eyelashes were so pale, they appeared almost white against her skin. "And then?" she asked, opening her eyes.

"And then, I don't know." I raked my hands through my hair. "Dump you in some kind of loud, public, and humiliating way at her party on Friday." It sounded so dumb now in the face of her calmness. Like, short of suffering some kind of temporary brain damage, there was any chance she would have ever fallen for it.

"Assuming I would find you irresistible enough to accept you in the first place," she said dryly.

Heat rose in my face. "Assuming, yeah." Hey, it wasn't

that big of a leap. I may not have had a girlfriend, but I'd never had trouble finding dates or, for that matter, hookups. Being Quinn Bradshaw's little brother had proven beneficial in that one regard, once Quinn himself was out of town and no longer an option.

"Okay, warning duly noted." She hefted her bag higher on her shoulder with a sigh. "Thanks for the heads-up." She started to turn away.

"Actually . . ." I began.

Ariane paused and gave me an amused look. "You do realize it's kind of pointless to ask me now, right? You just told me the whole thing is a revenge scam." She glanced out into the hallway, probably checking the time on the wall clock. It was getting close to the bell. There were fewer people passing by, not as many lockers slamming shut.

"I think we should go through with it," I said. "Not all of it, obviously. Not the end. But the rest of it."

She stared up at me for a long moment, her evaluating gaze so intense it felt like she was looking through rather than at me. "You're serious," she said finally, with the air of someone solving an equation and being faintly surprised by the results.

"Yeah." Did she think I was going to all this trouble for fun?

She shook her head in disbelief. "Why?"

My mouth tightened. Because Rachel had crossed the line. She'd used my real life as part of one her stupid ploys. But I wasn't going to get into all of that with Ariane Tucker. "It's a long story. But the short version is, I think she needs to see she can't mess with people like that."

"Uh-huh." Ariane sounded skeptical, but she wasn't

walking away. Maybe this would work after all. "What are you proposing?" she asked cautiously.

Yes. Now I had her.

I shrugged, forcing myself not to look too eager. I didn't want to scare her off. "Easy. We take the drama out of it. We play along until the end. Then when she wants a big show, some loud, humiliating scene, we just shake hands and walk away." Okay, so maybe that wasn't the most exciting plan ever, but it was pretty good considering I'd only come up with it ten minutes ago in the parking lot. And besides, it would drive Rachel *crazy*. Especially when, if I knew her, she'd be spreading the word for everyone to watch for a big blowup at her "social event of the year" Bonfire party. If it fizzled like a wet sparkler, she'd be completely humiliated. And it would serve her right.

Ariane frowned. "Why don't you just tell her no? Why go to all this trouble?"

Oh. I hadn't been expecting that question. I'd kind of been betting on her hatred of Rachel to make this a quick sell. And the answer . . . I wasn't sure if I had an answer other than I didn't want Jonas to do it. But I couldn't say that; it would only bring up more questions. Among them, why did I care what Jonas did with Ariane? And answering that would mean sharing more about my life—my dad, Rachel, all of it—than I was comfortable with at this particular moment.

I hesitated. "It's complicated," I said for the second time in one conversation.

Ariane eyed me with more than a hint of disdain. "Sounds like a cop-out to me."

"Whatever." I wasn't doing this for a life lesson from Ariane Tucker. "Are you in or not?"

She was quiet for a long second. "No," she said.

My heart sank.

"This could all be part of the game," she pointed out. "You let me in on it only to gain my trust and then pull the carpet out from under me at the last second."

That would be completely twisted . . . and probably not outside the realm of possibility, under other circumstances. But not today. "It's rug," I said automatically, my mind spinning, trying to figure out what to say to convince her.

She frowned. "What?"

"It's rug. Pull the rug out."

She made a face, and the pink in her cheeks returned.

"And I'm not going to do that," I said, trying to sound as convincing as possible without pleading. "You have to trust me."

"I don't." Then she turned on her heel and joined the much-diminished traffic.

Crap. I stepped out after her. "If you don't do this, she'll come after you another way," I called. "Rachel won't give up. She'll find your weak spot and make sure it hurts." She excelled at that.

Ariane paused and looked back at me, a bitter weariness in her expression. "Believe me, I know." Then she disappeared around the corner as the tardy bell rang.

CHAPTER 7

Ariane

PULL THE RUG *OUT, NOT THE CARPET. YOU KNOW BETTER.* I kicked myself mentally for that one all the way down the stairs to French III.

It was a dumb mistake, one that came from learning outside of standard context, and a dead giveaway that I was different. The rug/carpet mix-up dated back to before my early days of trying to grasp the nuances of spoken language. I thought I'd trained myself out of it years ago. That only went to show how much he'd taken me by surprise. Zane Bradshaw, of all people, had rattled me.

He'd meant it, what he'd said about getting back at Rachel.

Most of the time, reading thoughts is a crapshoot. The human mind is a roiling mass of half-finished observations, fleeting sensations and emotions, and imagined scenarios playing out on an invisible screen. That was one of the reasons my father had warned me away from using it as a sole basis for making a decision.

When someone is agitated, it's even more difficult to track a specific thought. Emotions rise up and block almost everything else out. But those emotions, while lacking the detail and the shades of gray found in conscious thought, can give you a baseline on a person's state of mind, albeit more as an internal scream of rage than, say, someone articulating, "Gee, I am angry."

Zane's mind was as messy and chaotic as everyone else's; no surprise there. But one thing had popped, loud and clear: he was angry with Rachel.

I wasn't sure what she'd done or why today was different, but he'd had enough. I understood that feeling, certainly, though it was a surprise to find it within Zane.

But what had me shaking was how close I'd come to agreeing. To see Rachel caught in the wheels of her own machinations . . . I wanted it so bad, I could taste blood. Or maybe that was just where I'd bitten the inside of my cheek to keep from saying yes.

"*Bonjour, Mademoiselle Tucker.* Good of you to join us," Miss Lenosi said as I crossed the threshold a full minute after the bell.

A wave of whispers and giggles swept the room, and my face burned. So much for keeping an even-lower-than-normal profile today.

Thanks a lot, Zane.

I took my seat at the back of the room and shifted my pack to the floor. I reached down to pull a notebook and pen from my bag, and noticed my hands were trembling.

Which was ridiculous. The worst was over. Zane wouldn't approach me again on the Rachel matter, or any other.

Except I wanted him to. One more push and I might

have given in, against all my better judgment. My human side was rattling its cage, screaming to be set loose.

No. I couldn't allow that to happen.

I forced myself to pay attention to Miss Lenosi's lecture, scrawling her words across my notebook page and correcting mentally for her atrocious accent. *Je vais* came out as *Juh vaze.*

But the idea of beating Rachel, scheming against her, with someone who was *her* friend . . . it made me want to laugh. It was dizzying and vengeful and everything Rachel deserved. I couldn't reach her grandfather—that would be far too dangerous—but in this small way I could turn the tables on both of them.

It was impossible, though. Against far too many of the Rules. And I didn't know Zane, didn't trust him. Even though I was pretty sure he wasn't planning to double-cross on his plan to double-cross, I couldn't be absolutely certain. It was an unnecessary risk.

I gritted my teeth. This was the balancing act I struggled with daily, sometimes hourly. I felt like I was nothing but a bunch of extremes all bound up together. The logical voice in my head pointing out facts and likely scenarios, and the roar of emotions, the rush of *want* and *need*, that would drown everything out if I let it.

Other than the sketchy info I'd found from years of careful Internet searches, I didn't know much of anything about the other part of my heritage, the ones who'd come from so far away. But logic—and various conspiracy Web sites—suggested that the Roswell aliens came from an advanced society. Creating technology that would allow them to break through impossible barriers—like traveling faster than the speed of light—could only come from intellectual superiority, a focus on science, logic, and strategy. They'd harnessed their potential instead of squandering it by focusing on petty divisions between race, religion, economic status, gills versus lungs, and whatever.

They—whoever they were—had risen above their primal instincts to achieve something amazing.

And as soon as they'd gotten here, however many thousands of light-years away, the human part of my heritage had shot them down, out of fear or hate or both.

Inspiring, right?

But it was important for me to remember that in this particular situation, as with most, giving in to my human side would be dangerous. Satisfying maybe, but dangerous. I *wanted*, *raged*, and *needed*, just like everybody else. But my analytical nonhuman side knew that giving in was risky; it might lead to decisions that would put my life or freedom in jeopardy. I wasn't above taking risks, but they had to make sense beyond the emotional appeal. Emotions were all too often what tripped the full-blooded humans up. They wanted something more than was practical or reasonable. The desire to feel a connection with another person, to actively love or hate someone—chasing after those things left you open and vulnerable.

Logic was sound, and it had saved me countless times.

Except once, my human side shouted. *Remember that?*

In the lab, that last night, it had been a gut instinct, the desire to survive at any cost, that had overruled the whisper of logic, encouraging me to come out from behind my cot at the urging of the guard, the man who would become my father.

I shook my head. That was different. In that case, it had been a matter of life and death.

It had been the middle of the night when the bomb went off. Not that I'd recognized it as such at the time. I'd found out later that people protesting against genetic experimentation on defenseless animals had sent GTX a package bomb. It had exploded in the mail-processing room, only one floor above my living quarters.

But all I knew then was that one moment I'd been asleep, and the next I was on the floor in the smoke-filled darkness, cowering behind my tipped-over cot while the walls shook and the ceiling rumbled. I wasn't even sure if I'd crawled there or I'd simply been dumped out by whatever force had rocked the room. Sirens shrieked overhead, hurting my ears, but I couldn't lift my hands up to cover them. My right arm ached in a familiar way that likely meant a break, and I clutched it tight against my chest.

The emergency lights flickered, trying and failing to alleviate the gloom. But I could see enough to recognize blood soaking through the white sleeves of my uniform. There were small cuts on my hands, and probably more on my arms. The games and books on my shelf had been shaken to the floor. Shiny bits of glass lay spread across the room, sparkling like diamonds in the unsteady light. And beyond that, the window wall, the one that occasionally masqueraded as solid, was fractured irreparably. A giant crack dominated the smooth surface, zigzagging into thousands of smaller breaks. At the bottom, the glass was gone entirely, fissures giving way to a gaping hole with sharp and jagged edges. The observation room, where Dr. Jacobs and the techs had watched me, was dark and somehow looked smaller than normal, filled with unfamiliar shapes. I realized that was because all the equipment had been thrown into a jumble at the center of the room and the walls appeared to be sagging. Wires were smoking and snapping.

It took me a second to gather the implications of the facts at hand: I was alone, unwatched, with an avenue for escape.

Immediately, the two opposing forces within me took up sides.

Run.

It could be a test, a trap.

Or it might not be. Run!

The latter voice was so loud in my head, I was up and on my feet, scurrying toward the broken window wall on shaky legs before I even realized it.

But the argument continued in my head.

You don't know how to live Outside. It's dangerous.

Not as dangerous as staying in here. You know what they made you do to Jerry. What do you think will happen next? Move faster!

But the problem was, no matter how loudly that voice yelled in my head or how quickly I moved, escape was not going to be easy. To begin with, the floor of the observation room was several feet higher than that of my cell—*the better to see you with, my dear.*

To climb out I'd have to reach up and somehow pull myself over the sharp edges of glass in the window with a broken arm.

I was standing there in front of the window wall, evaluating my options—*remove the rest of the glass; no, you don't have time for that*—when a shadow moved within the observation room.

Instinct drove me to hide. I skittered back behind my overturned cot and hunched down.

I peered cautiously around the edge as Mark Tucker appeared, shoving his way through the collapsed equipment in the observation room.

He wasn't my father then, of course. But I recognized him even with the dust in his hair and soot lining his face. He was the new guard, the different one.

Guards patrolled in pairs on a regular schedule on the other side of the glass wall. I'd never paid much attention to them because they didn't seem to notice me no matter what (screaming, pleading, bleeding) was going on right in front of them. I now know it was because they were hired for their discretion and paid well to ensure it.

But one day, not long after the . . . incident with Jerry, I was sitting in the corner of my room, refusing to watch a training video. How to assemble and disassemble an M16, if I remember correctly. I'd had my back to the video and was staring out through the glass wall. Dr. Jacobs was on the other side, casually threatening me, which I ignored. Passive resistance was the only defense left to me at that point.

When the guards came through to report in to Dr. Jacobs, I noticed something different. The guard closest to the glass wall . . . he was doing something curious.

After checking to make sure Dr. Jacobs was involved

in their discussion, I edged forward from the corner for a better look.

Though the man was focused on Dr. Jacobs, answering the questions asked of him, his hand, down by his side, was moving back and forth. A wave. A traditional manner of greeting when distance or situation does not permit spoken words, I knew.

I sucked in a breath and straightened up. This man was waving at me. He *saw* me.

Before I could respond—or remember that the proper response was to wave back—the monitors tracking my heart rate, blood pressure, and respiration began to flash brightly, attracting Dr. Jacobs's attention.

The waving guard and his partner walked on, and Dr. Jacobs turned his attention to the monitor readouts and then me, demanding to know what had caused such a response.

I'd ignored his questions, refusing even to look at him. I would not give up this secret, knowing already "Grandpa Artie" would only turn it into an experiment. Or the means to force me into doing something I didn't want to do.

But I'd watched more closely after that—every guard rotation, every shift coming through. What else did I have to do? But this one guard was the only one who waved. And to my shock, he did so nearly every time he came through. It wasn't an accident, either. When Dr. Jacobs was watching closely, the guard remained as still and obedient as all the others.

Now, that guard was moving toward the broken-window wall, and me, with purpose. He reached the edge and kicked at the remaining sharp pieces surrounding the hole in the bottom half of the window. When the shards fell inward, he bent down carefully.

"Come on, I know you're in there," he whispered.

I jerked back, retreating farther behind my cot.

"You don't have to be afraid."

In my limited experience, that statement was only a sure indicator that I *should* be afraid. And I was. I could get nothing from his thoughts but a vague sense of frustration and worry. That alone was a little frightening. I was used to being able to "hear" the noise of human thoughts, even if I couldn't always pick out specifics.

I heard his boots crunch on the broken glass as he shifted position. "If we're going to get you out of here, we don't have much time." The urgency in his voice finally registered with me. He was truly worried. Why? Surely, if he waited long enough, more guards would arrive to help him. He had nothing to fear.

I remained still, waiting, expecting him to call for assistance or charge in after me.

Instead he sighed. "I have a little girl, not much older than you. She's been sick for a long time. She hates being in the hospital, being poked and prodded. I can only imagine what it must be like for you. It's not right."

I could feel his outrage along with his love for his daughter, mixed with weariness and worry. Given how little I'd sensed from him before, he felt very strongly about both topics: my captivity and his daughter.

"But I think I can get you outside, if you'll trust me," he said.

I looked up sharply. He'd said the magic word. Well, the one that was magic to me. Clutching my arm to my chest, I scooted closer to the edge of the cot and peered out at him. "Outside?"

He nodded slowly, as if sudden movement might frighten me away. "Do you want to go outside?"

That kind of direct question was usually a test. I eyed him speculatively. "Dr. Jacobs would not want me to go."

The man didn't wave away my words or tell me that I was wrong. Instead he just looked at me. "What do *you* want to do?"

That was, as far as I could remember, the first time anyone had ever asked me that question. Normally, someone was right there telling me what to do. Issuing commands over the intercom.

But this man, he was waiting at the edge of the room for my answer. He wasn't charging in to drag me off, or shouting at me to do as I was told. He was *asking* me. I didn't realize until years later why that was struck me so deeply—my father was the first one to treat me as a *person*.

Half fearing that this was an elaborate trick, I stood up, my insides quivering with fear and anticipation. "I want to go. Outside."

He held out his hand for me. "Then let's go."

I hesitated for a moment, trying to think it through. Finally, the voice that had been shouting at me earlier kicked in. *Someone will come for you sooner or later. And this one, he defied Dr. Jacobs. Just like you. GO. NOW!*

And, my logical side rationalized, even if it did turn out to be a trick, I would likely be safer with him than any of the others who would come later.

So I left the safety of my tipped-over cot—my known world—to take his hand. It was the best decision I'd ever made. Except, perhaps, refusing to cooperate with Dr. Jacobs in the first place, but even that had had unforeseen consequences I still struggled with.

I was lucky that my father had chosen to associate his daughter with the small strange-looking child I'd been and taken the risk to save me. And I couldn't repay his leap of faith by taking more unnecessary chances. Not for Jenna this morning, and definitely not with Zane. His plan, tempting though it was, involved too many variables, too many opportunities for the situation to spin out of control.

So I would have to continue on as I was.

The disappointment tasted bitter, and I tried to remember that at breakfast, only an hour ago, I'd been relieved to find that my cover remained intact.

The phone in the side pocket of my backpack buzzed suddenly, startling me. I waited for Miss Lenosi to face the whiteboard and then reached down and pulled it free, to find a half dozen new text messages from Jenna. I must have missed them with all the noise in the hall.

> You're coming, right?
> I'm here. Where are you?
> Where are you?!!!!!
> Ariane? You promised!
> I can't believe you'd just leave me here!

And finally . . .

> Some friend you are.

I sighed. Unfortunately for both of us, today was not our day.

CHAPTER 8

Zane

IT TOOK RACHEL UNTIL LUNCH TO CATCH UP WITH ME. In line for food, I had my back to the rest of the cafeteria, but when I felt cool fingertips on my neck, I knew who it was.

"Are you mad?" she asked in a pouty whisper.

I sighed. At least she knew me well enough to know that I wouldn't be happy at what she'd said to Trey. But my anger at her had faded over the last few hours into a low-level simmering resentment. I probably had Ariane Tucker to thank for that little wake-up call. I wasn't sure what I'd been thinking or if I'd been thinking at all, going to her and proposing that wacked-out plan. I was lucky she hadn't taken me up on it. Rachel was just being Rachel; it was better to ride it out.

"Trey was being all sensitive, you know how he gets." Ignoring the tray in my hands, Rachel slipped her arm through mine, which jostled everything, knocking my milk container over into my mashed potatoes. "I had to say something to get him to understand."

Or she could have not kissed me in the first place. That would have worked. I still didn't know what was up with that. If she didn't want to have to smooth things over with Trey, she'd have been far better off keeping her mouth to herself.

She pulled my arm tighter between her breasts, and I could feel her warm, soft skin against mine, where the front of her shirt dipped low.

Did she think that would work on me?

"Come on, Zane," she pleaded. "Don't hold a grudge."

"Just because Trey has C-lunch doesn't mean he won't hear about this," I said, looking down at my arm held hostage.

Rachel let go of me with a sigh of disgust, confirming my suspicion that she was once again simply toying with Trey until it suited her to do otherwise.

"Two veggie burgers, please," I said to the woman behind the counter.

"Real men eat meat, Zane," Rachel said in a snippy, know-it-all tone.

"What do you want, Rachel?" I said, mimicking the rhythm of her speech.

She narrowed her eyes at me, suspicious that I was making fun of her. "I just wanted to find out if we're going to have company this week. I heard you were talking to our special friend."

"I talked to her." I took the plate of veggie burgers from the weary-looking lunch lady and nodded my thanks.

"And?" Rachel persisted.

"She said no." In truth, it had been more than that and less. I wasn't quite sure what had happened. For as much as Ariane had regarded my offer with cold disdain, I'd seen how she'd looked at Rachel yesterday—white-hot electric hate. Participating in this countergame of Rachel's should have been the easiest decision in the world for her. But she'd refused. Some of it might have been because she didn't trust me, and I couldn't blame her. She had no reason to, and what she'd seen us do to her friend Jenna yesterday probably hadn't helped.

I winced at the memory of censure on Ariane's face. She was right. Jenna hadn't deserved it. Maybe I should have spoken up and tried to stop Rachel, but "Rachel on a mission" fits pretty much in the same category as "runaway train loaded with explosives." Get out of the way or be counted among the dead.

"She said no?" Rachel gaped at me as if I'd spoken words she'd never heard before.

I took advantage of the momentary reprieve to pay for my lunch and head over to the table by the windows, where Matty and a few guys from the lacrosse team were already eating. Next year we'd be able to leave campus for lunch, even if it was only to go to the park across the street. But for now we were trapped, rats in the worst maze ever. The same corners, the same dead ends, the same boring cheese that had gone stale years ago. I'd enjoyed this once, hadn't I? I'd been happy to be Rachel's friend, pleased that I could follow in Quinn's popular footsteps, maybe even besting him slightly. After all, Arthur Jacobs had only one granddaughter, and she was my age, my friend. Not Quinn's. Even my dad had been pleased by that.

Now it all seemed tired and childish and not worth it.

I might have wondered when that had all changed, except I knew. To an exact date.

I'd spent years doing anything and everything that I thought might make my dad proud, including acting like a complete tool on various occasions, because, hey, that's what he would have done, right? In doing so, I'd paid little or no attention to the one person who loved me for who I was. If anything, I'd tried to keep distance between me and my mom, knowing my dad saw us as two of a kind.

It wasn't until after she was gone that it finally clicked. I'd been worrying about failing the wrong person. Nothing I did would ever be good enough for my dad, and by relentlessly seeking his approval, I'd lost my mom's.

Rachel followed me across the cafeteria. I could hear her heels clicking loudly a step or two behind me. People turned to see her coming, watching either with awe or great wariness as she approached.

Ignoring her and the inevitable storm to come, I set my tray down and dropped into an available chair, nodding at the guys.

"What do you mean she said no?" Rachel hissed in my ear. Instead of sitting down, she remained standing, sending out the message, consciously or not, that she was above us.

"Who said no to what?" Matty asked, his mouth full of food.

"Shut up and eat your pudding, Matty," Rachel snapped,

reaching down to shove his overloaded tray closer to him, her gold bracelets clanging against the hard tabletop.

"Coach told me I need to bulk up," he mumbled, his face flushing.

"It does occasionally happen," I said to Rachel. "Girls say no." And it did, but not usually to me.

Ariane's face, pale and accusing, flashed in my mind.

Rachel huffed impatiently. "I knew I should have sent Jonas."

"You can't now," I pointed out, pleased that part of my plan had worked out, at least. "She'll be too suspicious."

Rachel abandoned any pretense of casual friendliness, or friendliness at all. "What? So now you're on her side?" she demanded, folding her arms over her chest.

I was, actually. I liked Ariane, what little I knew of her. Maybe even more now because she hadn't fallen all over herself to get back at Rachel, though she clearly wanted to. I shrugged. "My point is, you're not going to get what you want from her."

"What is that supposed to mean?" she asked.

"It means she's not stupid. I think she's already accepted that you're out to get her, and she'll take whatever you're going to dish out." I had to admire that kind of resilience and determination. I might do better with my dad if I had half of that.

Rachel, however, looked offended. It was the fear she thrived on, and Ariane had taken that away from her. My admiration of Ariane—strange quiet thing that she was—edged upward another notch.

Rachel straightened up, her mouth thinning into a tight

line. "We'll see." She spun away from me in a whirl of red fabric and expensive perfume.

"Rachel. What are you doing?" I called after her, alarmed.

But she ignored me, making a beeline for the doors to the hall.

Shit. In trying to warn her off, I'd only pointed her straight to Ariane at full speed.

"Rachel better hurry before they finish with the cameras," Matty muttered.

"What are you talking about?"

Matty tipped his head toward the far wall, and I saw a guy in a black jumpsuit with a bright red GTX logo on a ladder, messing with some cables. "Didn't you hear the announcement this morning?" he asked, loading up his fork again.

I vaguely remembered hearing the loudspeaker going off when I was in the hall, tracking down Ariane.

"GTX donated a new security system to the school. They're installing it today." He swallowed and then chugged from his Gatorade bottle. "Cameras everywhere, man. Gonna be harder than hell to get away with anything now."

Huh. Wouldn't that be a nice piece of poetic justice if Rachel got busted by the same system the school had probably fawned all over her grandfather to get?

I sat back in my chair, smiling at the idea.

"Not that it matters for Rachel," Matty continued with a sigh. "That girl could get away with murder." He sounded envious, not angry about the injustice.

And he was right. My smile faded. The cameras could

catch Rachel doing just about anything, and the front office would find some way to excuse it or simply not see it. Especially if they wanted to keep her grandfather's favor and any other expensive equipment he chose to send the school's way.

Damn. I really hoped Ariane Tucker knew what she was doing.

CHAPTER 9

Ariane

"YOUR DAD MADE YOU STAY HOME THIS MORNING?" Jenna sounded skeptical.

I'd managed to delay the inevitable until after fourth hour simply by profusely apologizing via text and saying I'd explain my absence later, in person. But now, walking to the cafeteria, I was out of time and excuses for, well, not providing my other excuse.

"He didn't make me stay home completely," I said. "Obviously. I'm here. He just needed me to stay at home a little later."

I hated blaming my father for everything. But the best lies are the ones closest to the truth. And since telling her "I couldn't meet you this morning because it might draw more attention to me and therefore eventually destroy my carefully calculated guise as a normal and completely human student" was out, this was the next best thing.

Jenna hoisted her overstuffed bag up higher on her shoulder. She'd obviously been avoiding her locker between classes by the amount of books she was carrying. "Look, I don't mean to pry or anything, but is everything okay at home? Your dad seems to want *a lot* of together time." She wrinkled her nose.

I sighed. *Crap.* I was straying too far from social norms again. She was worried my father had an unhealthy interest in my life.

It was such a ridiculously fine line to walk between half-truths and arousing suspicion. Even if that suspicion was not, "Hey, you're an escaped science project," and more of the "Exactly how 'special' is Daddy's special girl?" it didn't matter. Getting adults involved—particularly those from some kind of governmental social services program—would be bad for my cover as a "normal" person.

"My mom is dead, and in two years he'll be alone," I said.

I'd discovered that bringing up a dead parent puts an end to almost any conversation. And since one of my "parents" was likely dead, it wasn't far from the truth.

At least I hoped he or she was dead. That sounds terrible until you consider the alternative. The source of the "foreign" material used in my creation—a nonterrestrial being who'd been minding his/her/its own business until it had been shot down, here on Earth, outside of Roswell in 1947, according to a variety of Internet conspiracy theorists—was surely out there somewhere, locked away in some secret facility, no doubt. I'd seen enough alien autopsy specials on television to know that.

But the thought of him or her alive and contained in some bright white room, alone except for when someone came in with oversized needles to remove samples for further cloning/hybridization, made me ill. The image of that same being dead and floating in an oversized jar of formaldehyde was equally horrific. But at least he or she would no longer be within reach of human harm. Lesser of two evils, and all of that.

I used to wonder if there was a family out there in a galaxy far, far away wondering what had happened when they lost contact with the one who'd been sent here. That same family would be mine, too, indirectly. But since I would never know, I couldn't allow myself to dwell on it.

My mother, a human surrogate, might be dead as well, for all I knew. GTX did not take project security lightly. It was only from information obtained through my father's GTX sources that I even knew I'd had a mother instead of donated human stem cells and an obliging petri dish or something.

I used to think about her, the surrogate, sometimes. Had they told her what I was? Had she been afraid? Maybe she'd hated me before I was even born. I'd seen enough TV and movies to know that the idea of hosting an alien or alien/human hybrid was often seen as terrifying and/or life-ending. (*V*, *Alien*, *Aliens*, etc., and the entire Stargate franchise.)

Or maybe she'd loved this creation that was some percentage of her own DNA and wished she hadn't had to leave me with GTX.

I had no way of knowing what was a realistic possibility and what was simply my human side, longing for a connection. So I tried not to think about her anymore, whoever she was.

But Mark Tucker was within my realm of knowledge, and I was genuinely worried about what my adoptive father would do after I was gone. Who would look out for him? Who would make sure he took his pills? Or call 911 if necessary? He didn't have anyone but me. He could have married again, started a new family. But instead he'd chosen to save me and given up the possibility of rebuilding his life. Once I was gone—and likely not ever able to return—he'd be alone. Lonely, perhaps. I knew what it was to be alone, truly alone, and I wouldn't wish it on anyone.

Jenna grimaced. "I know. I'm sorry about your mom." She hesitated. "But I think maybe you need to branch out. Try to have your own life and not—"

She would have pressed further, but a group of freshmen girls leaving A-lunch passed us. They, who should have been looking scared, hassled, or overwhelmed on their second day, had the audacity to giggle and whisper behind their hands while staring at Jenna.

Jenna's face turned bright red. "We're just going to go in, get our food, and get out, right?" she asked. "I've got passes to the library." She dug out a slip of paper from her bag and handed it to me.

I glanced at it. Signed by Mrs. Jurs, the guidance counselor. She was hopelessly ineffective at anything resembling guidance or counseling, from what I'd heard, but valuable, it seemed, in her generous distribution of hall and library passes.

"Fine." It had taken several text messages to convince Jenna to agree to this instead of skipping lunch entirely, which I could not do. I have to have food every few hours or risk fainting, which might mean the nurse's office—or worse, an ambulance.

But it wouldn't be a hardship for me to eat somewhere other than the crowded cafeteria. The audible noise was deafening; the mental noise was worse. It was a pit of anxiety and thinly veiled panic that began fifty feet down the corridor from the lunchroom doors, especially this early in the school year, when friendships and lunch table alliances were being formed and broken. I'd walked past SAT testing rooms that were calmer.

But I was concerned that hiding from everyone might send the wrong message. If Jenna wanted everything to return to normal, she was only putting off an inevitable period of awkwardness. The longer she delayed, the worse it would be, the more people would speculate and anticipate her return. The best way to reestablish the "normal" pattern was to resume it as soon as possible. I was something of an expert on this topic.

But I knew Jenna wouldn't want to hear it.

I wrestled with the decision as we approached the cafeteria doors, while Jenna remained uncharacteristically silent, no doubt gearing herself up for her entrance. Was it my responsibility to warn her of the flaw in her plan? Or would it be abnormal to have this kind of insight and share it?

The problem with overthinking everything in order to appear normal and mundane is that you sort of lose track of what insights a regular person would or would not have. Therefore, figuring out the right (a.k.a. the average, human, normal) thing to do was something I struggled with daily. Sometimes it was easy. If it was information I'd learned only by hearing someone's thoughts, no problem—pretend I'd never heard it and act accordingly.

But if it was something more subtle than that, a conclusion I should have reached by observation or years of experience, a conclusion or thought a full-blooded human *might* share if he or she was observant and/or moderately intelligent . . . then I had to decide what to do. What was the likelihood that Ariane Tucker, the version of me that I presented to others, would know something like this and be inclined to speak up about it?

God, it was so complicated, so many variables.

As we rounded the final corner, the noise increased and I winced at the blast of emotions and thoughts, all at a fever pitch. It was what I imagined the Colosseum must have sounded like in the days when religious persecution and entertainment were one and the same.

My stomach clenched, knowing Jenna wouldn't be the only one stared at. The two of us together would be twice the spectacle. I didn't want to go in there any more than Jenna did, but I was accustomed to looking past the emotion of the moment to find the logic.

"I'm going straight for the salad bar, and I'll meet you back out here," she said, digging into her bag for her wallet. She pulled her money free and tucked the bills into her pocket for faster removal.

Except the far more strategic move would have been to stay and suffer today in the hopes that tomorrow or next week would be better.

In the end, I had only my instincts, and they were screaming at me to speak up.

I hesitated, then said, "Jenna, maybe we should—"

A man in a GTX uniform crossed into the hall from the cafeteria, carrying a ladder, and my voice dried up in my throat.

Paying no attention to me, he leaned the ladder against the wall and climbed up to adjust a video camera on the wall, one that had not been there before.

Cold washed over me, and I couldn't move. It was like one of my nightmares, where the faceless men appeared in my bedroom to take me back to GTX and I couldn't run or hide. I let them drag me out the door, where a version of Dr. Jacobs, so much taller than everything around him, including my house, waited with that false expression of paternal fondness.

Jenna stopped outside the cafeteria when she noticed I wasn't with her, and turned around. "What's wrong?" she asked with a frown.

The tech on the ladder glanced down at us and then promptly returned to his work.

"Nothing," I managed to say through numb lips, barely able to breathe. "I need to make a call."

Jenna's bright blue eyes widened. "What? Now? Are you kidding me?"

I ignored her, fumbling in my pocket for my phone.

Jenna hurried toward me. "Wait until we get our lunch, please. We're almost there, and the rest of A-lunch is going to empty out soon." She sounded panicked. She wanted to try to sneak in during the five to ten minutes of transition between A- and B-lunch, while most everyone else was finishing eating or at their locker.

I shook my head, my neck so tight it felt as if it might snap. "I have to check in with my dad. I'm sorry." That was protocol for anything unexpected like this. Why hadn't he warned me?

I hit speed dial for my father's cell, ignoring Jenna's loud sound of disbelief, and turned my back on her and the GTX tech.

While the phone rang on the other end, I forced myself to focus and put the pieces together. The cameras meant surveillance. No doubt about that. My father had said they were ramping up the search for me. The fact that they were putting up cameras here, in my school . . . that had to mean they'd zeroed in on this location. That was bad. Unspeakably bad. I could almost feel Dr. Jacobs staring down at me. But they didn't know who they were watching for; they couldn't, or else they wouldn't have bothered with cameras. They would have just sent in a team to get me.

I lowered my guard and focused on the thoughts of the tech only fifteen feet behind me. He hadn't seemed remotely interested in me . . . and he wasn't.

God, that food stinks. Wonder what Mariella packed. A flash of a smiling dark-haired woman with a brown lunch bag in her hand. *Not that I'll get to eat anytime soon. So behind.* A second flash, this one a piece of paper with the words URGENT, PRIORITY stamped across it. *Ten more after this. They never should have scheduled us for this one today. I don't care who signed the order.*

"Ariane?" My father's voice on the phone pulled me from the tech's thoughts.

"Hey, Dad." The words sounded so stiff and stilted.

"Checking in, like you asked." That was a fabrication, but better than letting anyone who might be monitoring think I had another reason for calling.

Behind me, I heard Jenna huff in exasperation, and when I looked, she had disappeared through the double doors of the cafeteria. Evidently, going alone was better than going in late.

"Is everything okay?" He sounded alarmed but cautious.

"Sure, everything is great. Oh, hey, it looks like we're getting a new security system here, cameras everywhere. Did you know about that?"

Silence held on the other end of the phone, and my stomach plummeted. He hadn't known.

"Do I have a dentist appointment today?" I persisted. *Dentist appointment* was code for *Leave immediately*. Cell phone conversations were all too easily intercepted.

"No," he said finally. "I don't think so. Unless . . . your teeth are bothering you."

It took me a second to extrapolate his meaning. Run if I felt threatened. Well, easier said than done. I always felt some level of threat, and GTX in my immediate environment absolutely did not help.

"Not right now," I said.

"Let me check in about the dentist, and I'll get back to you. If you don't hear from me, proceed normally."

I winced. Even I knew *that* didn't sound like something a "regular" dad would say.

He paused. "I mean, come home and do your homework."

"Right, okay."

He hung up before I could say good-bye, and though

talking to him usually reassured me, there were too many gaps, too many pauses this time.

He should have known this was happening. He had sources in GTX for this exact sort of situation. Unless GTX was keeping things quieter than normal. That might mean they thought they were closing in on me. And/or maybe someone had finally figured out that we had a mole on the inside. My father might be under suspicion.

I couldn't shake the feeling of dread creeping up in me. GTX was nipping at my heels. The only question was how long would it take them to pin me down.

Glancing at the camera behind me and the tech fussing with it, I had to guess it wouldn't be long.

Urgency pulsed through me. I had to find a way to stop my little power outbursts and regain control. Immediately. My father had theorized that time, patience, and practice would eventually work. But I couldn't wait anymore.

I had to do something else. Now. But what? If I'd had other ideas to try, I would have tried them already.

I could feel desperation swelling in my chest, threatening to cut off my breath.

The bell signaling the official end of A-lunch rang, startling me. I forced myself to slowly draw in air.

Think, just think. But the noise from the cafeteria—both in my ears and my head—made that impossible. And standing here in the hall, pondering it all, right in the flow of traffic and ten feet from a GTX employee wasn't smart. Better to catch up with Jenna, get my food, and hide out with her in the library, where I could hear myself think.

I tucked my phone into my pocket and started toward

the cafeteria, but before I'd covered half the distance, a loud crash came from inside, followed by a piercing shriek.

Jenna.

I ran for the doors. Her distress was coming through loud and clear, but her thoughts were too muddled with the others for me to get a clear picture of what had happened.

I stopped at the threshold, the scene frozen in front of me like some kind of tableau or diorama entitled *Trauma in the Lunch Line.*

Jenna was on the floor in front of the salad bar, lettuce from a plastic container spread around her. A broken bottle glittered in an orangish-pink puddle of juice. Jenna's face was flushed, and her hands were up as if to defend herself from an invisible force.

A big shiny metal dog collar hung loosely around her neck, the prongs tangled in her blond hair. A box of Milk-Bones lay on its side, its contents pouring out of the open top.

Oh God, Jenna.

I rushed toward her, ignoring the voice in my head that warned me to stay away. And the second I moved, the entire cafeteria broke free from its hold of surprise, and jolted to life again.

The room exploded in hoots of laughter, catcalls, wolf whistles, and "Here, doggy, doggy" from all directions. Mr. Scaliari, one of the teachers on cafeteria duty, left his position against the far wall and jogged toward us.

I avoided the broken bottle and knelt down next to Jenna, shielding her from view as much as I could. "Are you all right?" I whispered. I didn't see any blood, and I wasn't sensing physical pain—more shock, horror, and abject humiliation. The entire area reeked of too-sweet juice, ranch dressing, and something far less pleasant.

Jenna looked up at me, her hands still up in the air and shaking. Her eyes were filled with tears. "I . . . I stepped in something."

I glanced around and discovered a half-squashed bag of what appeared to be dog excrement under the edge of the salad bar. Probably from the park across the street and definitely the source of the bad smell.

"And when I tried to move back, they put . . . What is this?" She lowered her hands to pull at the collar around her neck. Before I could stop her, she ripped it off over her head, taking chunks of her hair with it in the links.

When she recognized it, her mouth worked wordlessly, and tears spilled down her cheeks. She looked as if she was going to be sick, and my stomach twisted in agony for her. "Oh, Jenna, I'm sorry. I should have been with you."

But she didn't seem to hear me, her gaze focused on something behind me.

I stood and turned. Rachel Jacobs was there, wearing another of her flimsy spaghetti-strap tank tops—in red, of course. Her arms were folded across her chest, gold bracelets poking out, emphasizing her tanned skin and her slim wrists.

Two of her cronies—Angela and Deni or Demi?—sophomores desperate for her approval, were on either side of her, grinning like idiots, empty plastic shopping bags in their hands. They may have done the actual dirty work, but even money said that Rachel had done the planning and the shopping.

The worst thing was, Rachel didn't attempt to pretend.

She didn't hurry away or make some offhand comment to pretty up what she'd done.

She just stood there and smiled. But not at Jenna. At *me*. She raised her eyebrows, and I heard her, loud and clear. *Yeah, what are you going to do about it?*

My heart sank. *She'll find your weak spot.* Zane's words echoed back at me, and I looked around, spotting him easily. He was standing at the back of the room, a tray in his hands.

Mouth tight, he looked unsurprised and weary at the events unfolding in front of him. His gaze met mine. *I told you.* His thought came through as distinctly as if he'd shouted it in my ear, his emotion and intensity lifting it above the mental chaos of the cafeteria.

Rachel was torturing Jenna to get back at me. Fresh rage swept over me, and a high-pitched buzz filled my head. The overhead lights began to sway and flicker. A low rattling came from the hall, followed by several sharp metallic bangs. Lockers flying open.

The barrier in my brain had dropped again.

My stomach twisted. *Oh, no. No, no, no. Not now.* Not with all these people around, and with the GTX tech right out in the hall.

Panic turned my fingertips cold, and the lights shook harder. We were maybe seconds from more lightbulbs exploding, or worse. The energy that had once bent to my will, moving objects as I desired, now ran wild, uncontrolled. Without focus, it would simply arc outward to nearby targets.

I could feel the energy tingling up and down my arms,

seeking direction that I could not give. *No! Stay calm, breathe through it,* the voice of logic from somewhere deep within me commanded. *Get control.*

Great idea, except I had no clue how. I visualized a white stone wall and then a metal door. Then a metal door inside a stone wall and . . . nothing. I couldn't stop it. It was like trying to hold back an ocean of waves, one right after another.

The few people not distracted by Jenna's plight began to look up and point at the lights.

I turned to face Rachel—always know your enemy's movements—but she was no longer paying attention to me. She was staring at Zane.

. . . he looking at her? Shouldn't be looking at her. Little freak!

I froze. Her thoughts were loud and intrusive, breaking into the buzz of power that filled my head.

What, because she's some weirdo stray he feels sorry for? The more Rachel's thoughts intruded, the more distracted I became. She was the only thing I could hear—so damned loud!—overwhelming even the thrum of my power gone wild.

And what was she talking about?

With that thought, the barrier in my mind suddenly slammed into place, knocking me back a step. The rattling from the hall stopped, and the lights slowed their swaying and began to provide steady illumination again.

My ears rang with the chatter of the cafeteria, marking the return of my regular hearing.

Whoa. What was that? What had just happened? I rubbed my hands over my arms, brushing away the last prickles of fading energy. The barrier had dropped, all that power about to go wild . . . and then it stopped. I'd heard Rachel through all the noise, and when I'd focused on her thoughts . . .

"Mayborne, Tucker, Jacobs, Carson, and Lehigh. To the office," Mr. Scaliari spoke behind me, startling me. I'd almost forgotten his presence. "Now." He sounded irritated.

With a loud huff, Rachel spun off toward the doors, her two henchwomen trailing.

I turned slowly to follow, feeling wobbly and out of sorts. All of that uncontrolled energy and force that would have blown something up had instead retreated within me. Mr. Scaliari was supporting Jenna with one hand under her arm. She looked pale, though her cheeks were splotchy and red.

She was frowning at me. "Are you okay?" she asked.

No. But I nodded.

"Tucker, let's go. Move!" Scaliari pointed at the doors with his free hand.

I drifted through the doorway and down the hall, seeing everything through a haze—the GTX tech on his ladder, the brightly colored Bonfire Week posters, several lockers hanging open, groups of B-lunchers heading toward the cafeteria—as my brain whipped up and discarded possible explanations and scenarios.

Had I gotten my control back in one fell swoop? The wall broken by one moment of extreme pressure? That had been one of my father's theories, once upon a time, and it sure as hell would be good timing if that's what had happened.

But no, when I forced myself to focus on one of the open locker doors, I couldn't make it budge.

Jenna's voice was a low murmur behind me as she talked with Mr. Scaliari.

I bit my lip. Something had happened. Something was different. That was the first time the barrier had dropped and gone up again without stuff blowing up or flying around the room.

It wasn't controlled. I'd simply gotten distracted, and when I'd focused on Rachel's thoughts, the mental block had snapped back into place.

But that was more control than I'd had before. I'd spent years practicing, trying to regain the use of my ability. But maybe that was like trying to cook in the kitchen when I was still locked out of the house.

Perhaps all those years of practice hadn't worked because the barrier had to be gone—even temporarily—for there to be any hope of making the ability mine again. It sort of made sense: how could I direct something I couldn't even access?

A chill slipped over my skin. Was it as simple as that? The theory seemed sound. But to know for sure, I needed to test it. Get the wall down and then try to duplicate the results. Unfortunately, I knew of only one way to reliably make that happen.

Rachel. Proximity to her would likely spawn at least one more opportunity, maybe more.

I gave a mental groan. That was not a good idea. So dangerous.

Then I looked up at one of the newly installed cameras—*GTX* emblazoned in red on the side—staring down at me from high on the wall. Was doing nothing, and waiting for a retrieval team to catch up to my father and me, a safer option?

"Stop dragging your feet, Tucker. Keep moving," Scaliari called.

I gritted my teeth and picked up the pace. There was another problem. Since my life up to this point had generally revolved around avoiding Rachel as much as possible, it wasn't as if I could suddenly start inviting myself to her lunch table. Not with any chance of success, anyway.

That left me only with one option if I was I going to go through with this insanity.

I was going to have to take Zane Bradshaw up on his offer.

A zing of anticipation shot through me. Because no matter what my practical reasons were for agreeing to Zane's proposition, participating came with one giant bonus. A chance to beat Rachel at her own game, an opportunity to score a victory for myself, for Jenna, for all the people Rachel walked on like it was her right to trod on a person-paved path.

I wanted that. Badly.

"Tucker!" Mr. Scaliari shouted over his shoulder. At some point, he and Jenna had passed me. "Hurry up."

But first I had to go to the principal.

I'd never been in the principal's office before. It struck me as surprisingly mundane for all the fear and dread everyone accorded it. Four walls and a desk with a computer, a phone, and some family photos. But Mr. Kohler himself, a large man with an enormous shiny head, may have played some role in that fear and respect.

"No one else can verify your story," he said to Jenna, leaning back in his worn leather desk chair, which creaked under his weight.

"The entire cafeteria saw what happened!" Jenna protested, her face tear-stained. She smelled of spilled juice and the dog "present" Rachel and her followers had put underfoot.

"That's not what I'm hearing," he said. "And it's your word against Rachel's."

It turned out Rachel had had a purpose in speeding out of the cafeteria. She'd arrived at the office first and had the principal wrapped around her finger—and her side of the story—before we arrived.

And evidently, no one else was willing to speak for us. It was like that gangland documentary I'd seen. No one will talk, for fear of being included in the next round of punishment/killing.

"But if Jenna's story is true, then Rachel is the aggressor," I pointed out. "Why should Rachel's word be given equal weight? It's not as if you expect her to admit doing wrong, is it?"

Principal Kohler frowned at me. "Who are you again?"

I swallowed hard. "Ariane Tucker."

He nodded slowly, but I could hear him rifling through his mental files of students and not coming up with anything. Which was how it was supposed to be, after all. But once again it would have been nice to have had a reputation as a solid student, non-troublemaker, and credible witness in this scenario, instead of a blank spot in his memory. "Well, Miss Tucker, Rachel is a good girl."

. . . I think. She runs with a wild crowd, but they're kids. The things I did when I was that age . . .

I cocked my head to one side, listening to him ramble internally. *Good grief. He isn't even sure what he believes about her.*

"And her family has done a lot for this school," he continued.

Now, that was the truth. He didn't want to lose the favor the school had with GTX and Arthur Jacobs.

It always came back to him. That bastard would rule in hell or bribe his way into it.

"Can you play back the recordings from the new cameras?" I asked, trying not to seem as if I was holding my breath waiting for the answer. If the cameras were on, I was toast.

"The new system isn't up and running yet," Mr. Kohler said. "They're still in the installation process."

And even if they hadn't been, there was no way he'd use the GTX-donated system to bust Rachel. I didn't need to hear his thoughts to know that. Still, it worked to my advantage in this case. I let out a breath.

"Look, girls, most of the time, these things end up being a misunderstanding. A joke that went too far, as Rachel said." Mr. Kohler steepled his hands on his desk, attempting to project wisdom and confidence. "It will all blow over in a few days."

At least, he was hoping it would. He was worried. He didn't want the Maybornes to force the issue. That would make things awkward. There was all this emphasis on preventing bullying these days. . . .

. . . *We're raising a generation of wimps.*

Lovely.

"I'm going to talk to Rachel again and make it very clear that all jokes are off, okay?"

Jenna looked weary. "Fine." She dabbed at her face with a tissue.

"Wait here while I get passes for you." Principal Kohler levered his bulk out from behind his desk and headed to the outer office.

"Will your mother fight for you?" I whispered to Jenna. "He'll take that seriously."

"Are you kidding?" she said. "My mom was literally Miss Popularity. That was her yearbook title and everything. She won't understand."

I frowned. That, at least, explained Jenna's obsession with Rachel and breaking into the "elite" crowd. I'd been in the car with Dr. Mayborne once or twice before, to and from various shopping excursions with Jenna. She gave a constant stream of gentle-sounding suggestions—"Wearing your hair back would give you a slimmer look, Jenna." "A longer skirt would be more flattering to your shape." "You know, I've heard that bronze is the new silver, which could really help add some color to your face."—that would have worn down someone far tougher than Jenna just by the sheer volume.

Jenna tipped her head up toward the ceiling, blinking back fresh tears. "God. If I could only figure out what I did wrong."

I stared at her. "You didn't do anything wrong."

"You don't understand." Jenna shook her head, blond

curls that had probably taken an hour to create sticking to her overheated face. "Rachel wouldn't be nice to me only to turn on me."

I would have gaped at her naïveté, but this was Jenna. "She would do exactly that," I said, more harshly than I should have. "That was her intent in the first place."

Which was, I guess, the wrong thing to say.

Her face crumpled. "Seriously? You're supposed to be my friend and you say that? Like it's impossible that she could have been genuinely nice to me?"

"Yes," I said.

"Ariane!"

"Not because there's anything wrong with you," I said quickly. I wasn't explaining this well. I fumbled for the words to explain something that, to Jenna, would be completely foreign. "That's how Rachel is. She only sees people in terms of what she can get from them."

It made sense to me, as much as I didn't care for it. It was how Dr. Jacobs viewed the world; though in his case, it was less about mean-spirited entertainment and more about no-holds-barred scientific advancement.

I glanced toward the outer office to make sure Principal Kohler couldn't overhear. From the sounds of it, he'd gotten caught up in lecturing somebody about not using the bike racks for skateboard "stunts." "But listen, it's okay. I have a plan," I said to Jenna, with another involuntary shiver of glee.

Jenna frowned at me. "What kind of plan?" She paled. "Is this about getting back at Rachel?"

I opened my mouth to speak, but before I could say

anything, she cut me off, her hand up. "Look, I wish I was more like you, Ariane. That I didn't care about being alone and not having a life."

Stung, I straightened up. It wasn't that I didn't care about being alone or lonely. I just had to be careful in how I went about resolving the issue. I didn't have a choice in that.

"But I want a life, and I'm not going to get what I want by pissing off Rachel." She hesitated, then stood and slung her juice-stained bag over her shoulder. "Maybe we should take some time. . . ."

I realized with a harsh start that by "we," she meant *me*. That *I* should give her time, a chance to mend the imaginary fences she thought she'd broken in her "friendship" with Rachel without the added burden of me, another outcast. After all, in Jenna's mind, everything had been going great with Rachel until school started and the two of us, Jenna and I, were together again.

I swallowed hard against the unexpected lump in my throat. "Sure." I forced the word out.

"It's not forever, just until all of this gets straightened out," she said, backing toward the door.

Which would never happen because Rachel wouldn't change and Jenna would never see things the way they truly were. But I nodded, and Jenna smiled with relief. Then she turned and walked to the outer office. A second later, I heard her asking for a late pass to class.

I couldn't move. My fingers were wrapped so tightly around the metal armrests of the chair, I was worried they might break. I should have been grateful. Jenna, as my weak spot, would cause only more trouble for me with Rachel.

But I wasn't grateful. My chest ached with the hurt. Rachel had managed to win again, taking the only person I counted as a friend. And the worst part? It wouldn't change things. Rachel would still abuse Jenna, gaining her trust and then turning against her. And if she sensed Jenna's abandonment of me as a sign of my vulnerability, she'd probably take the opportunity to come after me again.

No. Just no. Rage welled up inside of me, and the picture frames on Kohler's desk began to jitter and dance.

Calm down. Breathe. I clamped down on the anger and forced myself to release my death grip on the chair arms, letting my breath out slowly. But then the lightbulb in Kohler's desk lamp gave with a quiet pop, followed by the delicate tinkling of broken glass, and something inside me eased, the built-up power released.

Shit. With a quick glance toward the door—I could hear the slightly whiny voice of the skateboard dude protesting loudly—I stood up and swept most of the glass off the desk into the trash, then straightened the pictures that had vibrated out of place.

It wasn't perfect, but it was better than doing nothing.

Which was pretty much the description of my plan. And I was going forward with it, Jenna or no Jenna.

I had to.

Rachel needed to see what it felt like to hurt, to lose for once. She and her grandfather had taken *everything* from me. Yes, it might save my life if I could regain control over the barrier in my brain and keep GTX from finding me. And maybe by keeping Rachel's attention focused on me, I could protect Jenna. But those were justifications, excuses for doing what I wanted—no, craved—with a frightening urgency.

See, this was the problem with creating a freak like me. I had the drive to win, to crush competitors who had no idea what they were up against, combined with an advanced ability to predict, plan, and manipulate. And you could bury all of that under layers of civility and rules, but it wouldn't go away.

It might have been my human side clamoring for blood, or my alien side looking for a chance to exercise strategic dominance over a lesser life-form. Either way, I was going to win.

CHAPTER 10

Zane

MY WHOLE BODY ACHED BY THE TIME LAST BELL RANG. The hallway around my locker had emptied out already—everyone dashing for the door as soon as they could—but I was moving slowly. The ibuprofen I'd snagged from Cami had worn off hours ago.

But it wasn't just the remnants of the hangover dragging me down. All afternoon I'd had to watch Trey mooning over Rachel; Rachel gloating at having coasted through the lunch trouble with nothing more than a stern warning from Mr. Kohler; and Cami, Cassi, Jonas, and Matty talking about the same things, the same people, as last year. I was so tired of all of this claustrophobic inner-circle crap.

And yet I stuck around. What did that say about me? But what was I supposed to do, cut them off? Join the goth crowd smoking behind the gym? Where else was I going to go?

"I'm in."

Startled, I turned to see Ariane behind me.

I slammed my locker shut and pulled my backpack up over my shoulders. "You're in what?"

"Your plan. The one you described this morning." She looked fierce, ready to spit nails. I couldn't blame her. But I couldn't help her either. Not anymore.

"It's too late for that," I said. "You saw what happened at lunch."

Her mouth tightened. "That's why I'm here."

"Zane, you coming, man?" Trey shouted from the other end of the hall, where he was waiting impatiently near the glass doors to the parking lot, car keys in hand.

"I'll meet you at the car," I shouted back. I turned to Ariane. "She'll never believe it. She already knows you said no. Forget it." There was no point in trying to fight. Just ride it out. Only another seven-hundred-odd days, right?

I started to walk away, but Ariane followed. "She'll believe it because she wants to believe it. She wants the opportunity to crush me more than she wants to think it through." I could hear the bitterness and disdain curling the edges of her words.

I stopped and looked at her. She wasn't pleading; she was too angry for that. Her eyes, that strange muddled blue, held barely restrained fury. I'd never seen or heard Ariane this emotional about anything, except in telling me off this morning. She was half my size but looked ready to break someone's arm off.

A flicker of interest in my original plan—and in this strange girl who made no sense—flared up again. "All right," I said. "What did you have in mind?"

She didn't sigh in relief or smile or say thank you, but the tension in her shoulders eased. "The same thing you proposed this morning. Bonfire Week."

I frowned. "The activities fair starts in three hours." Even from here I could hear distant echoing voices from the gym and the loud whine of what might have been a power saw as the various clubs set up their booths.

"I can be ready." She raised her eyebrows, her gaze taking me in from head to toe. A small but mocking smile played on her lips. "Can you?"

I grimaced. I must have looked pretty rough. No more drinking on weeknights. "Fine. Yes. Then what?"

Her brows drew together, crinkling her forehead. "What do you mean?"

I felt the tiniest bit vindicated at having figured out something before her. "I mean, we can't just show up at this stuff, the fair, the game, the bonfire, and that's it. If it's supposed to look legit, like we're into each other for real—and trust me, Rachel would expect that of any scheme of hers—then we've got to take it an extra step."

Ariane eyed me warily. "I don't like the sound of that."

"Do you walk to school?" I asked, ignoring the doubt in her voice. I waited for her to nod, though I already knew the answer. Trey and I had passed her often enough last year when we were coming in early for one thing or another.

"If I can get the truck for school, I'll pick you up tomorrow morning." My dad usually drove his work car, an SUV emblazoned with WINGATE CHIEF OF POLICE. If he could have had it personalized with his name, he probably would have. That meant the battered Blazer that Quinn drove was sitting unused in the garage. I could have argued for the right to take it to school, but since Trey had a car, it wasn't worth the fight unless I had a date.

"What? Why do you need to pick me up?" Ariane looked alarmed.

"The extra step," I reminded her patiently. "School pickup, drop-off, lunch probably . . ."

Ariane made a face, whether in memory of today's incident or the idea in general.

"But not at my house," she insisted. "You can't pick me up at my house."

In spite of myself, I felt the first tendrils of intrigue uncurling. She didn't want me at her house. Was it only me? Or everyone? "Okay," I said slowly. "Then how do you expect me to pick you up for the fair tonight?"

"We could meet in the parking lot and—" she began.

"Because no one would notice that and call us on it?" I asked. "Try again."

She scowled at me. "Fine. Two blocks from my house. Pine and Rushmore. But *don't* wait on Pine, go around the corner."

Uh-oh. I cocked my head to one side, staring at her curiously. "Are you sneaking out?" Come to think of it, I wasn't sure I'd ever seen her at anything outside of school, even regular extracurriculars like the fair tonight.

"No," she said, too quickly.

Great. "Look, I don't know what your life is like right now, but mine kind of sucks and I don't need more heat from my dad if your dad decides to get pissed about—"

"It's fine," she said. "He won't even be home. I just . . . I just don't want to answer a bunch of questions about what I'm doing if someone sees the truck in the driveway and mentions it to him." She shifted uncomfortably, avoiding my gaze.

Oh, she was so lying. Maybe not about her dad being gone, but about the sneaking out? Most definitely. But Wingate was a small town; no way we would stay a secret for long, which meant all of this would come raining down on my head at some point.

I hesitated, then shrugged. *Oh, what the hell.* My dad already hated me, what was one more reason for it? Hey, if her dad was Mark Tucker and this ended up making him cranky, maybe my dad would be pleased at having struck a blow at his mortal enemy.

"Fair starts at seven," I said. "What time do you want me to—"

"Quarter to. And don't be late," she added.

I resisted the urge to salute, figuring she might not take it well. I pulled my phone from my pocket. "What's your number?"

She narrowed her eyes at me. "Why?"

She was going to fight me every step of the way, even though this was her idea. This time, anyway. "How else do you want me contact you?" I asked slowly, as if to a child.

She frowned and made no move for her cell.

"Second thoughts already?" I asked, fighting disappointment. This was maybe the most interesting thing that had happened in months. I'd proposed my plan to her this morning out of anger and spite. I thought she'd go for it, and when she didn't, I thought better of her for it. And now . . . now she was coming back to me. I hadn't counted on that, and found I liked her even more for surprising me yet again.

She stuck her chin out. "No." She dug into her pocket and handed me her phone. I typed in my number.

"Here." I handed it back. "Call me."

She nodded and started to turn away.

"No." I snagged the edge of her bag to stop her, careful not to touch her directly. She'd been ready to bolt this morning whenever she thought I might make direct contact. "Now. So I have your number." You'd have thought she'd never exchanged numbers with someone before.

Her cheeks turned a pale pink. "Fine," she muttered.

She hit SEND on her phone, and as soon as mine rang, she hung up.

I typed her name in and saved it. "You know this could all blow up in our faces if Rachel catches on," I said, tucking my phone into my pocket. I found there was a part of me, bent on self-destruction, that was more than a little eager at the prospect, but I felt I had to warn Ariane. "If you think she's bad now . . ."

"She won't like it, but she'll believe." Ariane sounded absurdly confident.

I sighed. "Your funeral."

"Yes, it will be," she said solemnly.

Okaaaay. Before I could respond to that—I wasn't even sure what I would say—she turned and walked away. Her backpack—a plain green canvas rather than the pink sparkly or shiny black bags I was used to seeing from Rachel and her lot—pulled at her shoulders, and on the right side, where the neck of her shirt was bunched under the strap, I caught a glimpse of a square white edge. The bandage I'd seen last year.

My curiosity sparked to life again. Maybe tonight I'd start getting some of the answers I wanted. The missing pieces that would make her make sense.

When Trey dropped me off at home, I didn't retreat to my room as usual. Instead I cleared a space on the kitchen table and set the stage with my laptop open and books around it. I loaded and ran the dishwasher, but I didn't empty it. That would have been pushing it.

The trick to managing my dad was doing so without letting him catch on. There was an art to it. I'd watched my mom do it on my behalf for years. It meant choosing your words carefully, picking the right time, and positioning the situation and the desired action in a way that would make sense to him, right or wrong.

But after everything that happened last year, I'd been too pissed and confused to bother putting what I knew into practice. But now I wanted the truck, wanted to be able to pick up Ariane, enough to play his ridiculous game.

I was out of practice, though. I just hoped it would be enough.

If he kept to pattern, he'd show up between five thirty and six, and one of us would dig into the freezer for a casserole that some woman—either grandmotherly or looking to date my dad, it varied—had dropped off for us. Since my mom had left, my dad made a point of being home for dinner. Couldn't have people whispering about the poor neglected son left at home alone all the time, even if he was the "other Bradshaw boy." Appearances were everything to my dad.

I played at working on my homework—there was never very much in the first week anyway—while I waited and watched the clock. I'd be cutting it close for picking up Ariane, but it was a calculated gamble. If my dad had had a bad day, calling and interrupting him at work would trash my chances.

Killing time, I Googled Ariane. Yeah, it was a little stalker-y, but mostly I was just trying to find out what everyone else knew about her that I'd ignored or completely missed in the haze of last year.

Except it turned out Ariane Tucker was a ghost. Well, not really. But maybe as close to it as you can get and still be alive. In more ways than one.

There were lots of Ariane Tuckers in the United States, but they were the wrong age and/or living in the wrong place. This Ariane, the sixteen- or seventeen-year-old one in Wingate, Wisconsin, didn't show up at all. She didn't have a Facebook page or a Tumblr. No Twitter or Formspring either, as far as I could tell.

Then I tried searching her name in combination with the man I was guessing to be her dad, the infamous Mark Tucker.

Two listings came up. The first was an obituary from the archives of a newspaper in a small town in central Ohio. Dated from about ten years ago, it was for an Abigail Tucker, thirty-eight. She'd died in a single-car accident, a collision with a concrete bridge abutment on an icy night.

So Cami had been right. Ariane had come here after her mother's death. And Ariane *was* definitely related to the hated Mark Tucker. Interesting.

Then the second-to-last paragraph, right above the details for Abigail Tucker's funeral, caught my attention.

> *Mrs. Tucker is survived by her former husband, Mark Tucker. Ariane, the couple's six-year-old daughter, struggled valiantly in experimental treatment for a rare form of cancer, until several weeks ago when . . .*

I clicked for the next page, but got a 404 error, PAGE NOT FOUND. I tried again and got the same result.

I sat back in my chair. Cami said Ariane had been sick, but no one had ever mentioned that it was *this* bad. It sounded like she'd almost died. And then after surviving all of that, she'd had to deal with the fact that her mom was never coming back.

My mind immediately summoned up an image of the note on the kitchen table—a lone square of white paper on the polished wood—that Sunday morning. I'd stumbled in to find the kitchen empty and pristine. All the mess from Quinn's graduation party the night before had been cleaned up and put away. Not so much as a streamer remained on the wall. My mom must have been up for hours to get everything restored to normal in time for the next day, my birthday.

I'd been stupidly pleased. It was hard enough to have your birthday in the shadow of another big event, especially something for Quinn, but it would have been even worse if we'd been eating birthday cake on graduation plates, beneath balloons and banners that had been put up to celebrate him. Talk about proof that you're second best . . .

My mom, though, of all people, knew how it worked in our house. We were on the same side (or so I'd thought). She'd always done what she could to soften the blow of my father's disapproval.

I'd heard her moving around the house in the middle of the night—her footsteps much lighter than those of my dad or my brother—and thought nothing of it until I walked into the cleaned-up kitchen.

Smiling, I picked up the note. That was the last normal-ish moment I'd have for years. Maybe forever.

At first I thought it was a standard Mom note. *Running errands. DON'T eat Dad's leftovers from last night.* Or, *Picking up your cake at the bakery. Call and let me know if you've decided what you want for your birthday dinner tonight.*

But instead it was something entirely different, completely unexpected.

I just can't anymore.

—M

I'd failed so badly that even my mom, my one ally, couldn't stand to stay any longer. My dad had made her life miserable for years, and she'd probably thought about bailing a thousand times, but she'd hung in there long enough to get Quinn out the door and on his way to college. But I . . . I wasn't worth sticking around for. And she was right; I wasn't. Or at least I hadn't been back then. I was trying to be different now.

I forced my attention back to the screen in front of me and the information about Ariane. Despite the ominous tone of the article, she'd survived and was tougher than she looked. Maybe that was why she was so unrelenting and seemed a bit removed from all the high school idiocy going on around her. She knew there was more to life than what everyone else concerned themselves with.

That only increased my respect for her.

Her former illness might explain why she was excused from gym, as Cassi had pointed out last night. And considering it now, I wondered if the bandage on her shoulder was somehow related. Her treatment had been experimental, whatever that meant. It was possible she bore scars from her ordeal. Maybe that was what she was hiding beneath that bandage, not a tattoo at all.

The second listing for Ariane was from that same newspaper, published several weeks after the first article. I clicked on it, expecting an update on her condition, maybe an announcement about her triumphant return home. Instead it was a retraction, two terse and seemingly hurried lines.

> *In the February 28 issue, Ariane Tucker, daughter of Mark and Abigail Tucker, was reported to have died. We regret the error.*

I read it twice to make sure I wasn't missing something, but the meaning didn't change. How bizarre was that? How can you get somebody's *death* wrong? I mean, it happened all the time with celebrities—some famous person was forever announcing that he or she was still alive—but with a random little girl in Ohio? That seemed odd.

The back door banged open, startling me. My dad walked in, carrying a pizza box in one hand and a stack of mail in the other. He dropped them both on the island with a heavy sigh and then paused to rub the back of his neck, like the muscles were kinking up. His jacket was hanging open in the front, and he looked tired.

I froze. Uh-oh. This could go either way.

"Dinner," he shouted toward the back of the house, before noticing my presence at the table with a double take.

"Sausage?" I ventured, shutting down my browser and pretending I hadn't seen the surprise on his face.

He grunted an affirmative, shrugging out of his jacket and hanging it on the back of a chair. Judging by the size of the box, the pizza was a medium, barely enough to feed both of us for one meal. When I ordered I always got the extra large, enough for multiple meals.

But I kept my mouth firmly clamped shut. He'd taken the initiative to bring food home; that was unusual and a good sign. He'd done that occasionally when my mom was still around, surprising us with takeout or telling us to load up into the car for a meal at Morelli's. It was sort of his way of apologizing without actually saying the words "I'm" or "sorry."

I was cautiously optimistic.

Watching him as he flipped through the mail, I pushed away from the table to get a plate from the dishwasher.

A moment later, my dad followed suit, saying nothing about the fact that there were clean dishes finally. Then again, the absence of screaming was usually the best I could hope for. So far, so good.

I opened the pizza box and grabbed a half dozen squares and returned to my seat at the table, fighting the urge to scoop my laptop up with one hand and my pizza with the other and take off for my room. That was usually how "we" ate dinner: I retreated to my room and he stayed in the kitchen or disappeared to the basement family room.

I waited until he'd served himself and settled at the table, trying to get the timing right. But before I could speak, he beat me to it.

"How was school?" he asked, sprinkling pepper flakes over his pizza.

No sneer. No follow-up caustic comment. It was like he was genuinely asking. I almost fell out of my chair in surprise. "Fine," I managed. Either his meeting with GTX this morning had gone really well, or the exact opposite. It had happened in the past, on occasion, that after an apparently crappy day, he seemed to be relieved to be at home, where no one would judge him and find him lacking. Ah, the perils and pressures of social climbing.

I couldn't let his rare good—or not so bad—mood stop me, though; not when he'd given me the perfect opening.

"Except, what's the deal with GTX and the new security system at school?" I said, taking a bite of pizza and attempting to look casual. God, I was completely out of practice at this, and not nearly as good as my mom had been.

Unlike in probably every other house in town, I couldn't simply ask to borrow the truck. I had to distract, evade, and offer up a tidbit of interesting information to capture his attention, so that my request would seem incidental. Not a big deal.

"The new security system?" he repeated, tearing off a paper towel from the roll we kept in the center of the table.

He hadn't known about it. Good. Then this would have value if I played it right.

"Yeah, some guys from GTX were at school today putting in cameras and stuff." I pretended to focus on my laptop, which held nothing but the wallpaper image of a photo from the summer before last—a group of us all crowded together on the back deck at Rachel's house.

"Did Kohler say anything about it?"

I shrugged. "I think they made an announcement this morning, but just about it being installed. Not why."

"Son of a bitch." My dad pounded his fist on the table, making everything on it jump and rattle. "It's Mark Tucker. I'd bet my life on it."

This wasn't a huge surprise. My dad blamed Mr. Tucker for everything GTX-related that didn't go the way he wanted. And my guess was the money for the cameras and such was something my dad had been trying to sway toward one of his pet projects. I wouldn't have thought a security guy, even the head of the department, would have that kind of power, but what did I know.

Thinking of Mr. Tucker, always a shadowy and nebulous figure in my mind, as Ariane's dad raised more questions. "Why would Mr. Tucker want to put in a security system at school?" I just figured it was GTX greasing the wheels in some way, sucking up to the community again so no one would protest when they wanted to buy some piece of land or bulldoze a historical building for a new parking lot.

My dad shook his head in disbelief. "You don't listen to anything I say, do you?"

Maybe if you tried actually talking instead of yelling. I resisted the urge to say the words aloud. Instead I shrugged again, knowing he hated that, but it was the less inflammatory response.

He sighed heavily at my apparent ignorance. "They're still looking for that research project."

Oh, that. I knew about that. There'd been an explosion over at GTX a long time ago, right after my dad got the promotion to Chief. Then there had been whispers that an important research project had gone missing or been stolen. A laptop or all the files or maybe even the actual experiment, something big. But GTX would never openly acknowledge any truth to the rumors, and unless they officially filed a report, the police couldn't do anything about it. Most people probably would have been relieved to have less work, but my dad took it as a personal affront. He was convinced it was because they didn't trust anyone but their own people.

I frowned. "Why would GTX care about seeing what's going on in our school? It's not like anyone's using the chem lab to grow organs or something."

He impatiently waved off my words and unclipped his phone from his belt. "They're not looking for someone experimenting. They're watching for results." He stood up and turned his back on me as he dialed. "Someone giving their kid the growth hormones they stole."

"Growth hormones? Really?"

"My source said GTX has been looking to land a government contract for years. Bigger, stronger, better soldiers. Maybe even some experimentation with brain chemistry," he said, his voice distant, distracted.

I stared at him. He sounded paranoid and kind of ridiculous, like one of those alien conspiracy nuts he made fun of when he caught the UFO documentaries on the History channel while flipping past. As far as I knew, no one was sure what, if anything, had been taken from GTX the night of the explosion. And who was this source he was talking about? I couldn't imagine anyone in their right mind telling him anything like that. My mom would have been more likely to know someone on the inside willing to talk, if such a person even existed. She'd worked at GTX as an office assistant or something for a few years when I was little, back when my dad was working his way up to Chief. In fact, as I understood it, she'd quit only a few weeks before the explosion.

But, whatever. The tidbit about GTX and the security system had served its purpose, diverting my dad's attention and making everything else seem less important by comparison. "Hey, Dad, I need to take the truck for the rest of the week, okay?"

He frowned, evidently waiting for someone to pick up on the other end of the phone. "Why?"

I hesitated. I could lie and say Trey's car had broken down, but knowing my dad, he'd see Trey tooling around town, and I'd be screwed. "A girl," I admitted. It was the simplest explanation and close enough to the truth that he wouldn't be able to catch me in a lie later. "It's Bonfire Week. The activities fair is tonight."

He raised his eyebrows. Like maybe he thought there was hope for me yet, but he wasn't holding his breath. "Yeah? Rachel Jacobs?"

"No," I said, working to keep my tone even. "Someone you don't know."

My dad gave a disappointed huff.

And there it was. I winced inside. Back to business as usual. It shouldn't have hurt, not after all these years and so many similar moments, but somehow I just kept getting sucked into hoping. And I hated myself for it.

He jerked his head toward the cabinet where the keys hung on a hook. "Just don't bring it home with an empty tank." Then he turned his back on me again. "Hey, Chuck, it's me. Can you check to see if GTX filed permits for something over at the high school?"

I gathered up my laptop and books, balancing my plate of pizza on top, and escaped to my room. I had only forty-five minutes to eat and get cleaned up before I was due to pick up Ariane—an event that suddenly, in spite of everything leading up to it and the chaos it would inevitably cause, I was oddly looking forward to.

CHAPTER 11

Ariane

THE TEXT CAME AS I WAS FINISHING UP ANOTHER SESSION of Dream-Life and eating dinner hunched over the desk in my room.

Good 2 go. Got truck. See you in 45.

I'd been hoping to hear from Jenna; I'd texted her after school, with no reply. When I saw Zane's name on the screen, the last corner of crust caught in my throat, which suddenly felt a lot tighter. I coughed and sputtered, fumbling for my bottle of water.

I drank until the choking sensation eased. It wasn't that the text had taken me by surprise. Zane wouldn't have asked for my number in this situation if he didn't intend to use it. But seeing it right there, in black and white on my screen, was screamingly loud proof of how far I'd strayed from the Rules. What had seemed like a good idea at the time now felt like excessive craziness, tempting fate.

In my hours home alone, the fury and defiance that had been pumping through my veins had slowed to a dull trickle, and I could feel the cold sense of impending exposure sweeping over my skin, as if I'd been hiding beneath a pile of blankets and someone had gripped the edges to rip them away.

Only, I guess I was the one preparing to push those layers of protection away.

I texted back "Ok," before common sense could get the better of me. Even still, pressing SEND sent a spike of fear through me.

"What are you doing?" I muttered to myself, relieved that my father was not at home. Participating in this mess was bad enough; trying to hide it from him when I was this jittery would be excruciating.

On my laptop, my virtual boyfriend, Clark, disappeared from our virtual backyard in a flutter of red fabric.

Crap. I'd missed him again. I hurried to save the session.

Dream-Life (DL) was my *other* deep dark secret. The one Jenna liked to tease me about.

DL was an online game/community. You set up an account, created an avatar, purchased Dream-Life Dollars, and sent the virtual "you" on adventures and into lifestyles that the real you couldn't afford and, in some cases, most likely wouldn't survive. All from the safety of your laptop or mobile device.

It wasn't a big deal, except that I was uncomfortably aware how very different my DL was from the norm on that site. It was boring by anyone else's standards, including Jenna's—the one time I'd talked her into trying it last year. Most of the people who signed up did so to explore lives they could never have—hence, the name of the game. They wanted to be supermodels, or rock stars with groupies, or millionaires who go cliff diving.

I'd spent my credits on creating a two-story house in a relatively normal-looking suburban setting. With a pool.

It had driven Jenna crazy. But I didn't care. DL gave me the kind of worry-free interactions I could never have in the real world. In a virtual world, where people were constantly doing things that defied logic, I didn't have to concentrate so hard on doing or saying the right thing.

In Dream-Life I could have the easy, normal, stable existence I craved. I decorated my house, went to barbeques with "friends," swam in my pool, and talked with my online "neighbors" (who, admittedly, had occupations like "playboy philanthropist" or "rocket scientist/reality TV star"), all without looking over my shoulder for someone who might be watching. It was an amazing place to escape after a full day of being on guard.

And if it felt a little unsatisfying and artificial sometimes, then that was just the price I paid for peace of mind. It was more than worth it.

Plus, when in real life would I get to date Clark Kent? That had been the one fantasy element I had incorporated into my account. Other players created relationships or hookups with fellow DL gamers, to add that extra element of realism, I guess. (Because reality was what we were after here. Right.) But I'd elected to go another route, with a computer-generated option. I'd paired my avatar off with Superman's mild-mannered reporter alter ego. As the character was written in the program, he would occasionally disappear without explanation and reappear hours later while the "news" talked about a near tragedy being averted in some distant part of the world. He'd also sometimes demonstrate unusual strength or X-ray vision, but if my avatar questioned him on any of it, he'd deny it all. If I continued pressing, he'd go to another room and stop talking to me for the rest of my session.

But if I caught him in mid-transformation—hadn't happened yet—supposedly he would confess all and we'd live happily ever after or whatever.

I loved it.

Looking at my now-empty virtual backyard—and the missed opportunity—I grimaced. I never should have agreed to this scheme with Zane. I'd let my human side get the best of me.

But it was too late to back out now. I got up and took my plate into the kitchen to load it into the dishwasher.

Reaching for the dishwasher tablets in the cabinet, I noticed that my father's lunch dishes were still sitting in the sink—a plate with scraps of a half-finished sandwich and a glass with a quarter-inch of milk left in the bottom.

I frowned. He never left anything untidy. Part of his military training. Something had upset his routine, quite possibly the phone call I'd made about the new security system at school.

I grabbed his plate to dump the leftovers in the garbage, but when I opened the cabinet under the sink where we kept the trash can, I found the bag was almost full, a heavy glass bottle at the top. Scotch. And empty.

I guess he'd been more alarmed than he'd let on when I'd talked to him. Maybe he'd reached the same conclusion about GTX getting too close. All the more reason to carry on with my plan.

I took the bottle out, moving it to the recycling bin. Then I scraped his plate, rinsed the glass, and loaded them into the dishwasher, the sight of them unnerving me further. I might not be able to control much, but at least I could hide the obvious signs of disarray.

Thirty-seven minutes to go, the unhelpful voice in the back of my head spoke up, once I started the dishwasher.

I had to allow five or six minutes to cover the two blocks to meet Zane without rushing or looking like I was rushing. Which meant if I was going to change my clothes and attempt to re-tame my hair, I needed to hurry.

But I found myself dragging my feet in the hall to my room. A part of me was tempted to wear what I had on and forget about my hair—what was the point when all my wrangling efforts would be for naught the second I encountered a breeze, humidity, or a strong look?

And people would definitely be looking. Zane was *Zane Bradshaw*, which must always be said with the appropriate degree of female awe and giggling. And I was just . . . me. Most of my concern about my appearance was usually around blending in with the full-blooded humans, but I hadn't missed the fact that on a human scale of general attractiveness, I was likely considered to be somewhere on the low end. At best, midrange.

I mean, it would be one thing to be a female alien/human hybrid if that meant what it did in video games and comic books—I'd be six feet tall with golden skin, exotically colored eyes, like violet or something, and huge boobs. Unfortunately, reality had been far less generous. I was short, thin, and pale, and slightly "off" in some way no one could ever quite put their finger on.

My face burned at the idea of what people would say when they saw me with Zane. The discrepancy between us would be cause enough for chatter, let alone if I made an attempt to change my usual look in honor of said occasion. It would only make me seem more pathetic.

But I didn't want to give anyone a reason to question our ruse. I was supposed to believe this was for real. And a date with Zane Bradshaw—even if it was a "date"—was more than cause to make a larger effort with my appearance.

So I had to play the part of the duped—foolishly optimistic wardrobe and all.

I shut my door, hoping the comfort of my room and my possessions would soothe me. It had taken me years to adjust to the idea of having a space that was mine and things that belonged to me. I'd gone through a phase where I'd requested bedding and decorations in the loudest, most obnoxious colors I could find. I didn't want there to be a square inch of white in the entire room. I'd also held on to everything as "mine." Empty food containers and wrappers, broken hangers, clothing that I'd outgrown.

I'd been well on my way to becoming the world's (and possibly the universe's) youngest hoarder.

To his credit, my father hadn't pushed me, except to get rid of the empty food wrappers. And after a few more years I'd found a better balance.

My dresser and desk were mostly clear of clutter—I liked being able to tell at a glance if something had been moved in my absence, which so far had never been the case. The walls were a pale blue on top and light brown on the bottom—Sky Morning Blue and Antique Sand, according to the paint manufacturer. The bed, tucked in the corner with a view of the windows and the door—I would not be caught by surprise—was covered by a half dozen pillows and a fluffy comforter two sizes larger than necessary.

After so many years of a white room and a cot with scratchy cotton sheets, this was a luxurious escape, a place where I did not have to pretend for anyone. And it never failed to make me feel better, safer.

Except tonight.

Anxiety flapped around like a bird trapped inside of my chest as I opened up my closet. The problem with dressing up for my "date," among other things, was that my wardrobe was a continuous stream of nondescript clothing, featureless T-shirts (long-sleeved and short) in a variety of muted hues, and bland sweaters for layering in winter. Nothing that would cause anyone to point in admiration or envy, but not anything that would cause ridicule either.

There were other clothes I'd wanted—soft fabrics in bright colors on faceless mannequins in store windows, on television, and on the Internet. But I didn't buy any of them. It would have been more of a tragedy to see them hanging in my closet and not be able to wear them. It doesn't sound like much of a risk, I know, to wear pink, for example, or, hell, a skirt; and maybe if I'd started out as more fashion-conscious, it wouldn't have been a big deal. But once I'd started the habit of being bland, breaking it might have caused a stir.

I bit my lip, studying all the very unappealing options hanging in front of me. This would have been the perfect situation for Jenna's expertise—she always knew what we *should* be wearing, even if neither of us actually owned those particular items of clothing.

I left the closet, grabbed my phone off the desk, and dialed her one more time.

It occurred to me as the phone rang that if I went through with this plan with Zane, Jenna would hear about it. About Zane and me, out together. And she'd have no way of knowing—other than by recognizing the sheer absurdity of the concept—that it wasn't real. It would crush her.

I winced. I owed her more than a request for fashion advice.

But when her voice mail picked up—again—I couldn't help but recall the determination on her face earlier today when she'd left Principal Kohler's office. She'd made her choice, and it was Rachel.

If I told Jenna about what Zane and I were up to, would she tell Rachel? As much as I wanted to believe she wouldn't, the truth was, I wasn't sure. It might be just the "in" Jenna was probably racking her brain for right now.

I realized belatedly that the beep had sounded several seconds ago, signaling readiness for me to leave a message.

"Uh, hey, Jenna, it's Ariane. Again." I hesitated, not sure what to say but unable to hang up without saying *something*. "Listen, I know you're still upset with me. And I wish . . ." I swallowed hard. "I wish you weren't. I wish that we saw things the same way, that we saw Rachel the same way." I heard the hatred bubbling up in my voice when I said

Rachel's name, and clamped down on it. That would not help.

"Anyway, I just wanted to let you know that you may hear some stuff tomorrow." *Lame.* "But don't worry about it. Just ignore it. It's nothing. I mean, it's *really* nothing," I emphasized, trying to communicate everything I couldn't actually tell her.

"So, just call me back when you can, okay? Whenever you want," I added hastily. "I . . . I'll see you later, I guess. Bye."

I hung up, feeling both better and worse, and slowly returned to my closet.

After rummaging all the way to the back, I found a dark-green Henley with three-quarter sleeves. I'd ordered it online but never wore it because it was a little too tight, and the neckline, even with all the buttons buttoned, veered a touch too low in front. Then I dragged out my little plastic step stool—*hate* being this short—and dug around on a shelf until I found the right pair of jeans.

The only advantage I had in the fashion department was I was something of connoisseur when it came to denim. After so many years of wearing the cheap, easily found stuff, the discovery of premium fabric had come as a delight. Much like the luxury of having bedding with an actual thread count instead of the bleached hospital-grade sheet and thin cotton blanket I'd had in the lab, expensive jeans—softer, cut better, and longer-lasting—were a treat I would not give up. I'd stumbled across my first pair on a rare trip with Jenna to T.J. Maxx freshman year.

After that, I was hooked, and I discovered the joys of

eBay for finding brands the mall in Brookfield didn't carry and at a price that my allowance would accept. The best part was, as long as I kept the style pretty generic and wore a shirt long enough to cover up the emblems or designs on the back pockets, people couldn't tell. I mixed my Seven7s, Rock & Republics, and Sinclairs in with my Target purchases, and no one was the wiser. And I enjoyed the hell out of pulling *that* secret over on everyone. Strange, socially awkward Ariane Tucker had a jeans collection that would make Cami and Cassi Andrews, if not Rachel, Queen of Fashion herself, weep.

Hey, I had to have a hobby. There were a lot of hours *not* filled by school and Dream-Life.

I recognized a familiar velvety softness beneath my fingertips. *These.* I freed the pair from the bottom of a precarious stack.

These were the first of my collection. Lucky Brand. They'd come with a fortune cookie slip in the front pocket. *Happiness is in your future.*

Of all the horrible things full-blooded humans could create—bioweapons, global warming, "reality" television—jeans like these were not one of them. Though, my father might not agree if he saw what they normally sold for.

I hopped down off the step stool with the jeans in hand and set about changing my clothes.

Once dressed, I approached the dresser mirror for a quick look. A huge static-filled nimbus of pale hair surrounded my head, to my complete unsurprise.

I sighed. Taming the disaster that was my hair would be another battle, to be taken on momentarily, so I ignored it for now to focus on my apparel choices.

The jeans, faded and soft, helped create the illusion of curves where I was mostly sharp angles. The dark green color of the shirt made my skin look absurdly pale, but that, frankly, was a better option than the freaky grayish tone I sometimes had. Like the underbelly of a frog. A dead frog. (I longed to have the faintest hint of a tan. Or even a burn. But the sun that I'd yearned to see for so many years didn't affect me the same way it did full-blooded humans. I turned pink for an hour or two and then right back to white.)

The neckline of the Henley did scoop a little lower than I was used to, but it was nothing worse than what other girls wore to school on a daily basis. And besides, my chest was one area where the androgynous alien DNA had almost completely won out over the human, so it wasn't as if there was much to see anyway. Jenna's mom had once said I had an Audrey Hepburn–type figure, which I looked up, and as far as I could tell was a polite way of saying "flat-chested."

In any case, the back of the shirt rose high enough to cover the bandage on my shoulder blade, my one major requirement for clothing. Most shirts weren't thin enough that the identification mark would show through, but that was not a chance I could take. Hence, the bandage. If someone saw the GTX tattoo, that would be a tough one to explain.

The helpful countdown in the back of my mind piped up suddenly. *Seventeen minutes to go.* And I needed to be walking out the door in about ten.

So, good enough? I gave my outfit one last critical look and wished I felt a little more confident, but there was no time—and honestly, probably no hope—for much more.

I turned away from the mirror to head for the bathroom—where all manner of hair-taming products with varying degrees of ineffectiveness awaited me—and then stopped.

I stepped back to the dresser and pulled open the top drawer. Buried beneath a layer of bland shapeless shirts was a shiny white box. I pulled it out and opened it. An old and battered metal key—strange-looking in that it had prongs on the end instead of the typical ridge and valley pattern of a normal key—lay on a bed of cotton. The key had been polished enough that it gleamed dully around the dents and nicks in its surface. A pale green glass bead was wrapped around the center, and a thin chain with delicate gold links was looped through the opening at the top, where a key ring would have gone if it was a normal key.

When I'd first opened the box I'd had no idea what the object inside was, and my father had had to explain.

"It's a skeleton key. In old houses, one key would open all the doors," he'd said, keeping his gaze focused on the pancakes on his plate. "A woman at work finds them and turns them into jewelry. It . . . it made me think of you."

A symbol. So I would never be trapped anywhere again. If I'd been close to tears at any point since leaving GTX, it was then.

Normally I couldn't wear it. Way too attention-getting on the outside of my shirt and too bulky to hide beneath it. But tonight? Not a problem.

I slipped the chain over my head, and the key, cool and heavier than I expected, settled against my chest, above my virtually nonexistent cleavage. It felt right and more "me" than almost anything else I owned. I loved it, both for what it was and what it represented.

If nothing else, tonight's exercise in insanity would give me the chance to wear it proudly and without fear.

Too bad I couldn't say the same for my hair.

At precisely 6:37, my hair tamed into a ponytail and damp with fruity- and flowery-smelling styling products, I walked out of my house, pausing only to lock the door, my nerves-slick palms slipping on the metal doorknob.

I stuck my house key into my pocket and headed down the porch steps to the sidewalk, my stomach tight with anxiety. The sun was low, casting everything in a bright gold-and-pink haze. Up and down the street, people were enjoying their evening—taking a walk, bringing groceries into the house, playing with their kids in the yard—but I couldn't seem to focus on any of it.

Maybe Zane won't be there. I found myself oddly relieved and disappointed at the possibility. It would mean I could turn around and go home, as though this night were no different from any other, which would be good. But it would also probably mean that Zane had chickened out and returned to Rachel's side—if he'd ever left it—likely telling her everything that had transpired with him this afternoon. Not good.

As I walked, concentrating on putting one foot in front of the other, I tried to decide which would be worse—for him to be there or not. What would be my plan in either case?

But as it turned out, it wasn't up to me and my calculations. As soon as I reached the midpoint of the block I could see the back half of a battered dark gray SUV waiting around the corner.

Crap. He was here. My heart gave an extra-hard thump, and I was torn between hurrying toward him to get the inevitable awkwardness out of the way and fleeing without looking back.

Suddenly I felt ridiculous and exposed in the clothes I'd picked. I should have just worn what I wore to school. That was normal, predictable, no risk. I hadn't wanted to give anyone a reason to question Zane and me, but the truth was, they were going to question and gawk and whisper anyway. In my regular clothes I'd have been sure they were talking about the two of us together rather than my wardrobe choices.

I slowed, biting my lip. Maybe I should go home and change; it would only take a few minutes. But then I'd be late to meet Zane. And the neighbors would see me running back and forth, raising the odds that someone would mention it to my father.

No, better to proceed. I took a deep breath, straightened my shoulders, and moved forward at an even pace—a passable imitation of my normal stride. But I could feel home behind me, pulling at me like a magnet that wasn't quite strong enough.

When I turned down Rushmore, I found Zane leaning against the passenger side of the SUV, his head tipped down as he thumbed through something on his phone. He didn't notice me right away, so I took a second to let myself adjust. Seeing him there made something in me squirm—like one of those dreams where you run into someone where they have no business being, doing things they have no business doing. Except, well, in this case, I supposed, it wasn't him who was somewhere he shouldn't be, but me.

I was relieved to note that he'd changed his clothes as well. He now wore a plaid shirt, the sleeves rolled up well past his wrists, and darker jeans that looked slightly less like they might fall apart at any second. His dark hair looked a shade or two deeper than normal, damp from a shower maybe, but styled in the usual tousled spiky mess I remembered from class last year instead of hanging, defeated, in his face, as it had been this morning.

He *was* attractive, I realized with a bolt that went beyond the theoretical acknowledgment I'd always had of this fact. His face was symmetrical, without any of the uneven features that might have cast him into a less-attractive category—a nose too big or ears too wide. His hands made the phone look small, his thumbs typing adeptly on the screen.

No wonder Jenna fluttered around him, I thought, shifting uncomfortably, feeling more than ever that I shouldn't be here.

But those weren't the only physical changes I noticed. Something in him had eased. The tension in his shoulders seemed less. I was tempted to drop my guard and listen to his thoughts for a second—if he was relaxed because he'd lured me into some trap, I wasn't going to be happy.

But he chose that moment to look up from his phone. "Hey," he said with obvious relief. He straightened up, letting his hand with the phone fall to his side. "I wasn't sure if you'd show." He smiled as if he was pleased to see me.

"I said I'd be here, so I'm here," I said stiffly. Somehow it was easier to rebuff that unexpected smile with sharp words. "And you shouldn't park so close to the fire hydrant." I tipped my head toward the object in question, which might have been six inches too close to the front of his SUV. In other words, nine and a half feet away instead of ten.

He nodded slowly, eyeing me as if I might be a little off. "Okaaay. I'll keep that in mind."

Damn it. Even as the words escaped, I'd known it was the wrong thing to say, but I couldn't seem to stop myself.

"You ready?" He tucked his phone into his pocket and pulled open the passenger door.

Cool air rushed out. I could hear a faint dinging from inside, indicating the keys were in the ignition.

My heartbeat sped up, and I hesitated. This was wrong, against everything I'd been taught.

Don't get into a car with a stranger.

Never trust anyone.

The first was from a child-safety coloring book the police department had given out in grade school, and the second was my father's most important rule. But it was too late for worrying about that; I'd set the wheels in motion. Now it was my job to stay in front of them instead of getting crushed beneath them.

"Ariane?" Zane prompted, with a frown. I knew better than to draw this level of attention to myself; I should have been correcting my behavior—attempting to laugh it off or explain it away—just as I did whenever I got that reaction from Jenna. I'd strayed too far from "normal" again.

But right now it felt like too much, too overwhelming.

"Yeah, all right." I left the sidewalk, feeling as if I was leaving reality or sanity behind, and climbed up into the SUV.

Zane pushed the door shut after me, and the sounds of the outside world—lawn mowers and birds—died away.

My breath caught in my throat, and I wanted to claw at the door to let myself out. I have a hard time with confined spaces under the best of circumstances, and this was definitely not that.

But if I abandoned this opportunity, I probably wouldn't get another.

So I inched away from the door and squeezed my hands together in my lap to keep from reaching for the handle.

Zane opened his door and slid behind the wheel. "Are you all right?" he asked, and I could hear the concern in his voice. I didn't want to think about what might have been showing on my face.

He cranked the engine, and a blast of cold air roared through the vents and against my skin. I felt like I could breathe again.

I inhaled deeply and breathed out as slowly as I could without being obvious. "I'm fine," I said, my voice fainter than I would have preferred.

At least I would be. And soon, I hoped.

CHAPTER 12

Zane

I WAITED FOR ARIANE TO GET BACK IN CONTROL, LISTENING to her breathing slow down while I pretended to concentrate on driving. Sometimes there's nothing worse than people calling attention to your panic, asking you over and over if you're all right, watching you as if steam might suddenly pour out of your ears, causing you to deflate into some misshapen heap on the ground.

I knew because I'd felt that same panic every single time my dad told me with grim determination to go out to the yard "so we can throw the ball around" or made me try out for football.

I did not ask again if she was okay. It was obvious she wasn't. And why would she be? A lot of it might have been being in a vehicle after what had happened to her mom, even after all these years, but I was sure the fact that we were heading into one incredibly messed-up situation probably didn't help.

"You know, if anything, she'll be angrier with me than with you," I offered after a few minutes, trying to think of something reassuring to say. "I'm supposed to be her friend."

Ariane looked over at me, her hair a pale fire where it reflected the sunset behind her, and frowned as if she wasn't sure what I was talking about. Then her expression cleared. "Rachel. Yeah. But that's also why she'll end up taking it out on me instead."

She didn't seem particularly disturbed by the idea, which was weird. Especially because I would have thought that was part of what was driving her freak-out.

I would have asked if she still wanted to go through with it—probably should have—but she was here, and I didn't want to insult her. And some part of me resisted the idea. This was my chance to solve the puzzle of Ariane Tucker, and I didn't want to give it up.

"So . . . how do you want to do this?" I tapped a nervous rhythm on my leg, half afraid she'd ask me to turn around and take her home when forced to confront details of the tangled web we were weaving. But it had to be asked. We had to be on the same page—no, hell, on the same line on the same page—to make this work. I had to make Rachel think I was following through on her "suggestion," all the while pretending to be interested in Ariane. But Ariane had the far tougher job—she had to act like she believed me.

Funny how this was going to come down to acting skills, but neither of us was in drama. Not so funny, actually. If Ariane couldn't keep it together in front of Rachel, we were toast. I didn't want to deal with full-blown histrionics from

Rachel tonight. After all, it was one thing to turn the game around on her successfully; another to get caught in the act, midfail.

Ariane lifted a shoulder, seeming to have regained her equilibrium. "How do you normally do it?"

"What do you mean?" I asked, confused.

"I mean, I can't be the first person Rachel has ever wanted to punish this way," she said patiently. "If we know how you usually behave when you're pretending to like someone, we can go from there."

I took my eyes off the road to stare at her, all distant and cool as ice sitting there in the passenger seat. "You think I do this on a regular basis?" I demanded. "For what, fun?"

"It wouldn't be out of character for your group of friends," she pointed out.

"Well, I don't, okay? I'm not even doing that this time, am I?" I straightened up behind the wheel, both hands on it in a white-knuckled grip.

"You don't have much room to be offended," she said, sounding annoyed. "You stood there and let her torture Jenna. For all I know, you helped."

"First of all," I snapped, "I didn't know about the dog collar thing, but I tried to warn you that Rachel would do something. Second, there's a big difference between actively setting someone up for a prank and not leaping in to save the world every time someone's feelings are about to get hurt."

"Hurt feelings?" she scoffed. "You think that's what this was about?"

I sighed. "What difference does it make? None of this

matters anyway, right? It's high school. We're out of here in a couple of years."

"Only someone living inside the privileged circle would feel quite so comfortable saying that. You have the option to be bored, to not care, instead of dreading every day. It's the powerful versus the powerless, and guess which side you're on."

Yeah, that's my life, dripping with power and options. "You don't know me," I snapped. "You don't know anything about me."

Ariane opened her mouth to speak, but I cut her off. "And who are *you* to give me crap about speaking up, anyway? Always hiding in the back of the room, never talking to anyone, never making an effort. Easy for you to sit in judgment of the rest of us."

From the corner of my eye, I could see the color rising in her pale face, her hands clenching together in her lap as if she was struggling for control again; this time, though, over her temper. "I don't always get to do what I think is right," she said tightly.

"Yeah, well, neither do I." I smacked down on the turn signal, and the loud clicking filled the ensuing silence.

Cars pouring into the lot from the opposite direction held us captive in the intersection as we waited to make our turn.

One of us probably should have apologized, given that we were five minutes away, maybe less, from being each other's only ally in a crowded room. But I wasn't sorry for what I'd said, and I suspected she wasn't either.

Ariane cleared her throat and sat up straighter. "So . . .

I'm thinking if we're going to do this, our best bet is to make it relatively quick," she said, sounding very practical and logical, as if we were discussing some kind of biology project or something. "If we hang around for too long, people will start asking questions, and I don't think we're ready for that level of scrutiny yet." She looked over as if expecting me to object.

"Definitely not," I agreed.

"We should just make an appearance," she said. "Be sure people see us wandering the booths." She frowned. "There are booths, right?"

I looked over at her, startled. "You've never been?" I'd been going to the activities fair for . . . I don't know, forever. The whole town was invited. Some of the local businesses even kicked in with prizes and giveaways to help the clubs raise money. The irony was that participating in a booth seemed cool until you were old enough to do it, and then not so much. But it was something to do and there was ample opportunity to buy junky fair-type food.

Ariane shook her head. "I'm not . . . It's not my kind of thing."

Call me crazy, but I'd have sworn she was going to say "I'm not allowed." I had a vision of the shadowy figure of her father waiting for me with a gun when I dropped her off.

Great.

An opening in the traffic presented itself, and I took it. We joined the slow parade of cars looking for a spot. "Okay, wandering the booths. Check. Not a problem." I hesitated. "Uh, what about the other stuff?"

"What other stuff?" she asked with a frown, toying with what appeared to be a key on her necklace.

She wasn't going to make me spell it out, was she? No matter how I phrased this, it was going to be sound bad, but it had to be covered. "It's supposed to be a date," I said, hoping she would take it from there.

"Yeah, and?"

I let out a huff of exasperation. "And, I don't know, maybe we need to set some ground rules for, um, touching and stuff." I wasn't an idiot; I didn't want to cross boundaries, make her more uncomfortable than she already was.

"Oh." She bit her lip. "More rules," she muttered.

"What?"

"Nothing," she said. "What did you have in mind?"

"I don't have anything in mind," I said quickly. God, the last thing I wanted was for her to think I'd cooked up this scheme to get ahead in that regard. There would have been far easier ways to go about that, but she seemed to think the worst of me already.

She gave a surprised laugh, a high-pitched delighted sound that she immediately cut short. "Not what I meant," she said.

I relaxed.

"What are you proposing?" she said, her manner businesslike.

"I don't know. It's more up to you, isn't it?" I asked shifting uncomfortably in my seat.

"There." She pointed to a parking space in the lengthening shade of the bleachers.

I took it, turning the wheel quickly before the guy behind me got any ideas.

"Not really," she said, returning to our topic of conversation. "Not any more than it would be in a normal situation, if we're aiming to keep up the illusion that this is supposed to look genuine in some way. No one starts out a date by saying you can only touch me in these places and this many times, right?" She sounded uncertain.

Had she never been on a date? That wouldn't be impossible. But I guess I always figured that just because I didn't see her talking to people didn't mean she didn't. Therefore, the same thing with guys and dates.

"Right." I put the car in park.

"But," she said, frowning, "in a date situation, you'd want close contact, so the situation isn't quite the same. And it would look odd if we *avoided* touching each other."

I wasn't opposed to touching if she was okay with it. Part of me wanted to know what her hair felt like, if her pale skin was as smooth as it appeared.

Fake date or not, Ariane Tucker was intriguing to me, I realized, and not entirely in a mystery-to-be-solved kind of way.

"Even if we allowed standard personal space, it would probably be noticed," she continued, seemingly more to herself to me. "People who are attempting intimacy usually . . ." She cut herself off, catching my stare.

"You have really spent some time thinking about this," I said in wonder. She sounded like a professor.

"Nothing wrong with being observant," she snapped, the angry blush returning to her face.

There was observant and then there was clinical, obsessive, detail-collecting. But I was smart enough to keep my mouth shut.

"When it's only the two of us, where no one can hear us,

we can be ourselves, no pretending," she said decisively. "In obvious view of others, we'll attempt to project a . . . cozy infatuation."

I raised my eyebrows and tried not to laugh. "What does that mean?"

"Close proximity, some whispering and longing looks. Probably holding hands." She sounded less than thrilled. "But no kissing," she added sharply.

I lifted my hands off the wheel as if to show I was unarmed. "Okay, no kissing. Got it."

She took a deep breath as if to steel herself. "Are you ready?"

No. "Sure." I turned off the car and grabbed the keys from the ignition.

"Let's say, one hour, maximum, and then we're right back here. Agreed?" She looked over at me expectantly, and I felt like she was about to suggest we synchronize our watches. Or, since neither of us was wearing one, compare cell phone times at least.

"Yes, ma'am," I said.

Someone, somewhere, should put her in charge of an army.

CHAPTER 13

Ariane

THE SCHOOL LOOKED DIFFERENT AT NIGHT. SOFTER, THE edges of the buildings less severe in the setting sun. It might have been all the brightly colored balloons tied near the entrances to the gym, or maybe the presence of so many seemingly happy families—most of them with excited children in tow.

I pushed open the door to Zane's SUV, taking care not to hit the truck parked next us, and slid down, right as Zane rounded the back corner in a hurry.

When he saw me, he let out a sigh and stopped. "I would have . . ." He gestured at the door.

Oh. He'd meant to open it for me. Traditional custom, slightly old-fashioned, but still accepted practice on date-type outings.

I grimaced. "Sorry. I didn't think about it." Obviously I was not accustomed to going out. *Way to advertise your inexperience there, Ariane.*

"It's all right." Zane looked around, his gaze following the groups of people heading toward the gym. Then he turned to face me and offered his hand, palm down, with a hint of challenge in his expression.

Ah. He'd picked up on my reluctance to be touched. My fault for reacting so badly when he'd come up to me yesterday. It's just . . . he'd taken me by surprise.

That was why he'd made such a point about setting boundaries for our "date," I realized, my face heating up. It was kind of considerate of him. And surprising. If he'd been more like what I'd expected, he wouldn't have bothered.

And he was right: I wasn't comfortable with people touching me, especially unexpectedly and without permission. But I wasn't sure if that would hold true for the reverse—me making contact with someone. Honestly, I'd never tried it, spending most of my time and energy avoiding even casual grazes.

Zane raised his eyebrows, and hell no, I wasn't going to let him win. I'd agreed to this, so I'd go through with it.

Sticking my chin out defiantly, I lifted my hand to his, and he closed his fingers around mine securely. His palm was warm and dry, and I could feel rough spots—calluses from lacrosse, probably—rubbing against my skin in a not-unpleasant friction.

He grinned and gently tugged me forward to follow him through the gap between his SUV and the truck, and into the parking lot. Knowing what I did about our arrangement, I expected to feel reluctance or distance in his grasp, but he held my hand as if he meant it.

Once, early in my learn-to-be-more-human stage, I read

an article that said you could tell a lot about people by the way they held hands. Palm-to-palm with fingers interlaced indicates an intimate relationship, usually of a romantic variety. When only the hands are involved, the person whose palm is up is seeking guidance and reassurance. Children always have their palms up when being led by their parents. The person whose palm is down feels protective, responsible for the one they are leading.

I couldn't help but notice that Zane's hand was palm down over mine. He felt responsible for me, if only in some small way. I didn't know what to think about that. I was, in the end, responsible for myself, thank you very much. But it was nice.

I shook my head. It was dumb to think that way. I couldn't let myself get distracted.

I refocused my attention on the crowds around us, everyone heading to the gym, where I could hear music and the louder sounds of laughter and conversation pouring from the open doors. "There are so many people here," I murmured.

"It's Wingate," Zane said.

I looked at him questioningly.

He shrugged. "Nothing else going on."

I'd never thought about it. The extent or frequency of social events in town was not a top concern for me on a normal day, or, you know, ever. This would, however, make encountering Rachel interesting, which was to say dangerous. It was one thing to nearly lose control in front of a third of the school in the cafeteria, but something else entirely with what appeared to be a good portion of town in attendance. Some of whom worked for GTX, guaranteed.

My stomach knotted with anxiety.

"Will the game tomorrow night be the same or—" I began.

"Zane!" A loud female voice called from somewhere to my left. "Over here!"

I stiffened, and Zane stopped dead, his hand tightening on mine.

We both turned to look at the same time. It was not Rachel, thank God. It was . . .

I frowned. I didn't know who it was.

An older woman, probably in her late forties or early fifties, dressed in a brightly flowered shirt and khaki pants that were a size too small, waved frantically at Zane, her smile decorated in a particularly obnoxious shade of pink lipstick. She hurried toward us as fast as she could, given the two sticky and sort of dirty-looking children she dragged in her wake.

Zane groaned quietly. "Just . . . hang in there. I'll try to get us out of this as soon as I can, but if we run, she'll tell my dad, and I'll never hear the end of it," he said under his breath. Then in a louder voice, he called, "Hi, Mrs. Vanderhoff."

I watched her approach, the heat making her pant. She didn't look particularly dangerous, but I could feel a low level of dread coming off Zane without even trying to sense it. *Huh.*

"Where is your father this evening?" she asked when she was close enough, waving her hands in front of her reddened and sweaty face as if that would serve as some kind of air-conditioning. "Did he get the casserole I left for him? We haven't seen you at church lately."

Honestly, I wasn't sure what Zane was supposed to respond to first.

He smiled stiffly. "He's working tonight. You know, protect and serve. And yes, we did. It was delicious. Thank you." He shifted his weight, his hand tight around mine, and I could tell he wanted to bolt.

The children collapsed at their mother's—grandmother's?—feet and promptly began punching each other. Mrs. Vanderhoff didn't seem to notice. "And how is your brother? Doing well in Madison, I hope. Such an honor for him to win that football scholarship."

Poor thing, this one's never going to be what his father was. Such a disappointment. Black sheep. Just like his mother.

She was so loud. Some humans were just natural broadcasters, thinking in screams instead of whispers. Rachel was one, this woman was evidently another. I tried to focus on the music in the distance to block her thoughts out.

"I think my dad talked to Quinn last week. He's busy, but I think he's enjoying it," Zane said with strained politeness.

"Such a good boy, Quinn." With a fond but pitying smile, Mrs. Vanderhoff reached up and patted Zane's shoulder. "It's just too bad you didn't inherit your father's skills as well," she said with a tsk and a sad shake of her head. "But God blesses us all in different ways."

And yet she managed to make it sound as if God had not blessed Zane at all. *What a bitch.* I didn't even like Zane, and I thought that was cruel.

What was worse, I could now feel shame rising up in

Zane, taking the place of dread. He believed her.

"Yes, I suppose that's true," he said with a tight smile. "But we should be going and—"

"Oh, you should have seen your father play, back in the day." Mrs. Vanderhoff clasped her hands to her substantial chest. "The way he could throw a ball, and how fast he could run, so strong . . ."

I'D HAVE RIDDEN HIM LIKE A PRIZE STALLION UNTIL HE WAS BEGGING FOR MERCY.

Gross. I made a sound of disgust. Normally I was better at hiding my response to what I heard, but that had been so unexpected. And boomingly loud. Like screaming into a megaphone.

"Who's your friend here?" Mrs. Vanderhoff asked, turning her attention to me with a forced smile and heavy suspicion.

Zane hesitated, then said, "This is Ariane—"

"Just Ariane," I said quickly. I didn't want her tracking me to my father.

"And where do you go to church?" She looked me up and down carefully.

Strange little thing. Not at all a match for one of Jay's boys, even if it is this one instead of the older one. Must be the sex. Boys will lie down with anything these days.

"I don't." I saw no point in lying about it when she'd already judged me and found me wanting, in more than one sense of the word.

She narrowed her eyes. "I see." *Definitely the sex. Just like his daddy. If Jay Bradshaw had kept it in his pants a while longer, he could have married my Mindi, and . . .*

"Mrs. Vanderhoff, we should get inside." Zane sounded a little desperate. "We don't want to miss out on the good booths."

"Of course, dear, I understand," she said. But her hand, with bright pink fingernails to match her lipstick, reached out. "A few more minutes, though, won't—"

"And the sex," I said brightly to Zane. "Don't forget. We have to leave lots of time for sex."

Mrs. Vanderhoff froze, her claws extended.

Zane let out a strangled sound and turned away quickly, pulling me with him. "Bye, Mrs. Vanderhoff!" he called.

"Sorry," I said as he rushed us toward the gym. "But she was a hypocrite." I hated people like that. They were akin to Dr. Jacobs and Rachel and all the others, only not as direct about it. "And so mean to you—" I clamped down on my words. When had it become my job to defend Zane Bradshaw? This little pretend game of ours was already going to my head.

"I can take care of myself," he said, his tone sharp.

"Then why didn't you?" I asked, exasperated.

He slowed, then stopped just outside the door, where a clown was handing out balloons to everyone waiting to go in. "Because sometimes it's easier to let it go," he said with a frustrated sigh.

"Not for me."

"I've noticed," he said dryly. "But you don't have to deal with my dad."

I frowned. "What's wrong with your dad?"

He waved the words away. "Nothing. Never mind."

He let go of my hand long enough to step forward and

snag a balloon from the clown. A blue one. He returned and lifted my arm to tie the string around my wrist, taking care to leave the loop loose enough to be comfortable. The warmth of his breath on my skin and the feel of his attention made something shift inside my chest, like some delicate item—one of those expensive, paper-thin china teacups I'd once seen on *Antiques Roadshow*—on a precariously tilting shelf.

"There. Now you're official. Your first activities fair." He let go of my wrist.

"Thank you," I said. The balloon bobbed near the top of my head, generating static I could hear and making loose strands of my hair stick to it. Of course.

I plucked at the string, trying to get used to the sensation of it around my wrist. "Will you get into trouble for what I said?" A thought that had not occurred to me until much too late.

His mouth tightened in a wry smile. "Probably." He glanced over at me. "But it was kind of worth it." He pushed the balloon away to free my hair and tucked the strands behind my ear.

The teacup in my chest gave another dangerous lurch. And it was only afterward that I realized: we were in public, in plain view of everyone. He was just acting. I needed to remember that.

The activities fair turned out to be four aisles of booths, from plain tables to sophisticated constructions that must have been brought in in pieces and assembled here. Every club and organization I'd ever heard of (and some I hadn't) had a presence. A heavy canvas tarp had been put down to protect the polished gym floor from all the "street" shoes and the rough/sharp edges of booths, tables, and chairs. When I'd asked Zane why they didn't hold this outside, he'd rolled his eyes. "They're worried about damage to the football field."

There were games, fake fortune-tellers, and food. So much food—cotton candy, popcorn, brownies, cookies, cakes—it was ridiculous.

And now Zane was trying to talk me into yet another example of activities fair ridiculousness.

"No, I do not want French kisses from the French Club," I said firmly, laughter in my throat threatening to bubble free. French kisses from the French Club. Who approved that as a fund-raising idea? And worse yet, who would pay?

In the last thirty minutes, we'd wandered through two of the four aisles. Zane had insisted on buying me the suspiciously named Puppy Chow, which turned out to be peanut butter, chocolate, and some kind of cereal mixed together in a powdered-sugar-dusted bag; and I'd won some kind of small stuffed animal of indeterminate species—it might have been a dog or possibly a bear—at the ringtoss. Technically, Zane had gotten it for me after I'd protested, maybe a little too loudly, that the ringtoss was a scam. The rings were way too small to fit over the bottles. Zane had given the bored kid in the booth five dollars, and the kid had dropped a ring over the top of a bottle for Zane. Which was, in my opinion, completely against the spirit of the game. But then again, they were handing out dog-bears as prizes, so whatever. . . .

"Oh, come on, it's fun." Zane tugged at my hand in an effort to pull me along to a pink-tulle-draped table at the end of the aisle, where, surprisingly, a sizable crowd had gathered. "What do you have against French kisses? I think maybe it's a phobia." He shook his head in mock dismay. "Maybe we should visit the Psychology Club."

"We don't have a Psychology Club," I pointed out, my feet sliding on spilled shaving cream, which had come from an enthusiastic throw at the football booth. (For a dollar, you could throw shaving cream pies at various players, but apparently everyone with a decent sense of aim was already on the team.)

"You're changing the subject," Zane said with a grin.

Yes, yes, I was. I didn't have a phobia. It was just plain old fear. I'd never done it before—kissed anyone, in any way—and it struck me that while there were lots of easy things to fake and/or disguise, a first kiss probably wasn't one of them. What if I did it wrong? Or what if something about my mouth screamed *not human*, something I wasn't aware of? No thanks. And even without all of that, why would I want to kiss some random stranger?

I eyed the pink and fluffy French Club table with suspicion. "No, thank you."

"Even if I promise you'll like them? French kisses are good," he teased, with amused warmth in his expression that made him seem less burdened, happier. Not that I'd ever thought of him as particularly unhappy. And yet tonight he was brighter, more *alive* somehow, than I ever remembered seeing before.

I shook my head with a smile. "Even if."

But then he let go of my hand and grinned at me. "Wait here." He headed off toward the line.

Was he going to bring someone over here for that purpose? Surely not. Zane didn't strike me as the kind of person who took pleasure in other people's discomfort, what little I knew of him.

Exactly. That's the problem. I didn't know him, not really, not at all. And the real Zane might very well find forcing me into a publicly humiliating situation "funny." He'd seemed to be against what had happened to Jenna, but that didn't necessarily mean anything in this situation. Everyone defines humor differently.

My hands went cold with panic as I watched Zane step up to the French Club table and say something to the guy behind it. The cozy cocoon of pretend we'd wrapped around ourselves had vanished.

The danger with pretending is that if you do it well enough, it starts to feel real. Sometimes, just for a few minutes, when Jenna and I were busy talking about school or boys or whatever, I forgot myself. Forgot that I wasn't the Ariane Tucker everyone thought I was, a regular human girl. And in those moments it felt like a huge weight had been lifted from me, the ever-present boulder of dread I hauled around. Of course, when I remembered myself, the burden felt ten times as heavy. But it was worth it for those few seconds of escape.

I had no business forgetting who I was or what I was about with Zane. If anything, forgetting should have been impossible. The entire situation was contrived, fake, forced.

But I never before realized the lure of make-believe

when *both* people are in on it. None of this actually meant anything; I knew it and so did Zane. So I could do whatever I wanted. I could pretend I was a real girl. Pretend I had nothing to hide. Pretend to like this guy holding my hand so carefully. Pretend he liked me back. Pretend there were no Rules.

At least until that boulder caught up with me and knocked me down.

Like right now. Zane laughed at something the French Club guy said, and that first pinch of worry I'd felt bloomed into a full-blown wave of anxiety. I would *not* be made to do something I didn't want to do. Not again. Period. I'd spent too many years in the lab under Dr. Jacobs's control.

I turned and walked back the way we'd come, my heart beating triple time as the crowd closed around me.

It was so loud, both in my ears and my head. I wasn't sure how I'd managed to ignore it for so long, the distant buzzing static of so many thoughts battering against my guard all at once. No, I did know. I'd been pretending to be someone else, someone who couldn't hear the flotsam and jetsam floating through people's minds, and for a while that illusion had worked well enough to distract me.

But now there were too many people in here, and they were all too close to me, and it felt like they were staring. I wanted to put my hands over my ears—not that that would help anything—and bolt for the door.

I made myself keep walking, one foot in front of the other at a normal pace, suddenly highly aware of the GTX cameras watching overhead.

"Ariane?" I heard Zane calling behind me. I didn't stop.

"Hey, Ariane, wait! Where are you going?" He caught up with me and touched my shoulder cautiously.

I flinched, much to my chagrin, and he jerked his hand away immediately.

"What's wrong?" He sounded baffled and maybe a little hurt.

I turned to snap at him, wary of whomever he'd dragged with him from the French Club booth, but I found only Zane with a concerned expression on his face and a small plastic bag of cookies in his hand. Cookies that appeared have to have a Hershey's Kiss in the center and strips of paper wrapped around them, fortune-cookie style, printed with what appeared to be French phrases.

Oh.

My face burned. "Those are the French kisses?" I said, knowing it before I asked, and feeling both stupid and angry.

"Yeah, they sell them every year. Peanut butter cookies with Kisses in the middle. It's a— Wait." He frowned at me. "Did you think I was going to bring someone over here and make you . . ." His eyes widened. "I would never do that."

"How was I supposed to know?" I demanded.

Zane lifted his hands in exasperation, the plastic bag of cookies swinging from one fist. "Because *who* would do something like that?"

"I don't know, someone who finds hemorrhoid cream on lockers entertaining?" I shot back.

His mouth tightened. "I keep telling you I'm not like them."

"So you say."

He stepped closer to me. "You know, at some point you might have to trust me. Just a little." Frustration came off him in waves, as if what I thought of him somehow mattered. Then he turned away, raking his hand through his hair. "This was a mistake," he muttered.

I shifted uncomfortably, surprised by the guilty ache in my chest. The truth was, I already trusted him way more than was comfortable, simply by being here; but he'd have no way of knowing that. And I'd been the one to push him into this after his initial prompt. I was using him far more than he was using me.

And . . . we'd been having fun. Now the illusion of two people having a good time and enjoying each other's company was shattered, and we were left with the prickly reality of two relative strangers.

I approached him cautiously and touched his sleeve. It felt weird but also right in some way to be the one to reach out.

Zane looked down at me, surprised.

"I'm sorry," I said, searching for the right words, ones that would explain without giving too much away, which was an impossible task. "This"—I gestured to the activities fair around us—"is not really my . . . thing. So I'm doing my best to adjust."

He opened his mouth, but I rushed to finish before he could speak.

"And you're right. You, personally, have never given me any cause to doubt you, other than guilt by association, which I suppose isn't *always* the most accurate judge of character." I let out a slow breath. "There."

He gave a short laugh. "That is possibly the most begrudging apology I have ever heard."

I stiffened and let my hand drop.

"But," he said quickly, "I appreciate the sentiment." He grabbed for my hand, and I allowed it.

"Okay?" he asked, and I wasn't sure if he meant the hand holding or the situation in general.

But I nodded. Both were as okay as they were going to get, I supposed.

Zane tugged me closer as we headed down the crowded aisle. "I didn't mean to upset you," he said. "I would never do anything to deliberately embarrass you. I know what it's like."

I looked up at him, startled by the grim set of his mouth and flush of color in his cheeks. And I caught the flash of an image in his mind, a red-faced man standing over him, the man's mouth open and screaming while people in the background—mostly little kids in football uniforms—stared.

His father? Probably. I'd never seen the Chief close enough to be sure of that assumption—nor did I want to. Then I remembered what Mrs. Vanderhoff said, the nasty busybody. How it was such a shame Zane wasn't up to the standards set by his father and his brother. So maybe he did know something about being humiliated and considered not good enough. But that didn't explain why he was friends with Rachel.

Unless it did.

If you've been on the outside, been ground beneath the

heel of others, probably the safest place to be is on the side of those doing the grinding. Even if you don't enjoy it.

It wasn't an excuse, but it was an explanation.

I relaxed a little and took the bag of French kisses. I would be able to eat the cookies and maybe even some of the much-hyped Puppy Chow. Both had peanut butter, a staple in my diet.

"So what next?" Zane said with a bit of forced cheerfulness in his voice, as we slipped and slid our way past the football team again. "You want to maybe challenge the Mathletes to a fraction-off or bob for apples against the cheerleaders?"

I raised my eyebrows.

"I know, I know, not very creative," he said with mock disapproval. "I think they're kind of counting on the fact that wet T-shirts help donations. The cheerleaders, not the Mathletes," he clarified. "Though, the other way around might be an interesting choice."

My mouth quirked into a reluctant smile. He was funny, also an unexpected discovery.

"Zane!" someone shouted.

I didn't even react at first. People had been shouting his name all evening. Most of the time they'd been satisfied with nodding at him and staring at me, or, in the case of guys, bumping fists with him and ignoring me.

No reason to suspect this would be any different, except, this time, when Zane stopped and turned toward the voice, tension passed from his hand through mine, like he was touching a live wire.

His back blocked my view, so I couldn't see who'd called

to him. But then slim arms bearing a series of gold bangle bracelets appeared around Zane's neck.

Rachel.

I jolted with surprise. Normally I'd have heard her thoughts well in advance of her approach, but the mental noise from the crowd had evidently drowned her out.

It was only at that moment that I realized Zane had angled himself to hide me from view. Was he protecting me? Or ashamed? Well, the latter would be sort of dumb considering our plan; but then again, in that case, the former didn't make much sense either. He still had hold of my hand though, his fingers now laced through mine and squeezing a little tighter than was comfortable.

"What are you doing here? I didn't think you were coming," she purred, loud enough for me to hear. She slid her fingers through his hair.

A flash of jealousy and possession tore through me, taking me by surprise. He wasn't mine, not really. But he wasn't hers either. If she'd been the slightest bit attuned to body language, she would have picked up on the stiffness of his posture. Not that something as minor as his discomfort would matter to her.

"I was stuck at home forever," she continued, her voice shifting to more of a pout. "My grandfather came over for dinner, and he wouldn't shut up about the lights blowing up yesterday. He had all these questions. God. It's just electricity."

I froze, and if I could have felt my fingers, I might have been squeezing Zane's hand as hard as he was squeezing mine.

"And he kept asking about who was there, who I was hanging out with." She gave a halfhearted huff of annoyance, but her tone suggested she was secretly pleased at being the focal point of such attention.

"I think he's going to try to surprise me with that trip to Europe for all of us that I've been asking about for, like, ever. Anyway, by the time I got over here, Cami and Cassi were already . . . What are you doing?" Her voice sharpened and her arms disappeared from around his neck. She must have (finally) picked up on the awkward way he was standing with one arm—the one holding my hand—almost behind his back.

He stepped aside slowly, perhaps even reluctantly, revealing Rachel in another of her endless series of expensive red dresses (this one with thin straps and a floaty skirt), ridiculously tall heels, and her hair styled in loose waves more appropriate for a photo shoot than bobbing for apples or throwing shaving-cream pies. "Rachel, you know Ariane."

Rachel's eyes widened and her mouth dropped. It might have been funny except I sensed the shock ripple through her and I knew an explosion was in the offing. Evidently, no one had texted her to let her know of our appearance here together. I couldn't blame them. Rachel wasn't known for being kind to messengers.

"Zane," she said through clenched teeth, "can I talk to you? Now." Her thoughts were an incoherent jumble of confusion and fury, and her nostrils were flaring, perhaps in an effort to get oxygen. With her mouth that tight, certainly nothing was passing through there.

I loosened my grip in preparation for letting go, but he

surprised me by tightening his grasp. "We were about to go bob for apples," he said.

We were?

"But we'll catch up with you later," he said, his tone a decent imitation of easy and relaxed, if, again, you couldn't feel the grip of his hand. Which I could. I could also feel his fury bubbling beneath the surface, but not at Rachel's current presumption. It felt older than that.

I stared at him. *What are you doing? Are you trying to piss her off?* Not that I minded, exactly. An angry Rachel was better for my plans. But Zane didn't know that. And as someone who proclaimed to be a fan of "letting things go," he certainly wasn't acting accordingly. What was going on here?

"It'll just take a second," Rachel said with a forced smile. She reached out and snagged his wrist. "It's about what we talked about yesterday. Remember?"

She had the nerve—or idiocy, I wasn't sure which—to tip her head less than subtly toward me.

Really? Even without the added help of my nonhuman heritage I wouldn't have been slow enough to miss that. I fought the urge to roll my eyes.

Zane lifted his chin in determination. "I remember. We'll talk later."

Rachel's eyes narrowed. "Now would be better."

I sensed a sudden burst of surprise and pain from Zane, and looked down to see Rachel digging her nails into the vulnerable flesh of his wrist.

What. The. Hell.

It wasn't a serious injury obviously, but still. It was the

idea—that Rachel felt she could hurt people who defied her. Apparently, it was a Jacobs family trait.

A burning hatred zipped through my veins, warming my whole body, and I couldn't stop myself. I stepped up, putting myself slightly closer to Rachel and partially in front of Zane. "He said later."

Her gaze snapped to me, and the shock—the horrible thrill of being at the center of her attention—was energizing. "I wasn't talking to you."

I forced myself to shrug, though it felt as if all my joints were stuck in place with the thickness of the tension. "I don't care." The buzz of power slipped along my skin, and I had to work to keep myself from smiling.

Overhead, the lights began to flicker, which, in theory, was great. Exactly what I'd wanted to test my hypothesis. Except this time, people around us—huge groups of them—seemed to notice. Some of them even stopped and pointed upward.

I tried to concentrate on shutting my power down. To find the quiet spot that let me hear Rachel's thoughts, as I had in the cafeteria. Once I'd gotten distracted, the barrier had snapped right back into place.

But this time the tingly waves dancing down my arms and legs grew stronger, the crowd was too loud in my head, and Rachel wouldn't shut up to let me concentrate. "I mean, who do you think you are?" she demanded. "Zane is my friend. It's not up to you to tell him what to do."

If I hadn't been in the middle of trying to shut down a crisis, I would have pointed out that being his friend didn't give her that right either, no matter who I was.

But I could feel the power building and slipping away from me. The lightbulbs were rattling and so were the stacked metal bleachers against the far wall. Coach Kiler stormed out of the football booth, shouting for someone to shut down the music and fans. I wasn't sure whether he thought there was an overloaded breaker or he wanted to hear better to determine where the problem was originating. Either way, not good.

I stared at Rachel, trying to focus, but her mouth kept moving without sound, the overwhelming static of building power in my head blocking out her actual words. *Shit.* If I lost control here, people would be hurt. It was unavoidable. Even if just the lights blew, someone would get trampled in the panic, or catch glass in the eye.

Hurting innocent people had never been my intent. I could feel sweat breaking out on the back of my neck. I had to stop this. I'd been so foolish to take the risk.

Zane's face appeared in front of mine, his forehead crinkled in concern. *Ariane, are you okay?* I couldn't hear him, but his mouth moved slowly enough that I could read his lips.

Then, over Rachel's shoulder, movement caught my attention at the football team's booth. The players were filling their tinfoil pie plates with mountains of shaving cream and using each other as targets. Making a huge mess of themselves and the booth.

My attention zoomed in, hyperfocused. I could smell the soapy, aloey scent of the shaving cream, almost feel the weight of the plates. I had a second to recognize that this sensation—a weird, intense attention to detail—felt familiar in a very distant way. And then pie plates and shaving cream exploded in a hundred different directions.

I jumped, startled. People ducked and shouted in surprise as the plates flew by and shaving cream landed on them. But better that than shattered lights and broken glass, I thought.

The wall in my brain snapped back into place, and the energy abruptly cut off. But that didn't stop what had already been set in motion.

Several globs of shaving cream flew past Rachel and spattered onto Zane's shirt and my face. *Ew.* The overheated gym had turned it more liquid than solid, and it trickled down my cheek on impact.

I let go of Zane's hand to wipe it away and noticed that Rachel seemed to have seized up in front of us. Her eyes were squeezed shut, her hands by her face in fists, and her shoulders hunched up by her ears. Well, at least she'd removed her claws from Zane's wrist.

Zane and I looked at each other in confusion, and I lifted my shoulder in an "I have no idea" gesture.

"Rachel?" Zane called hesitantly.

Her eyes snapped open, and if her nostrils had been flaring before, she now resembled an angry horse.

"Are you . . ." Before Zane could finish the question, Rachel turned away, her dress clinging wetly to her legs.

And once she had her back to us, it was clear why. She was covered in shaving cream, from tiny dots near her ankles to huge sprays of it across her shoulder blades.

"Matty!" she shrieked, and one of the football players, a heavyset kid with a stunned expression and his hair sticking up in sweaty spikes, cringed.

She charged toward him, leaving us behind, forgotten.

I laughed, giddiness sweeping over me in the absence of the soul-crushing fear that had dominated only seconds before. I had done that—made a mess of Rachel by blowing up the shaving-cream pies. I hadn't been able to bring the barrier up, but I'd redirected the power. I'd been in control, if only for a few seconds. It was a step in the right direction.

Zane looked at Rachel, the shaving cream splattered across her back and hair as if she'd been caught in the crossfire of a violent crime against the giant marshmallow man from *Ghostbusters*; then he looked at me, giggling, perhaps a little manically, with relief.

"Uh, I think maybe we'd better go," he said.

"Are you sure?" I asked, trying rather unsuccessfully to choke back my laughter. "Maybe if we stick around, someone will attack her with aftershave."

Zane shook his head, but the corners of his mouth turned up in a reluctant smile. "I think you have a death wish," he whispered, putting a hand on my shoulder to steer me between the booths, where, presumably, we could make it to the door without attracting Rachel's attention.

No. Not a death wish. Just very little left to lose.

CHAPTER 14

Zane

IF I'D THOUGHT I WAS INTRIGUED BY ARIANE BEFORE, IT was nothing compared to how I felt after the activities fair.

Outside, in the much cooler air, she was glowing in the harsh white parking lot lights. Not literally. That would have been weird. But it was as if an energy suffused her, so much so that she could have been visible in the dark. And her hand gripped mine like she needed the tether to keep from floating away.

"That was amazing." She wasn't shrieky or girly—not her style, I'd come to notice—but her voice was shaking with . . . excitement, nervousness, a mixture of both? I couldn't tell.

I dug my car keys out of my pocket and steered us toward the truck. "You know this is only going to make things worse for us," I said, but I couldn't help but smile in response to her euphoria. It was not an emotion I'd ever seen from her before.

"Tonight? I don't care." Ariane tipped her face up toward the sky and laughed, a freeing sound. The light bleached all the color from her, emphasizing the pale color of her hair and the unusual lines of her face. She was beautiful but not in any kind of conventional way. She looked . . . foreign. In the way that people from Iceland or Estonia, or wherever, looked different—slightly higher cheekbones or pointy chins or something. Just enough to trigger the realization that they weren't from around here.

I wondered if her mother had been from outside the U.S. Her obituary hadn't made mention of it.

It wasn't something I could ask without sounding like a major creeper, and it didn't matter, except it was one more piece of Ariane that didn't quite fit. I was beginning to wonder if maybe *nothing* about her made sense, and that, in and of itself, was the pattern.

I pushed that thought away and made an effort to rejoin the conversation. "I can't figure out what the hell Matty was thinking," I said. "He knows better than to go up against Rachel."

Ariane slowed, frowning. "It was an accident. He wasn't aiming at her. They were goofing around in the booth and things got out of hand," she said decisively, almost as if she were trying to convince herself.

"I don't know," I said. "That's not what it looked like." But then again, I'd missed the start of what happened, distracted by the increasing tension between Rachel and Ariane. And the lights . . .

"Hey, did you see the lights? Flashing all crazy like they did yesterday in the hall before they blew up." It was strange. I was pretty sure I'd seen the same kind of thing in the cafeteria today when Rachel was taking out some of her aggression on Jenna. The stupid thing was, I kept thinking about what my dad had said about someone using the GTX research to experiment on a kid. Now, granted, the entire idea was whacked-out beyond all measure, a conspiracy theorist's wet dream. And yet I couldn't help but notice that the weird stuff with the lights only seemed to happen when Rachel was around . . . and pissed. Maybe I'd watched too many reruns of *The Incredible Hulk*, but the idea of scientific experimentation and "you wouldn't like me when I'm angry" kind of went together. And Rachel certainly would have been an easy target, given who she was. But why go to all the trouble of making it seem like the research project had been stolen?

Unless that's what they wanted people to believe.

Whatever. I would definitely not be bringing up any of that, now or ever. My dad had the crazy angle covered when it came to GTX.

I realized suddenly that Ariane had gone quiet, and, looking over at her, I noticed some of her happy glow seemed to have faded. "Hey." I swung her hand to get her attention, as we approached my car. "You okay?"

"Yeah. I mean, no," she said finally. "I didn't notice the lights."

I stared at her. "How did you not see—"

"I was too busy watching Rachel dig holes into your arm," she said, her mouth pressed into an unhappy line.

At the reminder, I grimaced, looking down at my arm. I couldn't see much in the dim light—just slightly darker marks on my skin—but I could feel the cuts, small stinging souvenirs of Rachel's disapproval. "It's fine. Not a big—"

Before I could say more, Ariane dropped my hand and grabbed my other arm, pulling it across my body and bringing it closer to her so she could see it in the dim light. The balloon I'd tied around her wrist at the beginning of the night bobbed in my face until I pushed it behind my shoulder.

She ran her fingertips lightly over my injuries, sucking in a sympathetic breath so quietly I wasn't even sure I was supposed to have heard it.

She tucked my arm beneath hers, as a captive, and bent her head for a better look, revealing the pale and vulnerable back of her neck and a glimpse of the whiter-than-white edge of that mysterious bandage.

But I found I didn't care so much about that mystery right now. I could feel the warmth of her skin through her shirt and the rise and fall of her ribs as she breathed, and maybe even the underside of her breast against the inside of my elbow. It . . . she felt good. To be that close to someone and have her want to be that close to me, because I was me, not because of Quinn or my dad or because I was friends with the right people. We were alone out here; there was no one to pretend for.

I cleared my throat. "You defended me," I said, unable to keep the amazement out of my voice, the words escaping before I could stop them. "Against Rachel."

Ariane looked up at me sharply. "I didn't mean to offend your manly sensibilities."

"You didn't. It was . . . nice." No one had stood up for me like that in a long time.

Our gazes locked, and with the noise and the lights of the activity fair in the gym behind us, I could feel the connection thrumming between us. Her hands fell away from my arm, and I reached up to touch her chin, to tilt her face toward mine.

She stepped away, ducking around my hand. "You should make sure to disinfect those cuts when you get home," she said, avoiding eye contact. "There are millions of germs beneath human fingernails."

Human fingernails? What other kind of fingernails were there? I stared after her as she made her way to the passenger side of the SUV. Then I shrugged. At this point, I shouldn't have been surprised by anything from Ariane, I guess.

I unlocked and opened her door, and she didn't even glance at the hand I offered to help her up. But I wasn't dumb. I knew what I'd felt, and I knew I wasn't the only one. I shut her door and went around to climb in behind the wheel. But maybe she had the right idea. This was already complicated enough, and who knew how much of that connection was due to these forced circumstances? Better to leave it alone.

I stuck the keys in the ignition and started the car. *Oh, screw it.* "Speaking of home, how about something to eat first? Everyone in town is here. We could get chili cheese fries at Culver's and eat in peace, probably have the place to ourselves." I was surprised at how much I wanted her to say yes.

Ariane glanced over at me, startled, and for a second I thought I saw a flash of emotion cross her face—longing or loneliness, or both.

"I'd better not." She turned to look out the window.

I backed out of the parking spot and tried to ignore the rush of disappointment.

"Besides," she said, digging into her plastic bag to produce the Puppy Chow and French kiss cookies, "I think Reginald and I are set in terms of food for the night."

"Reginald?" I asked, confused. I put the car into drive and headed out toward the street.

Ariane dropped the cookies and snack mix into the bag and held up the stuffed animal from the ringtoss game. "Yes, Reginald. The dog-bear." She frowned. "Or bear-dog. Whatever you prefer."

"Reginald, the dog-bear," I repeated.

"Or bear-dog," she reminded me.

"That's terrible," I said in mock solemnity. "He's already not sure what he is—a dog, a bear . . . a bog . . ."

She giggled.

"And then you tag him with the name Reginald?" I shook my head.

"What's wrong with Reginald?" she demanded, a smile pulling at her mouth.

"Where do I begin? Is he an English lord of some kind? No. He's a bog. And all the other bogs will make fun of him."

"I have heard that the bog community is known for being close-minded," she said thoughtfully. "But maybe he can be a dear instead of a bog. You know, a d-e-a-r."

I pretended to gasp in horror. "You can't switch allegiances like that! Don't you know anything about the fierce infighting within the bog-dear communities? They hate each other. Especially after the stuffing incident."

This got the reaction I was hoping for—another reluctant laugh from Ariane. "I'll probably regret this, but I'm going to ask anyway. What was the stuffing incident?"

"Shhh! You can't talk about it so openly. They're both very sensitive about it." I leaned closer to her, careful to keep my eyes on the road. "It involved a spy with a tail transplant and ear elongation surgery. And a bog-dear forbidden love."

She rolled her eyes, but she was smiling. "You are ridiculous."

"No, I'm serious. They're crazy for that romantic shit. And you only say that because you have no idea what the bogs and dears have lost in this conflict."

"'Many Bothans died to bring us this information,'" she intoned.

It took me a second to place the familiar words. "You're a Star Wars person?"

"You have no idea," she said, with a rueful smirk that I didn't completely understand. "I mean, not dressing up and waiting for days in line, but yeah."

She paused for a moment, her gaze focused out the windshield but not on anything particular. "Have you ever noticed, though, how all the aliens are either scary or ugly?"

I frowned. "You've thought a lot about this."

"You haven't?" She gave me a knowing look. "You recognized a minor quote from a movie that's almost older than both of us put together."

"Okay, so I might have watched it a few times." In truth, it was something I'd never discuss or even bring up with anyone besides Ariane, but I'd been obsessed with those movies as a kid. Not a huge mystery there. Come on, it's a story about a guy with an overbearing father who is always trying to force him into stuff he doesn't want to do.

"The slave girl that Jabba fed to the Rancor before Luke," I said finally. "She was pretty hot."

Ariane gave me a skeptical look. "She wasn't an alien."

"How do you know that?" I countered.

"She looked totally human!"

"Uh, she was green and had tentacle things coming out of her head. What would you call that?" Some part of me couldn't believe we were arguing over Star Wars; it was so far from my normal life, but it was also the best night I'd had in a long time.

"Good makeup and a slinky costume?" she shot back.

"You're just mad because she doesn't fit your aliens are ugly/scary theory," I said with a laugh.

She glared at me. "Her look was created to be attractive to humans. That's just as bad as making her ugly or scary. It's faux alien, not realistic. I mean, *I* didn't even notice she wasn't . . ." She took a deep breath. "You know what? Never mind. Forget it." Ariane shifted in her seat and returned her attention to the window.

Somehow, I seemed to have offended her. She was taking this conversation seriously; I kind of loved that. "Realistically, I don't think any of them are particularly human," I offered. "Not the way we think of it. Tatooine isn't exactly in our—"

Ariane suddenly sat up straight, staring out the window. "Wait. Stop."

"What's wrong?" I tapped the brakes automatically at the urgency in her voice.

She looked at me like I was crazy. "We're here." She pointed at the darkened street.

"We're in the middle of the road," I said, in disbelief.

"Here is good," she said crisply. "It's only a couple of blocks to my house."

I recognized the intersection as the same one where I'd picked her up.

"No way. I'm not going to drop you off in the dark to walk home." Okay, yes, this was Wingate, so the odds of something happening to her were small, but still. It felt rude, disrespectful to her in some way—like I was pretending not to know her or something. Plus, if her dad was going to be pissed that she'd gone out, how angry would he be if he found out I'd dropped her off in the middle of the street? I let my foot off the brake. "Which house is yours? I won't pull into the driveway if you don't want."

"Let me out," she said, the steel returning to her voice. She put her hand on the door handle, and for a second I thought she might jump out while the car was moving.

"Ariane, I'm just—"

"Are you going to keep me in here against my will?" she asked in a stiff voice. The last thing I wanted was to scare her.

"No!" I said, frustrated. "I just want to make sure you get home okay."

"I'll be fine. Now, stop. Please."

It was the "please" that got me. It was softer, more of a plea than a demand. How could anyone resist that?

I sighed and slowed down to pull over. "Just . . . can you tell me why? Is it your dad? Because, you know, I can introduce myself and—"

"It's not that," she said sharply, leading me to believe it was exactly that.

"Then what is it?" I asked, playing along.

Ariane hesitated. "It's complicated."

"I seem to remember someone telling me earlier today that wasn't a good enough answer." I reached the curb and put the truck in park.

Ariane bit her lip, then said, "It's the only one I've got." She pushed the door open and hopped down, pulling her balloon out after her.

"Wait," I said. "What about tomorrow?"

Her hand on the door, Ariane glanced up at me, blinking hard against the brightness of the dome light. "What about it?"

"A repeat performance of tonight," I prompted. "The daytime version."

"I can't meet you there?" she asked, her shoulders sagging.

I frowned. It hadn't been that bad tonight, had it? Aside from the encounters with Mrs. Vanderhoff and Rachel, I thought we'd had a good time.

Before I could say anything, Ariane nodded with a sigh. "Fine. See you tomorrow morning." She started to shut the door and then stopped. "Here, though," she said pointedly. "Not at my house."

"Got it," I said, drumming my hands on the wheel, a nervous fidget. I hated leaving her to walk in the dark. It seemed wrong. Like tempting fate or something.

"I mean it."

"I said okay."

She gave me one last stern look, as if reinforcing her point, and then slammed the door. The glow from the dome light faded, but I waited—I never promised I wouldn't do that—watching her cross the street and then walk up the sidewalk until she vanished—presumably into one of the houses on that side of the block.

The tightness in my stomach eased with the assumption that she'd made it home okay. And it was right then that I realized I might be in way over my head with this game of pretend.

CHAPTER 15

Ariane

WHEN I SLIPPED THROUGH THE FRONT DOOR, THE HOUSE was dark and still except for the murmuring and flickering of the TV I'd left on in the family room. I let out a breath I hadn't realized I'd been holding. Of course my father wouldn't be home yet. It was barely nine; he wouldn't be home for hours. And yet the guilt of sneaking out and obliterating nearly every one of the Rules made me feel certain he'd be waiting for me, grave disappointment and censure carved into his face.

But he wasn't.

I went into the family room, clicked off the TV, and hurried down the hall to my room. I needed to get everything put to rights and be asleep (or look as if I were) before he arrived home. I had plenty of time, but I could feel my crimes written all over me—in what I was wearing, in the sagging balloon tied to my arm, in the plastic shopping bag containing fair snacks and the stuffed bog/dear

Reginald. And judging by my reflection in the mirror, I was nowhere near sleepy or even a reasonable facsimile of it. My cheeks were flushed, my hair was all over the place, and my eyes . . .

I stepped closer to the mirror. My eyes looked brighter even behind the dulling plastic of the blue lenses.

I'd enjoyed tonight. I mean, any evening that ended with Rachel coated in shaving cream and shrieking had to be on my top ten of all time. But it was more than that. Zane was not who I'd thought he was. Or, if he was that arrogant, privileged jerk, there were other sides to him, other facets: the little kid who, if the memories/images in Zane's head were to be believed, had once had *Star Wars* sheets on his bed, so great was his obsession. The guy who knew what it was to be different and not good enough.

Not that learning those things about Zane changed anything. My opinion of him was irrelevant. This would be over in a day or two, at the most, and then things would return to normal. Or maybe slightly better than normal, as Rachel would finally have a taste of what it felt like to lose, and I'd learn more about regaining control over my "lost" ability.

That last part made me queasy. In all honesty, I didn't really want my ability back. At least not any more than was strictly necessary to keep those weird power flare-ups at bay. But limiting myself wasn't an option. I needed to be able to protect myself and my father if GTX came after us.

But my brain had put up this barrier for self-protection, and for good reason. I didn't want to be the person who could do what I'd done in the lab, near the end of my stay there. And some part of me believed that if I brought the barrier down permanently and regained control over my ability, I'd finally be the success Dr. Jacobs had been longing for, and he'd, I don't know, somehow sense that and find me. I knew, logically, that wasn't true, but I couldn't stop thinking about it, especially after seeing Rachel in action tonight, hurting Zane for not cooperating. It brought back lots of bad memories.

"I've got big plans for you, my dear," Dr. Jacobs used to say from the observation room window, the one that made up the entire fourth wall of my little room. "You will save lives."

What he'd failed to mention, though, was that I'd have to take other lives in the process. Not that it had started out that way.

The new tests began when I was six. (Only a month or so before my father would rescue me, actually; though I didn't know that then, of course.) And this time, Dr. Jacobs and the techs didn't want blood or bone marrow or brain tissue—much to my relief. Instead, these tests were more like tasks. Just games, tricks for treats—all of them with the promise of a potential trip Outside if I performed "up to standards."

The first series of tests: move the big rubber red ball to specific locations in my room (far right corner, five feet in the air) without touching it. No problem. I'd been doing much the same on my own for as long as I could remember. I could lie on my cot and float a book from the shelf across my room over to my waiting hands just by focusing on the spine of the one I wanted. Levitation. Easy.

Second series: my favorite lab tech, Mara—she talked to me like I was a person and smiled at me instead of avoiding my gaze—would stand with an open bag of my favorite candy in her hand and a plastic cup on the floor in front of her. My task? Stop the peanut M&M's Mara dropped before they fell into the cup (or onto the ground, her aim wasn't so good sometimes). And I got to eat the candy I "saved." Yummy.

Then, once I'd mastered that, I had to redirect the falling candy to different target cups set out across the room, on command. And at faster and faster speeds. Bullet speed, in fact. For the last test, Mara used rubber pellets, and one of them actually tore a hole through the far side of a disposable cup, sending plastic splinters into the air. I got to keep the whole bag of candy that time. (It wasn't until years later that I understood what they were training me to do. Redirecting bullets is a handy skill if you have the need for that sort of a thing.)

The third series of tests, though, that's when everything changed. Mara wheeled in a glass cage on a metal cart. In it, a tiny brown-and-white mouse scurried through a bed of cedar chips, running between a shiny metal wheel in the corner and a water bottle hanging down the side of the cage. I was entranced. I'd never seen a live animal, of any variety, before. And, foolishly, I thought I was getting some company in my lonely little room, even if it was only for a few days.

My first tasks with the mouse were simple, innocuous. Use my mind to keep the wheel from moving when the mouse tried to push it forward. Then I was supposed to hold the mouse still, again without actually touching him.

"From across the room, darling," Dr. Jacobs said over the intercom.

High on previous successes and with the carrot of Outside dangling in front of me, I didn't even hesitate. Of course I could stop the mouse from moving. There were complexities to this task, involving energy, molecules, the vibration of atoms, and various other aspects of the science that I didn't care about. It was simply enough that I could do it.

But I took special care not to hurt Jerry. We were, in my six-year-old head, friends. (I'd named him after the clever cartoon mouse; though, my Jerry, sadly, showed nowhere near the initiative or intelligence of his namesake. But I was hopeful.)

At night, when the tests were done and everyone had gone home, I had the comforting noise of Jerry shuffling through his cedar chips or running on his wheel to keep me company. I talked to him, too, whispering so no one could hear. He didn't respond or acknowledge my existence in any way, but I knew that would change eventually.

I was training Jerry to trust me. I picked out the sunflower seeds in his food before he could eat them and used them to lure him closer so I could pet him. (There's a bit of irony for you—the experiment training another experiment, using the same methods that had worked on her. Or maybe it's just evidence for the nurture side of the nature vs. nurture debate.)

In any case, my week or so with Jerry was probably the happiest I ever was in the lab.

I really should have known better. My studies should

have clued me in on what was coming next. The daily curriculum now included videos with diagrams of mouse anatomy. Find the heart. Understand how it works.

But I was oblivious. Until Dr. Jacobs spelled out exactly what he wanted.

"Kill the mouse," he said to me late one afternoon over the intercom, barely looking up from the sheaf of papers on his clipboard.

"What?" I stared at him, not understanding. I looked to Mara, standing next to Dr. Jacobs in the observation room, for guidance. But her eyes were wide with surprise.

"Sir—" she began.

"Just stop the heart. You can do it," Jacobs said to me impatiently, with a glare at Mara.

Mara, in turn, gave me a forced smile and a stiff encouraging nod. But I could feel her fear.

I didn't move. I knew I could do what he asked—find Jerry's rapidly beating little heart by picturing it as I'd seen it on the diagram and telling it to STOP. But I wouldn't; Jerry was my friend.

Something in the quality of my stillness must have registered with Dr. Jacobs. He put his clipboard down with an exasperated huff. "Darling, you've been doing so well, so far. You want to go Outside, don't you?" His smile was tight, threatening somehow.

My mind flashed back to Leo and his bloodstained grin. *Freak. They're never going to let you out of here.*

I frowned. He'd been telling the truth, I'd felt that for sure. But I didn't get any sense of deception from Dr. Jacobs, either. Someone had to be lying.

Dr. Jacobs never specified when *you'd be let outside or in what condition*, my logical side pointed out suddenly. I recognized it as a negotiation strategy commonly employed among humans. It was called *leaving a loophole.*

A rush of heat filled me, driving me to clench my hands into fists. I hated Dr. Jacobs in that moment, not just for asking me to kill Jerry, which I wouldn't do, but for making me hope for something that he had no intention of delivering.

Dr. Jacobs took my continued silence as assent. "Very good." He scooped up his clipboard and resumed flipping through pages.

"No." My voice came out small and soft. I could feel sweat breaking out on the backs of my knees and in the crooks of my elbows. Refusing always had consequences. But unlike the other times—where techs like Leo were sent in to force cooperation—this was one thing Dr. Jacobs couldn't make me do.

Or so I thought.

At the sound of my refusal, all activity in the observation room stopped, the techs' gazes moving to focus on Dr. Jacobs. Things had been tense lately. Men in military uniforms—so many buttons and medals on their shoulders—had taken to appearing in the observation room on occasion, where they were seemingly unexpected and not particularly welcome.

Dr. Jacobs put his clipboard down with a loud snap. "Now, Wannoseven, I don't think you're—"

"No," I said again quickly, before I could lose my nerve. I was shaking from head to toe.

Mara tried again. "Sir, I think she's become attached to the—"

But Dr. Jacobs was beyond listening to either one of us.

He had my cot removed that night, leaving me to sleep on the cold, hard floor. When that didn't work, he stripped the cell of everything but Jerry's cage.

By that time, though, I was starting to enjoy his frustration. And he knew it.

So he took away food. Not just mine, but Jerry's too.

I started to see the effects on Jerry after a day or two. He no longer left his nest of cedar chips to run on the wheel or drink from his water bottle, which I refilled at the sink. I checked on him constantly, making sure his sides were still puffing in and out with breath.

On the fifth day of my rebellion, Dr. Jacobs, Grandpa-freaking-Art, had turned out the lights, leaving me alone in the dark.

Remembering those days in the pitch-black, I shuddered and left my bed to turn on my desk lamp and closet light, making my room as bright as possible.

I would never forget that kind of dark. It was like nothing I'd ever experienced before or since. My eyes had created hazy, crazy designs out of nothing in a panicked attempt to see something, anything. And the thick quality of the blackness was such that I felt like I might choke on it.

But the silence had been the worst.

I couldn't hear *anything*. No noise except for Jerry and me. No thoughts, no feelings. Just empty, abandoned silence.

Would they just leave me here? Forever? Jacobs had already told me—multiple times—I had no value to him if I was uncooperative.

So . . . my only excuse is that I was six and hungry and

scared. And trapped in a small room in the dark. Maybe forever.

Still, that's not enough. Not for what I did.

When Jacobs returned to check on me—three days later, I found out—Jerry was dead and I was curled up in a ball in the corner. As far from Jerry's cage as I could get within my own cage.

I don't remember much of those three days, other than the paralyzing darkness and the occasional shuffle of Jerry in his cedar chips . . . and then the ear-ringing silence of being completely alone and knowing what I'd done. It was horrible.

When the lights came back on in my room, they were blinding. And Dr. Jacobs's voice boomed congratulations in what was probably his normal speaking voice, but it felt like screaming to my ears. He ordered all my privileges returned in double portions.

But none of that mattered, not when I squinted up to see Mara coming in to wheel Jerry's cage away and she wouldn't even look at me, her fear a distinct pulse in my head. Only this time, she wasn't afraid of Dr. Jacobs. She was afraid of me.

Sick shame filled me. Dr. Jacobs had made me like him; I'd hurt something smaller and weaker than I was.

Too weak to stand, I rolled onto my stomach and dry heaved until I passed out.

I'd woken up, hours later, hooked to an IV for nutrition, with a tech (not Mara; I never saw her again) fussing over me. And it hadn't taken long for Dr. Jacobs to start up the testing again. Or, to try to, anyway.

Something had happened in the dark. A switch inside

me had flipped. Whether it was the trauma of the dark, or killing Jerry, or both, it didn't matter. I could not access my ability anymore. Nothing Jacobs did after that made a difference, carrot or stick. And he'd tried both. More candy, more promises of Outside, followed by days without food or light.

But it didn't matter; I couldn't have done what he asked even if I'd wanted to. I was empty, hollowed out. Whatever had been there before was now gone. After that, if I wanted something from across the room, the only way for me to get it was the human way—walking over to retrieve it.

Jacobs had been enraged and threatened to "dispose" of me in the days leading up to the explosion that would allow my father to free me. But I . . . I'd been relieved. He could no longer control me; *I* couldn't even control me, so to speak. The ability to obey his demands had been taken away from me, and with it, the fear.

But now I was supposed to be working to get all of that back. And even though having my telekinetic ability restored would actually make me more powerful, it felt more like I was daring Dr. Jacobs to come and find me.

I shook that thought away. With effort, I refocused my attention on hiding the evidence of my illicit evening.

I tucked the Puppy Chow and French kiss cookies into my schoolbag. I couldn't leave them in my room without risking my father's attention. And I'd learned during my hoarding stage that food stored in unusual places attracts bugs, which . . . gross.

But at school, I could keep them in my locker or share them with Jenna.

I flinched and snapped my bag closed. No, I would not

be sharing them with Jenna. She hadn't returned any of my texts or calls. She'd been serious about putting some distance between us.

Except tomorrow she'd hear someone, somewhere talking about Zane and me, and then she'd hate me forever.

I sighed and crossed over to my desk. Maybe that was for the best. Maybe my father was right: I was too attached to Jenna when she didn't even know the real me. At least if she was avoiding me, I wouldn't have to see the hurt on her face when I couldn't explain what was really going on. How it was all fake. How I didn't really like Zane and he didn't like me.

That last thought surprised me with the pang of hurt that accompanied it.

Don't. Don't be that stupid girl. Nothing had changed. My goal was the same and that had to be my focus.

I opened my desk drawers to look for scissors. I needed to cut the balloon off my arm, pop it, and hide the evidence at the bottom of a garbage can, preferably under the nastiest, smelliest trash I could find. Subterfuge. It was my specialty. Well, one of them.

So Zane was attractive and less of an ass than I'd originally thought. That was no reason to lose sight of the point of this exercise. Even if his smile did funny things to my insides and his hands were big. Which was nice.

I remembered the feeling of his hand, gentle but certain on my back, steering me out of the gym. And I shivered. Which was ridiculous. I'd been holding his hand all night—why this would have made a difference, I wasn't sure. It just felt more personal.

And then in the parking lot, when I'd responded without thinking about it, taking his arm to look at what Rachel had done. The heat of him had radiated against me, and I'd been all too aware of that small distance between us, as if an electric connection existed, leaping across the space. He'd looked at me with warmth in his gaze, and I'd felt small but not in a bad way, not in the way I was accustomed—where the world felt dangerous and enormous, and I was on my own. Instead it was more like being protected, shielded from all those searching for me, wanting to hurt me.

He'd thought about kissing me then. I hadn't heard it in his mind—hadn't needed to. It was written on his face. Not that that would have been a good idea. And yet I couldn't stop thinking about it.

Another shiver ran through me.

I found the scissors under a half-empty package of printer paper and used them to snip the balloon free from my wrist, the cool metal moving smoothly against my skin. Another surgical cut at the base of the balloon and it deflated quickly and quietly.

I knew I should cut it into little tiny pieces so it would be completely unrecognizable in the unlikely event that my father would catch of a glimpse of it.

But I hesitated, scissors hovering above the remains. Something in me protested the destruction. It wasn't as if I'd have many nights out like this in the future, fake or not.

My father often talked about my life, post-Wingate. The kind of freedom I'd have, all the things I'd get to experience. But the wistful tone in his voice set off alarms in my head; his description of my future life seemed to have a fairy-tale quality to it rather than something he expected me to actually experience.

And he was right. Because even in the best-case scenario, where I managed to escape Wingate without bringing GTX down on us, I'd have to set up a careful anonymous life somewhere. Always watchful that I didn't get too involved, didn't allow others to become attached. There was too much at stake.

Aside from the difficulty of constantly staying on my guard, never being seen without my contact lenses in, and avoiding situations where the strange tattoo on my shoulder might be revealed (pool parties, summer days, and, um, more intimate moments), there were other complications.

Caring about someone, or having them care about me, was too dangerous. It left vulnerabilities that GTX could manipulate; it opened up the possibility of being hurt or hurting others, even unintentionally. That final experiment in the lab—beyond its value in blocking off an ability I no longer wanted—had taught me that.

The Rules, as much as I hated and railed against them, kept me—and everyone else—safe. So my father's Rules were not just rules for living in Wingate. They were Rules for the rest of my life. Which included never falling in love or letting anyone fall in love with me.

Not that that was what was happening here with Zane, but it was a reasonable facsimile. And with the safety of a built-in end date, it was the closest thing I could allow myself to have. I couldn't destroy evidence of it.

Right then, I knew where the balloon—and Reginald—should go.

I put the scissors down and I went to my closet. I dragged out the stool and raised myself to my tiptoes and dug behind my stacked jeans until I felt the sharp edge of cardboard.

I wrestled it free, doing my best to avoid a denim avalanche, and hopped down from the stool.

It was an oversized shoe box labeled "Old School Papers," and was possibly the world's most obvious hiding spot. Fortunately, most of its contents didn't look all that unusual and wouldn't raise an alarm with anyone but GTX.

With a cautious glance toward the dark and quiet hallway, I pulled the lid off. Memories immediately leapt to mind with the sight of everything inside.

This box was what remained of my hoarding tendencies, only instead of little bits of everything I touched, it contained physical reminders of the things that had been important to me.

A ticket stub from the first time my father had taken me to a movie.

A carefully cleaned-out wrapper from my first taste of french fries (gloriously fried potatoes! GTX had been way more into giving me green vegetables and tofu, figuring "my people" were healthy vegetarians or advanced enough to pop pills for nutrition instead of eating anything).

A photo of the original Ariane Tucker—a pale dark-haired girl with a huge smile and purplish shadows under her eyes—swiped from an old frame I'd found buried in a box in our basement.

A magic coin trick from the first cereal box I'd finished in my father's house.

Scrunched up in the corner, the tiniest fragment of ripped white fabric, maybe only an inch by inch, with my GTX designation. GTX-F-107. The same mark that I bore on my back. They'd labeled all my clothes, and when I'd escaped, my father had destroyed the shapeless shirt and pants made of scratchy cotton. But I'd torn the designation out of the neck of the shirt before giving them to him. I didn't want to forget where I came from.

An important thing to remember, especially on a night like tonight.

I set the box on my desk, tucked the deflated balloon and string inside, and retrieved Reginald from the grocery bag.

I put him on top, remembering Zane spinning that story about bogs and dears, and how he'd grinned, so pleased with himself when I laughed.

Stupidly, my eyes welled with tears.

Enough, I told myself. I put the lid on the box, shutting away Reginald's malformed ears and cheap black button eyes.

I returned the box to its hiding spot behind my jeans, shoved the stool back into place, closed my closet, and headed to the bathroom.

Snapping the light on made me blink, temporarily rejecting the additional brightness as well as the glimpse of myself in the mirror with reddened eyes.

I busied myself with my contact case and solution.

Remove my lenses, wash my face, brush my teeth, put on pajamas, and get into bed. That was all I had to do. Then everything would be as if I'd never gone out at all tonight—except for the guilt of lying to my father and the empty space I could feel growing in my chest.

I should never have agreed to any of this with Zane, no matter what the benefits. Pretending made things too real.

I carefully took my contacts out and closed the case. Then, steeling myself, I looked in the mirror.

I usually avoided my reflection unless I had my lenses in. My eyes were so dark—so wrong, no distinguishable pupil—seeing them in their natural state always sent a shock through me. With normalish-looking eyes, my unusual features were softened. But with my distinctly nonhuman eyes uncovered, the point of my chin seemed so obvious, and the too-severe slant of my cheekbones, the faint grayish hue to my skin . . . it all screamed ALIEN.

I flinched and glanced away. I'd gotten used to not seeing myself this way.

I finished in the bathroom and returned to my room to put my necklace away and change into my pajamas—yoga pants and a T-shirt made of the softest cotton I'd ever felt.

I was climbing into bed when my phone, in the pocket of my jeans which were now slung over my desk chair, chirped with a text message.

"Jenna." I breathed with relief and scrambled out from under the covers.

But it wasn't Jenna. It was Zane.

> 7:30 ok? See you tomorrow am.

I couldn't help but notice that he didn't give me a chance to decline, only the opportunity to change the time. He was right. We'd committed to this path and now we were stuck.

I fought a smile. I should not have felt quite so pleased about that fact. Definitely not.

I went to put my phone in my bag so I wouldn't be

scrambling to find it in the morning, and realized it was flashing one unread message.

I frowned. It must have come in while we were at the activities fair, where it had been too noisy for me to hear the chime.

Still hoping to see Jenna's name—I didn't text anyone else, ever—it took a second for the "DAD" designation to sink in.

Dad. My father *never* texted.

My heart rate skyrocketed, and my hands shook as I pressed the button to read the message.

> Pulling a double. Will be home tomorrow after you leave for school. Don't forget to feed the fish.

I relaxed. Nothing about the activities fair. But a double shift? Normally he knew about those weeks in advance. I frowned.

I bit my lip, thinking it through. The reference to feeding the fish was our signal that everything was okay. So I had to assume that it was either a normal work scheduling hiccup—which had never happened in my memory—or he'd chosen to stay after for some reason. He'd done that occasionally in the past when he needed to talk to someone who worked a different shift. But it was usually only a few hours, staying in late or going in early, never a whole second shift.

It clicked in my head. The cameras. The ones GTX had installed today. I'd bet anything he was checking into it further. Trying to find out what had happened, how he'd not known anything about it.

I felt a little sick. He was really worried.

I forced myself to take a breath, and let it out slowly. He'd told me to feed the fish (which, by the way, we didn't actually own). He wouldn't have done that if he was concerned about my safety.

But something was keeping him at GTX, away from home and out of routine. And even without specific details about what that something was, I knew it wasn't good.

I texted back. *Fish fed. See you tomorrow afternoon?*

And though he normally didn't respond to messages or phone calls at work unless I indicated it was urgent, the silence following the chirp of my text felt ominous.

It was going to be a long night.

CHAPTER 16

Zane

I WHISTLED ON MY WAY DOWN THE HALL FROM MY ROOM to the kitchen. I'd slept better than I had in a while. Yeah, it was a messed-up situation, so maybe it was a little wrong to be having so much fun. But to be honest, I wasn't interested in inspecting it. When good things happening were in such short supply, I was going to take them any way I could.

Ariane hadn't texted back last night to tell me a different time or not to pick her up, and I knew her well enough now to be sure she'd speak up if she had a problem with either. I was counting that as a win and looking forward to seeing her again with an anticipation that might have scared me if I looked at it closely.

But as I said, I was firmly anti-inspecting today.

I pushed open the door to the kitchen and nodded a greeting at my dad, who was once again at the island with his coffee and his paper. He scowled at me, and the last tuneless note—I wasn't whistling a song so much as making a cheerful-sounding noise—died on my lips.

"Sorry." I wasn't about to tangle with him this morning. Last night we'd almost been getting along—by our standards, anyway. I didn't want to push my luck.

I moved past him, giving him plenty of room, and grabbed the bread bag, only to remember that I'd choked down the last of it yesterday.

Oh, well. I crumpled up the bag and tossed it into the garbage. The Blazer needed gas; I could grab something at the store on my way to pick up Ariane.

I started across the kitchen, heading toward my backpack and keys on the counter near the back door.

"You're certainly looking pleased with yourself this morning," my dad said in that all-too-casual tone that signaled danger.

My heart sank. Clearly the temporary near-peace we'd enjoyed last night was over. I calculated my odds of grabbing my stuff and getting the hell out before he blew up. They weren't good. And even if I made it out now, I needed the car for tonight and tomorrow. He'd have no problem taking it away from me if he decided I was being disrespectful. And since I had to live here . . .

I let out a slow breath that I hoped he wouldn't hear and braced myself for what was coming. "Yeah," I said, forcing an easy tone. "Guess I had a good time at the fair last night."

"I heard I missed some excitement," he said, still sounding fake mellow as he studied the newspaper.

Oh. Okay. I let out a silent breath of relief. This I could handle. He was cranky because he thought he'd missed out on an opportunity to herd people to safety.

"It wasn't much," I said. "Just the lights flickering. Too much stuff running at once, I guess." And maybe the presence of the mystery kid who my dad was convinced had been injected with GTX's missing research. Who might possibly be Rachel Jacobs herself.

I thought about bringing it up, in the hope of distracting/placating him, but I wasn't sure I could manage it without letting skepticism leak into my tone.

"Yes, Mrs. Vanderhoff mentioned in her voice mail that it was interesting there for a few minutes." He looked up, his mouth pinched.

Oh, fuuuuu—

"Mrs. Vanderhoff's very long message on my cell phone at six this morning also included how pleased she was to have seen you last night, and so disappointed that my son would speak disrespectfully to her."

I winced. There it was. The key word: *disrespectfully*. I wouldn't be getting out of this so easily. That was my dad's major hot button. Respect, or lack thereof.

Even though, technically, I hadn't said much of anything at all, and Mrs. Vanderhoff deserved the shock she'd gotten from Ariane.

I waited for him to demand the identity of my "date"—that would be the only thing that could make this worse, learning I'd been out with the daughter of his mortal enemy—but apparently, Mrs. Vanderhoff's "concerned" diatribe had focused on me as the perpetrator.

"Do you have any idea how hard it is to do what I do? No, of course not," he answered for me, snapping the paper closed and standing up to jab a finger at me. "The last thing I need is you making it more difficult by smarting off to important people in this community."

Delores Vanderhoff was the organist at our church and the biggest gossip in town. She was important mostly because of her ability to disguise malicious conjecture as truth and rev the rumor mill into high gear.

My mom would have known how to defuse the situation, to point out that Delores was "talking to hear herself make noise" without making my dad even angrier. Unfortunately, she had not passed that skill on to me. "Dad, Mrs. Vanderhoff is freaking out over nothing, as usual," I argued. "You know what she's like. It was just—"

"Zane, I don't care if she was shouting that the sky was falling because it's raining. You nod politely and duck when she tells you to."

I wanted to scream. I'd been hearing a version of this lecture for as long as I could remember. It's called "Everyone else is always right even when they're wrong." Everyone's opinion of us mattered more than the actual truth. Quinn had mastered this lesson by lying and listening to lies with a polite smile. That was my brother—the politician.

But the injustice of it rubbed me raw.

"My ability to serve this town depends on people trusting me, respecting my ability to control difficult situations. What do you think it says to them if I don't have control over my own kid?" He was in my face now, his coffee breath sour. "What you say and do reflects on me, and I won't have you representing my name poorly."

Again. Even more. He meant those things even if he wasn't saying them.

My dad made a disgusted noise. "You know, I'm the one who stuck around. Your mom left you high and dry. I'm the good guy here."

I was pretty sure if you have to argue that you're the good guy, you're defeating your own argument. But I kept my mouth firmly shut against those words, though my jaw ached from holding everything in.

"The least you could do is show some gratitude," he said.

Resentment burned deep in my gut. Gratitude for his sticking around and being a parent so grudgingly? Gratitude for hating me and everything I reminded him of?

He thrust his hand toward me. "Keys."

I gaped at him and his open hand. "What?"

He snapped his fingers. "Keys. You don't think you've got car privileges after all that, do you?"

A haze of fury clouded my vision. He could have taken the keys before I got down here, but no, he had to rub my face in it like I was a puppy making a mess.

I clenched my fists, and Dad shifted his weight, eyeing me closely as if expecting—or challenging—me to rush at him.

A single clear thought penetrated. *Stop.* A warning whisper that sounded like my mother's voice: *Think about this. Be careful. Play the game and play it right.*

If I let things get physical, I might win, but I'd still lose. My car privileges would be gone forever, and my life in this house would be about ten degrees warmer than hell.

So . . . the question was, what did my dad hate more than his family being imperfect in front of others?

It took me a second, but then it clicked. Like one of those

little-kid jokes. What was worse than one instance? Several instances of his family being proven imperfect. Which gave me an idea.

"Fine," I said, barely managing to force the word out. I stepped to the side, snagged the keys from the counter, and held them out to him. "I need you to call some parents, then."

He grabbed the keys and then paused, his hand out. "What?" he demanded with a frown.

"Well, the girl I'm driving to school, for one. I told her parents I'd be picking her up and dropping her off this week. She doesn't have a ride, otherwise."

My dad opened his mouth—whether to protest or to ask her name, I wasn't sure—but I didn't wait.

"And Rachel Jacobs's dad," I said quickly.

His mouth snapped shut.

Of course *that* would work. I forced myself to keep a neutral expression. "I promised Rachel I'd be a DD for her party tomorrow night. I guess some people drink at the bonfire before they come over." As he well knew, just as he knew there would be drinking at Rachel's party afterward; though I wasn't dumb enough to wave that flag in his face. "Her dad insisted that there be sober people with cars on call, in case." In reality, he'd requested no such thing (though he should have). I doubted he even knew about the party.

My dad narrowed his eyes. "I should make you call them and explain why you're inconveniencing so many people because of your disrespect."

I felt the first flicker of possible triumph. He'd said

"should." In his mind, the only thing worse than his having to call to explain would be my doing it when he couldn't control what I would say. "Okay," I said, trying to sound neutral.

He gave a loud huff of frustration and chucked the keys at me.

I managed to catch them before they hit my face.

"Saturday morning. The Blazer's back in the garage and you are grounded." He pointed a censorious finger at me.

I nodded.

"And don't you dare make the mistake of thinking you won this round, Zane." He stalked out of the kitchen, presumably to get ready for work.

I didn't think I'd won anything. It was more a temporary stay of execution. And yet it was more than I'd ever attempted before. I hadn't out and out defied him, but it was way closer than anything I'd previously done.

Oddly enough, remembering my conversation with Ariane last night about Mrs. Vanderhoff's bullying, I couldn't help but think that Ariane might have been pleased at what I'd done this morning.

Not right now, though. Now she'd be angry because I was running late. I wondered how long it would take her to assume that I wasn't going to show up. Probably not long. She still didn't trust me. The weird part was how much I wanted her to.

Again: not looking at anything too closely this morning. With a hint of my good mood returning, I grabbed my backpack and hurried out.

CHAPTER 17

Ariane

THREE MINUTES LATE. I PACED THE SIDEWALK, A COUPLE concrete squares away from the actual intersection of Pine and Rushmore. Three minutes—though a devastating break in pattern for someone like me (assuming there was someone else like me) wasn't much for a so-called normal person. I knew that from years of observation. Being three minutes late didn't even require an apology, from what I'd seen.

Unlike, say, five minutes . . .

The next two minutes ticked by with excruciating slowness, but I felt every second of them. Exposed, left standing here, open for scrutiny by anyone glancing out their window or driving by.

And still no sign of Zane. I tensed with the sound of every car approaching, even if it was from the wrong direction. And every time, it wasn't him.

Had something changed? Last night, the closeness between us had seemed natural and easy, despite the circumstances. But reviewing it in the harsh light of day, I couldn't help but wonder if I'd gotten it wrong.

Maybe I'd enjoyed last night more than he had. Maybe he'd simply made the best of a bad situation and humored me. I mean, in theory, this wasn't about fun for either one of us.

I hadn't picked up on any obvious deception in his thoughts last night—not that I'd been actively listening in. But people attempting to hide something tend to be rather loud about it in their thoughts—a consequence, I suspected, of trying to be subtle in their words and actions. Unless they'd been trained in lying or done it well for a really long time.

I sighed. More and more, I realized that my father was right. Hearing people's thoughts was not nearly the advantage the scientists who'd tinkered with my genetic makeup thought it would be.

It led you to shaky and unreliable conclusions, and made you feel that you knew someone better than you actually did.

The worst part was not that Zane was late or maybe not even showing up, but rather that I *felt* it. My chest was tight with disappointment, and a weird stinging sensation in my eyes suggested tears.

They indicated that this fake situation had some kind of real meaning, enough to affect me, which I did not want or need. Particularly today, when I was already worried about what was going on with my father, what he'd found (or not found) at GTX.

I swallowed hard and added another sidewalk square to my pacing. I would not—could not—let this *nothing* with Zane get to me.

At 7:36 (and 30 seconds, give or take), according to my cell phone, I started walking to school. Waiting for someone who was seven minutes late (or not coming at all) seemed to be a particular threshold of patheticness I didn't want to cross.

I'd gone about a half a block when Zane's SUV pulled up to the curb. And despite the internal complaining I'd been doing about hearing thoughts and feelings, I sensed him before I saw him. The frustration and worry coming off him was intense and seemed legit, as far as I could tell.

Still, didn't make it right. I kept walking.

He rolled down the window on the passenger side. "Ariane, I'm sorry," he said, out of breath, as if he'd been running instead of driving. "My dad was being a dick, I had to get gas, and I'm just . . . late." He lifted his hands helplessly.

I faced him. "You couldn't call or text?" I waved my phone at him.

"I was afraid you'd leave anyway." He gave me a sheepish smile.

"Right on that one," I muttered.

"Come on, you going to get in?" he wheedled.

Before I could answer, he parked and scrambled out and around the front of the SUV. "I brought you breakfast." He held up a grease-spotted bag sporting the familiar golden arches.

My stomach gave an interested—though, thankfully, quiet—rumble. I hadn't been able to choke down much of my peanut butter toast this morning (Thursday is always toast day). It had been too strange, eating breakfast alone.

I raised my eyebrows. "You had time to buy food?"

He held his hands up, one still clutching the bag. "Only while the tank was filling, I swear. The other day you said you forgot to eat breakfast. I thought maybe if that was a regular thing . . ."

I looked at him, startled. I *had* said that—a lie to try to distract Jenna, but he'd obviously been listening. *Before* we'd entered this little arrangement of ours.

"Aaaand I thought it might make you less mad at me for being late." He gave me a lopsided grin that did funny things to my insides and made me look a little too hard at his mouth. He had a very nice one. Empirically speaking.

Despite my best efforts, I could feel myself relenting. His open-faced sincerity was hard to resist. "That might work on other girls . . ." I began. Then my stomach gave a particularly loud rumble. I sighed. "And it's totally going to work on me, too."

He grinned again (causing my heart to do little flips that should have been anatomically impossible for either species I belonged to) and opened the door for me.

I crossed the grass and got in, setting my bag on the floor. He closed the door after me and jogged to the other side.

"We're going to be late for school," I said, when he opened his door. I couldn't help noticing the two paper cups of orange juice in the drink holders between us, straws in their wrappers tucked behind them. He really had been planning on our eating together.

"Nope, we just have to eat as we go." He climbed in and slammed the door. Then he set the bag on the armrest between us. "I didn't know what you liked, so I got a little bit of everything." He gestured toward the bag. "Biscuits, burritos, McGriddles . . ."

I peeked inside the bag. "Hash browns," I said, spotting the familiar wrapper, and snatched it. My obsession with fried potatoes was not limited to french fries. The crunchy outer goodness with that lovely soft but textured inside—yum. I'd have to watch my intake to make sure I didn't fill up on carbs instead of protein (because I'd faint somewhere, oh, around fourth hour), but they were so good.

Zane looked at me oddly as he put the truck in gear. "Very glad I didn't fight you for those. I might have lost fingers."

"Shut up," I said without heat, around a mouthful of hash browns.

He laughed. "You want to hand me something in there?"

I frowned and looked into the bag again. It was pretty full. He hadn't been kidding about there being a variety of items available. "Like what?"

"Clearly not the hash browns." He gave me a mischievous smile. "Whatever, I don't care. I eat all of it."

I rummaged until I found a breakfast burrito. That seemed like a guy breakfast item.

I held it out to him.

He raised his eyebrows. "Can you maybe . . . a little help?" He tipped his head toward his hands occupied with the steering wheel, his attention focused on the road.

"Oh. Yeah." I peeled back the wrapper enough for him to start eating and handed it to him, our fingers brushing in the process.

I tried to ignore the weird little jolt the contact sent through me.

"Thanks," he said.

I unwrapped my straw and stuck it through the lid on

my cup. I hesitated for a second, and then went through the same process for Zane's. Why not?

Being here with him, it felt oddly intimate, not closed in and too close, as it had yesterday. The clean fresh scent of his shampoo and the delicious smells of salt, grease, and syrup filled the front seat. The low murmur of the radio was comforting, lulling. It felt cozy and real. More so than eating in a restaurant, or anywhere else.

"So what do you think today is going to be like?" I asked, more to fill the silence and calm the queasy, anxious-but-eager feeling in the pit of my stomach.

Zane bobbled a bite, and cheesy egg—steaming hot in the cool air—dripped down his chin. He winced.

Ouch. I grimaced in reflexive sympathy and dug into the bag for napkins.

"Here." Without thinking, I reached out to help, intending to wipe away the egg—it was, after all, the most expedient solution. But in a moment of colossal miscommunication, Zane tried to hand me the burrito and take the napkin, resulting in confusion and too many hands going in different directions.

I retreated immediately. "Oh. Sorry." My face burned. "Did you want to, um . . ." My hand flapped uselessly, holding the napkin. Of course he did. Who wanted someone you didn't know that close up in your face?

"Nope, go for it," he said. "Clearly I cannot be trusted to feed myself."

I leaned over and removed the offending bit of egg and cheese, careful not to block his line of sight. But it was closer than we'd been since last night, and something about the daylight made it seem so much more real.

He smelled good. Really good. Something that seemed to be exclusively him made me want to bury my face against his neck.

My heart thumping too hard, I scooted back into my seat before I did just that and humiliated myself. What was wrong with me?

Zane cleared his throat. "So . . . today. Probably like last night, times a thousand. People will be asking questions. Especially when they can catch either one of us alone. You gotta be ready for that."

I nodded. "What am I supposed to say?"

"Tell them . . . it just happened."

I snorted. "No one is going to believe that."

He shrugged. "They'll be way more interested in what we're doing now than how we originally hooked up."

Just the words "hooked up" made me blush again.

He polished off the last of his burrito and crumpled up the wrapper. "But it's probably better for the illusion, and to avoid that kind of thing, if we meet up between classes and walk together—"

I frowned. "We have no classes together. It'll be out of our way."

He gave me a sideways smile—his teeth were so white against his tan skin—and my traitorous heart gave another improbable leap. "You're such a romantic."

He tucked his wrapper under his leg and then snagged a quick drink of juice.

"Hit me again." He nodded toward the bag.

I pulled out a McGriddle, the paper sticky with syrup.

I peeled back the wrapper and handed it to him, taking care to keep my fingers out of the way of his. I didn't like the disconcerting feeling of touching him—wanting to and being scared to at the same time. Too much conflicting data for my brain to process.

"Thanks," he said.

We were getting close to school, and I still needed to boost my protein. I had peanut butter crackers in my bag for an emergency, but this was not that, yet.

I rummaged in the bag one last time and found an egg-and-cheese biscuit. Good enough.

We munched in silence for a few minutes, and I watched the school rise up in the distance. It looked nothing like it had last night, once more all sharp edges and imposing.

Thinking of the activities fair, I had to ask, "What about Rachel? What should we expect from her? Other than smelling like she bathed in cheap aloe." It was a petty dig, but I couldn't resist.

Zane shook his head with a rueful smile. "You're enjoying this."

"Maybe a little," I admitted.

He sighed heavily. "She's been texting me since last night. I told her I was just doing what she asked me to. But it doesn't matter. She'll find some way to retaliate, to punish us for being there when she got hit with the pies. She doesn't handle being embarrassed very well." He grew quiet. "She didn't used to be this bad."

"Are you sure she's the one who changed?"

He looked up sharply, and I wanted to take back the words.

"I'm just saying, she's been mean for as long as I've known her, and you . . . you're different." I fumbled to explain. I knew about his mom leaving; everyone did. Thanks to Jenna, I had all the details I could have ever wanted. According to the rumor mill, his mom had taken off on his birthday, after sticking around for his brother's graduation the night before.

Add that to the images I'd gotten from his head of his father screaming at him, and I had to wonder if all of that was contributing to this version of Zane. The new and improved. One who now seemed to think for himself instead of following Rachel's directives blindly.

"What I'm trying to say is," I said carefully, "would you have thought twice about doing what she asked if it was a couple of years ago?"

"I don't know," he said in a clipped voice, making the turn into the school parking lot.

Which we both knew meant no.

He crumpled his food wrapper with more force than necessary. "They're my friends," he said.

"I know." But I was beginning to think he deserved better. I couldn't say that—not without poking at his defenses with a too-sharp stick. For some reason, Rachel and her crew represented something important to him, and he wasn't about to let them go.

I was trying to figure out how to end, or change, this conversation that I hadn't meant to start in the first place, when his expression darkened.

"And maybe some people change for the worse," he said, his mouth tight.

I followed his gaze, not sure what he was talking about at first. We were in a line of cars heading toward the section of graveled lot where Zane and his "friends" socialized before school. No gym cattle call for them.

I located Rachel first, leaning against her car, Trey's arm slung around her shoulders. The twins were nearby, arguing over a scarf, judging by the way one would snatch it from the other and then the other would strike back.

But another girl stood in front of them with her back to us, her blond hair perfectly curled and bobbing with her enthusiastic hand movements as she talked.

I recognized those details immediately even though I couldn't see her face.

Jenna. I sucked in a breath.

Her shoulders held a new level of tension, and she was keeping her distance from Rachel, as if not quite sure how close she wanted to get. But still she was there. On sacred ground, among Rachel's circle of friends.

Exactly where Rachel wanted her this morning.

It wasn't hard to see where Rachel was going with this. Aware of Jenna's (obvious) crush, she wanted her to see me with Zane. But Jenna wasn't the target this time. I was. Rachel had to know this would destroy my friendship with Jenna. Or whatever was left of it, anyway. I'd realized that was a possibility, but in setting us up like this, Rachel had all but guaranteed it.

"Damn it." My hands curled into fists against the fury rising up in my chest. Zane had said Rachel would punish us for the shaving cream. I just never thought she'd go this far. She wasn't just cruel; she was conniving. Which only went to show that it was a mistake to overestimate her capacity to act like a normal, feeling human instead of a sociopath.

"I take it you didn't have a chance to tell Jenna," Zane said, weariness in his voice.

I shook my head stiffly. "I tried. She's not speaking to me. After the other day, she thinks being seen with me will blow her chances for being friends with Rachel. And 'Oh, hey, btw, I'm fake-dating your longtime crush' isn't exactly text message material." I wondered what Rachel had said to Jenna to convince her it was safe to approach again, after yesterday's incident in the cafeteria. It probably wouldn't have taken much; Jenna wanted to believe. Maybe Rachel had sold her on the idea that it was a joke that had gotten out of hand, hazing gone awry. Or maybe she'd simply apologized—hard to imagine, but I was willing to bet Rachel wouldn't let one fake "I'm sorry" stand in the way of a bigger and better opportunity to hurt.

"What do you want to do?" Zane asked, surprising me. Did that mean he'd call the whole thing off right now if I said so? We were three car-lengths away, enough time to drive down a different lane and, well, run.

But no, it was too late for that. Even if Jenna didn't see us together for herself, she would soon find out that we were at the activities fair last night. We were well past the point of no return.

"We have to go through with it," I said grimly. I was not going to let Rachel win this round.

"Are you sure?"

My gaze locked with Rachel's through the windshield, and she gave me a smug smile.

Yeah, let's see how you like this. Nobody plays me, get it?

As usual, Rachel's thoughts filtered through the rest of the white noise and past my resistance at a decibel that would make ears bleed.

I flinched.

She thinks I'm stupid, trying to turn this around on me. I'll show her. I can't believe Zane doesn't see she's scheming to get back at me. Unless he does and he doesn't care. Unless he really likes her. Rachel's smile faltered, insecurity rolling off of her.

Oh my God. Now I understood. The rumors were true. Rachel was in possession of tender feelings when it came to one Zane Bradshaw.

But I couldn't dwell on that, or even take time to think it through.

"Ariane?" Zane prompted, sounding tense.

"Rachel's not just trying to cause chaos this time. She's calling our bluff, and she's using Jenna to do it," I said. "If we back down now, we're done." Hate for her boiled inside me. I couldn't walk away now. Not when letting Rachel win would do nothing but make life more miserable for everyone involved. Not when I was so close to regaining control.

Zane shifted uncomfortably in his seat. "You do know that I never meant to . . . I mean, I tried not to do anything that would make Jenna . . ."

"Not your fault that you're apparently irresistible," I said, hearing the ice in my words.

"Doesn't sound like a compliment when you say it like that," he muttered.

He parked on the opposite side of the lane, away from Jenna, Rachel, and the others, giving us some space. At the far end of our row a black van with the bright red GTX logo rose above the other cars. The sight of it made my breath catch in my throat. It was probably another tech finishing up the camera installation, but the van served as a solid reminder of what was at stake. We had to keep the game going.

"Ready?" Zane asked, grabbing his backpack.

"No," I admitted, but I pushed the door open anyway.

He met me at the rear of the SUV and extended his hand. After a second, I took it, feeling surprisingly comforted by the contact. His grip was warm, firm, and familiar. I felt more grounded, touching him. Was that why people did this? To feel less alone?

His thumb brushed over the back of my hand, a single reassuring stroke, and something tight in me eased. This was horrible, yeah, but I wasn't here by myself.

Without my telling him to, Zane led the way, which was a small relief. It was hard enough to do this, let alone take the lead.

"Hey guys," he said. "Rach." He nodded at Rachel, who didn't even bother to hide her triumphant grin. Exactly how stupid did she think I was?

"Zane!" Jenna turned, curls bouncing, her face lighting up immediately. With her tunnel vision focused squarely on him, she missed me at first. I watched as her gaze traveled down his arm to where our hands were joined and then shot over to my face.

"Ariane?" she asked, sounding confused.

I watched her deflate, the excitement and eagerness leaking out of her, replaced by disbelief and hurt.

Oh, Jenna. I bit my lip.

"What is this?" She looked from me to Zane and back again. "I don't understand."

"Uh-oh." Rachel oozed closer—as much as anyone can ooze in stilettos on a gravel surface. "Do we have a love triangle?" she asked, her voice thick with mean-spirited amusement.

"I think you're forgetting a side," I snapped, staring her down. Maybe not my best comeback, but I wanted her to know that I knew.

Trey frowned. "What does that mean?"

I could see Zane's equally confused expression from the corner of my eye.

But Rachel got it. Her mouth turned white around the edges of her perfectly applied lipstick. She flounced toward her car with Trey following. "Rach, I don't understand. What was she talking about?" he asked.

"So . . ." Jenna edged closer, as if we were something that might explode if approached too suddenly. "This is what you were talking about in your message? This is what you wanted me to ignore?" Her voice cracked, and I could see her throat working as she struggled to hold back tears.

Guilt squeezed my chest, but before I could answer, Jenna shook her head. "You don't even know each other. And Ariane, you hate these guys."

An offended gasp rose up from somewhere nearby, probably from one of the twins.

I pulled my hand free of Zane's—dimly aware that I missed the contact immediately—and edged closer to Jenna. She looked ready to bolt. "Look, we just need to talk about it. . . ." I hesitated. Which we couldn't do here, and then there would be the issue of how much I could explain. As much as I wanted to trust Jenna, she had a huge blind spot when it came to Rachel.

None of that mattered, though; Jenna was already retreating, her face flushed and shiny with tears. "No."

"Jenna." I started to follow her.

She held her hands up. "You stay away from me. I don't want to talk to you. I don't even want to see you. You're such a freak!" The last words were shouted as she ran for the building.

I winced, feeling her words dig into me, followed by the confirming titter of laughter from Rachel and her friends.

"Run, Jenna, run," Rachel said with a cackle, stepping up with her cell phone to snap a picture.

This time I didn't have to think, didn't have to force the focus. An unexpected tingle of power told me the barrier was down, and then Rachel's phone spun out of her hand, colliding hard with the side of her car.

"Oh my God!" She was on her knees immediately, scrambling for it. "Trey, you idiot, what is your problem?"

"I was nowhere near you!"

"You were the only one near me!"

They continued bickering, but I ignored them.

I'd done it. Taken another big step toward regaining control. I wasn't entirely back to rights—I still needed Rachel to trigger whatever it was that pushed the barrier down—but I was closer, much closer. However, the triumph of the moment felt flat and artificial—tinny music on bad computer speakers.

What was the point, I had to wonder, of fighting so hard to learn to protect my life if I was destroying it in the process?

And how was I distinguishing myself from Rachel and her evil pillar-of-the-community grandfather if I was doing exactly what they did? Lying to get what I wanted and not caring who got hurt in the process.

I suppose there were good intentions and all of that, but I wasn't about to kid myself that Dr. Jacobs didn't write himself the same blank check of an excuse.

"Hey," Zane said, startling me.

I turned to see him approaching cautiously with a concerned expression.

"She'll be okay, you know," he said. "She was just surprised."

I made a face. "Yeah, people usually are in an ambush."

He sighed. "You're being too hard on yourself. You didn't set this up."

"No," I said, "but I made it possible."

And that, to my mind, was more than enough.

CHAPTER 18

Zane

ARIANE WAS QUIET THE REST OF THE DAY. I FOUND myself deflecting the attention on our behalf, glaring at people who approached, and tugging Ariane down side corridors to avoid the worst of the staring.

Oddly enough, that seemed to do more to convince people that we were real than presenting ourselves for inspection and answering questions with cutesy but vague responses. By the end of the day, most of the spectators had retreated to watch and whisper at a safe distance. And that was only the most devoted of the big mouths. Most everyone else had already shrugged it off and gone on about their lives. Even Rachel had stayed away except for amused stares from across the hall and communiqués via text. My phone had been vibrating nonstop with long gloating messages and various instructions on how to "keep Ariane on the hook."

Now, after the last bell, with most everyone gone, Ariane leaned against the locker next to mine while she waited for me to switch out books and grab my homework for the night (not much, thankfully). Her expression was much as it had been all day, perfectly smooth and impassive. She might have been happy and hiding it, or miserable and keeping it quiet—it was impossible to tell. But I knew that something—lots of something, most likely—was churning beneath that impenetrable surface.

I paused in shoving my chemistry book into my locker and looked over at her. Her face showed nothing new, but her hands, folded around the strap of her bag, were fidgeting, her fingers playing with a loose thread. Winding it around her index finger until it was tight, and then unwinding it. Over and over again.

"Are you sure you're okay?" I hated hearing the words come out of my mouth. I'd only asked her that about ten times, but I wasn't sure what else to do.

"Fine." Which was the same thing she'd said the last ten, now eleven times. In the same flat, unemotional, I'm-not-really-here voice.

I made a disgusted sound.

That seemed to startle out of her semicatatonic state. "What?" she asked, blinking and looking at me for the first time in hours.

"You're not. You're obviously not."

Her brow wrinkled. "What?" she asked again.

"Fine," I said with exasperation. "You're not fine. That's just what you're saying so you don't have to tell me what's going on."

"Zane—" she began, with a shake of her head.

"I'm serious. I may not be an expert on Ariane Tucker."

Not yet, but I was trying. "But even I know you're usually a little more than a good imitation of a statue."

She looked startled.

"I've even known you to smile. Every once in a while." Usually in the presence of fried potatoes. Today, at lunch, the only thing she'd eaten with any kind of enthusiasm had been french fries. "We're in this together. Talk to me."

"It's nothing."

I leaned closer to her, though the hallway was deserted. "Is this about Jenna?"

She stiffened, and I saw the first cracks in her composure. "I don't want to talk about it."

"Too bad," I said cheerfully. "I didn't want to talk about Rachel this morning, but you didn't give me the option." I slammed my locker shut.

She narrowed her eyes. "You weren't exactly bubbling over with information."

I slung my backpack onto my shoulder and dug my car keys from my pocket. "Not my favorite topic. Come on, let's go."

She straightened up, looking more alert and interested than she had all day, and followed me down the hall. "You never said what she did that made you so angry."

"No way." I shook my head. "We're not talking about me. We're talking about you." I shoved through the door to the parking lot and stepped back, holding it open for her.

She crossed the threshold and turned to face me. "Technically, we weren't," she corrected. "We were talking about you, and you were attempting to deflect the attention to me, when I am far more interested in—"

"You feel guilty. About Jenna," I said, leading the way to my car.

She clamped her mouth shut.

I sighed. "I'm not stupid, Ariane. I saw you this morning. If Rachel was a grenade and you could have thrown yourself at her to save Jenna, you'd have done it."

"Now, that's an interesting mental image. Rachel as a grenade," she murmured.

"But you don't have anything to feel guilty about." I hated seeing her like this, all closed in and shut off. Back to being the mysterious girl I didn't and couldn't ever know instead of someone who laughed at my dumb stories and quoted Star Wars.

"Because we're not real, I know," she said.

"No," I said firmly. "You don't have anything to feel guilty about because you didn't take anything from her. I do not have feelings for Jenna. Never have. Don't I get a say in the matter?" I asked, attempting to tease her into lightening up.

"No," she said with a mirthless smile.

I sighed and unlocked the SUV. Ariane got to her door before I did and opened it for herself, sending me a challenging look.

I raised my hands in surrender and headed to my side.

Inside the stifling hot interior, which still smelled vaguely of breakfast, I chucked my backpack into the backseat and started up the engine, turning the AC on high. Ariane seemed undisturbed by the heat, sitting there calmly with her seat belt on already and her bag at her feet.

"Unlike some people," she said, so quietly I could barely

hear, "I don't have as many options to choose from when it comes to abandoning one friend for another."

I reached out to turn the fan down so her words didn't get lost in the noise, half afraid that the quiet would scare her off.

"And before you say anything, I'm not feeling sorry for myself. . . ." She sighed. "It's just, Jenna understands, or she did anyway. She never asked questions or tried to pry into my personal life—"

I laughed in disbelief. "So, in other words, you were friends as long as the attention was focused exclusively on her."

"It's not like that. She's not like that," Ariane insisted.

"Really? Because people who are your friends are *supposed* to want to know about you. And do I need to remind you that she's the one who stopped talking to you because she thought it would make Rachel like her better?" I asked, disgusted. "Look, I don't know Jenna as well as you do, but I've seen her in action. She'd run you over with a truck if she thought that would get Rachel to pay attention to her. And you deserve a better friend than that." The words slipped out before I could stop them, and I wished them back, wincing in anticipation of her reaction. I barely knew her; who was I to say what she deserved?

But she didn't gasp in fury or shoot back with some kind of cutting remark. She gave a strangled kind of laugh. "I thought the same thing about you this morning, when you were talking about Rachel."

Her gaze met mine, and a thick electric silence fell between us.

She bit her lip—I'd noticed she did that when she was nervous or uncertain—and I was suddenly possessed with the desire to touch her mouth, to stop her from hurting herself even with that small pain, and to kiss her.

But before I could move, she broke eye contact and shifted to stare out the window.

A lost opportunity, one accompanied with more regret that I ever would have imagined. I frowned. What was going on here? I'd started this whole thing to get Rachel off my back and maybe to satisfy some of my curiosity about the strange girl in math class. How had it gotten this far?

Putting the SUV in gear, I pulled out of the nearly empty lot and started toward the intersection where I knew Ariane would insist on being dropped off.

Silence, of the awkward variety this time, held for several blocks.

"Speaking of feelings for you . . . Jenna's, I mean," she said suddenly, her face flushing red. "I've been wondering why Rachel was going to all this trouble."

"A natural love of mayhem and messing with people isn't enough?"

"No, not really . . ."

It took me a second to connect the dots between the first part of her sentence and the last. *Feelings for you . . . Rachel.* "Rachel?" I laughed. "No."

"Oh, come on, haven't you wondered why she's so determined to involve you in all of this?" She turned toward me in her seat, warming to the topic, something she'd evidently been thinking about for a while. I was beginning to wonder if there was ever anything Ariane didn't consider for hours or days before saying something. "If she wanted to punish me, there are easier ways."

I nodded, tapping an uncomfortable rhythm on the steering wheel. "Which is why what you're suggesting doesn't make sense. If she . . . liked me"—God, I could barely force the phrase out—"she wouldn't push me to pretend to pursue someone else for one of her games."

"You're not thinking about it the way she does," Ariane said. "If she can get you to do what she wants, it means you're hers."

"She already has Trey for that," I pointed out.

"Exactly, he's no challenge, so it means nothing to her. But with you"—she tilted her head to one side, eyeing me speculatively—"she knows you aren't as eager to jump, and it drives her crazy. She wants you to want her."

I flashed back to Rachel kissing me the other night, right in front of Trey. "That is messed up." But not entirely out of character, the part of her I knew that maybe the others weren't as aware of. "How do you know? That that's what Rachel's thinking, I mean."

Ariane hesitated. "I understand how she thinks. Maybe I'm more like her than I'd prefer."

I knew she was blaming herself for Jenna again. "No. You're not." I stopped, trying to decide whether I wanted to go where this was headed—I didn't talk about this, with anyone—but then the words were out, sounding loud and awkward. "I'm sure you know about my mom."

"I know what people say," Ariane responded carefully.

"My favorite ones are the Witness Protection Program

and running off with some rich guy she met on the Internet," I said.

Ariane stiffened, and I knew she'd heard both of those.

I focused my attention on the road and made myself keep talking. "I think it's a lot simpler than that. My dad's a dick, and she couldn't take it anymore. And, unlike Quinn, I wasn't enough of a reason to stick around."

Ariane made some small noise—sympathy, surprise, a combination of both—but she didn't interrupt.

Which was good, because that had been harder to say than I thought, even though so much time had passed. I cleared my throat. "So anyway, one night last year, I'm at a party at Rachel's, and I was drinking. Okay, I was drunk," I admitted ruefully. "And the party is a total rager, so I'm just trying to find a quiet corner that's not already full of broken stuff or covered in puke, you know?"

Out of the corner of my eye, I saw her nodding, though I was pretty sure she'd never been to one.

"And I find Rachel in her dad's study, and she's crying." I pulled around the corner at Pine and Rushmore and parked.

"If this ends with you having sex with Rachel, you can stop now," Ariane said with distaste, her hand on the door. "There are those rumors, too." She raised her eyebrows at me in challenge.

"Never happened," I said.

She nodded slowly, as if relieved.

"Anyway, she starts talking to me about stuff she's never even hinted at before, and we had been friends forever. Her mom is in some kind of semipermanent spa/rehab joint in California, and it's a mental thing, not just alcohol or pills.

Her dad is always gone, traveling for GTX, shaking hands and schmoozing. Her grandpa is the only one who cares about her, and he's always busy at work."

Next to me, Ariane went rigid.

"I'm not telling you this stuff as an excuse for her," I said quickly. "Just trying to show you how the conversation was going."

Ariane seemed to relax.

I leaned back in my seat, tracing the lines of the emblem in the center of the steering wheel with my finger. "Anyway, so . . . she's upset, and I've been drinking, and it suddenly seems like a good idea to talk about my mom. How she left and didn't tell us where she was going. I mean, forget telling my dad, but what about me? And sticking around for Quinn's graduation party one night but not for my birthday the next day?" I let out a slow breath and forced a smile. "It's enough to give you a complex, you know?"

I dared a quick glance at Ariane, to find her watching me intently.

"In any case, we, uh, ended up, um, comforting each other." It had not been sex or even close, but I didn't feel it was in my best interests to go into detail about what it had or had not been. "Then someone set off a two-liter bomb in the backyard and everyone scattered, and we never talked about it again, except to agree that it didn't happen. Until yesterday morning when Trey shows up at my house, trying to talk me into going along with Rachel's plan even though he knows I've been all messed up and different since my mom left, blaming myself, and it isn't my fault . . . blah, blah, blah." I took a deep breath. "He never would have come up with all of that on his own. Trey and I have never talked about that kind of stuff. And I don't *want* to talk about it or hear people talking about it ever again. Most of that had finally died down. But I knew if I kept telling Rachel no, all of a sudden it would be about poor, messed-up Zane again. . . ."

"Oh." Ariane drew in a quick breath. "She used what you told her against you. Manipulated Trey into manipulating you. That's what made you so angry." Her eyes were bright, and I realized she was on the verge of tears. For me.

"And that's how I know you're not like her."

She sat up straighter. "She should never have done that." She sounded fierce on my behalf, like she would take on Rachel for me, and a rush of warmth and unexpected gratitude flooded through me. "I would—"

I didn't let her finish. I leaned over the armrest between us and kissed her, a brush of my mouth over hers. Testing the waters.

Her lips were soft, and I felt her catch her breath in surprise.

My heart pounding (ridiculous from such a nothing kiss, but it was happening), I backed off immediately. "Okay?"

After a second she nodded, so wide-eyed I could see the edges of her tinted contact lenses, and some part of my brain registered that there was a decent chance this was her first kiss. Her father was pretty strict. And I'd never seen her even talking to another guy.

I felt kind of honored. I'd have to take it slow and make sure she had time and room to speak up, which was pretty much my policy anyway. Though most of the time, in recent months, at random party hookups, I'd been the one trying to keep up or slow things down. Girls sometimes got aggressive, especially with a Jell-O shot or three in them.

I kissed Ariane again, and this time she tipped her face toward mine, responding. And such a simple thing was a huge turn-on; it sent a bolt of heat through me. I was going to have problems if this went on for too long, as innocent as it was.

Her hands were cool and tentative at first, at the back of my neck and then moving with more confidence over my shoulders and through my hair.

Reaching up to touch her face, I could feel her delicate bones beneath soft skin—she never seemed fragile or small except for when I touched her. Her personality made her seem bigger, more powerful.

I slid my hand beneath her hair, which was heavy and soft and held the heat of her body, making me want to touch more. I tipped her chin at a slightly stronger angle and tasted her mouth, and she let out a gasp, her hands clutching tighter at my collar.

God. This little game we were playing didn't feel much like a game anymore.

CHAPTER 19

Ariane

A PART OF MY BRAIN WAS BUSY PONDERING THE PECULIAR twist reality had taken that ended with Zane Bradshaw kissing me. And me kissing back.

But the rest of me was just *feeling*. Focusing on sensations that made everything else fall away. His tongue was in my mouth, and it didn't feel weird. At all. And when I summoned the courage to respond in kind, his hands tightened on me. He liked it. A thrill went through me at the idea that I'd caused him to react. It was such a heady sense of power and vulnerability. For as much as I wanted to make him feel good, I knew he was trying for the same thing.

His chin was rough with stubble, and he smelled so right. A switch clicked on in my brain. Suddenly I wanted to be closer. I fumbled blindly to unbuckle my seat belt. It ended up thwapping both of us in the side of the face, making Zane laugh.

"Careful," he said into my mouth. He broke off our kiss long enough to shove the belt between us. It retracted with a loud clunk, and then I was moving, pulling my legs onto the seat so I could kneel instead of sit, bringing myself that much closer to him.

He showed his appreciation with his hands at my waist, pulling me against him, as much as possible with the armrest in between us. I could feel the heat of his chest against me, the way his breathing had picked up so much faster, like mine. And I wanted more.

As if reading my mind, he slipped his hands under my shirt in the back, and I stopped breathing at the sensation of his fingers against my bare skin. He traced dizzying patterns, skimming over my bra and higher.

I cursed the armrest divider between us, though I wasn't entirely sure what I would do if I could get over onto the other side.

Then his questing fingers reached the edge of the bandage on my right shoulder blade, and he froze.

A shock wave rolled through me. I'd forgotten about the bandage. *How* could I have forgotten that?

I pulled away from him, breathing hard.

"I'm sorry." He dropped his hands down to my waist.

"No, it's okay. It's . . . nothing." Except a very vivid reminder of who I was and why I shouldn't—couldn't—be doing this with him. With anyone.

He hesitated, then asked, "Is it from before? From your treatment?"

It took me a second to realize what he was talking about. The experimental treatment that had supposedly saved my life just before I came to live with my father. "Sort of. Can we . . . not talk about it?"

He nodded and let go of my waist. "Sure."

Disappointment thundered through me. *Way to kill the mood, Ariane.* But what else was I supposed to do? I couldn't explain, and while he seemed satisfied for the moment with my nonanswer, how long would that last? It reminded me of a ghost story I'd heard kids tell during lunch in grade school. About the woman with the red ribbon at her throat. She married a man who loved her but couldn't stop asking about the ribbon at her throat, even after she told him not to. Then one night, while she was sleeping, his curiosity got the better of him. He pulled at the ribbon and her head rolled off.

It wouldn't be quite that dramatic, but if Zane got a glimpse of what was under the bandage, I'd be equally condemned.

"I have to go." I swung my legs to the floor and fumbled for the door handle.

"Ariane."

I glanced back at him. His mouth was red from our kissing, and all I wanted was for it to happen again. I caught myself leaning toward him and couldn't quite stop.

He leaned in to meet me halfway. "You're okay?" he whispered against my mouth.

I nodded. "I'm fine." Except for the part where I wanted his mouth on mine again, always, and I wouldn't be able to have it.

Yeah, I was great. Tears pricked my eyes, and I bent down to scoop up my bag before he could see.

"Then I'll see you tonight?" he asked, still oh-so close.

I blinked rapidly. "What?"

"The game?" he prompted.

I forced my kiss-fogged brain to process. "Oh, right." The varsity/JV exhibition game was tonight's Bonfire Week activity. Another event at which Zane-and-Ariane were supposed to make a public appearance. But there was a problem. My father. He would be home tonight, after working a double shift last night/today. "I don't know."

I could tell my father a small white lie and say I had a school event I was required to attend. He wouldn't question it. He'd have no reason to doubt me. Because I'd never lied to him before. Honesty was part of the deal when someone puts their life on the line for you.

Guilt pulled at me, and I hesitated.

"Please?" Zane flashed me a grin that I felt all the way down to my toes. "You'll have fun, I promise."

How was I supposed to resist that?

By remembering that this isn't your life? A nagging voice spoke up in the back of my head.

"I'll try," I said, feeling like a horrible person. I wasn't even sure who I was lying to, Zane or myself. "I'll text you."

I shoved the door open, but before I could I slide out, Zane touched my arm.

"Are you sure you're okay?" His forehead crinkled with concern, and his gray-blue eyes searched mine.

I nodded. "Fine. I'll see you later," I said, not trusting myself to say more over the growing lump in my throat.

I stepped out of the SUV quickly, shut the door, and gave a wave good-bye.

I started walking, but Zane didn't pull away immediately. I was around the corner and well on my way, probably out of his line of sight, before I heard the engine rev. If I'd let him, he'd have pulled into my driveway and waited until I was in my house with the door locked behind me. He was . . . sweet. Like any of the things that were after me could be stopped by a simple dead bolt.

I closed my eyes for a brief second against the ache in my chest. Oh God, what was I doing? This was so crazy.

Of all the Rules my father had given me, there were some that had hung over my head every second of every day. *Never trust anyone. Remember they are* always *searching.* It was a rare moment when one or both of those wasn't occupying some part of my brain. Even *Don't get involved* and *Keep your head down* made relatively frequent appearances.

But *Don't fall in love* had always seemed to be sound advice in a theoretical sense, highly unlikely to have any practical application. Like, in case of alien invasion, make sure you have plenty of clean socks. Good advice, but probably not necessary.

Okay, maybe that wasn't the best example, given who and what I am, but you get the idea.

My point is, of all the Rules I'd broken or worried about breaking, #5 was one I'd hardly thought about. It had never seemed within the realm of possibility.

But right now, #5 was screaming in my head, all capital letters and flashing neon, as the last Rule I'd not yet broken and one in serious jeopardy of joining the others in shattered bits on the floor.

What frightened me the most, though, was how scared I *wasn't* at the idea.

I remembered the feel of Zane's hands on my skin, and shivered, my breath catching in my throat.

I shook my head and kept walking. *Don't be ridiculous. This is an artificial closeness generated by a forced situation and layers of lies.*

Except the closeness didn't *feel* artificial. On my side or his. He liked me, was intrigued by me. That right there should have been enough to send me running in the opposite direction, but after so many years of being invisible, it was nice to be seen. To be noticed. It sent an unexpected warmth through me, made me feel alive in ways I hadn't anticipated.

All the more reason to stop now. This has no future. And you know it.

That was true. It was too dangerous—for both Zane and me—to keep going like this, particularly if GTX continued to close in. So, tomorrow night, once Rachel's party was over, our "relationship" would be done. It would have to be. And if Zane wouldn't end it, I would.

A thought that should have brought relief made my eyes fill with tears.

It wasn't fair. I'd been good. I'd spent the last ten years avoiding getting too close to anyone, usually without too much trouble. And now, the first time that I actually wanted someone in my life enough to take a risk, it was impossible, the worst timing in the history of ever.

I wiped away an errant tear with the back of my hand, hating the way my contacts were blurring. Hating that I had to wear them. Hating that GTX existed. Hating that I was who I was.

Because that's what it came down to. This pain was

simply the cost of doing business, the price of being me. Nonnegotiable.

And it sucked.

My only consolation was that I'd have the next twenty-four hours with Zane; a poor prize, when you stopped to think about it. But it was all I had.

So for now I would break Rule #5 into a million pieces—and once this was over, the giant reset button pressed, I'd walk away with the memories. That was the best I could do, the *only* thing I could do.

Taking a deep breath, which did nothing to ease the ache in my chest, I followed the sidewalk up to my house and slipped the key into the door as quietly as possible.

Odds were, if my father was sleeping, opening the door wouldn't be enough to awaken him, but I didn't want to take any chances. Not right now when I'd probably see him and burst into tears and tell him everything. Better to steer clear until I had a better grip on my stupid feelings. (Life would be so much easier without them; they were always causing problems.)

But as soon as I crossed the threshold, I knew avoiding him would be impossible. A roiling mass of complicated emotions—disappointment, fear, fury—poured forth from someplace in the back of the house. The kitchen, most likely.

I stopped, shocked. I rarely picked up *anything* from my father, and to feel his emotions this strongly meant he was having trouble keeping control. Not good.

A rush of nerves pushed away the last of my sadness. Something was definitely wrong. Not so wrong that he was scrambling to get me out of the house, but it couldn't be anything remotely good to generate this kind of reaction.

Smart money is on someone recognizing you or hearing your name at the activities fair last night. I grimaced. All it would take was one person mentioning something to my father about his "daughter" being there.

I locked the door, then forced myself to move toward the kitchen, hopefully in a manner that did *not* suggest that a large portion of my thoughts was occupied with creating a series of believable fibs to cover a variety of situations. *School assignment to be at the fair . . . No, I wasn't holding hands with anyone. . . . The lights? No, I didn't notice . . .*

My stomach ached at the idea of lying to him, but telling the truth just wasn't an option. He'd make me stop everything.

But as soon as I reached the kitchen, it became immediately clear that the situation was far worse than anything even my most expansive lie would cover.

First, my father was sitting at the table, still dressed in his rumpled work clothes, which meant he hadn't been to bed yet even though he'd been awake for more than twenty-four hours.

Second, several inches of scotch in a tumbler sat at his right hand, with a mostly empty bottle next to it.

Third, and most damning of all, a laptop sat open on the table, surrounded by messy layers of grainy black-and-white photos. It took me only a second to recognize them for what they were—photos from a surveillance camera feed. The supersized time and date codes at the bottom were dead giveaways.

And there was only one surveillance camera feed that would provoke such a reaction from my father. The newly installed one at the school.

Oh no. I froze in the doorway, thinking of all the things he might have seen. Stupidly, it had never occurred to me that he would try to view any of it. GTX had surveillance teams (administrative drones, mostly) specifically for this purpose—finding me—and he wasn't on any of them.

And, oh God, never mind my father. What about GTX?

My heart lurched. Had they seen what I'd done with the shaving-cream pies at the activities fair? I thought I'd been hidden well enough in the crowd. But maybe not.

"Are you going to just stand there?" my father asked.

I swallowed hard, my tongue sticking to the roof of my painfully dry mouth. "Does GTX know? Did they see . . ." I fumbled for the words.

"I pulled the footage," he said. "You're damn lucky I decided to keep an eye on the feed."

I sagged against the doorway in relief, and my father glared at me.

"How could you be this reckless?" he demanded.

"It's not what you think," I said quickly. Which was a mistake. Never be the first one to go on the defensive. I'd been taught better than that. But I was rattled.

"And you, of course, know what I think."

I flinched. He was so calm, not even close to yelling, which was chilling and more frightening. Screaming at me would have been better. Then his outsides would match his insides. I pushed harder against my barriers to block out the noise coming from him.

"No. You know I can't hear you most of the . . ." I

swallowed hard. "I was using it as a figure of speech, a colloquialism."

"And what is this? More colloquialism?" He slid a photo across the table, and with nothing to stop the glossy paper, it landed, faceup, on the linoleum floor with a sharp smack.

The angle was weird—taken from high above—so it took me a moment to place what I was seeing. A crowd of people, so indistinct it wasn't easy to make out individual faces, but the booths on either side of the aisle were clear. The activities fair. And there, in the center of all of it, a tall boy in a plaid shirt was laughing. At his side, a much shorter girl, whose hair was so pale it looked white in the field of grays and black. She looked happy, too.

"Why didn't you tell me?" My father, sounding exhausted, ground the heels of his hands against his eyes. "This is dangerous, Ariane. That's why the Rules exist."

"I can explain." Though, I couldn't, not all of it. And I was on the defensive again, damn it. I'd never win this way.

"I gave you the Rules for very specific reasons, and you—"

"It wasn't a real date," I said. "I was using him to get close to Rachel Jacobs. See?" I stepped up to the table and flipped through the photos until I found one that showed Rachel standing in front of us, pulling on Zane.

I held it up to my father.

"When I'm around her, the block in my brain goes away. Yesterday in the cafeteria, she was picking on Jenna—"

My father sighed. "Ariane."

"Just listen! She was picking on Jenna, and the energy started to go out of control, but I stopped it. Last night, she was hurting Zane—"

"Zane?" he asked with a frown.

Uh-oh. I squirmed inwardly before answering. "Bradshaw."

His expression darkened. "The police chief's son? This is the police chief's son?" His voice rose.

I ignored him; I was on a roll. "The lights were flickering and everything, but I managed to send it into those shaving-cream pies instead of all over the place. I *controlled* it." I flipped through more pictures and slapped down one of Rachel covered in white goop.

I kept going before he could interrupt again. "And this morning, I knocked Rachel's cell phone out of her hand. I didn't even have to work that hard to do it."

He sat up straighter in his chair, his gaze sharper now. "You're telling me that you've done it? You're back in control?"

I hesitated. "It's not as—"

He slid the tumbler across the table to me and nodded toward it. "Show me," he commanded. "Move it."

I thought about trying, but it would have only been for show. I could always feel it when the barrier dropped. And right now it was very much in place.

I took a deep breath. "I can't," I admitted. "I don't have it quite yet. I still need Rachel around to, I don't know, trigger it. She's the key, but I'm so close—"

His mouth tightened. "It's not her. It's you. It's always been you, your head, your block. The conditions *you* set for it to go down. It's a combination lock *you* established."

I stared at him, startled by the depth of frustration in his voice.

He sighed. "There's a pattern to your power outbursts. I wasn't sure before, but now it's pretty clear. When someone's suffering at the hands of a more powerful person, your block vanishes. And when it comes to Rachel"—he gestured to the laptop and photos—"you identify with her victims in particular. Probably because you put the wall up to protect yourself from Dr. Jacobs. You won't defend yourself, but your subconscious won't allow others to suffer if you can do something about it."

I blinked. I'd never thought about it that precisely. But he was right. When I saw someone abusing their authority on someone who was powerless to defend themselves—most often Rachel and her multitude of victims—it kind of made me crazy.

"The trouble is, as far as I can tell, you don't have any control once the barrier is down," my father finished.

"Okay, fine," I argued, "but now I know what the combination is, and I can keep working on my control. That's more progress than we've made in years, right?" I heard the desperation in my voice and hated it.

He nodded slowly, but I could sense the words bubbling beneath his surface. He was going to say more. He was going to tell me to stop.

"All I need to do next is figure out how to keep the barrier down or control it without needing Rachel to do something horrible first," I said quickly. "I can do that. I've got two more opportunities to—"

"Ariane," he said with a tired but knowing look. "What about the rest of it?"

"What do you mean?" I asked, wary.

"I mean, the police chief's son," he said, biting off each word.

Oh. "I only agreed to go out with him to get closer to Rachel so I could practice. It isn't real." It hurt just to say that. It was real, far more than either of us had intended or I could allow.

My father laughed, except not like it was funny.

I stiffened.

"Ariane, kiddo, you are good at so many things, but you're terrible at hiding this kind of emotion." He reached out and tapped another photo of Zane and me at the activities fair. This one had been zoomed in, and I could see us clearly. Zane in mid-gesture, explaining something with wild hand movements, and me watching him intently, as if waiting for the end of the story or joke.

"It's written all over your face," my father said. "You're a blank screen when you're sad or angry or frustrated or scared. Like right now." He nodded at me. "You wipe it all away. You probably had no choice in that—a survival mechanism at GTX. But when you're happy, genuinely happy, it shows."

He paused. "The first time you tasted french fries, I saw it." He laughed. "Light shining through dark glass." He held up the photo of Zane and me. "Same thing here."

I swallowed hard. "It wasn't supposed to be real," I whispered.

My father smiled bitterly and raised the scotch bottle in a kind of salute before taking a drink. "Pretending to feel something you don't can often lead you to the real thing, in some form," he said in a thickened voice, his eyes watering from the sting of the alcohol. "Trust me. But you have to end it now."

"No." The word escaped before I could stop it. It felt like it came from someone else.

My father looked up, startled.

And rightly so: I'd never openly defied him. Ever. And just saying it now almost killed me, but I couldn't live with myself if I stayed quiet. I would give up Zane and everything he represented (happiness, warmth, company) after tomorrow night, but I'd *promised* myself the next twenty-four hours.

"It's just . . . I'm so close to figuring it all out and I . . ." I took a deep breath and stopped. Stopped lying to myself and to my father. I wasn't fooling either one of us.

I curled my fingers into my fists, feeling the reassuring bite of my nails into my palms. I was real, and I was here. "I don't want to let this go," I said. "Not yet. I won't have this chance again with anyone, and Zane . . . he's different." I blinked against the sting in my eyes, remembering the pleased-with-himself grin he got when I laughed at his ridiculous bog/dear story. I knew I would play that moment in my head over and over again, years from now. And feel his hands on me, not hesitating, afraid, or clinical.

"Do you understand?" I pleaded, moving to drop into the chair next to my father. "I know it's selfish and dangerous, but it's already started. I won't ever have this again."

He opened his mouth to speak.

But I shook my head. "You talk about my life once I get away from Wingate, but we both know it's a lie."

He stopped, snapping his mouth shut in surprise.

"It's going to be me, alone, for the rest of my life, if I'm lucky," I continued, trying to keep my voice from quavering. "And I'm grateful for that chance at freedom." My voice broke. "But I want this. Please. I know it can't be anything . . . real. It's only a day or so and then it'll go away. And if it doesn't, I'll end it. But please, just let me have this." Let me have the silly stories he'd come up with, the heat of his hands, the feel of his mouth against mine. I wanted to store those moments up, food before an endless winter.

My father sighed. "Sometimes I forget how young you are." He smiled sadly.

And I knew I wasn't going to like what was coming next.

"Just because you end it doesn't mean it's over." He held up a photo. "If GTX finds about this, even if it's weeks or years from now, they'll use the threat of hurting him to get you to do what they want."

I hadn't thought about that. But it was true: I wouldn't stop caring about Zane just because we weren't together. Therefore, Zane would be a good source of motivation, as far as GTX was concerned.

The image of Zane pacing the floor in a small white room like the one where I'd been held for so long popped into my head, and I wanted to throw up. He wouldn't know why he was there, he wouldn't understand what was going on, and I would be the one who'd put him there. Everything they'd do to him—and they could do unspeakable things in the name of motivation—would be my fault.

I couldn't do that to him.

My dream of the next twenty-four hours crumbled into dust and blew away. My eyes burned at the loss, and my all-too-human heart gave an extra hard thump of anguish.

"You've hung a bull's-eye around that poor kid's neck, and he has no idea," my father said, his disappointment in me so deep it thickened the air until I felt as if I couldn't breathe. "It has to stop. Immediately."

I nodded slowly. What else was there to say? I'd broken the Rules almost beyond repair. And now I'd pay for that. I just had to hope I'd be the only one.

CHAPTER 20

Zane

AT DINNER, IT WAS CLEAR THAT MY DAD'S MOOD HAD NOT improved much from this morning. And the salad only made it worse.

Since my dad had brought home pizza last night, it was my night to "cook." I could have pulled one of the many casseroles out of the freezer, but I'd gotten sick of eating those about six months into my mom's absence. We'd never gotten the hang of thawing them out completely.

So after I'd dropped off Ariane—my head still spinning from the feel of her skin under my hands—I'd swung by the store to pick up some bread and I'd snagged one of those frozen ready-made lasagnas on my way through.

On a whim, I'd picked up one of those salads in a bag, a brand I recognized from what my mom used to buy. I was just momentarily tired of all the grease at home and school, and wanted something different.

Now, at the dinner table with my dad and the salad

between us—in the same glass bowl my mom had used—you'd have thought I'd brought home roadkill and dropped it in front of him.

"What is this?" he demanded, his mouth curling up in disgust.

What does it look like? "Salad," I said. And remembered, suddenly, vividly, my mom lecturing all of us on eating more vegetables, including salad.

Oh, damn. Talk about waving a red flag. After this morning he probably thought I was taunting him, deliberately making a reference to my mom. He'd never admit it, but she'd dealt him a serious blow by leaving. I think he had loved her—or at least needed her—in his own messed-up way. And, of course, it had done serious damage to his ego that *she* would be the one to want out.

But I wasn't trying to send any kind of secret message. I just freaking wanted one food item that wasn't covered in cheese.

"Dad—" I started.

His phone chimed, and he turned away. "Bradshaw." He paused, listening to the person on the other end. Then he gave a hearty laugh that rang false to my ears. "No, you're not interrupting. It's not a problem."

Ah, concerned citizen. Probably of the female variety. We got a lot of that around here.

I tuned out the rest of the conversation. I guess from the outside, my dad looked like a pretty good dating option. He had a steady job, a prominent position in the community, and he was still in shape for a guy his age. Plus, he had that whole sympathy thing going for him—abandoned by his wife with a kid still in high school.

But if these women just stopped and thought about it, they'd have to realize there was more to the situation than what they could see on the surface. I mean, did they think my mom left because everything was too awesome to bear? Then again, maybe they'd just tagged her departure as another example of genetically predisposed poor judgment. She was, after all, a McDonough. And blood will always tell, or whatever.

"Well, it's not the same as being on the field or watching my boy out there, but I wouldn't miss it," my dad said with another laugh.

My phone buzzed, and I slipped it out of my pocket and checked it beneath the table. I expected to see Rachel's photo on the screen yet again, demanding the latest Ariane update.

But the screen was blank except for a name, Ariane. Affection tugged at me. I needed to take a picture of her so it would come up when she called. I wondered if she'd let me.

I got up and headed toward the hall before answering.

"Hey," I said. "Please tell me you're ready to go. Because I am so ready to get out of here." I checked over my shoulder to make sure my dad was still yakking it up.

"I can't." Her voice sounded flat, dead.

It sent a chill through me. I pretended to misunderstand. "Okay, so later? How about—"

"No, I can't go tonight. Or for the rest of this week. It's done. What we were doing is done," she said in that same mechanical voice.

I took a step back, absorbing her words like a blow. "What happened?"

Her breath sounded ragged; she'd been crying. "Ariane?" I asked, alarmed.

"It's nothing I can explain to you, so let it go, okay?" I could hear the steel in her tone even as she was trying not to sniffle.

Her dad. He'd found out. Had he hurt her? My jaw tightened. I'd always known something was up at home for her.

"I'm coming over," I said.

"No, you can't," she said sharply, which only further convinced me I was right to be concerned.

I made a quick decision. She'd be pissed at me, but I wouldn't be able to live with myself if I let this go.

"Here are your options," I said.

"Zane—" she protested.

I ignored her. "You can either meet me at Pine and Rushmore in fifteen minutes so I can see for myself that you're okay, or I'm going to drive up and down your street honking the horn and yelling your name until you come out or someone calls the cops."

She sucked in a breath. "You wouldn't."

"You're going to take that chance? I have an in with the police around here. I could probably get away with that for a lot longer than most." My dad would leave me to sit and rot in jail for as long as he could on a disturbing-the-peace charge. But it would be worth it.

Ariane gave a frustrated sigh. "All right. But not until later. Dark."

"Fine." From what I'd overheard, my dad was going to the exhibition game, which would make it that much easier. "Eight."

"I'll be there," she said. "Don't come to my house. And don't honk."

"Ariane . . ." I hesitated. "I'm not trying to be a jerk. I just want to make sure you're okay."

"I'm okay." But she didn't sound like it.

Ariane was waiting for me when I pulled up. At least I was pretty sure it was her. At our usual meeting place, my headlights caught a slight figure in a gray hoodie, despite the warmth of the evening.

I parked, and she climbed in, bringing the scent of lemons with her. But she left the hood up even once she was inside.

"What are you doing?" I asked.

"What do you mean, what am I doing? You're the one who blackmailed me into this meeting," she said, her head turned away from me.

My stomach tightened with dread. "Look at me."

"Why?"

"Please?"

She turned toward me, and I pushed her hood away. Her face was clear of the bruises I'd half expected, but her eyes were red and swollen.

"Happy?" she demanded.

"Not yet." I took her hand in mine and pushed her sleeve up. Nothing but smooth white skin all the way up past her elbows. I knew from experience if someone bigger is going to grab you, they usually do it on your forearm. I checked her other arm and found the same thing, which was to say nothing at all.

She gave an exasperated sigh, but didn't fight me when I checked both arms again. "My father doesn't hurt me. He would never do that."

Something about the formal way she said "my father" set off warning bells in my head.

I released her, and she tugged her sleeves into place. "So, I'm here. You can see that I'm fine. Are we done now?" she asked in a clipped tone, but I noticed she wasn't reaching for the door.

I shook my head. "No way. What's going on? Are you in the Witness Protection Program or something?" I tried to joke.

She defiantly tipped her chin. "If I said yes, would you let it go?"

But I was on to her by now. "Depends. Is it true?"

She sighed. "Sort of. And that's about the best answer I can give you." She looked away. "I shouldn't even tell you that much."

So she was in hiding. I frowned. "Does this have anything to do with your being declared dead and then not dead?" It occurred to me that being declared dead was a pretty good way to keep people from looking for you. And with the delay in the retraction notice, there might be people who still thought she was dead.

She jerked around to stare at me.

"I did some research," I admitted.

She tensed, as if she might bolt from the car. "What did you find?"

"Nothing much. An article about your mom's accident, and a retraction notice about your 'death.'" I grimaced. "Sorry, I didn't mean to bring up—"

She relaxed. "No, it's okay." She waved a hand at my words. "It was a long time ago."

Which struck me as an unusual response, when she'd been on the verge of panic a few seconds ago.

Once again, I tried to put the pieces of Ariane Tucker together. Who she could possibly be hiding from? Her mother's family? A grandparent who wanted to keep her? Or, given how intensely she was taking the situation, maybe it was a relative who *legally* had rights to her.

"You know, my dad is a jerk," I said, "but if this is a custody thing, he could probably—"

"No, absolutely not," Ariane said. "It's under control." She swallowed and fidgeted with the zipper on her hoodie. "Just . . . go back to your normal life. Tell Rachel I freaked out on you, talking about prom or something already, and you couldn't take it anymore. She'll enjoy that." She smiled bitterly.

It must have been serious if Ariane was willing to let Rachel think she'd gotten the better of her, even for pretend.

I focused my gaze on the steering wheel, seeing it but not. "What if I don't want to go back to my normal life? What if my normal life kind of sucks?" I forced a laugh. I'd had more fun in the last couple of days than I'd had in more than a year. Ariane didn't try to control me or want me to be somebody I wasn't. It was a relief.

She touched my arm, her fingertips cool and tentative. "I'm sorry," she whispered. "But this is better for everyone."

She blinked quickly, and I saw tears on her eyelashes. "And besides, who are we kidding? This would have been over on Saturday morning anyway. Maybe even Friday night after Rachel's party." Her voice was choked.

I looked at her sharply. "You think this is still about getting back at Rachel?" I asked, stunned.

She didn't say anything.

"Forget it." I turned away in disgust, my face hot. Obviously, she didn't feel the same way I did. And now I felt like an asshole. I'd thought after this afternoon that we'd both recognized it was something more, but apparently, that was just my overactive imagination. God, was I that desperate? Making up connections where none existed?

Ariane's hand tightened on my arm. "Are you saying it's not?" she asked quietly.

"I talked to you about my mom," I said stiffly. Which was all the answer I could manage, but probably wasn't enough. How could she possibly understand what that meant to me without seeing the inside of my head—

She stood up, half bent over, and scrambled around the armrest between us, dodging the steering wheel. Suddenly, with her knees on either side of me, I had a lapful of girl, which I hadn't been expecting. Not that I was complaining. She was warm and weirdly light even for her size; but when she leaned forward into me, heat spread from every contact point between us, and I stopped thinking about anything else.

"I'm sorry," she said, her mouth moving over mine. "I wish it could be different."

Before I could say anything in response, she was kissing

me like I was her last, best chance at breathing.

I clutched at her waist and felt the warm, smooth skin in the gap between her sweatshirt and jeans. I couldn't stop myself from sliding my hands up her sides, beneath her shirt, my thumbs over her ribs. . . .

She sucked in a surprised breath and pulled away slightly.

"It's not about this. You know that, right?" I asked, panting and struggling to focus on finding words. I didn't want to scare her away. But there were so many competing voices in my head, most of them telling me to stop talking and roll with it. "We can slow down—"

"I know," she murmured.

But she didn't. Slow down, that is. Instead, she leaned in and kissed me again. And slid her hand between us to tug at the top buttons of my shirt.

Oh God. How far was this going to go?

I barely had time to wonder about the impracticality of anything more—front seat of a truck on a public and fairly well-lit street—before she stopped, wrapping her arms tight around my neck and burying her face against my shoulder. And a second later, warm tears dripped against my skin.

What the—

Confused by the sudden shift in her mood, I pulled my hands out from under her shirt and touched her hair hesitantly. "Are you okay? I didn't mean to—"

"You didn't," she said, her voice muffled against me.

Okaaay.

After a moment, she sat up and wiped her eyes. "I have to go." She reached over and popped open my door.

I stared at her in disbelief. "Ariane. Wait."

"Don't text me again. I won't respond." Her tone was crisp, businesslike, and the coolness of it tore through me. "Don't come back here. Not tomorrow, not ever. When you see me in the halls . . ." She hesitated. "Don't see me. It's easier that way." She slipped off my lap and out of the truck.

"Have a good life, okay?" She smiled uncertainly, the corners of her mouth wobbling. It made my heart ache. "You deserve it." She slammed the door and hurried away.

I sat back, stunned, and watched her disappear around the corner in my rearview mirror.

Ariane Tucker was as much a mystery to me now as she'd been in the beginning. And I'd let her go.

What other choice did I have? She was obviously determined not to speak to me again, to retreat into the closed-off cocoon of a life she'd had before. Which frustrated the hell out of me.

What kind of life is it when you're running scared?

About the same kind of life as when you let other people make your decisions for you? I heard Ariane's wry voice in my head.

Yeah, except I was trying to change that. Ariane wanted to go—she thought she had to, for some reason—but I wasn't going to give up so easily. Not this time. I hadn't fought to find my mom because she'd made it clear she wanted nothing more to do with me. But that wasn't the case here.

I pulled my phone out of my pocket and hit Rachel's number.

CHAPTER 21

Ariane

PEOPLE WERE STARING AT ME WHEN I WALKED INTO THE gym on Friday morning before school, but that was no surprise.

It had been almost twelve hours since I'd ended things with Zane, and clearly he'd done what I'd asked and told Rachel about it. The rumor mill was actively churning; I could hear the whispers and feel the looks. And, of course, my red and swollen eyes were clear confirmation that something was going on. Nothing short of huge (and way too obvious) sunglasses would hide them well enough.

I'd had trouble sleeping last night. I'd tried to lose myself in Dream-Life, which had never before failed to distract me from the suckiness of real life. But not even another of Clark's disappearing acts—he'd returned with mysteriously fresh French baguettes—could charm me. It had just seemed ridiculously fake and empty, so I'd shut it down without even saving the latest session.

Then I'd woken up this morning after only a few hours of fitful rest to find my pillowcase wet and my eyes puffy. I'd been crying in my sleep. How could a few days make such a difference? I'd been alone for ten years—more if you counted my time in the lab. But this morning, walking to school by myself, studiously ignoring the section of the parking lot where I knew Zane would be, I felt bereft. Lonely.

I got a sudden flash, the sense memory of his hand on the back of my head, soothing, while I cried all over him.

God. Get it together, Ariane. I hadn't even seen him this morning. How much worse would it be then? I blinked rapidly and wished for those sunglasses. I made myself keep moving, across the gym floor and to a reasonably empty section of bleachers.

A barrage of whispers and giggles followed as I made my way, but none of them touched me. Aside from thoughts about Zane, which struck with the sizzle of an exposed nerve, a vague numbness had settled over me. As if I were experiencing the world through a layer of cotton. What did I care what these people thought or said about me?

I climbed up to a relatively populated row—no sense in isolating myself near the top, making it easy for everyone to watch and speculate—and sat on the end. Conversation in my immediate vicinity died for a long moment, and then it started up again in "hushed" voices that I would have had to be deaf not to hear.

It would get better in a few days, I told myself. By Monday, something else would have happened to occupy their time and attention. They'd forget all about me and my ill-fated, extremely temporary relationship with Zane Bradshaw. Full-blooded humans have notoriously short attention spans.

If only I could say the same for myself.

I'd found something I could never have, and now the only solution was to pretend it had never happened, to go back to being the version of Ariane Tucker I'd been before.

Except I didn't know how to get back there. I didn't know how to turn off the want.

I'd have to ignore it now, even as it dug into me, pleading for attention. A just punishment, I supposed.

It will fade. It will get easier. That was my new mantra. I kept repeating it over and over again in my head, praying it would eventually turn out to be true.

This morning I'd dragged myself out of bed, through the shower, and into some clothes, keeping to the schedule I'd held for years before this week. It had never felt like so much work. As if there wasn't enough air in my lungs for the required tasks.

I was doing the right thing. I was keeping Zane safe. That was the only saving grace, the only thing that kept me moving.

Still, I'd dreaded facing my father over the breakfast table and seeing the censure mixed with pity on his face. Thankfully he was gone by the time I got there.

That should have alarmed me, but I couldn't seem to make myself care. I'd seen a mysterious black van on our block (which turned out to be a florist, according to the name on the side; though whoever heard of a florist's van being black?) and hadn't even flinched. If there was immediate danger, my father would have warned me. And if it was another vaguely ominous yet distant threat that would make my life even more miserable for a few days or week, well, no thanks. I was full up on the misery meter at the moment. Try again later, GTX.

A burning rush of hatred and fury rose up inside me. GTX was the root of all of this. Without them, none of this would be happening. But without them, I wouldn't exist. The fact that I should theoretically be, in some way, grateful to them made me want to scream. My lungs burned with the need to shout, to empty myself out. To declare GTX's inhumanity, to let the world know what they were capable of, even as the cool and impassive flashing red lights of the security cameras recorded it all.

"Um, are you okay?" A tentative voice at my elbow asked.

I looked over, my neck so tight with tension it hurt to move. The girl sitting next to me, a freshman, most likely, was watching as if I were one match-flick away from exploding.

"Fine," I said, forcing out the word through clenched teeth, which pretty much shouted I was anything but.

It, however, also had the advantage of scaring the girl into silence. Blinking rapidly, she scooted a few inches away from me.

Some distant part of me knew I should I apologize, even wanted to, but I couldn't. I couldn't find the space inside myself for another emotion. Everything was jammed in there too tight, and pulling on one thing might send all of it spilling out.

I concentrated on keeping my composure, inhaling and exhaling. I would not lose it front of all these people. I would not—

The crowd around me rustled and stirred suddenly, a giant creature woken from a nap, and a chaotic surge of thoughts rose up from the background of static in my head.

I tried to ignore it. I didn't need one more thing to juggle right now.

But the noise in my head only grew louder.

Resisting the urge to put my hands over my ears, I glanced around to try to find the source of the disturbance.

It wasn't hard to find what—or, in this case, who—was sending shock waves through the minds of the student body.

Rachel Jacobs, who had never deigned to mingle with the peasants in the gym before school, was mincing her way carefully across the polished floor. Cami and Cassi trailed behind her, their identical heads tipped down over their phones as they texted, probably each other.

The sight of Rachel immediately inflamed the battle I was fighting inside myself. If there was ever a representation of GTX's indulgences, excesses, and thoughtlessness, it was Dr. Jacobs's granddaughter herself.

I gripped my seat on the bleachers, willing myself to stay still and silent.

Rachel moved as if the floor were made of ice instead of wood. Which is what happens when you wear stupidly inappropriate footwear—today, five-inch heels with ribbons wrapping up her legs—on a regular basis. Clearly, *she* had never had to worry about the possibility of running for her life or scaling fences to escape a retrieval team.

Her nose was wrinkled in distaste, as if the giant cavernous room smelled, and it kind of did—sweaty socks, too much Axe, and nerves. The rest of us simply dealt with it.

If hate was detectable by an infrared camera, I'd have been the white-hot center of the room. Everyone else watched with awe, fear, or surprise. I just wanted her gone.

She moved closer to the bleachers, her hand raised to block the overhead light while she searched for someone, and I tensed. If Rachel was here, it was for a purpose. Probably a nefarious one. Unfortunately, at this distance and with all the background noise of other minds in proximity, I couldn't hear what she was thinking or who she was looking for.

But I had a good guess.

I spun around in my seat to find Jenna. It took me a few minutes to locate her in the upper-left quadrant of bleachers by herself, her gaze fixed on Rachel. She was pale, watching the inevitable approach of another round of destruction march ever closer.

It had been bad enough, what Rachel had done to Jenna's locker and to Jenna herself in front of a cafeteria full of people, but in here, in front of the whole school except the privileged twenty or so in the parking lot, that was a whole new level of warfare.

I found myself standing up without realizing I'd come to the decision to do so. I couldn't have Zane, but I sure as hell did not have to sit here and let Rachel torture Jenna again.

Jenna may not have been the friend that Zane thought she should have been, but then again, neither had I.

I charged out of my row to the stairs, my only goal to put myself between them before Rachel zeroed in on her.

"There you are," Rachel said loudly.

I froze, then turned to watch as she charged straight at *me*. Well, wobbled, more accurately. Regardless, she was coming my way.

A direct confrontation, though? That wasn't her style.

My heart pounded harder, and I longed for the barrier in my head to drop. I would give her a show she wouldn't forget.

Too many people. Too many witnesses, the worried voice whispered in my head.

I didn't care.

Rachel climbed up the first three stairs, and I stepped down to meet her halfway, blood boiling so hard I thought there might be steam emerging from my ears. Like in those old cartoons I'd once taken so literally.

"What do you want?" I demanded, the muscles in my arms shaking with the tension of holding myself back.

"I'm having a party tonight, and you should come." She smiled, but her gaze held a hardness that reflected her true feelings.

I nearly toppled down the remaining steps between us. *What?* I couldn't have been more surprised if she'd offered to braid my hair.

"I don't—"

"Zane seems to think I might have given you the wrong impression the other night. That I might have scared you off."

He what? I stared at her in confusion. He was supposed

to have told her that it was over. I didn't understand what was going on.

"We can't have that, can we? Zane's friends should be my friends. So, party, my house, tonight. It'll be fun." Her dark eyes gleamed with anticipation.

Come on, come on . . . you know you want to go. Rachel's thoughts momentarily broke through the mental noise of the crowd. *I've seen how you look at him. So wrong. I haven't worked this hard for nothing. . . . People will be talking about this for years.*

Okay, now I was getting it. Rachel was still hoping for the opportunity to humiliate me in the most public and agonizing fashion possible. But what was Zane playing at? He was behind this, I was sure. I just didn't know why.

Maybe he wanted to see me again. He'd been so surprised last night; I'd completely blindsided him with walking away.

No. I couldn't afford to think that way. I shook my head, resisting the urge to rub at the ache in my chest. "I can't—"

"Unless I've scared you off for good," Rachel said with a thin, haughty smile, triumph glittering in her gaze. *I win either way.*

My logical side fired off a warning. *Ignore her, Ariane. You know better. She's just pushing your buttons.*

But it was too late. I set my jaw. "I'll be there." My father would be at work. I could get to Rachel's party, be completely *not* destroyed by whatever she intended, and get home long before his shift ended. Which meant I would win. Score one for me in the battle of Ariane versus GTX. It wasn't a big victory, but one more than I'd ever had before.

And Zane would be there.

"Good," Rachel said. Then she turned and click-clacked her way down the stairs and across the floor.

With her departure, the adrenaline flooding through me faded. I sat down on the steps, right where I stood. How had this gotten so complicated in such a short period of time?

A party at Rachel's house. A place where Dr. Jacobs had surely visited countless times. He wouldn't be there, but something about passing so close to his shadow . . . I shivered.

Sudden movement to my left, followed by a wave of disgruntled thoughts, caught my attention. I stood up to see Jenna, her face red, which meant she was crying, clambering down the bleachers instead of the steps, forcing people to move out of her way.

I sighed. Obviously she had witnessed what had happened with Rachel, and even if she hadn't been able to hear our conversation, she'd made the leap that it was a friendly encounter. How did full-blooded humans keep making that mistake? Couldn't they see beneath the pretty face to the malice below? Yes, I had the advantage of sometimes being able to hear Rachel's thoughts, but still. Didn't they see the sharp edges to her smile? The truth in her behavior, if not her words?

Guess not.

Jenna stumbled on the last bleacher and landed on her knees with a thud that echoed through the huge space. And even from this distance I could see her face grow redder.

A jeering round of applause went up from those close by, and I winced.

Oh, Jenna. More humiliation on top of humiliation. I couldn't leave her like that. I owed her more than that. We'd been friends once, and maybe we could be again, if she'd allow it.

So when she staggered to her feet and ran out of the room, I headed down the steps to follow.

Unless you were Rachel, there were only two places you could flee to before the start of classes: the school office or the bathroom. After our less-than-successful visit with the principal the other day, I was betting that Jenna had chosen the latter.

The girls' bathroom immediately off the gym was quite possibly one of my least favorite places in all of my experience. And lest you have forgotten, I spent a goodly amount of time trapped in a secret room underground.

This bathroom was rarely used except during this pre-start to the school day and by those professing "emergencies" during P.E. It was small, dimly lit, and reminded me of a dank prison cell with its fractured gray tile floors and graffitied walls.

I pushed open the door quietly, wrinkling my nose at the overwhelming stench of industrial cleaning supplies.

The lone stall door, bearing the mark of someone's early morning boredom in the form of a huge swooping heart with "Maddy + Josh 4EVA," was closed. The muffled sounds of sniffling came from behind it, along with a piercing stream of harsh thoughts.

. . . so stupid, ugly, fat, no wonder you're such a loser. God, you should just kill yourself. . . .

Uh-oh. I tapped on the stall door hesitantly. "Jenna?"

"Oh my God," she wailed. "What do you want? To dig the knife deeper into my back?"

I flinched. I deserved that, I guess. "I wanted to make sure you were okay." I made a face at my own words. Obviously she *wasn't* anything near okay.

Jenna whipped the door open suddenly and so hard it collided with the metal stall wall with a loud smack.

I took a startled step back.

"Do I look okay?" she demanded, emerging with her face flushed and shiny with tears.

"Jenna, I am so sorr—"

"You know, I was your friend," she said, advancing on me and pointing with her hand full of wadded-up toilet paper. "Even though you're freaky and weird and you can never go out anywhere and I think your dad keeps you locked up in the basement or something."

My face grew hot, hearing her say it like that. It was not far from what was once truth.

"All the strange restrictions and messing up words and not understanding random stuff that even little kids get." Jenna threw her hands up in the air.

My whole face was on fire now. She'd never said any of this before. And she'd hidden it well because I'd never picked it up in her thoughts, other than the occasional "huh, that's weird" kind of a moment. "I'm sorry it was so difficult," I said stiffly.

She picked at the toilet paper in her hands, separating the cheap two-ply into thinner single sheets. "My mom said that I should aim higher, but I defended you," she said over a hiccup. "When I picked you to be my friend, I thought, Here's someone I can trust. She doesn't care about being popular. She doesn't even care about being normal. Next to her, I've got a shot at being noticed instead of always being second best." She raised her gaze to the ceiling as if reenacting the realization.

A yawning emptiness opened up inside me. Zane had been right. Jenna was my friend, but only as long as it was on her terms, as long as I stayed in the little box she'd put me in, the obedient (and slightly weird) friend. The second things changed in a way she didn't like, she called it all off.

How had I missed that? Had I been that desperate and lonely?

"Now you're the one all best buds with Rachel, and you don't even like her," she raged.

"Are you angry that Rachel chose me, a freak, for *special* attention?" I demanded, with extra emphasis on the "special" because Jenna, of all people, should know how much Rachel's definition of that varied from the rest of ours. "Or is it that she chose a freak over you?"

Jenna's eyes widened, but she rallied quickly. "You don't even appreciate what you're being offered," she said. "Your dad *wants* you to stay home all the time."

I frowned, not making the connection. "What exactly do you think I'm getting?" I asked.

"The perfect life! Once you're in, you're good. You never have to worry about people liking you or fitting in or being alone on a Friday night or your mom telling you that you just must not be trying hard enough," she said in a longing voice.

Dr. Mayborne strikes again. Jenna's mom was worse than I'd realized. "Yeah, being popular, a solution for all the world's problems." I sighed, thinking about what I knew about Zane and how Rachel treated him. "You know it doesn't work that way."

"You're still going," she accused.

I stared at her in disbelief. "Yeah, because Rachel is trying to set me up, and I'm not going to let her get the best of me," I snapped.

She sniffled and looked up, hope lighting her face. "Really? That's all?"

I clamped my mouth shut. I shouldn't have said anything. It was too much of a risk. "Forget it." I started to turn away.

"You know it's not real with Zane, right?"

I froze, then faced her. "What?"

She didn't seem to hear me. "It can't be. It just can't be," she repeated softly, as if trying to convince herself. "People like him don't choose people like you."

I jerked back as if she'd hit me. She wasn't wrong, exactly; I couldn't deny that. How often would someone like Zane Bradshaw choose someone like me? Not very. But I couldn't believe that a person who was supposed to be my friend would say that.

She looked like the Jenna I knew—pink cheeks, scattered curls, overly careful attention to her accessory selection—but not. All of this had started because I'd broken the Rules to defend her against Rachel. But apparently that had been a huge mistake. Jenna was *nothing* like who I thought she was. Yeah, I'd lied about who I was during the course of our friendship—it couldn't be helped, given what I had to hide. But I'd done my best to be as honest as I could. She, evidently, hadn't bothered. She wasn't a true friend. She never had been.

My eyes stung with tears, which surprised and infuriated me. I bit down hard on the inside of my cheek to stop them, and headed for the door. I could feel the walls of the room pressing in on me.

"No, Ariane, wait!"

I paused, my hand on the door, and glanced at Jenna.

She dabbed under her eyes with the shredded toilet paper without looking at me. "So, um, do you think you can get me in at Rachel's tonight?"

I closed my eyes. Any hope I'd ever had of our being friends again died a swift and painful death. Some part of me wished we could go back to before, when I didn't know what I meant (or didn't mean) to her. But now that I knew, there was no forgetting, no getting past it. Zane had said I deserved more; I wasn't so sure about that. I just couldn't handle one more person seeing me as *something*, useful or not, instead of *someone*.

I opened my eyes. "Bye, Jenna," I said, and walked out.

CHAPTER 22

Zane

BY FIFTH HOUR, THERE WAS STILL NO SIGN OF ARIANE. I'd figured it wouldn't take her long to seek me out once Rachel had delivered her "invitation" in the only way that Rachel could: condescendingly. Which Ariane would take as a personal challenge and respond the only way she knew how: by saying yes.

But instead . . . nothing.

No texts or phone calls. No hissed conversations in the hall. Not so much as a glare in the distance, which would have required my seeing her, and I hadn't. But Ariane had to know why I did what I did, right?

After confirming again with Rachel at lunch that the encounter had gone as I'd expected ("Yes, Zane, for the twelfth time, she said she'll be there. God! What is your problem?"), I went looking for Ariane.

She let me find her at her locker. I say "let" because the first seven times I'd walked past, on my way to class, the drinking fountain, etc., she hadn't been there. She might have been avoiding me, or maybe I just had crappy timing.

"You sicced Rachel on me," she said, her attention focused on trading out her books. She was so cold and distant compared to last night.

I rolled my eyes, jamming my hands into my pockets. "You didn't give me a choice. Would we even be having this conversation if I hadn't?"

"It doesn't change anything. I can't . . . we can't . . ." She avoided looking at me. "You know that."

"I don't know that," I said in exasperation. "Because I still have no idea what's going on." I paused, waiting for her to fill the silence with some kind of explanation. But she stayed quiet, concentrating on what she was doing at her locker.

Okay, fine, if that's how we're going to play it. . . . "It does change something," I pointed out.

Ariane glanced up at me sharply.

"You're going to the party tonight when you weren't before."

She gave me a sour look. "Because you manipulated Rachel into manipulating me."

I snorted. "Yeah, that was a real stretch of my abilities." The two of them had done all the work themselves—I'd just given Rachel the idea.

I thought I saw the start of a smile before she shook her head. "What do you want, Zane?"

"Look, I just want . . ." Actually, I hadn't stopped to think about *what* I wanted. Only that I didn't want it, whatever *it* was, to end with last night. "I want to see this thing through," I finished lamely. "Don't you?"

"Without sounding too self-pitying, it absolutely does not matter what I want." She shut her locker and turned away from me.

I followed her. "It matters to me." I winced at the supreme cheesiness of the line even though it was the truth.

And it worked. She looked up at me directly for the first time. Her eyes were bloodshot and more swollen than last night—it must have been hell to put in her contact lenses this morning. "That," she said quietly, "is why I should be putting as much distance as possible between us."

I sighed, tired of trying to understand her enigmatic answers. "Look, you've got secrets. Fine. I understand."

She gave me a wry smile.

I sighed again. "Okay, no, I don't understand, but my point is you can trust me. You don't want to talk about it? Fine. But don't cut me out." I stuffed my hands into my pockets again, feeling absurdly vulnerable.

Ariane cleared her throat. "Because it's a challenge."

"No," I snapped, frustrated. "Because you are the most interesting person I've met. Ever. Because you take my side without weighing whether that's best for you or not. Because you're real and you don't care what anyone else thinks."

And what I couldn't make myself say out loud: Because I want to be *that* guy. I want to be the person you trust. To be worthy of someone who really knows me instead of being their second—or last—choice.

I'm not dumb. I didn't miss the parallels between this situation and my mom. Ariane had a secret, just as my mom had when she was planning her escape; and this time I wanted to be included, taken along instead of left behind.

But even knowing that some of this was driven by the forces of my past didn't change how I felt.

"If you knew the truth, you wouldn't be so quick to sign on," Ariane said as we dodged people—and curious glances—in the hall.

"So tell me," I said.

"You know I can't," she said, exasperated.

I grinned smugly. "Then I guess I get the benefit of the doubt for now." I put my arm around her shoulders and pulled her close.

"This is only for tonight," she warned, but I could feel her relaxing into my side.

And if she wanted it to be just for tonight, that was fine. After the party was over I'd work on getting her to agree to tomorrow or next week. I wasn't into her because she was a challenge, but I certainly wasn't afraid of the challenge she presented.

"And we're not going to the party together. We just happen to be going to the same party," she said with a sniff.

I raised my eyebrows. "Yeah? How are you going to get there?" I asked, betting she hadn't gotten that far yet. Rachel's house was on the other side of town.

She stopped, genuinely startled. "Damn."

"I'm guessing a taxi might attract attention that you don't want. . . ." I shook my head in mock seriousness.

She glared at me. "Don't gloat. It'll stunt your growth."

I laughed, surprised. "I don't think that's how it works. And besides, even if it did"—I gestured at the height difference between us—"I think it's a little late for that. For me, at least." I frowned. "You, on the other hand, are apparently the gloatiest of all gloaters."

She pursed her mouth. "Funny."

I bumped her hip with mine—well, her side, thanks to that height difference. "You just don't like it when I'm right."

"No, sometimes I wish you were right all the time," she said, her gaze distant.

I could feel her mood veering off into the melancholy gloom I'd found her in. "Come on, walk me to class and I'll let you lecture me about the debilitating effects of drinking coffee as an infant or of not eating my toast crusts."

"Your parents gave you coffee?" She sounded aghast.

And I couldn't resist. "Straight from the pot into a bottle." I held my hand up in an "I swear" gesture, struggling to keep a straight face.

She believed me for about a half second. Then she shoved me. "Shut up." But she was smiling. And that was all I wanted.

CHAPTER 23

Ariane

One more night. Just one. It won't make that much of a difference.

That's what I told myself over and over again throughout the rest of the afternoon and with every step on my way home. Zane had offered me a ride, but since I was already acting in direct defiance to my father's wishes, I didn't want to push my luck. Or fate or karma or whatever.

My guilty conscience was already working overtime, making me jumpy. Since talking to Zane, I'd been on high alert, waiting for my phone to chirp with a text from my dad telling me I was busted (if he was monitoring the security camera feed, that was more than possible) or that we needed to run.

But so far, my phone had remained silent. So much so that I'd taken it out of my bag and turned it off and then on again to make sure it was working.

Now, on the sidewalk, I tensed every time a car passed,

expecting the shrill screech of tires and brakes, and either my very angry father or a GTX retrieval team to storm into my path.

But all was quiet except for regular traffic and the same dumb black van from this morning. This time, though, it zoomed past me. It had a large white banner on the side, proclaiming DORIS THE FLORIST, TULIPS ARE BETTER THAN NONE!

It made me edgy, but if it was a front for GTX and they knew who/what I was, they wouldn't have been wasting their time driving around.

I was being paranoid. I was pretty sure.

Approaching our house, I couldn't help but notice it had an abandoned air to it—the empty driveway, the curtains pulled tight. But that had to be my imagination, my fear that my father would be taken and hurt because of my actions. Right?

I hurried up the walkway and, with shaking hands, managed to get the key in the lock. Once inside, I peeked into the kitchen, half convinced that the table and chairs would be turned over, dishes shattered on the floor. But everything was as I'd left it. My single spoon and bowl in the drying rack. No one had been here since I'd left this morning, as far as I could tell.

I let out a relieved and guilty breath. My father was probably still at work, though he'd put in more than his required hours this week. He was watching out for me again—as always.

I looked at his chair, where he'd sat last night, drinking away his disappointment in me.

Was it worth all of this?

I bit my lip. I'd have the rest of my life to follow the Rules. I just wanted one more night off to put Rachel in her place.

I retreated to my bedroom, dropped my bag on the floor, and climbed onto my bed, sinking into the fluffy comforter and pillows. But they offered no relief, no feeling of escape or safety. If anything, they felt claustrophobic, surrounding me too closely.

I stared up at the plastic stars dotting the ceiling and realized for the first time I'd recreated the outside in here. Stars overhead, a blue sky on the upper part of the wall, the darker sandy color of the earth below it. Guess that answered the question of how scared I was of life, even as recently as three years ago. I'd brought the outside in rather than venturing out on my own.

Frustrated, I fought my way off the bed and started pacing the length of my room, as I'd once walked my GTX cage.

I stopped in front of my closet and yanked open the louvered doors. If I was going to go through with this tonight, I needed something to wear. And from the second Rachel had challenged me to show up, I'd known what it should be.

At the back of my closet, shoved behind all the grays, whites, and earth tones, a pink shirt screamed like a neon sign.

Jenna had given it to me last year for my (Ariane's) birthday, annoyed by the lack of "happy colors" in my wardrobe. The color listed on the tag was "dusty rose," which sounded awful if you thought about it literally; but it was a pretty, soft pink fabric.

The style was a deep V-neck with the material gathered slightly under the chest for emphasis, which was good because I needed all the help I could get. Then it descended into deliberately ragged layers, one on top of the other. It was fashionable and shouted, "Look at me."

It was much too flashy for my regular wardrobe, so I'd never worn it. And, I realized suddenly, Jenna probably never expected that I would. She preferred me as I was—pale, colorless, bland, nonthreatening.

Before I could talk myself out of it, I shoved my other clothes to the side and pulled the "dusty rose" shirt off the hanger.

It was as pretty as I remembered, the fine fabric catching on my fingertips. Jenna had spent serious money on this gift. And suddenly I wanted to wear it, wanted to prove her wrong. That I could be someone who would wear this shirt and be comfortable in it. That I wouldn't just be the freaky girl whose only purpose was to make average girls look better.

I pulled my gray Henley over my head. The air felt too cool against my skin, and I shivered.

Then I squirmed my way into the new shirt—it was tighter than most of the other things I wore. And for good reason. I turned to look at myself in the mirror. As I'd suspected, the crisscross of the fabric in front aided in the appearance of a B-cup, and the layers of ruffles below the chest created the illusion of someone with more distance between breasts and hips.

I backed up a step or two for a better look. It made me appear taller, too. Not that I would resemble any definition of that word standing next to Zane, but the illusion was more than I had otherwise. Pair it with another of my favorite jeans—maybe the ones with the Swarovski crystal designs on the back pockets—and I'd be set.

In the mirror, my face was flushed, and my pale hair stood up in crazy, static-filled tufts.

But I looked . . . happy. Not normal, exactly, but a better version of me.

And I wanted to be *her* tonight, that girl in the mirror. Maybe not tomorrow, maybe not next week. But for tonight.

I turned to pull the tags off the shirt and caught my first glimpse of a problem. The neck that tapered down to a fine point in the front started out much wider at the shoulders. So much so that the edge of the bandage covering the GTX identifier on my shoulder blade was visible.

Get one of the clear bandages, my inner voice argued. *Or a smaller one. You have options!*

I did. But there was only one option I was interested in.

Using the mirror for guidance, I plucked at the bandage with shaking hands. After a second, the edge came free, and I managed to wrest the entire thing away. It came off a twisted and mangled bit of cotton and sticky tape. And the four-by-four-inch space of my skin—covered every minute of every day for the last ten years except for the few seconds it took to change the bandage—felt absurdly sensitive, as if the nerve endings had multiplied in the constant dark. The fabric of my shirt felt cool and slippery soft against that place.

Before leaving the room to shower and then wrestle with my hair, I double-checked to make sure the tattoo wasn't visible above or through my shirt.

It wasn't. My back was a solid wall of dusty rose.

So, tonight, for one last night, I would do what I wanted. I'd break the Rules and be the Ariane Tucker *I* wanted to be.

CHAPTER 24

Zane

FEELING ODDLY NERVOUS, I ARRIVED AT PINE AND Rushmore a few minutes early and parked around the corner, as usual. I wished she'd have let me pick her up, but I knew better than to try *that* argument. I hoped the owners of the house on the corner didn't mind my waiting here again, because the last thing I needed was someone calling the police. My dad was still pissed that I'd talked him into the SUV for one last night. I'd stayed holed up in my room—emerging only to grab a plate of half-thawed chicken casserole—to avoid the possibility of another fight that would cause him to renege.

Fortunately, no one on the street seemed the least bit interested in me or my truck. Most of the houses were lit up—people watching television, finishing dinner, or getting their families to bed. It was almost nine. In fact, the only other vehicle in sight was a dark utility van parked on the other side of the street, its engine running.

Squinting at it, I could just barely make out the lettering on the side. Something about tulips. A florist's van?

I frowned. Kind of late in the day for flower deliveries, wasn't it?

I might have thought more about it, but then I caught a glimpse of Ariane in the side mirror as she came around the corner and moved through the light of the streetlamp. She was wearing pink, definitely a brighter color than I'd ever seen her in. And her hair was down and loose around her shoulders. I felt like I was seeing *her* for the first time.

I fumbled for the handle and got out of the truck.

"Don't," she warned, her shoulders tense, when she saw me.

I held up my hands in defense. "I wasn't going to. You look . . . amazing."

She dropped her gaze, but she was smiling. "Thanks."

I stepped around her and opened the door. "You ready for this?" I asked.

Her smile faded. "Probably not. But this is what we've been working toward, right?" She slipped past me and climbed into the truck.

I shut the door, suddenly feeling uncertain about my plan. Maybe this wasn't the best idea. Goading Ariane into accepting the invitation had only been an opening move, something to keep her talking to me. But if tonight was my only chance to convince her that this thing between us was worth pursuing, Rachel's bonfire party probably wasn't the right environment to help me win the fight.

I jogged around the Blazer and got behind the wheel. "You know, we don't have to go tonight," I said. "There will be other parties. Other opportunities to watch Rachel lose her mind when she learns she can't control everyone and everything in her path." I gave Ariane a grim smile.

"Yeah, like when she kills you for not showing up after you made her invite me."

"I'm serious, Ariane. We don't have to go."

"No," she said, "let's just get this done."

"Okay," I said reluctantly. I put the truck in gear and headed in the direction of Rachel's neighborhood. But I couldn't shake the unaccountable feeling of dread in my gut. My phone had been disturbingly quiet for the last couple of hours—no texts or calls from Rachel—which should have been a good sign, except it felt wrong somehow. "How about afterward?" I persisted, feeling some gnawing need to establish a further connection, future plans that would cement us together.

She frowned. "What about it?"

"Well, we're not going to want to hang around while Rachel tries to keep from going nuclear in front of everyone."

She raised her eyebrows, surprised. "I thought . . . I figured you'd want to stay."

"No way. We're going to walk in, wait for Rachel to pull the trigger on our 'breakup,' and stick around long enough to see the look on her face when she realizes we've gotten the better of her. Fifteen minutes, tops, and we'll be out of there."

"What did you have in mind?" she asked.

"How do you feel about bowling?" All right, it wasn't my best idea ever, but it was the first thing that popped into my head.

"You mean in general or the eternal question—sport or game?" she asked with a hint of a smile. "I've never played, so I couldn't say."

"Bowling is an eternal question?" I asked, trying not to laugh.

"Yes," she said with an air of absolute confidence.

"I want to ask," I said, "but I'm a little afraid of what the other eternal questions might be."

"It's not a comprehensive list, but Star Wars versus Star Trek, Dumbledore or Gandalf, and foosball: game of skill and chance or exercise in futility," she said promptly.

I stared at her in wonder. "And how did you come across these eternal questions? Do you have a reputable source or—"

"Years of study," she said, sounding distracted. She leaned forward in her seat, staring out the window. "Wow."

We were in Rachel's subdivision already, and the *thump-thump* of bass from the party rattled my windows from several houses away. Cars, trucks, and a few vans lined the street on both sides. For all of Rachel's talk of exclusivity, it looked like most of the school was here, and the bonfire wasn't even over yet. I'd thought by arriving ahead of the crowd we'd be able to avoid most of the drama. But Rachel must have invited everyone to come over early. Maybe this was designed to function as much as a pre-party as post. Or maybe she'd just wanted as many people as possible to witness what she was going to do to Ariane.

"Yeah," I said grimly. "She's not going to miss a chance to show off. She had to work to steal this party away from Lauren-Whitney Tate."

Ariane looked at me questioningly.

"The bonfire party is always supposed to be at a senior's house, but Rachel convinced everyone to come here instead." I wasn't sure what she had promised to get them to show up, but whatever it was, it had worked.

I slowed down to look for parking, finally finding a spot between Matty's beat-up Volvo and a bright and shiny Kia that I didn't recognize.

I cut the engine, but neither of us moved to get out.

I twisted in my seat to face Ariane. "At the risk of repeating myself, are you sure you want to—"

"No." But she pushed her door open and slid out.

So I guess that answered that. I hurried to follow, catching up with her in the middle of the street.

Taking her hand in mine, I led the way to the wrought-iron gate that divided the backyard from the front. From the corner of my eye, I could see Ariane taking it all in. Rachel's house, a two-story stone monstrosity bathed in floodlights with a hand-to-God pair of matching turrets, was worlds away from the neighborhood of small square houses where she lived.

"Just . . . stay close to me, okay?" I said, feeling as if I were about to introduce a newborn puppy to a pack of hungry wolves. Which was dumb because Ariane had proven time and time again that she wasn't afraid to defend herself or others. It was more the sense of her being untainted, I guess.

She nodded, her expression serious. Too serious.

I squeezed her hand gently. "So, out of curiosity, how do you come down on those eternal questions?"

"Star Wars but only the original three, Dumbledore, and exercise in futility," she said with a faint frown, as if I'd suggested that there might be another way to answer.

I laughed. And suddenly I was glad we were on our way in to see Rachel. The sooner we were done with our "fake" relationship, the sooner I could convince Ariane that giving a real one a shot would be worth it. Starting with bowling, of course.

As we cleared the edge of house, she slowed down. "Something's wrong," she said in a voice so quiet I could barely hear. I turned to look at her. Her head was tilted, her forehead wrinkled in concentration, as if listening for something.

I frowned. I didn't hear anything except the buzzing of a speaker with the bass blown, the shouts and splashes of people in the pool, and laughter and conversation at a level that could probably be heard three blocks from here.

I might have written it off as cold feet, but Ariane didn't seem nervous or upset, just perplexed.

"Are you sure? We can leave," I offered, hoping she'd take me up on it.

She frowned. "It's probably nothing." But she didn't sound convinced.

And as soon as we started up the stairs to the oversized deck, it was clear she'd been right. There was an air of tension, a sense of waiting, hanging over the party. How Ariane had picked up on that before we even saw anyone, I didn't know. But I didn't have time to worry about that right now.

Heads swiveled toward us, and regular conversation dropped off to be replaced by whispering and stares. Confirmation of that gut-level dread I'd been feeling.

I turned to Ariane. "Let's go. We should—"

"You're here!"

I glanced back to find Rachel wobbling her way around the hot tub toward us. She was barefoot and very drunk in a short red dress that swirled around her tanned thighs. "Now the fun can start," she said with a wide and too-perfect smile that in no way disguised the mean glint in her eye.

Oh, this couldn't be good. I frowned. Why the hell was Rachel drunk? She should have been clearheaded and reveling in triumph, not sloppy and staggering.

"Zaney," she said, pouting at me as she stumbled closer, almost tripping over a cooler at the edge of the hot tub. "Remember when we used to call you that?"

I looked for familiar faces in the crowd, for help. But Cami and Cassi were huddled together on the far side of the pool, watching like trauma victims hoping the serial killer was too distracted to remember they were there. And Trey was in the far corner alone, surrounded by discarded red cups and glaring at me.

My God, how bad had it gotten before we arrived? Rachel could be vicious when she was drunk, but most of us in her inner circle were usually spared. Something strange was going on here tonight.

"Yeah, I remember," I said.

"And then your mom left and you got all boring and sad." She heaved a big sigh.

Ariane stiffened.

"You don't want to talk to us anymore, you don't want to have any fun." Rachel's eyes sparkled with tears.

"Rach . . ." I started toward her, feeling a tug of sympathy—we'd been friends for years, no matter what was happening now—but Ariane's hand tightened on mine.

"Don't," she whispered.

Without warning, Rachel went from bad to bat-shit. "And then I have to find out from Princess Monkey-face Ass-kisser over there that you're double-crossing me with that freak," she shrieked, her face nearly as red as her dress.

I followed her gaze to find Jenna Mayborne standing awkwardly by the pool steps in a skirt that looked too tight, a blush rising from her throat into her cheeks.

Oh, shit.

"Jenna," Ariane breathed, her voice cracking with hurt.

I made a decision. It wasn't how I would have preferred to do it, but I didn't have a lot of options. "I'm not double-crossing you," I said to Rachel. "It's real." I wrapped my arm around Ariane's shoulders.

Ariane looked up at me, shocked.

Rachel threw back her head and laughed. Several people around her giggled nervously.

I stayed still, and Ariane slid her hand around my back. Which had an immediately nullifying effect on the laughter, nervous or not. And even though now was so not the time to be worrying about it, I couldn't help but feel relieved. Maybe this would work out after all, assuming we could survive tonight.

"Right, Zane." Rachel swayed closer. "Like I'm going to believe that. Even *you* have better taste." But her voice held a note of vulnerability, and I suddenly remembered Ariane's theory about why Rachel had been so insistent that I be the one to follow through on her plan.

I grimaced. "Rachel, I'm sorry, I didn't mean to—"

Apparently that apology did more to convince her than any attempt at an explanation.

"Son of a bitch," she said with a hiccupping gasp, and staggered back, knocking into the open cooler again, sending ice water sloshing over the side into the hot tub. Somebody squealed.

"Come on, let's get out of here," I said to Ariane. It hadn't gone down exactly the way I'd anticipated, but it was over, at least.

She hesitated and then nodded.

As we turned away, I saw Cami and Cassi edging closer to Rachel, their hands out, whether in defense or in an attempt to be soothing.

"Rach, it's okay," Cami murmured behind us. "It's no big deal."

"Yeah, Rachel, who cares. It's just Zane. It's not like *you* wanted him. . . . Wait. Unless you did?" Cassi sounded confused and even spacier than normal, but volume certainly wasn't an issue. Anyone at the party who *hadn't* been clear on what was going on definitely knew now. Which only made things worse; the scattered whispers became more concentrated and mixed with giggles. People laughing at Rachel. Not good.

I closed my eyes for a second. Cassi, for the win.

I tugged at Ariane's hand, urging her silently to hurry.

"Rachel, don't!" Cami shouted.

Ariane stiffened next to me a split second before something slammed into the back of my knee, sending pain ricocheting upward through my thigh and knocking me off balance.

Reeling, I looked back in shock. A full beer bottle lay just behind me, spinning. And Rachel was digging into the cooler to reload.

"Rachel, what the hell are you—" I began.

She let fly, and I ducked instinctively. The bottle hit the deck, shattering this time, spraying beer and glass in a dozen different directions. The girls closest to me shrieked, their bare legs dotted with foam and speckles of glass. One of them stumbled back, bending down to clutch at her ankle, blood oozing from between her fingers.

Shit. This was getting out of control. I started toward Rachel, my knee screaming in protest.

"Rachel, stop," Cami begged as Rachel dug into the cooler a third time, coming up double fisted, a bottle in each hand. Trey finally seemed to realize something was really wrong, and headed toward us. But he wasn't going to get here fast enough.

Cassi reached in to grab Rachel's hands, but Rachel shouldered her away, and Cassi's feet tangled over the long cooler handle. She fell, her head hitting the edge of the hot tub with a sickening crack.

Everyone froze, horrified. Everyone except Rachel. She was tunnel-vision focused on me.

I never saw the last bottle coming. To be fair, I don't think she was aiming it specifically for my head—she wasn't really aiming anywhere, just chucking anything and everything she could reach in my general direction. And I was distracted, watching as Cami dropped to the ground next to her twin, her mouth a silent O of distress and shock.

The bottle struck the side of my face, opening a white-hot

line of pain on my cheek. The world spun for a moment, giving me an odd view of Ariane. She was taller than me somehow. That was when I realized I'd fallen to my knees. Ariane was motionless, her strange eyes wide and fixed on my face. Then color rose through her pale face, and her mouth turned into a tight line.

"It's okay. I'm fine," I managed through numb lips. I wasn't, though. I could feel warm blood trickling down my cheek and dripping off my jaw, and everything around me had taken on a strangely dreamy, distant feeling. *Head injury. Concussion, maybe. Stitches, definitely.* A voice in my head, logical and unmoved, cataloged my injuries.

People were starting to panic, the air filled with the scent of spilled blood and beer.

"Rachel, put it down!"

"Call 911! Cassi's not waking up!"

"Shari's bleeding!"

But Rachel, swaying unsteadily, ignored them, a bottle still in her hand. Her gaze narrowed in on Ariane, a new target now that I was down.

I looked up to tell Ariane to move, to run, knowing it was too late—but she was already in motion. Heading *toward* Rachel.

Rachel gave an enraged screech and threw the bottle at her.

"Rachel, no!" I flinched, anticipating the thump/shatter of the bottle connecting with Ariane and the ensuing cry of pain.

But instead I heard a collective gasp from the crowd.

Ariane was facing Rachel without fear, her palm out and

up, as though defending herself. But the bottle, the one Rachel had hurled at Ariane, was hovering in midair, about six inches from Rachel's hand, which was frozen in a throwing position.

"They want you to stop, Rachel," Ariane said, her voice calm and matter-of-fact.

I shook my already wobbly head in disbelief, trying to clear the image. Getting hit with that bottle had done even more damage than I'd thought. No, wait, everyone else was staring, too, at the bottle fixed in space like it was some kind of freaky Criss Angel illusion.

Ariane remained impassive as Rachel tried desperately to lower her arm, struggling against some invisible force holding her in place. "How are you . . . what . . . Let go of me, you freak!" Rachel spat, confusion and fear taking precedence over anger.

A weird rippling sensation spread across my skin and made the hair on my arms stand up, and suddenly Rachel wasn't moving at all anymore. Her eyes grew so wide I could see the whites of them from where I was.

"They told you to stop. But you just couldn't resist making him bleed. Hurting innocent people for your own agenda," Ariane said, advancing on Rachel, hatred pouring from every word. "Maybe you'd like to know what it feels like to be on the other side of that decision. Not that you're innocent, of course."

She moved closer. Rachel's face turned red and then an alarming shade of purple. She clutched at the left side of her chest, giving a horrible-sounding gurgle that came from deep within her throat. And still Ariane approached, her hand out and steady, her steps calm and sure.

Ariane was doing this. Somehow. She was making this happen to Rachel.

Dark veins pulsed in Rachel's forehead and throat as she fought to breathe.

I staggered to my feet. "Ariane." I forced her name out, my voice cracked and rusty-sounding. But it was enough.

She started as if she'd completely forgotten my presence. As if maybe she'd forgotten everyone and everything but Rachel. The beer bottle dropped to the ground with a sudden thud. And Rachel fell to her hands and knees, coughing violently as she sucked in desperate breaths.

Ariane slowly turned to face me. The flush of anger had drained away, leaving her even paler than normal—almost gray—as she took in all the people watching.

Her throat worked like she was struggling to find words or she might be sick. She looked small and vulnerable, but there was also something completely unfamiliar about her. Something foreign and frightening.

She fixed a pleading gaze on me, and I looked away, my head spinning with everything I'd seen. Who was this girl? The same one I'd been kissing in my truck just last night? I couldn't make my brain reconcile all the conflicting facts. The question circling my brain was the same one I'd had all along—who is Ariane Tucker? Only now it had a far more ominous tone to it, and I felt even less sure of the answer.

"I . . . I'm sorry," she said to me in a choked voice. Then she turned and bolted for the stairs; and everyone, including me, let her go.

CHAPTER 25

Ariane

I ALMOST KILLED RACHEL JACOBS.

My face hot with tears, I lurched through the gate into the darkened side yard, forcing myself to breathe through the urge to gag. Now was not the time for crying or throwing up. I needed to think.

The barrier dropped and I almost killed her. In front of everyone. In front of Zane.

She didn't give you a choice! She was hurting people. She was hurting Zane.

The all-too-clear image of Zane with blood running down the side of his face, his expression dulled with shock, floated in front of my eyes. And right behind him, Rachel had been preparing to hurt him further. And no one was doing anything about it. No one was stopping her.

Just like her grandfather. Just like GTX.

The bubble of fury, resentment, and fear that I'd been suppressing for days, no, years, had burst forth and something inside me had clicked. Like the combination lock my father referenced last night.

When I'd lifted my hand, it was as if there was no barrier in my head, as if there never had been one. I wanted Rachel to stop, so she did.

I didn't have to struggle or force it into being. No sense of a wall coming down or a door opening up. It was like reaching out for something that had once been impossible to get and having it fall into my hand.

Natural. Simple. Easy.

If only I'd stopped there. But I hadn't.

I'd wanted Rachel to hurt, to be afraid, and that urge had consumed me, blocking everything else out. Her face had turned red and purplish and the vein in her forehead protruded, her heart struggling to keep beating against my will.

And then Zane had called my name. The way he'd looked at me, his face pale beneath the blood, it had just cut straight through me. I'd heard the bitter clanging of fear in his head, like one of those old-fashioned alarm bells that wouldn't shut off.

Then he wouldn't look at me at all. He'd been scared or horrified or disgusted or maybe all three.

And some part of me—soft, hopeful, human—had died in that moment.

Even though I knew better, I'd allowed myself to believe that, with Zane, *who* I was outweighed *what* I was. And that only made things so much worse now.

The force of his rejection slammed into me all over again, stealing my breath, and I had to fight the urge to curl up into a ball in the middle of Rachel's lawn.

I forced myself forward, toward the street, folding my arms across my chest in a vain attempt to stop the tremors shaking my whole body.

It had been a mistake to come here. A mistake I'd added to by not walking out the second I'd realized that Rachel was out of control. Even if it meant leaving Zane behind. That's what the Rules dictated.

It's a little late to be worrying about the Rules now, isn't it? my logical side pointed out. *You have bigger concerns.*

I was whole again, what I'd once been, with all the inherent flaws and dangers. It wouldn't take much to turn me into the weapon Dr. Jacobs had wanted from the beginning. And I'd just done the alien/human hybrid equivalent of skywriting, *COME AND GET ME. I'M RIGHT HERE!*

It wouldn't take long for word to spread about what had happened. Even if none of the people at the party understood what they'd witnessed, the inevitable cell phone videos would be out floating on YouTube, Twitter, Facebook, and God only knew where else in a matter of minutes.

I had to be smart. Make this time count. It was a head start, nothing more.

Following the protocols my father had established, I pulled my cell from my pocket and chucked it into the grass, trying not to feel as if I'd thrown away my life preserver in the middle of drowning. But it was too risky, too easy for GTX to track.

Now all I had to do was get to the half-empty Wygreen shopping center on the other side of town. The Dumpster behind the abandoned Linens-N-Things would have a duffel bag of emergency supplies and cash duct-taped beneath it.

I never should have kissed him. None of this would be happening now if I'd just kept my distance.

Except I couldn't quite bring myself to wish it all away, even after tonight.

Going to the activities fair, pretending to be a regular girl, and forgetting the truth for a while, that had been worth it. And last night, the feel of Zane's hands on me, moving without hesitation . . .

I crossed the street, cursing my stupid too-human heart. This was so not the time to be getting distracted by—

Headlights flashed suddenly, trapping me in their glare. Blinded, I threw my hands up to block the light.

Engines revved, and I heard rolling doors slide open. I blinked furiously, willing my eyes to adjust. But when they did, I saw what I expected, what I feared: men dressed in black with the bright red GTX logo on their shoulders pouring out of vans parked on the street—black vans with the florist logo that I'd seen earlier today. *Retrieval teams.*

My heartbeat exploded in my chest, and I couldn't breathe. My legs went weak and shaky, caught between the urge to flee and the primal instinct to freeze. But a tiny part of me remained calm, unsurprised. Of course GTX was here. They'd always been somewhere around, lurking in the shadows; the only question had been when they would catch up with me, when they would figure out I'd been right here in Wingate the whole time.

But how had they found me so quickly? How had they known I was here? Those were questions I'd have to leave for later.

The first wave of men, plastic restraints in hand, approached in a standard five-formation but without nearly enough caution.

Because no matter how life-destroying tonight's encounter with Rachel had been, it had given me one advantage: the frustrating combination lock on the wall in my head no longer existed. It didn't need to.

The wall was gone. The second I saw the retrieval teams coming toward me I felt the bubbly tingle of power race along my skin, and my head began to ache like a muscle longing to stretch. It was an overwhelming sensation, and it took everything I had not to give in to it.

"Stay away," I said in a choked voice. The warning came from deep inside me. I didn't want to hurt anyone, but I knew I could.

The foremost man on the retrieval team held a hand up. "It's okay. We don't mean you any harm." A trickle of sweat ran down his face beneath his helmet.

I didn't believe him. I wasn't sure if he even believed him.

But it didn't matter. That was all it took.

Something half forgotten welled up inside me and took over, running attack scenarios.

Holding the men in place was a possibility, but it would take a great deal more effort, and it would be hard to contain so many of them. Three teams of five. Fifteen men. Or I could go full-on Darth Vader—

No, there was a much simpler option.

Hit center mass. Force to injure and incapacitate. No kill.

That formerly lost part of me calculated angles, speed,

and force in a blink. And then I *shoved* at the closest team. Not with my hands—that would have ended in disaster—but with all that lovely power dancing along my skin.

The force of the effort took my breath away for a second, but the results were immediate. The five men closest to me flew backward as if a giant arm had come along and swept them away. They collided with the cars parked along the side of the road, cracking windows, denting doors, and making car alarms shriek.

The grim determination to grind my competitors into nothing, to win not by a little but by utter annihilation, was something I kept buried. An inheritance of uncertain origin. Perhaps it came from beings who'd set out to conquer this tiny blue-and-brown ball of dirt—there were those rumors, too, that the single ship in 1947 had been a scout for a larger invasion—or maybe it was from my human side, a primal instinct left over from the caveman days of few people and even fewer resources.

Either way, tonight, when I called on that legacy, it answered, rising up inside me with hot fury. I smiled fiercely, daring my challengers to come closer.

The remaining retrieval teams slowed their approach, reevaluating, and at a command I couldn't hear, they pulled guns from holsters on their backs. Loaded with tranquilizers probably. I would have preferred to confirm that from their thoughts, but I couldn't afford to lose focus.

I only needed one small break here, a chance to slip away into the shadows . . .

A strangled noise came from behind me, and I turned to see Zane at the corner of Rachel's house, staring at the scene playing out before him, a stack of napkins pressed against his bloodied cheek.

The GTX teams reshuffled suddenly, drawing my attention back to them. One of the teams broke off, giving me a wide berth and heading in Zane's direction. I didn't know if that was because they knew who he was or if they just wanted to suppress the possibility of a witness.

Either way, I wouldn't let GTX have him.

No. With a thought, I shoved the team approaching Zane. They flew sideways, landing on the sidewalk with satisfying thuds and grunts of pain.

Behind me, I sensed movement rather than heard it, and turned in time to see darts coming at me. I knocked them down, sending them clattering to the pavement.

That had been close—the retrieval teams had used Zane as a distraction. Obviously GTX was not going to give up easily.

No matter. I would simply have to try harder. I could beat them. They were only human.

I started toward Zane; consolidating our position would make it much easier to defend us both.

"Ariane."

I stopped dead, startled. The voice was familiar. Too familiar. One I would recognize anywhere. It was the voice that had called me out of the darkness and smoke so many years ago.

"Father?" The word caught in my throat, escaping only as a whisper, and this time, my concentration was shattered beyond repair. How did he know where I was? He shouldn't be here. GTX would find him, kill him.

Panicking, I spun around and squinted into the shadows, where his voice had come from. And that was the only opening the team behind me needed. I didn't hear the gunfire, just felt the dart enter my back with a tight pinch, right below the GTX tattoo on my shoulder.

Icy fear washed over me, and I stumbled forward, trying to run.

But the drug was powerful . . . and fast. My legs wouldn't obey. I tried to reach up and remove the dart, but my hand felt heavy, as if it had been baked into the middle of a concrete block.

My knees wobbled, and I went down hard on the asphalt, unable to stop my fall. My head struck the road, igniting a sharp blast of pain, and my vision swirled.

I struggled to keep my eyes open and focused. *Get up, get up! Come on! MOVE!*

I needed to reach my father and get us both out of here.

But I couldn't. I managed to stay alert long enough to see Zane retreating, slipping back toward the party; and then, on the other side of me, a gray-haired man in a GTX security uniform emerged from the street shadows. . . . My father.

My father, in his black security uniform with the bright red GTX logo on the sleeve, loomed over me. "I told you, Ariane," he said, his voice bent and weirdly distorted by the drug shutting my body down. "Rule number one: Never trust anyone."

CHAPTER 26

Zane

"START FROM THE BEGINNING," MY DAD SAID UNDER HIS breath, keeping an eye on the gap in the privacy curtains for the approach of a doctor or nurse. "What exactly did you see?"

"I told you, I don't know," I said wearily. My head was throbbing, and my newly acquired stitches were itching and stinging; but worse than either of those things was a weird feeling of disorientation, dislocation. Like I'd somehow stumbled into a movie. "It didn't make any sense."

It was almost one in the morning, and we were still in the emergency room, waiting for someone to take me for X-rays. Somewhere, on one of the floors above me, Cassi Andrews had already been checked in. She'd been conscious but out of it by the time the ambulance arrived. When the 911 calls came in with the Jacobs's house as the address, my dad had gone out with his guys, unsurprised and yet less than pleased to find me there.

But his displeasure at discovering me among the partiers had been quickly replaced by intense interest when he started hearing the panicked stories about Ariane. How she'd stopped that beer bottle in midair. How she'd somehow made Rachel choke without touching her (or how Rachel choked and Ariane did nothing to help—the story varied). How I was the one who'd brought her to the party.

"I was leaving, going home." Or going to try to talk to Ariane. I wasn't sure if I'd even made up my mind before I'd left. "And they shot darts at her. I watched it happen right in front of me." I shifted the bag of ice on my left knee, which had swollen to twice its normal size, thanks to Rachel's attack. Between that, the stitches, and the possible concussion, I was kind of a wreck.

But nowhere near as bad as Ariane. I'd watched her take that dart and seen her fall with nothing to cushion the impact. The sound her head made hitting the road . . . I swallowed hard to keep my stomach from revolting.

She'd saved me. Those GTX guys had been coming at me—I don't know why, maybe just because I was there?—and she'd swept them away. Looked at them, waved her hand, and they'd flown through the air like they were being pulled on cords.

I shook my head, feeling dazed. I didn't understand any of this.

"Start from the beginning," my dad prompted again, awkwardly laying a heavy hand on my shoulder in what was meant to be an attempt at comfort.

I tried not to cringe. The gesture felt so unnatural coming from him. "Okay," I said.

Making serious effort to keep my good leg from jouncing with the edgy, fractured-feeling energy coursing through me, I started over, beginning with our arrival at Rachel's party. I'd already been through this story several times with my dad, and each time it came out a little less jumbled, which was probably why he kept asking me to repeat it.

Now, hours later, I wasn't any clearer on what had really happened, except that Ariane had done *something*, and men in GTX uniforms had freaking kidnapped her in the middle of the street.

When I got to the part about the silver-haired guy calling to Ariane and how she seemed to know him, my dad slapped his palm against the table. "Son of a bitch. I should have known Mark Tucker was involved. That guy was squirrelly from the start."

Mark Tucker. Ariane's father?

I gaped at my dad. "You think he stole drugs and gave them to Ariane?" How could somebody do that to their kid, turn them into an experiment? It made me feel sick. Had she even known what was happening to her?

I frowned, thinking back on it. She hadn't seemed scared, not right away. In fact, facing off with Rachel, she'd been anything but scared. Calm, collected, and *pissed*. But that was about it.

With the GTX guys, though, it had been different. I'd had a clear view of her, caught in the vans' headlights, and I'd recognized the tension in her shoulders, the carefully blank expression on her face. It was just how she'd looked when I'd first approached her with my idea about Rachel—angry, afraid.

My dad frowned. "It doesn't make sense. If Tucker stole from GTX, why would he use GTX personnel to capture her? Why would he need to capture her at all?" He shook his head. "This stinks of some kind of conspiracy. Exactly what I was afraid of when GTX refused to liaise with the police department." He pointed at me as if I'd had something to do with it.

I resisted the urge to roll my eyes. This was what he'd been afraid of? Really? I never could have dreamed up this scenario in my worst nightmare. But trust my dad to relate everything back to his disappointed GTX ambitions.

"This girl has been running around in our community for years," he continued, working himself up into his speech-to-the-public mode. "We have no idea what kind of danger she presents to us, to the children she's been in contact with."

This time I did roll my eyes. "She's not a danger. She's just a girl." Except even as I said it, I remembered Rachel's face turning purplish red, and I realized I wasn't so sure. I was having trouble reconciling Ariane, the girl in my truck, the one with the shy smile and a kiss that screamed of desperate loneliness, with the one who tossed full-grown men around like chess pieces.

"What are you going to do?" I asked.

My dad tapped his fingers on his chin. "Have to play this one carefully. GTX won't want to let me in on it, but if we—"

"I mean, about Ariane," I said quickly.

He sighed in exasperation. "Zane, what do you want me to do? She's a minor in the custody of her father, her legal guardian. And if what you told me about tonight is true—"

I looked at him in disbelief. As if I'd make any of that up.

"—then she's probably better off contained, where she can't hurt anyone."

"She didn't hurt anyone," I protested. "Not until they tried to hurt her or someone else." And I'd seen every one of those GTX guys get up and limp off, albeit with help from their comrades. Rachel had also recovered just fine. She'd been spitting mad and screeching when I'd seen her last, getting loaded into the back of a squad car.

"Why are you so concerned about this girl?" he asked. "I've never heard you mention her before."

I exhaled loudly. "She's a friend, okay?"

His eyes lit up with sudden interest. "How much time have you been spending with her?"

For some reason, his new enthusiasm made me uncomfortable. I didn't like where it was leading. "I don't know. A lot, the last few days."

He nodded rapidly. "Starting when?"

I had to think. So much had happened recently. "Wednesday."

"The day after the incident with the lights exploding at the school?"

"Yeah. I guess."

"Were you there when that happened?"

Where was this going? "Yeah." I'd been there all the other times, too, when the lights had acted weird. In the cafeteria and the activities fair and . . .

Oh, God. It had been Ariane all those times as well.

The belated realization struck like a slap.

My dad didn't seem to notice. He nodded with a tight smile, distracted. "Good. Good." He clapped a hand on my shoulder, heedless of my grimace. "Stay here. I need to make some calls."

"Dad, I don't understand—"

"They're going to want you," he said impatiently. "Want you to stay quiet. Want to talk to you. Something. That gives us leverage."

I stared at him dumbly, still not getting it.

"You're a witness. That's our ticket in. We can force their hand with this, make them involve our department," he said with a grin.

And then I got it. GTX would probably deny that anything had happened tonight, and that was *if* anyone bothered to ask them. No one else at the party had even seen the GTX guys take Ariane, so there was no connection between what she'd done and the company. And even if someone did put the two together, who would believe jumbled and outrageous-sounding stories from a bunch of drunken kids over the word of Wingate's largest employer? Never going to happen.

But if my dad, the well-known and respected police chief, threatened to get involved and make a fuss over what I'd seen, GTX would have to, at the very least, acknowledge his existence, if only to keep him/us quiet.

My dad was going to use this—use me—to break into the GTX circle of trust, something he'd been after for years. He wanted to be number one on Dr. Jacobs's speed dial when there was trouble, and he thought this was the way in.

I felt sick.

"Be right back," he said, pushing aside the curtains and stepping out.

I sat there and listened as my dad ignored hospital cell phone rules, calling in favors, checking in with his various cronies, and generally making it known to the rumor mill that he had a valuable source in the form of me, his son.

He was probably right. Based on what I'd seen tonight, GTX would want to shut that down, and they'd probably humor him . . . temporarily. And my dad would be happy with me, with the situation for a while.

And Ariane? What about her? She'd probably end up stuck in a small room somewhere in the bowels of the GTX complex, with people poking and prodding at her.

I remembered how she'd first flinched away from being touched. God, no wonder.

I rubbed my hand over my face. She'd probably had people all over her for years, in a scientific capacity. And yet she'd rallied. She'd trusted me. She'd taken my hand even though she'd been leery.

My eyes burned at the memory of last night. Her determination to walk away. And her tears. If only I'd known. When I'd joked about the Witness Protection Program, she'd tried to tell me, in her own way, that she was hiding.

I shook my head. She didn't deserve the fate she was likely headed for.

My dad let loose with his interview laugh on the phone, the big booming one that said *Everything's okay as long as I'm around*. Then he stuck his head back in my room and winked at me.

The shock of it took my breath away. My dad saw me as worth something for the first time, I realized. The younger son, the other Bradshaw boy finally had value. After all those years of trying to make my dad proud, trying to make him see me, I'd actually succeeded.

But there was no rush of relief or joy or even just satisfaction at the accomplishment. I was empty. Hollowed out.

I looked down at my hands, remembering the sensation of Ariane's hand in mine. Light, tentative but trusting.

And suddenly I felt smaller and less important than ever.

CHAPTER 27

Ariane

YOU KNOW THOSE FIRST FEW MOMENTS AFTER WAKING from a bad dream, when you're convinced that your nightmare is real, and there's an impossibly large coil of dread in your stomach? But then slowly, details from the dream slip away and reality slides into place. You didn't miss your bio final, you didn't walk into school naked, the evil corporation that created you didn't recapture you. . . .

Oh, wait.

I felt an all-too-familiar rough cotton sheet pressed against my cheek. Then the overwhelming smell of antiseptic mixed with cedar chips.

No. I opened my eyes to see the edge of a cot draped in a white sheet, and a spotless white tile floor stretching out underneath me.

No, no, no! I couldn't be here. I couldn't be back in this place. My stomach lurched, and I struggled to push myself up, but my arms and legs felt floppy and awkward, as if they belonged to someone else. Hot tears flooded my eyes, unsticking the contact lenses that had dried out during my unconsciousness.

"Careful now. Go slowly, my dear." Dr. Jacobs's voice, echoing a little through the overhead intercom, was as gentle as ever.

I froze, breaking into a cold sweat at the sound of it.

"You're still under the effects of the sedation. Don't want you falling and hurting yourself. You've already got a nasty bump to the head."

Once he mentioned it, I became aware of a dull throbbing at the back of my head. A souvenir from my adventures with the tranq dart in the street. It was real. It was all real.

A surge of panic gave me the strength to flop over onto my back and roll into a semi-upright position, using the wall for support. The room looked as I'd left it, as if there'd never been an explosion the night I escaped. In the far right corner, the toilet, the shower, and a sink, behind a curtain that could be pulled for privacy. Directly across from me, white plastic shelves of teaching toys and games, books, and videos for the flat screen embedded in the wall above the shelf. In the far left corner, a rolling tray with a glass cage on top. Inside, a little white mouse ran on a metal wheel, pausing every few seconds to lift his nose up and sniff the air, as if he knew something was wrong.

I couldn't breathe. I pulled at the neck of my shirt, struggling to suck air into my lungs, which felt more like two shredded plastic bags for all the oxygen they were capable of holding at the moment.

White sparkly spots flitted through my vision, signaling

the approach of unconsciousness. I flopped forward, bringing my head down to my knees, on the command of some distant voice in the back of my brain that remembered the protocol to prevent fainting. *Being passed out and vulnerable right now is a bad, bad idea,* that same voice whispered.

But I was beyond appreciating that bit of wisdom.

I can't be here. I can't. I can't. The refrain, once started, wouldn't stop, growing louder and louder and blocking out everything but a dull buzzing in my ears.

"It's just a panic attack. Breathe through it. You'll be fine."

The sound of my father's voice over the intercom, calm and comfortingly familiar, broke through the static in my mind and triggered my last firm memory—the one of him standing over me in his black GTX uniform, reciting Rule #1: *Never trust anyone.*

My head snapped up. My father. He was here. And he . . . he'd *betrayed* me.

The little bit of air that I'd managed to take in caught in my throat, and my brain refused to process, stuck in a loop of disparate facts. He'd saved me, protected me. And he'd called GTX down on me? It didn't make sense. Why now? Why at all? There had to be another explanation.

Except . . . what other scenario, besides betrayal, would end with me back in this room?

Unfortunately, I already knew the answer with a sickening certainty—there wasn't one.

As though a switch had been flipped inside my brain, my panic converted to fury, hot and reassuring, eating away all my fear and confusion.

I turned my head carefully, my neck wobbly, toward the wall on my left. It held both the sheen of glass and the illusion of opaqueness.

"Show me. I want to see you." My voice came out cold and tight with a fine tremor running through it.

The white wall went translucent in a blink of an eye, and the observation room came into view. The room itself was several feet higher, like my quarters had been dug deeper into the ground. *The better to see you with, my dear.* The line from a book of fairy tales, one I'd read in this very place, ran through my head, and I shuddered. Monitors, machines, computers, printers—diagnostic equipment of all kinds lined the left and right side of the room. Several lab-coated professionals sat in front of them, their heads down, studying the data being spat out.

Dr. Jacobs stood dead center in the window-wall, less than ten feet from me. Picture the kindest, most grandfatherly-looking man you can imagine. Curly gray hair, plump apple cheeks, twinkling dark eyes that seemed to find the amusement in everything. That is, unless I chose to tell him no. I knew from experience those laughing eyes could change to hard little marbles, cold and uncaring, in the space of a single word.

My father stood immediately to the left of Jacobs. His GTX uniform was pristine, as if the events of tonight had left him untouched, and his gaze was fixed at a point well over my head.

At the sight of him, contradictory impulses screamed within me—the first to run to him and seek comfort, and the second to back as far away as I could from this stranger who'd shared a home and a breakfast table with me for ten years.

"You turned me in?" I asked him. "Why? Because I broke your Rules? Because I went to a party?" In spite of my best efforts, I could hear the pleading in my voice along with a cracking that mimicked the pain in my chest.

The muscles in his jaw tightened, but he kept his gaze fixed on the wall above my head.

"You're not even going to look at me?" I demanded, knowing I sounded hysterical. "I think I deserve at least that."

"Oh, don't fuss," Jacobs said impatiently. "He didn't betray you. For that, he would have to have been on your side to begin with."

Those words hit with a virtual thunderstrike in my head. What did that mean?

My father turned to glare at Dr. Jacobs, who waved his hand dismissively. "It's not like she wouldn't have figured it out eventually."

I stared at them both; the gaping hole in my life I'd just discovered had turned out to be a bottomless pit. "What are you saying?"

Dr. Jacobs shrugged at me. "You didn't leave us much choice. You were refusing to cooperate, and you're far too valuable to destroy." He smiled and tilted his head closer to the glass as if preparing to tell me a secret. "Do you know you are the only one at this facility to have survived and thrived for this long?"

GTX-F-*107*. 106 before me. I'd suspected as much, but having it confirmed made me feel ill. How many of my kind—some mix of human and other—had lived and died in this little room?

Jacobs nodded, pleased with himself. "I think the illusion of freedom was good for you."

It sounded like . . . Was he saying my whole life on the outside had been a lie?

No. That couldn't be. I shook my head, wincing at the resulting pain. But my brain, slowly pushing off the last effects of the drug, worked through the logic, against my will.

The attack on GTX the night I'd escaped could have been real, or the whole thing could have been engineered to create a solid story.

I hadn't been stupid, even at that age. If they'd opened the door and let me walk free, I would have been suspicious. Maybe not right away, but eventually.

Instead I'd been spirited away . . . from the scene of a major crime at a highly security-conscious company, hidden in an oversized gym bag that, somehow, no one had even questioned or bothered to check.

I felt dizzy suddenly. My escape had been too easy. Way too easy.

"Our psychological expert suggested that the block in your abilities might be unconscious and that the only way to 'undo it,' so to speak, was for you to feel safe again. You also needed practice in pretending to be human and blending in." He frowned. "You always were an odd little thing." He brightened. "So we just moved to Phase Two—cultural indoctrination—of the project a little sooner than planned. We couldn't have you wandering around on assignment, saying and doing things that would call attention to yourself. Now you can pass through a crowd unnoticed."

I'd fallen right into their plan, I realized. Walked in step with it as if I'd known what they were intending all along.

"But the Rules," I protested weakly.

"We had to do something to keep you from getting too involved, too close to the good citizens of Wingate," Dr. Jacobs said. "Letting you wander with some autonomy was quite the risk for us, even with Tucker supervising. Our entire project could have been shut down if you'd decided to tell someone the truth."

The Rules hadn't been about protecting me. They'd been covering their asses. All the time, effort, and worry I'd devoted to those Rules . . . I'd just been helping them, aiding in my own captivity.

Hot acid rose from my stomach into the back of my throat, and I made it to the toilet, barely, before vomiting.

My life as I knew it was over. No, worse than that—my life as I knew it had never existed. My head was throbbing, a tight band of pain around my forehead and through the back of my neck. Every part of me was screaming to shut down. To close my eyes and simply pretend I was somewhere else.

In the background, I could hear Dr. Jacobs yammering on, as though he hadn't noticed my distress. More likely, though, he simply did not care. ". . . it's taken us far longer to get to this point than I'd initially hoped. We'd anticipated it would only take a few months for you to break through the block, not ten years." He laughed. "So we're running short on time. Laughlin has set up trials for next month in Chicago. But I know you will soundly defeat the hybrids from his lab," he said with pride in his voice. "I've heard rumors that they can barely speak."

Hybrids. That caught my attention, and I turned my head carefully in his direction. Did he mean others like me? There were others like me, still alive? And defeat them how?

The name, *Laughlin.* It sounded vaguely familiar, as though I'd heard it before, years ago.

"First things first, though." Dr. Jacobs clapped his hands briskly, the sound delayed a millisecond over the intercom from the action I saw through the window. "You must change your clothes and take out those contact lenses. You look ridiculous. Like a monkey wearing a suit and glasses."

I looked down at myself. I was still wearing my pink shirt, though it was torn at the shoulder and streaked with dirt and grease from the road. I couldn't see myself in the mirror, but I could feel the lenses, gritty in my eyes. In any other situation I'd have been glad to get into something clean and take out the contacts, which I hated anyway. But to do so at Dr. Jacobs's command?

I didn't move.

Dr. Jacobs sighed. "You're not going to start this again, are you? Not even here a few hours and already you're forcing me to resort to threats. Young lady, I don't like to threaten."

No, he *loved* to threaten. I ignored him, turning my attention to the man I'd once trusted with my life.

"Was your daughter even real?" I asked, swallowing hard over the lump in my throat. "Or was that just another manipulation? Something to make me feel like I could trust you?"

Mark Tucker's gaze darted toward me for a second, and I saw that his eyes were rimmed with red. Stress, lack of sleep, or did he actually care?

"I took a photo, did you know that? From the box in the basement," I continued.

He looked at me, startled.

"I think it's a school picture," I said. "Probably her last one."

He winced.

"Was that something I was meant to find, a GTX tech's weekend adventure with Photoshop?" I persisted. I needed to know what was real, needed to see something from him, some kind of reaction. "I mean, it was a hell of a bargain, two made-up daughters, one to fool the other—"

"Ariane—"

Jacobs intervened. "Enough of this. Mark, thank you for your service. Finish your rounds and wait for me in my office." He waved him off—it was so odd to think of him as "Mark," but I would *not* think of him as my father. Never again.

Mark waited a beat, staring Jacobs down before turning abruptly and leaving the room.

"You've really got him quite conflicted. I believe he's grown quite attached to you." Far from sounding disturbed by this, Jacobs seemed almost pleased, like I'd performed some kind of admirable trick. "We had to put the cameras up in the school when we learned your powers were returning and he hadn't reported it."

Only because I hadn't yet reported it to him, I thought bitterly, pushing myself to my feet slowly, my knees protesting their time on the hard tile floor.

"And he refused to bring in the Bradshaw boy last night. Did you know that?"

I looked up sharply, caught off guard. Damn it. He'd surprised me, mentioning Zane so casually. There went any chance I might have had at pretending I didn't know or care about Zane.

"Oh yes, we know all about him," Jacobs said.

Even though I'd expected this—my fath . . . Mark Tucker had warned me—I still felt the blood rush from my head at the implied threat. "You can't touch him," I said quickly. "He's a minor and one of your precious humans."

Jacobs shrugged idly. "If I have his father's permission, I can do anything I want."

Would Zane's father give him over that easily? Not if he knew what Jacobs intended, but nothing was stopping the good doctor from lying. Plus, he had that whole pillar-of-the-community thing going for him. I couldn't be sure Zane's father would check into the situation thoroughly before sending Zane over.

My shoulders sagged. And even if Zane's father did manage to keep him away from GTX, what would be next? Would Jacobs haul in every person I'd ever spoken to? Everyone who'd been, if not kind, at least not cruel? I couldn't do that. I couldn't let him hurt innocent people on my behalf.

"Now, we have a lot to do before the trials next month," Jacobs said, consulting a clipboard. "The Department of

Defense is such a stickler for documentation and details."

You could kill him, my logical side offered softly. Even with the wall between us, all I had to do was direct that newly recovered power in my head to squeeze his heart until it no longer had the strength to beat—just as he'd had me do to Jerry. Just as I'd almost done to Rachel.

He's old. It probably wouldn't be that hard. The cool and unemotional analysis made me feel vaguely nauseous again. I didn't want to be that person. That's who Jacobs wanted me to be, even if he didn't want to be the target.

A tapping on the glass wall startled me into paying attention again.

"You may think I don't know you, but I've spent years reading Mark's reports, and I've studied the photos and videos from our surveillance teams. I've seen that expression on your face before, particularly when confronted with my delightful granddaughter. So bloodthirsty," he said with a chuckle. "Exactly what we wanted. But let me clear one thing up for you: that door"—he pointed to the transparent door set in the glass wall, through which I could see the start of a generic white hallway—"only opens to my palm print."

And I knew from experience that nothing short of an explosion would take out the glass wall.

Which meant killing Jacobs wouldn't do any good. He'd die on the other side of the glass and the door would still be locked. I'd be trapped in here, unable to escape, waiting for someone to find me. And I wasn't foolish enough to believe they didn't have a contingency plan, with or without Jacobs. If I became too violent, too uncooperative. Against my will,

I looked up at the air vents in the ceiling. The room was airtight. I was sure that was not a coincidence.

"I think maybe you need some time to settle in," Jacobs said decisively, putting his clipboard down.

The mouse in the cage, as if sensing a change in the air, abandoned his wheel and scurried to the far corner of his habitat, scattering cedar chips.

"A fresh uniform is under your pillow," Jacobs said. "As always."

Without meaning to, I glanced over at the cot, seeing the neatly folded pile of white fabric beneath the pillow. I'd spent years trying to disappear, to not be seen as an individual among the humans. That uniform would accomplish it in a second. The moment I put it on I would become nothing. No one. Again.

"We can work on getting you some more age-appropriate reading materials and videos. Perhaps some of the items you enjoyed during your time with Mark?" he offered.

Just the idea of my possessions—reminders of my life outside—being trapped in here with me, like a mockery of the freedom I'd thought was mine, made me want to scream.

"I want you to be comfortable here. This is your home, after all," he said with the same gentle smile he'd given when he'd left me to go hungry in the dark, years ago.

Tears of frustration and fear burned in my eyes, and I turned away swiftly before he could see them.

"Oh, 107, do dispose of that mouse sooner rather than later, would you please? I feel as though I can smell the stench from in here."

Then the intercom clicked off, and when I risked a glance over my shoulder, the glass wall had flashed to solid, leaving me alone in a deafening silence.

Time passed slowly in the white room, with nothing to break the monotony. I'd forgotten about that.

I sat on the edge of the cot, attempting to take up the least amount of room possible. The lights had been dimmed to the "nighttime" setting. I was tired, my head hurt, and I wanted nothing more than to lie down, close my eyes, and try to gather my fragmented thoughts. (As if having a better grasp on the situation would change anything.)

But it felt like if I allowed myself to relax, I was accepting my fate, resigning myself to whatever Jacobs had planned.

And I couldn't do that.

So the uniform remained folded beneath the pillow. And I'd named the mouse out of sheer obstinacy. "Pinky" was alive and well, spinning furiously in his wheel, first one direction and then the other, like he wasn't sure which way he was supposed to go.

I watched Pinky spin and tried to stay awake, a small act of rebellion and the only one available to me at the moment.

I didn't know how much time passed—and I might have dozed off while sitting up, despite my best efforts—but suddenly the wall flashed to transparent, letting in the light from the observation room, and startling me into looking up.

On the other side of the window, my . . . Mark Tucker approached. And my heart lifted with hope even though I *knew* better. It was as though the years of habit, of trusting him, relying on him, just weren't ready to die.

The sole lab tech in the observation room stepped in front of him, trying to stop him.

The intercom wasn't on, so I couldn't hear what Mark said, but I saw the tech cringe and then scurry through the door. Some kind of threat, no doubt.

A second later, Mark's voice sounded in my little room. "Ariane."

Hearing him say my name—was it really my name anymore?—tore at something fragile inside me.

I shifted on the cot, giving my back to the glass wall. "I don't want to see you. Ever again," I said, disgust thick in my voice.

"I'm not going to beg you to understand," he said finally. "I'm not sure there's anything I can say that would make this okay."

Hmm. You think? With effort, I swallowed back the words. Engaging only made it worse, reminded me of all the conversations and moments from *before*, when I hadn't yet known he was a lying, traitorous bucket of pond scum. When I'd believed he actually cared about me. It hurt to remember that time. And I hated that it hurt almost as much I hated my own stupidity and foolishness for believing to begin with.

"I just wanted you to know, my daughter is real. Was real," he said, and I heard the pain in his voice. "Everything I told you about her was true."

"Except?" I prompted dully without turning around. There had to be something I was missing.

"Except Dr. Jacobs promised me the best in experimental treatment for her if I took this . . . assignment," he said.

And there it was. My heart fell. Of course. He would have done anything for *his* Ariane. "But it didn't work," I said, clearing my throat against the lump growing there.

"No, it didn't," he confirmed. "But the research they're doing here, it's important, so I agreed to stay on. They told me that your immune system attacks and destroys irregular cells and cell growth. If GTX can keep their funding and figure out how to recreate that in full-blood humans, do you know what that would mean? No more cancer. No more sick children spending their short lives in and out of hospitals."

I sat back, stunned. I knew they'd taken all those tests and samples years ago for a reason; I just hadn't known what it was. Assuming that Jacobs was telling the truth, the good of the many always outweighed the good of the few. Right? What was one not-so-human child in light of all those who would be saved? Except when that not-so-human child is you.

"But if I'd known then what I know now. If I'd known you . . ." He shook his head. "I am so sorry," he said, his eyes bright with tears. Tears for me. Not for the other Ariane.

"Then get me out of here," I said, choked by a swell of emotion.

He swiftly wiped his eyes. "I can't. I wish I could. Jacobs has the door set only to—"

"His palm print," I said, disappointed. I'd hoped, foolishly, that the good doctor had been exaggerating for effect. "I know. He told me. Wanted to make sure I didn't kill him in an escape attempt. Though, I'm still considering killing him just for the fun of it." The brittle bitterness in my tone startled even me, and I realized I wasn't entirely sure if I was joking.

To my further surprise, my fath . . . Mark didn't seem shocked by my statement of (potentially) murderous intent.

He looked over his shoulder, anticipating the return of the frightened lab tech, no doubt. "You heard Jacobs mention the trials with Laughlin and the other hybrids."

"What do you know about that?" I asked, suddenly suspicious.

"Not much. Jacobs expects you to win."

I made a frustrated noise. "But what does that mean?" I had visions of arena combat, boxing matches or competitions to see who could redirect the most M&M's.

"I'm not sure. But"—he hesitated—"I know it's to the death."

I froze. "What?"

Mark glanced at the door as if he'd heard a noise, before leaning closer to the intercom. "You may not believe that I care about you, but I do," he said quietly. "And that's why I'm telling you: commit, Ariane. Undergo the training Jacobs sets out for you. Kill the mouse. Do what he tells you, whatever you have to do in order to survive. It's your only chance."

Then, as the lab tech returned with several reinforcements, Mark Tucker straightened up and walked away without a backward glance.

CHAPTER 28

Zane

I WASN'T SURE WHETHER IT WAS MY POSSIBLE CONCUSSION—and the medical requirement to keep me awake—or my dad's newfound discovery of my value that prompted him to bring me to work with him.

Either way, we went straight to the station after the ER doctor pronounced me only slightly broken.

My dad left me to cool my heels in the waiting room under the vigilant eye of the desk sergeant, while he closed the door of his office to, no doubt, continue his GTX scheming.

In the hard plastic chair I was painfully aware of every bump and bruise from the night, and there was nothing except an ancient copy of *Ice Fishing Quarterly* to distract me from the ceaseless churning of my brain.

Was Ariane okay? Had she woken up yet? Had she woken up at all?

I'd assumed that they'd knocked her out. But who knew what was really in those darts?

My chest felt tight at the idea. The memory of the girl

laughing in my truck, crawling into my lap to kiss me contrasted so sharply with my last image of her, lying so quiet and still on the pavement, like a puppet whose strings had been violently and irrevocably severed.

Thinking of her helpless like that, it made me feel ill.

I remembered what she'd said to me earlier: *If you knew the truth, you wouldn't be so quick to sign on.*

And last night, when she'd tried to wish me well. To say good-bye.

She'd known this was a possibility. She'd been trying to protect herself—and me. But I'd pushed her into continuing. I'd goaded her, through Rachel, into going to the party last night.

God, I was such an asshole.

Ariane had accepted me for who I was, without expectations or demands that I be better. And how had I repaid her? By turning my back on her. Maybe not literally, but only because I'd been too busy staring at her, just like everyone else.

And why? Because of something outside her control. If my dad's theory about the missing growth hormone research was right, it was all Mark Tucker's fault. I mean, I was pretty sure Ariane hadn't asked her father to steal drugs and give them to her, or whatever it was that he'd done to her.

She probably hated me for being a coward. I couldn't blame her. I hated myself for that too.

I'd wanted Ariane to trust me, encouraged her to take that leap, and then, at the first test, I'd been proven completely unworthy. Even worse, it was my fault she was in that situation, at the party and facing off with Rachel, in the first place.

Now Ariane was gone, and there was nothing I could do. She was with GTX. I *hoped.* That was the best alternative I could come up with.

And if GTX had somehow known what was going on, known what her father was doing to her, did that make the situation better or worse? Human experimentation—I was pretty sure that was illegal and something GTX wouldn't want a lot of people knowing about.

Still trying to wrap my brain around what had happened, and my own part in it, I stared out through the heavily tinted windows of the waiting area, watching the sun come up in shades of gray.

I wasn't the only one up—or still up—at dawn, though. To my surprise, some of my classmates were apparently still in custody from the party last night. And as I sat there waiting for my dad, other parents I recognized—including Trey's very pissed off dad—came in to collect their wayward and hungover offspring. Trey gave me a sheepish and pained nod as he passed me.

Rachel was the last one to emerge from the cells at the back of the building, at the behest of a nervous and timid-looking man with a briefcase. I didn't recognize him; he was probably someone in the employ of Dr. Jacobs. A lawyer, maybe.

The man stayed at the desk, filling out the paperwork required, but the second Rachel saw me, she made a beeline. "This is your fault," she hissed, jabbing an accusing finger at me, her high heels swinging in her hand. "You and your freak girlfriend."

I was *not* in the mood for Rachel. "Yeah, and you had nothing to do with it," I snapped, sitting up straight.

"What the hell was that last night? You put people in the hospital. And Cassi's going to be okay, by the way, in case you were wondering."

She glared at me. "Did you miss the part where that Ariane girl almost killed me? I couldn't breathe!"

"You seem to be breathing just fine now," I said dryly. "And she was only trying to stop you." Okay, and maybe a little more. A little vengeance had been at play, perhaps. Ariane had been angry, I knew that. But she'd shown more control and caused less damage than Rachel, who had no such excuse.

"God, she has you completely under her spell." Rachel narrowed her eyes at me. "You know she has freaky mind powers." She gave an exaggerated shudder. "I'm glad they're going to be chopping her up and putting her under a microscope or whatever."

Everything seemed to slow down in that second, leaving Rachel's words hanging in the air like some kind of horrible cartoon speech bubble. "What are you talking about?" I managed to ask.

She didn't hear me. "I mean, seriously. Did you know I had to spend the whole night back there? The dirt is never going to come out," she said with fury, looking down at her dress and her filthy bare feet.

I snapped my fingers, earning her attention and another glare. "Rachel, focus. What did you just say about Ariane?"

She rolled her eyes. "Ariane, everybody always wants to know about Ariane," she said in sneering, mimicky tone. "When I talked to my grandfather to get me out of here, that's all he wanted to know. Nothing about how I was or the fact that I was in freaking jail," she said bitterly. "He was all, 'What exactly happened? Who talked to her? What did it feel like when she targeted you?' You mean, aside from almost dying, Grandpa?" she scoffed.

"Rachel—"

"And she's not even a person, you know? She's a thing. An experiment."

The thick layer of hate in her voice stunned me. "Just because her dad stole some drugs and—"

"No," she said sharply. "Grandpa said they've been treating her for some kind of weirdo condition or something for years."

I stared at her, not sure if I should believe what she was saying. "He told you about Ariane?"

"When I wouldn't answer his stupid questions at first, yeah."

"Did he . . . do you know what's going to happen to her?"

Rachel frowned. "What difference does it make? She's locked up, which is exactly where she belongs." She touched her chest carefully, as though there were bruises from her ordeal, but I couldn't see anything. "Wait," she said, holding up a hand and cocking her head to the side in disbelief. "You don't actually *care*, do you? She is a complete freak of nature, someone who should never have been walking around free. She's dangerous."

In the face of Rachel's determination to make me see how wrong I was, the vague shape of an idea began to form in the back of my brain. I needed to see Ariane. I couldn't just let her disappear, not without at least trying to find her. And Rachel loved nothing more than being right and taking the opportunity to rub it in your face.

"So you say," I pointed out.

"You need more proof than last night?" she demanded. "I almost *died*."

I shrugged.

Her mouth tightened. "You want to see her."

"Unless you can't get me in," I said.

"I can get anything I want," she fired back immediately.

"Good. Let's go. She had me fooled, and I want to see for myself." I stood up, my heart beating way too fast. Would Rachel really go for this? Would it be this easy?

"No," she said, regarding me with suspicion.

Damn.

"You can't just stroll into a secure facility, Zane," she said with scorn. "It takes time." She eyed me speculatively. "Tonight, maybe."

"Fine." I sat back down easily, as if it didn't matter to me. Maybe it really did take time. Or maybe Rachel just wanted to see me squirm. Either way, I didn't care. As long as she got me in.

"They've probably got her locked up in chains or something," she said, testing me.

I shrugged again. "Just want to see for myself."

"Oh, you'll see," she said with a dangerous smile. And I knew I had her for sure. Rachel *wanted* me to witness Ariane being treated like the bizarre science experiment she believed her to be. Now, whether Rachel could actually pull it off and get me inside GTX, that was a whole other issue and one I couldn't control. I'd done my best and that would have to be enough. It *had* to be. I couldn't just abandon Ariane. I'd given up and stopped fighting on far too many important things in my life already.

"Mr. Erickson," Rachel bellowed, in the direction of the nervous-looking man, "let's go!"

The man hastily scrawled his signature across one last piece of paper, scooped up his briefcase, and hurried after her.

Once they were out the door I slumped back in my chair, the rush of adrenaline fading and the pain in my head returning.

"What was that all about?" my dad called, startling me.

I swiveled in my seat to see him at the desk, frowning after Rachel and her lackey.

I hesitated. If I told him what I'd gotten Rachel to agree to, he'd probably be thrilled and insist on tagging along to GTX. Protecting his "in" to the company. And that would draw way more attention to us than I could afford. It might even stop the whole thing dead.

I couldn't take that chance.

"Nothing," I said finally. "Just Rachel being Rachel."

He nodded slowly, clearly skeptical. "Don't mess this up for me, Zane," he warned, pointing a finger at me.

I nodded, maybe a little too quickly, and he turned away and went back into his office.

I let out a slow breath. If and when my dad found out that I'd gone to GTX without him, he'd be furious. As in, an all-consuming make-my-life-hell kind of fury.

So, in other words, he'd despise me only a little more than he normally did.

Totally worth it.

CHAPTER 29

Ariane

DR. JACOBS SIGHED LOUDLY WHEN HE SAW ME SITTING on the edge of the cot, still not wearing my uniform.

Hours had passed since Mark Tucker's visit, I was pretty sure. The lights had grown brighter—the daytime setting—some time ago, so it was probably early Saturday morning by now. I hadn't moved except to draw my knees up to my chest to combat the chill of the air system kicking into higher gear.

"107, while I appreciate your determination, which will serve you well in future—" Jacobs began.

"Were you telling the truth?" I asked, my voice raspy from disuse and lack of sleep. I'd been waiting for him, to ask this. "What you said to Mark, I mean. About my immune system and maybe saving people who are sick." I hadn't been able to shut off the thoughts circling in my brain.

Dr. Jacobs stopped, and closed his mouth with an audible click. Then he gave a forced laugh. "I suppose I shouldn't be surprised that he managed to slip in here and talk to you."

I waited.

He cocked his head to one side, eyeing me. "Would *that* make a difference to you?"

Oh no, I wasn't falling for that. "Is it true?" I persisted, my chest tight.

"I have always been honest with you—"

"If not particularly specific," I shot back. That was always his loophole. I hadn't forgotten who I was dealing with.

He ignored my slam. "—so, yes, the research is promising. But we need the funds from the military for additional work, and for that, we have to win at the trials. Trials you are not qualified for yet."

I didn't even want to know what constituted being "qualified."

Shivering, I hugged my knees closer. If he was telling the truth about the research, then suddenly everything I wanted seemed so much smaller and insignificant. Who was I to put my dreams and wishes ahead of those who were just trying to *survive*?

"But 107, the most important thing is for you to accept who you are, to live up to your potential. You are a miracle of human ingenuity and scientific development." He sounded way too pleased with himself for his role in said miracle.

Yuck.

"You weren't created for high school, dates, and football games," he said with disdain.

My mind instantly flashed back to those heated moments in Zane's truck, and a blush spread across my face. How much had GTX seen?

"You are meant for so much more," Jacobs continued. "To use your skills, take down the enemy, save lives. This is who you are."

I stood up and crossed closer to the window wall. "You mean, someone who blindly follows orders, jumps at the command of whoever is holding my leash, and hurts or kills people without compunction, including other hybrids like me?" I asked. "That's what you really mean, isn't it?"

His mouth tightened. "Mark talks too much."

"I assume it's true, then." I folded my arms.

Jacobs waved away my words impatiently. "None of that matters right now. Everything I'm asking you to do at this moment is something you've done before." He leaned closer to the wall and stared me down as if he could will me into action. "Change your clothes. Kill the mouse. Baby steps, 107. That's all."

Yeah, and if I let him, he'd baby-step me right into Hell.

I returned to my cot.

He sighed. "You know I can make this painful for you."

I swallowed hard. I did know that. All too well. And it might not even be torture for torture's sake, but simply more medical tests. Those were bad enough.

He shook his head. "I don't understand why you're fighting this."

"Because fighting is the only thing I have left," I snapped. Whatever pain he inflicted on me would still be less than what I'd feel the second I gave in.

"If I opened the door to your room right now, where would you go?" he demanded. "Who would be looking for you? Who would be happy to see you?"

His words struck deeper wounds than I glared at him. "The Rules—"

"Oh yes, the Rules limited your life so severely." He rolled his eyes. "Do you honestly believe that's true? That if you'd suffered no such restrictions, your human life would be full of friends and loved ones?"

I opened my mouth to argue.

He tsked at me. "Do you think I don't know how hard it was for you to blend in? To adjust, to fit in?"

I felt the truth of his words sink in, but I shook my head. "Because I was afraid to stand out," I protested. "I thought you were hunting me—"

"That wasn't the only reason, and you know it," he said quietly. "You don't belong in that world, and you must have felt that every day of the last ten years, whether you're willing to admit it or not."

To my horror, my eyes welled with tears. "You should know; you made me this way," I choked, my vision blurring.

"I do know," he said in an almost gentle tone. "And that's why I'm telling you. You belong here with us, 107, doing what you were created to do."

Another tech appeared behind him, holding out what appeared to be a cell phone. Dr. Jacobs snapped off the intercom and turned to hear whatever the man had to say.

I took the opportunity to twist around on my cot so Dr. Jacobs couldn't see me blinking rapidly to keep from crying.

My head was spinning, and I was so tired and suddenly unsure. Why *was* I resisting? My outside life was a lie. And he was right: there was nothing—and no one—to go back to. What was the point?

I sniffled, trying to take a deep breath and clear my thoughts. My whole life I'd been caught between two sides—emotional against logical, human vs. other—warring inside me. And as I sat there, I realized that for the first time ever, they were dangerously close to agreeing.

Surrender now, and survive to fight another day. If you push too hard, he might decide you're not worth the effort, logic whispered.

You could help people, my emotional side urged. *Maybe not in the way he wants, but if you can save one person from what happened to the real Ariane Tucker . . .*

"No," I whispered.

"What, my dear?" Jacobs returned to the intercom, though he sounded distracted.

I turned to face him. "No," I said, raising my voice even as the sheer weight of hopelessness descended upon me. I still wanted a life of my choosing. I couldn't change that, even if it would be better for me to forget it and do as I was told.

Dr. Jacobs didn't respond right away, more focused on the cell phone than my refusal.

He looked up with a distant smile. "Well, clearly, more incentive will be required."

Incentive. I tensed. What did he mean by that? Nothing good.

"Fortunately, I believe I'm in a position to get exactly what we need, and soon." He waved the phone at me with an all-too-pleased expression.

Panic lit up my insides. Who was on that phone? My fath . . . Mark Tucker? Zane?

"Wait. Wait!" I shouted, lurching off the cot as though I could follow.

But Dr. Jacobs ignored me and charged out of the observation room, into whatever lay beyond it, leaving only a gape-mouthed tech staring after him in his wake.

CHAPTER 30

Zane

I HADN'T BEEN SURE IF RACHEL WOULD ACTUALLY FOLLOW through on her promise to get me into GTX, even after I'd gotten her text midafternoon:

> Tonight. 9pm. Pick u up.

But now, just moments from arriving at GTX, I had to admit that it seemed like she might really be intending to do exactly what she'd said.

"I could have just met you there," I said, resisting the urge to hold the handle above the door as Rachel took the turn onto the GTX campus a little too fast. Of course, driving myself would have meant sneaking the truck out too, which would have made things more difficult. But it might have been safer.

"Are you kidding? I'm not missing a second of this," she said with grim smile.

Right. Being there to witness Ariane's humiliation and my belated realization that I'd been completely and utterly wrong was the only reason Rachel was going along with this.

I turned away and watched the light from the street disappear as we wound our way deeper into the heavily wooded GTX property. The company was backed up to a forest preserve, creating the illusion of a small city rising up out of nowhere.

I'd been to GTX a few times on field trips in grade school, but tonight the sprawling complex looked even bigger than I remembered. Most of the lights were off, so it appeared to be this hulking indefinable mass barely detectable in the darkness. A sleeping monster.

Rachel's name and attitude got us past the guardhouse, to the parking garage, and into the main building, but when we crossed the expansive and fancy lobby—as in marble floors and a gold statue of Dr. Jacobs in a water fountain—to the elevator bank, we ran into trouble.

Rachel passed up the two standard elevator doors for a smaller one on the far side. The entrance was guarded by only one guy behind a desk, though he was certainly big enough to be two. Dude was dressed in the standard black GTX security uniform, and it looked like they'd stitched together two uniforms to make his. The nameplate on the tiny-by-comparison desk indicated his name was Joey.

I slowed down, but Rachel was not the slightest bit intimidated. She marched past him to stand in front of the elevator and then looked over at him with an impatient huff. "Push the button already."

Oh, boy.

But the mountain named Joey seemed unconcerned. "That's Dr. Jacobs's private elevator."

"Yes, I know," she said with exaggerated slowness. "Do you know who I am?"

He shrugged one enormous shoulder. "Doesn't matter. Dr. Jacobs doesn't want to be disturbed."

"Call him," she said, her hand on her hip. She'd changed for our nighttime adventure into jeans and a red tank top with a gold scarf tied around her neck. With her huge, expensive-looking bag slung over her shoulder and her toe-tapping impatience, she looked every inch the privileged granddaughter of the CEO.

And still Joey wasn't going for it. "No," he said flatly.

"Uh, Rachel, maybe we should just . . ." I began.

She glared at me and then turned her attention back to Joey. "Call him. He's expecting us."

"He's what?" I asked, stunned.

With a skeptical expression, Joey picked up the phone and punched a few buttons.

"Your grandfather is expecting us?" I whispered.

"Of course," Rachel said, exasperated. "How else did you think we were going to get where we needed to go? It's classified or top secret or something. They're not putting her up in a conference room with the accounting department."

Oh, this couldn't be good. I'd envisioned sneaking in, maybe stealing a few minutes alone with Ariane, making sure she was okay. And for a moment or two I might have even entertained the fantasy of getting her out, like hiding her in a cart of laundry or something.

(Okay, so clearly, escape plans are not my forte.)

But a documented, official visit, one that other people would be aware of? I wasn't counting on that, and the ramifications that it would bring, mainly in the form of making my dad really, really pissed.

Joey put the phone down with a loud clack, catching our attention. "Dr. Jacobs says you can go up," he said with a frown.

I kind of felt the same.

Joey pushed a button and the doors opened, revealing an interior that looked more like something out of a fancy house than a corporation—heavy carpeting, shiny wood walls, and the smell of money.

Rachel sailed ahead, and I followed slowly. Some part of me was screaming that I should just forget it and get out now. But I'd come this far, and another chance in the future seemed pretty damn unlikely. Rachel would lose interest, and I'd lose her as my access point.

The doors closed silently, and we began moving upward with barely a jolt.

The elevator doors opened onto hallway filled with more of the same luxury. Plush carpeting, polished wood walls, and artwork in gold frames.

Rachel moved with confidence to the double doors at the end of the hall with me a step or two behind her.

She pushed open the doors and stood back to let me in. A massive desk stood in front of a wall of windows overlooking the dark GTX park. Two smaller chairs huddled before it, similar to the "you're in trouble" seats in the principal's office. A leather couch sat on a thick Oriental rug. Dr. Jacobs was nowhere to be seen (except in the form of a portrait hanging over a well-stocked minibar).

Rachel flopped onto the sofa and stretched out with a

casual disregard for the expensive leather beneath her heels.

"Now what?" I asked, stuffing my hands into my pockets and fighting the urge to pace.

"We wait," she said with a shrug.

In the hallway, the elevator chimed and we both looked in that direction. Rachel sat up quickly and swiveled to sit in a more formal position.

Heavily padded footsteps sounded for a few seconds before Dr. Jacobs pushed through the half-open doors. He spotted his granddaughter immediately. "Rachel, sweetheart. I'm so glad you're here."

Then he looked at me, a curious, evaluating expression passing over his face. "You must be Zane."

"Yes, sir." I stepped up and offered my hand.

He shook it. "Jay Bradshaw's youngest," he said with a hint of amusement in his voice. "Does your father know you're here?"

I hesitated. "Not yet."

He laughed as if this were the funniest thing he'd heard all day.

I winced. I couldn't escape the feeling that I was missing something. This was way too easy.

"So, what can I do for you on this fine evening?" he asked, sounding almost giddy as he moved to pour himself a drink.

I hesitated. If Rachel was to be believed, it was not Ariane's father who was primarily responsible for her existence and her capture tonight, but rather the man standing in front of me. Choosing the right words would be important.

I fought against a swell of helplessness. This was so much

more Quinn's area, or my dad's. "Well, uh, sir, I was hoping that it might be possible to—"

"He's in love with your pet," Rachel interrupted with a mocking smile.

I glared at her.

"Well, you are."

I should have known that working with her was a bad idea.

But Jacobs didn't seem angry or annoyed. He paused with the glass on the way to his lips. "Really?" he asked, intrigued. "I was given to understand your interactions with her had their basis in a prank." He leveled a look at Rachel, who shifted uncomfortably on the couch.

"Yeah, in the beginning, but . . ." I paused, mindful of Rachel's hawklike attention to my every word. "I'd just like to see her. Please," I added.

Rachel snorted.

Dr. Jacobs put his glass down on the minibar, below the painting of himself wearing a stern but paternally fond expression. "Well, certainly. I'm glad she has friends."

I stared at him. "What?" This was not the captor-captive dynamic I'd been expecting.

"I am not her friend," Rachel said sharply at the same time.

Dr. Jacobs smiled at me. "She's not a prisoner here. It's for her own good."

Except, how many bad, bad things had happened to people under the label of "for your own good"? I knew of a few in my life alone.

"We tried introducing her to fully human society," Dr.

Jacobs added, "but you saw how well that turned out."

Fully human . . . The words echoed in my head. Meaning what? Ariane wasn't?

"Come on. This way," he said cheerfully, leading us out into the hall.

I hung back a bit as Dr. Jacobs called the elevator. Something was wrong here. I couldn't quite put my finger on what it was, other than that he seemed blissfully unconcerned with our presence at GTX and our interest in something that had to be classified.

"This isn't right," I whispered to Rachel. It shouldn't have been this easy. We hadn't signed any papers or even promised to stay quiet. I mean, maybe Dr. Jacobs was counting on Rachel's family loyalty, but what about me?

He must have had something in mind. I had no idea what that might be, and I did not like the feeling.

"No kidding," Rachel said bitterly. "Did you hear the way he talks about her? He's never that interested in me."

Not exactly where I'd been going with that, but okay.

The elevator doors opened, and Dr. Jacobs stepped in, Rachel on his heels with her arms sullenly crossed. After a moment, I followed. I was just getting this sudden overwhelming premonition that I didn't want to go where this elevator would take me. And that maybe, somehow, nothing would be the same when I came back up. I wasn't stupid; being an inconvenient witness who asked too many questions might prove to be a fatal condition. I probably wasn't the easiest person to dispose of quietly, given my dad's job, but I wasn't sure enough of that to completely rule out the possibility.

I swallowed hard as Dr. Jacobs inserted a key into the elevator panel and the doors closed.

Too late to worry now.

It seemed to take forever before we slowed in our descent and then stopped. The elevator doors opened onto a blindingly white hallway, as sterile as the one upstairs had been plush.

Without another word, Dr. Jacobs stepped off the elevator and exited into the too-bright hall. I could see a large opaque glass door with a couple of steps leading down to it. Closer to the elevator, an open doorway loomed on the right, with the low sounds of conversation and a rhythmic beeping coming from within.

"Come along." Dr. Jacobs headed toward the open doorway.

I wasn't sure what I was expecting to see inside the room. Some kind of prison cell with Ariane behind metal bars, maybe. Instead, this room resembled a high-tech lab. It was filled with equipment, computers, monitors, printers—a dozen or more things beeping and humming all at once.

Two harried-looking lab techs in white coats looked up, startled.

"Sir—" one of them began, frowning at Rachel and me.

Jacobs waved the tech's concern away. "Go. Now," he ordered. "Close the door after you."

After a second of hesitation, both techs pushed away from their computers and left the room.

Once the door closed after them, Dr. Jacobs turned to us with an eager smile. "Do you want to see her?" His hand hovered over a panel at the front of the room. I hadn't noticed it before, but the wall seemed to be made of glass painted white. Or something . . . It had a glossy sheen to it.

"I know she'll want to see you," he continued.

"Yes," Rachel snapped.

"No," I said at the same time, my attention caught by a set of monitors to Dr. Jacobs's right. I stepped closer for a better look.

The bottommost flat screen showed a small white room with a cage containing a small animal—a mouse or a hamster maybe—on a little running wheel, and a cot on the right-hand side. A girl sat on the cot, her back against the wall and her knees drawn up to her chest. It took me a second to recognize her as Ariane. She seemed so much smaller due to the overhead angle of the camera and the white prison-type uniform she wore. If she'd been easy to miss at school, she was damn near invisible here. Her pale blond hair looked darker, damp maybe, and stuck to the sides of her face. It made the point of her chin and angles of her cheeks strikingly prominent and distinctly strange.

"Fascinating," Dr. Jacobs said near my ear, making me jump in surprise. I hadn't heard him approach.

"She must care for you a great deal." He looked at me with renewed interest. "She changed her clothes," he explained with some excitement, as if that should mean something to me. Then he squinted at the screen again. "But," he said with a sigh, "it appears the mouse is still alive."

I gaped at him, having absolutely no idea what to do with that nonsensical statement.

"She knows we're here," Jacobs whispered, sounding delighted.

Glancing back at the monitor, I found Ariane standing up and staring directly into the camera. My heart stuttered in my chest. The wide darkness of her eyes shocked me. I was used to seeing them as the murky blue of her contacts. There didn't appear to be any difference between the irises and the pupils—all dark.

"She must be quite tuned in to your thoughts," Dr. Jacobs said.

I didn't know what to say. "She can hear what I'm thinking?" I immediately tried to reconstruct everything I'd been thinking in her presence over the last few days. *Oh God.* My face burned in embarrassment, thinking about what she might have "overheard."

"Not all the time," he said, as if I'd asked something absurd. "It would be far too overwhelming for her human side."

There it was again: that strange emphasis on the word "human." If she wasn't human, what was she?

"But strong thoughts or emotions come through clearly." Dr. Jacobs cocked his head to one side, frowning at me. "Exactly how close are you to my girl?"

Just the way he said that was skeevy, *too* interested, and I shuddered. Ariane . . . how bad was it for her to be trapped here with him?

"Enough talking," Rachel snapped. "Let's get this freak show on the road."

Before anyone could say anything, she pushed forward and punched the button Dr. Jacobs had indicated earlier.

I sucked in a breath, not sure what would happen, and the wall in front of us shifted from white to translucent.

And there was Ariane, on the other side of the glass, staring back at us.

CHAPTER 31

Ariane

ZANE WAS *HERE.* AND HE WASN'T ALONE. I BARELY HAD time to accept that jarring bit of reality before the glass wall flickered and went translucent.

Zane was standing next to Dr. Jacobs, staring down at me, his mouth open slightly as if startled by the sight of me. He appeared unharmed, thankfully, except for a distinct pallor to his skin, like the kind that came with receiving a major shock.

Oh God. I closed my eyes, my face burning with humiliation. Being a freak is one thing. Being a freak in a cage is so much worse. And if Dr. Jacobs told him about my nonhuman heritage . . .

Most people didn't even think aliens really existed. And among those who did believe, "my" relatives had a bad rep. Little, gray, and creepy. Known for cattle mutilations, abductions, and an extreme fascination with probing of all kinds. Not that any of those rumors were true, as far as I knew. Except for the being little and gray—that bit was accurate, as far as I could tell, based on my own physiology and the Internet, of course.

"Zane," I whispered, not sure what to say, afraid of making things worse. I didn't want to see him look at me with disgust; that fear would transform me from Ariane, a girl he knew, to a *thing*. An alien freak.

And yet, that was pretty much unavoidable at this point.

It wasn't that I expected anything from him in the future. Obviously. But I guess . . . I wanted Zane to think of me somewhat fondly, without the memories being completely tainted. How very human of me.

It's not what it looks like. I can explain. I wasn't lying to you, not exactly. I'm sorry. None of those options seemed to fit the situation.

"See? I told you," Rachel said with a smirk.

Up until now I'd ignored her and her loud thoughts in favor of focusing on Zane. But now I realized she was the one in front of the wall control. She'd brought Zane here and then pulled the cover off my cage, so to speak. I didn't know whether it had been at her grandfather's request or out of her own desire to torture me. But either way, she was still a bitch.

I stared her down, and she didn't move, just watched me, her eyebrows raised in challenge. And never in my life did I more fully hate the wall keeping me in here.

The air bowed and flexed around me, and from the corner of my eye I saw Dr. Jacobs move swiftly to check a monitor a split second before a wooden chessboard from the shelf of toys and games smashed into the wall.

Rachel shrieked and jumped back, her hands flying up unnecessarily to protect her face.

I smiled, filled with gritty satisfaction at that small victory, and followed up by sending the chess pieces into the wall in front of her like a hail of bullets.

Which wasn't particularly smart because they broke apart the second they hit the glass, sending the splintered remains ricocheting at high speed back toward me. Plus, Rachel barely even flinched, having figured out that nothing could get through the wall.

I redirected most of the shrapnel, but I missed one or two and felt a sharp jagged edge snag my cheek as it passed, opening a cut in a bright spot of pain.

In the room above, Dr. Jacobs ignored everyone and everything, grabbing a fresh printout and comparing it against something in a bright orange folder. Zane was shouting at Rachel, pointing at me, and she shouted right back, jabbing an accusing finger at him. The intercom was off, so I couldn't hear what either of them was saying.

I couldn't resist one more swipe at Rachel and sent the Risk board at the wall with a loud smack.

Distracted by Zane, Rachel jumped in surprise, and then glared at me.

Dr. Jacobs looked up, half dazed, and stepped between Rachel and Zane to adjust something on the control panel, and the intercom popped to life. He backed away and gestured toward Zane with a "go ahead" motion before returning to his folder and papers with a frown.

"Ariane," Zane said. "Are you okay?" He sounded worried, which simultaneously warmed and broke my heart. I could hear Rachel's strident voice in the background as she talked to her grandfather, but not what she was saying. She was too far from the mic. Thankfully.

I raised my sleeve to wipe at my cheek. The blood looked so red on the white, but not red enough, probably. Not human enough. "I'm fine. You shouldn't be here."

Zane looked around the observation room and then at my little white room with a frown. "I don't think anyone should be here."

For some reason, this show of faith, even after all he'd seen, brought tears to my eyes.

I looked away. "I'm dangerous." The words slipped out before I could stop them, my worst fear spoken aloud.

"Yeah?" He shrugged. The gesture was a little stiff, but he was trying. "I bet you're hell on checkers, too."

I couldn't help it, I laughed, though it came out resembling a sob.

"Listen," he said more quietly. "Is there someone I can call? Someone who can help you or—"

"No. You need to leave right now," I said. If Dr. Jacobs would even let him. As I watched, the doctor stepped around his granddaughter and picked up the phone on the wall, pressing a quick succession of buttons before hanging up. Something bad was coming, I could feel it. "Zane, I'm serious. You need to contact your father." He might not be much help, but something was better than nothing. "Do you have your phone?"

His mouth tightened. "I'm not going to leave you here."

"You don't have a choice."

He pulled his cell from his pocket and looked at it. "No bars," he said after a second.

Of course. "Does anyone know you're here?" I asked, hearing the desperate edge in my voice.

Zane frowned. "What are you not telling me?"

Behind him, two men in the black GTX uniforms I knew all too well stepped in.

No. I rushed at the wall and pounded on it. Zane stepped back, startled.

"You don't have to do this," I shouted at Dr. Jacobs. "He didn't do anything. Please!"

Jacobs didn't spare me a glance; he simply nodded at the security team.

"I'll do it!" I said in a panic. "I'll do anything you want. Leave him alone." I couldn't watch them drag him away to whatever fate Dr. Jacobs had devised for him. It would be clever and cruel, I knew that much.

Zane looked from me to the security guys. "Ariane, what's going on?" he asked, tension in his voice.

"Don't," I pleaded with Dr. Jacobs.

Then I watched in shock as they clamped their hands on Rachel, not Zane, and pulled her from the room. She was too startled even to scream.

Dr. Jacobs, his expression grim, followed.

"Run," I urged Zane in a low whisper. I had no idea what was going on, but an opportunity like this would not happen again. "Go before he gets back."

"I can't," he whispered. "The elevator is locked."

"What about a place to hide? Did you see anything?"

"What is going on?" he demanded.

"He's going to try to use you to make me cooperate, to make me kill," I said flatly.

Zane's eyes widened. "What?"

The door to my little prison opened, and Rachel tumbled in, a blur of dark hair, red shirt, and gold scarf. She landed on her knees as the door snapped shut.

I couldn't have said which of us was more surprised.

Rachel scrambled to her feet, her ankles wobbling in her too-tall heels. "You do not touch me, you little freak. You stay away."

Somewhere along the way, Rachel had failed to notice that I didn't need to touch her to cause harm.

She backed up toward the door and turned to pound on it. "Let me out!" she shrieked.

Dr. Jacobs appeared in the observation room again, his face drawn. If I didn't know better, I would have said he was upset. But then again, that would have required a soul.

"What is this?" Already, my room felt smaller with Rachel yelling. I seriously hoped this was not Dr. Jacobs's attempt to motivate through negative reinforcement. As in, Rachel would stay in here with me until I cooperated. That might actually work.

Dr. Jacobs approached the microphone. "The GTX reputation is at stake. The trials are in less than a month, and we don't have time to waste. I've tried to appeal to your logical side, but perhaps I've been going about this all wrong." He held up the orange folder in one hand and the new printouts in the other. "It seems your emotional response is the key."

Zane looked at me in confusion. "Trials?" he mouthed at me.

I ignored him, focusing on Dr. Jacobs. What did any of this have to do with Rachel being in here?

"I can't haul young Mr. Bradshaw around with us everywhere, jabbing at him like some kind of oversized voodoo doll to get you to behave. You'll never *win* that way," he said, his disappointment clear. "I need you to remember who you are. You are not human, no matter how successfully you may masquerade as one."

I winced.

Zane edged closer to the microphone. "You keep saying that about her," he said, his gaze bouncing between Dr. Jacobs and me. "Why?"

He doesn't know?

Jacobs looked startled, as though the answer should have been obvious.

"Don't," I said quickly. "Please."

But he didn't hear me, or pretended not to. "She is, quite simply, a masterpiece," he said to Zane. "My crowning achievement, a seamless blend of human and foreign DNA—"

"Stop!" I protested. "He doesn't need to—"

"In layman's terms, a hybrid. Human and extraterrestrial," Dr. Jacobs finished.

My shoulders slumped.

"Extraterrestrial. You mean . . . alien?" Zane gaped at him. "Like, little green men?"

"What?" Rachel stopped her pounding on the door to stare at her grandfather and then me.

"Gray, actually," Jacobs said to Zane. "But you've got the right idea."

Zane paled.

Crap. I closed my eyes for a second, opening them just in time to see Rachel bend down and pick up some of the scattered chess pieces from the floor and throw them at me.

They bounced off me harmlessly. "I cannot be in here with this . . . thing," she shouted at her grandfather, and bent down to scoop up more game pieces.

Pushed well past the point of patience, I reached out mentally and held her still. "Enough already."

Rachel struggled to move, but got nowhere for her efforts. "Let me go!"

"No," I snapped.

"Excellent," Dr. Jacobs murmured, watching us intently.

I froze, a very bad idea occurring to me in the form of a question I should have asked from the beginning. "What are the requirements for the trials?" I asked, feeling a slow swell of dread. "What do I have to do to qualify?"

"There's just one," Dr. Jacobs said in that clipped, clinical tone I'd learned to hate. "End the life of an enemy combatant with documented proof of such."

"What?" Rachel looked at me, her face pasty white.

Yeah. That's what I was afraid of.

CHAPTER 32

Zane

Alien. The word echoed in my head, blocking out everything else. The idea was ridiculous, laughable even.

Except . . . Ariane was short and thin, so breakably fragile. Her pale skin was not that of a redhead; it was more of a pure white, maybe what would come from blending human skin color with that whitish gray of an alien. And all the things she could do—that wasn't normal.

I took a step back. One of the flat-screen monitors caught my attention. It was flashing data, numbers, and charts I couldn't make much sense of. At first.

One screen was labeled HUMAN and seemed to be indicating norms for blood pressure, temperature, heart rate, respiration, and other measurements on a human-shaped diagram. A second later the screen flipped to a different diagram, one I recognized almost as quickly as the first, though it took my brain a second to process what I was seeing.

Under the label FOREIGN, the screen showed similar diagnostics scrawling across an image of small body—thin arms and legs, large head with a demonstrably pointed chin. The only thing missing was the traditionally gray skin and the oversized dark eyes.

I swallowed hard. What Dr. Jacobs said was true. Ariane really wasn't human. At least, not entirely.

"Her death. And verifiable proof of it?" Ariane asked, her voice thinner over the intercom than in real life.

That brought me back to the conversation at hand. I looked up sharply, unsure what was going on. It sounded like a negotiation.

Dr. Jacobs nodded.

"What will you give me if I choose to cooperate?" Ariane asked.

Definitely a negotiation. Involving death? "Wait, what?" I stepped back up to the intercom.

Rachel rushed up to the window, her face blotchy and smeared with tears. "Get me out, Zane! She's going to try to kill me!"

"Not try," Ariane said with a shrug.

She could do it, I knew that. She'd almost done it last night.

"Grandpa?" Rachel whispered, her gaze searching his face.

But he looked away.

Rachel gave a shriek that was equal parts terror and outrage and ran to the door to pound on it. "Let me out! Someone let me out!"

Wide-eyed, I looked to Dr. Jacobs, who sighed heavily.

"We're all called upon to make sacrifices in the name of science. We need a documented death to enter the trials. And"—he opened the orange folder in his trembling hands and held it out to me—"it seems 107 responds to Rachel as a threat, based on recent incidents."

I shook my head. His words made sense individually, but put together they were word salad. "Trials. What are—"

"A competition between 107 and other similar, though inferior, creations from my opponents," he said impatiently. "An important government contract is at stake."

He was serious. The man next to me, whose face was in the paper every other day, who had a freaking permanent place on the parade stand next to my dad every summer during the Wingate Fourth of July parade, was proposing murder in order to enter some kind of *game*.

"You can't just go around killing people as part of an experiment," I said, aghast.

He tsked at me. "Don't be so naïve. If you'd paid any attention at all to history, you'd know there's a long tradition of doing exactly that. Collateral damage. Acceptable for the greater good."

"But Rachel's your granddaughter!" I blurted, unable to formulate a stronger argument through my shock.

"I should ask someone else's family to make the sacrifice instead?" he asked mildly. "This is my life's work. I bear the cost.

"What do you want in return?" he asked Ariane, resuming their discussion.

I stared at them. How in the hell had I ended up here? Then again, maybe it wasn't so bizarre that Dr. Jacobs was suggesting killing his own flesh and blood when the girl I'd been making out with just the other night was *half alien.*

I turned my attention to Ariane, looking so small and yet so dangerous on the other side of the glass. Despite the new information I had, this was the same girl who'd sat in front of me in Algebra II last year. The one who'd seemed so lonely and vulnerable, wounded by the depictions of aliens as scary, ugly, or violent. The one who'd intervened last night to stop people—humans—from being hurt.

I leaned closer to the microphone. "Don't," I said to her. "You don't have to do this. It's crazy."

"Crazier than my being in here? Crazier than what I am?" she asked, her dark eyes damp and shiny with tears.

Damn. I tried a different tack. "Remember how you were all over me about making my own decisions? This is the same thing." I could hear the desperation in my voice. This was important—not just in terms of Rachel's life, but in who Ariane was going to be. I could sense the fork in the road looming ahead. This would change her. How could it not?

But Ariane didn't respond. She just looked from Dr. Jacobs to me, calculating in some way.

I kept pushing. "Rachel is a pain the ass, yes—"

Rachel took time out from her panicked flailing at the door to step back and glare at me.

"—but she doesn't deserve to die. Please."

Ariane tipped her head to one side, her strange, too-dark eyes considering. "If I do this, you release Zane," she said to Jacobs. "Never bother him again. That's what I want."

"No!" I shouted.

"Of course," he said immediately, as if it were nothing to him.

"What?" Rachel shouted, her hands clutched in fists.

"He's lying to you!" I couldn't be sure of that, but it only made sense. Why would he do what Ariane wanted when he wouldn't even refer to her by name? And if he was willing to have his own granddaughter killed, he sure as hell wasn't going to leave me alive as a witness.

Ariane nodded slowly, but I couldn't tell if she was responding to me or Dr. Jacobs.

"Stay away!" Rachel stumbled out of the corner, trying to put more distance between herself and Ariane, a hopeless effort in such a small space. She reached the bookcase and started hurling books toward Ariane, who raised a hand and shunted them aside without even looking.

It was frightening and impressive.

Then Ariane turned to face Rachel, who went very pale and still.

"No," she whispered, visibly trembling. Her cheeks were wet with tears and her nose was running.

My stomach twisted.

"You aren't seriously going to let this happen, are you?" I asked Dr. Jacobs.

He reached out and snapped off the intercom. "We need the funds from winning the trial. That's all. Are you honestly telling me that one spoiled girl's life is more important than all those who will be saved through the medical and military advancements from this project?" He gave me a forced, polished smile, his eyes blazing with a creepy passion. It reminded me of my dad's arguments for the greater good that were more about his own advancement.

Jacobs was slick, I'd give him that. But even if everything he said was true, it wasn't his choice to make. To control Ariane's life. To end Rachel's because he needed his stupid proof. No way.

I turned away from him and focused on Ariane. *I know you can hear me. You can't come back from this. Please!*

She tensed but didn't look at me. Instead she stepped toward Rachel, her hand out and her mouth moving quickly with words I couldn't hear.

Rachel looked both pissed and terrified.

Oh God, Ariane was really going to do it. I turned away. "I can't watch this."

"Don't worry. It'll be over quickly," Dr. Jacobs said. "All we need to do is document her actions and confirm the death—"

I bolted for the exit, and he didn't try to stop me. That was because the door to Ariane's prison was not just locked but sealed. A scanner with the outline of a hand on the glass sensor was set into the wall.

I heard Rachel scream—Jacobs must have turned the intercom back on—and through the transparent door I watched Ariane back her up against the wall simply by walking toward her.

With a cold smile, Ariane leaned toward her, whispered in her ear, and Rachel screeched to bring the house down, tears dark with mascara rolling down her cheeks.

Then Rachel suddenly went quiet, the silence ringing in my ears. It was last night all over again as Rachel clutched at her chest, her face turning red.

"Ariane!" I pounded on the door. "Stop!"

Rachel dropped to her knees with a painful thump, and Ariane moved out of the way, as cool as you please.

A moment later, Rachel collapsed forward onto the floor, her whole body limp.

Ariane turned to look up at Dr. Jacobs in the observation room. "Satisfied?"

He ran into the hall and down the few steps, a stethoscope around his neck and a case marked with a heart and a lightning bolt in his hand. A portable defibrillator? I'd seen them at the police station.

"Move," he shouted at me.

I stepped aside as he slammed his free hand against the palm scanner, and the door hissed open.

He rushed inside, and I followed. The door snapped shut behind us.

Rachel wasn't moving, her eyes closed and hands lying slack at her sides. I'd never seen her so quiet and still. I hadn't always liked her or agreed with what she did, but she was still one of my oldest friends. Or, she had been.

I stared at Ariane. I couldn't believe she'd done it.

She avoided my gaze, folding her arms over her chest in a defensive posture. "You reap what you sow," she said quietly, her attention focused on Dr. Jacobs.

"Really?" I demanded. "That's the only thing you have to say?"

Dr. Jacobs knelt at Rachel's side and turned her over. He put the stethoscope in his ears and cracked open the defibrillator case in preparation. At least he was going to try to save her.

He looked up at the camera in the corner of the room. "Documentation of GTX entrance qualification," he said in a loud voice.

But only after he got what he wanted, of course.

"Time of death—" he began.

Before he could finish, Rachel sucked in a deep breath and sat up, sputtering and coughing.

I stumbled back, shocked.

Rachel glared at Ariane. "Do you have any idea how hard it is to hold your breath for that long?"

CHAPTER 33

Ariane

FRANKLY, I THOUGHT RACHEL OVERSOLD IT. SO MELO-dramatic, falling to her knees. Please.

But given that she was working with the three seconds of instructions I'd managed to whisper to her, it wasn't so bad. And apparently it had been believable.

Zane sagged in relief as she coughed and sputtered.

Dr. Jacobs jolted as though he'd been electrocuted. Then he stood abruptly and began backing toward the door.

"No." I reached out and held him still, without moving from where I stood—all the lessons in this very room paying off.

"You didn't do it," Zane said in wonder, as he moved to Rachel's side to help her up.

I was not entirely successful at squashing the spurt of jealousy at the sight.

"No, instead she almost killed me because I had to hold my breath for freaking forever." Rachel scowled at me. "What took you so long?"

"I'm sorry. Would you have preferred the real thing?" I asked.

She gave an indignant huff.

"You two conspired," Dr. Jacobs said, sounding like a man who wasn't sure what he was seeing. "But you hate her. You perceive her as a threat," he said to me, as though he was piecing events together. "And emotion is the trigger for you."

"Except, as you so clearly pointed out to Zane, I'm not just one thing or the other," I said, working to keep my voice even. My whole life I'd been torn between the two voices in my head, feeling like I had to choose a side: I was either an alien weakened by my humanity OR a human tainted by the strangeness of my "foreign" DNA.

But the truth was, I didn't have to choose. I was both. And that was an advantage, not a flaw. At least in situations like this, where someone was trying to manipulate me by counting on my allying myself to one side or the other.

"I might hate Rachel, but that doesn't make me stupid." I smiled tightly. "And you of all people should know the strategic value of a common enemy." I looked to Rachel, who shrugged at her grandfather.

"She wanted me to pretend. You wanted me to die. Not a hard choice," she said bitterly. "You just wait until Mom and Dad find out about this."

He gave a strained laugh, startling all of us. "Darling, even if they believe you, do you think they will care?"

Rachel stiffened and then started toward him, murder in her eyes.

"Ignore him," I said to her. "Let's just focus on getting out of here." I was suddenly aware that all I'd done was trap Zane and Rachel in here with me.

"I don't take orders from you," Rachel snapped, but after one final glare at her grandfather, she backed off.

"I'm going to let you go," I said to Dr. Jacobs, "and you're going to open the door for us."

He laughed again, but with less confidence. "Why on earth would I do that?"

"You will," I said. "The only question is whether it'll be the easy way or the hard way. I'm betting that scanner doesn't recognize whether you're conscious or not. Or alive or not."

Zane frowned.

Dr. Jacobs looked at me, surprised. "You're threatening me now?" A faint smile crossed his face. "Perhaps I haven't failed as thoroughly as I thought."

"Just open the door." I released him but stayed ready. He'd have to move fast to get through the door before I could stop him, but I wouldn't put it past him.

Only, he didn't even try. He didn't do anything, remaining fixed in place as if I still held him there. "You'll never make it out of the facility," he said.

"So you say," I said, but I could feel an urgency creeping up on me. Killing him would be the smart thing to do. But I suspected it might only make things worse later down the line. I'd be a murderer, on top of everything else.

"Even if you do escape, where will you go?" he asked gently. "You have no money, no resources."

Evidently he didn't know about the duffel bag of cash and supplies stashed under the Dumpster at the abandoned Linens-N-Things. Or maybe the bag wasn't there. I'd never seen it with my own eyes. Mark Tucker had just told me about it. It was hard to know what to trust when your whole life turns out to be a lie.

But it didn't matter; there was no way in hell I was staying here. He had to know that. Why was he even trying?

"There are far worse things out there than your life here," he persisted.

I frowned. I was missing something. If he was so sure I wouldn't get out, then why was he bothering to—

His gaze darted toward the door, and I caught the first clear whisper of his thoughts.

. . . should be here any minute, lazy bastards . . . pay them to make regular rounds.

He was waiting for the guards. "So, the hard way," I said with a nod.

With a gesture, I shoved him into the corner that was my little bathroom. His head hit the shower tiles with a loud but satisfying smack.

Zane winced. "Ariane!" For the record, Rachel wasn't the least bit perturbed.

I hurried over to check on the doctor. He had a bloody gash on his temple, but he was still breathing, a state I was willing to bet I'd regret at some point.

"Help me drag him," I said over my shoulder. I wasn't sure skilled and careful levitation was in my repertoire yet, and I didn't want to waste time trying when we could move him the human way almost as quickly. "We need to hurry. The guards have a regular rotation. They'll be here any minute."

Rachel and Zane joined me—the former with an annoyed sigh—and with an effort, we dragged him over to the wall scanner. I was careful not to look at Zane in the process. Since he'd been here, I'd done only what I had to do, but I couldn't possibly have proven myself to be more strange, more alien than if I'd set out to do just that. I didn't want to know what he thought of me.

I lifted Dr. Jacobs's limp hand up to the scanner—it barely reached from his position prone on the floor—and the lights across the top flashed. After a second or two, during which I thought my heart might stop from fear, the door clicked open.

"Go," I said, dropping his hand. The two of them rushed out, and I followed, just a step or two behind.

In the hall, as the door clicked shut behind us, I waited for an alarm to sound, for someone to shout, but there was nothing but cool silence. Instead of feeling relieved, though, I felt only the growing pressure to get as far away from here as possible.

I looked at Rachel and Zane waiting in front of the elevator. The door was open, but they weren't going in.

"What's wrong?" I asked, suddenly envisioning guards inside, their weapons pointed.

"He had a key. . . ." Zane began.

Oh, damn. The key to the elevator. Some strategy expert I was turning out to be. I glanced back at Dr. Jacobs, out cold in my former room.

"Go back in and get it," Rachel snapped, her tone at odds with her anxious fidgeting, her fingers wrapping and unwrapping around the ends of her scarf.

"I can't," I said. "The scanner is set only for him."

"Maybe there's another way out," Zane said, not sounding particularly hopeful.

No, there wouldn't be but . . .

"Come on." I hurried past them into the elevator and pressed the button.

"Not much point without a key," Rachel singsonged. She was still leaning against Zane, though I was convinced that was, by now, thoroughly unnecessary.

"Shut up," I said. The doors rolled open, revealing a wood-lined elevator with thick red carpeting. I'd been unconscious or in a duffel bag during my previous rides in here. Nice to know Dr. Jacobs didn't spare any expense when it came to his accommodations.

Inside, I found the keyhole right next to the panel with buttons. It looked pretty standard. Just insert the key we didn't have and turn. So, if it wasn't wired in some way to resist tampering . . .

I knelt down for a better look.

"Oh my God," Rachel muttered.

I ignored her, focusing on the tiny moving parts inside the lock. Manipulating smaller items with precision was a lot more difficult than throwing stuff around, but opening practice locks had been one of the many skills GTX had taught me. Can't have your super-alien spy stopped by a good old Schlage.

The lock clicked, sounding loud in the quiet of the elevator, and the floor numbers lit up. *Yes.* I stood up and reached for the lobby button, the fastest way out of this hellhole.

"No," Zane said quickly. "It's guarded. And you look . . ."

I glanced down at myself, in my white jumpsuit with numbers on my shoulder and blood on my sleeve. *Like an escaped experiment. Like a freak.*

I nodded, my face hot. "Right." I pressed the only other button. Fifth floor.

"It's Dr. Jacobs's office," Zane said. "Maybe he'll have a sweater or a lab coat or something."

Rachel laughed bitterly. "Yeah, like that'll help."

Zane glared at her.

"What?" she demanded. "We came in as two people, but we're leaving as three. More than a little suspicious, don't you think?"

I stepped closer to her. "Are you volunteering to stay behind?"

She blanched and then gave me a hostile look, but she shut up.

"Ariane." Zane moved to stand next to me. "You're still bleeding." He studied my face with a worried frown.

The cut on my cheek. It must have been deeper than I'd thought.

Zane lifted a hand as though he would touch me, but checked himself, color rising in his face.

"Sorry," he murmured.

Well, I guess that answered the question of what he thought of me now. "It's fine. I'll be fine once I'm out of here," I said stiffly, turning away to face the doors. Except I had nowhere to go. I hadn't just lost my freedom in the last few hours; I'd lost my home, my family, my life. And the only guy I'd ever cared about was afraid to touch me.

Yeah, I was great.

My eyes stung with tears, and without the contacts, my vision was swimming that much faster. I tried not to blink. I would not cry in front of Rachel, not in the middle of an escape. That was just ridiculous.

"Hey," Zane said quietly. "I didn't mean . . . I just . . . This is a lot, you know?"

Yeah, I knew. I'd lived with who I was and where I'd come from every day of my life. But he hadn't had nearly the same adjustment period. And I wasn't sure if any amount of time would be enough.

"Ariane—" he said.

"I said I'm fine." But my voice wobbled, belying my words. Damn it. If he didn't stop talking, I was going to have to curl up in the corner and die. Which would be most inconvenient, given all the trouble I'd gone through to escape.

Rachel snorted.

"Shut up, Rachel," Zane and I said at the same time, with varying degrees of exasperation.

"Yeah. Like I'm the problem," she said, but with far less aggression than normal. Clearly, her near near-death experience had thrown her for a loop. Or maybe it was learning that her grandfather viewed her as expendable. I almost felt bad for her. Almost.

Zane gave me a commiserating glance, so familiar, so normal, it almost made me laugh even as it broke my heart. But I ignored the pain and drank in the moment, wanting one last bit of "normal," or as close as I was going to get.

I was glad I'd had it, because as soon as the elevator doors opened, everything changed again.

CHAPTER 34

Zane

ARIANE TENSED A SECOND BEFORE I SAW HIM. *THEM*, rather. My dad, in full uniform, with Joey the mountain on one side of him and another guy in GTX black on the other.

The surprised look on their faces when they saw us was comical . . . until they pulled guns on us. Real ones, not the kinds with darts.

"Dad, what are you doing?" I asked, shocked.

"I told you, I have contacts at GTX. When you disappeared, did you really think I wouldn't find out where you'd gone?" my dad demanded.

I'd never really thought his mysterious GTX sources actually existed. Apparently, I'd been wrong.

"Come on out of there, son." He waved me forward, never taking his gaze or his aim off Ariane.

"You can handle this, right?" I whispered to her. I'd seen what she'd done with those tranquilizer darts in the street.

She lifted her shoulder. "I've had more practice with

M&M's," she whispered back with a frown.

"What?" I asked, confused.

"Excuse me," Rachel yelled from behind. "I'm a Jacobs. You need to let me through." Without waiting for a response, she pushed past Ariane and me.

I winced in expectation of shouting and possibly gunfire, but my dad nodded at her. "Come on."

She stepped neatly to the side and tossed a strained but smug smile at us as she headed into her grandfather's office and out of harm's way.

Clearly, any lessons she might have learned tonight had had only a limited effect.

"Zane, follow Rachel. We'll take care of this," my dad said.

"Go," Ariane said to me, never taking her gaze off the men in front of her. "I'll be fine."

Except she wouldn't. Even if they didn't shoot her, she'd end up right back downstairs in that horrible little room. I had no doubt of that.

She was trying to protect me.

That realization broke something open in me. She, who'd had one seriously crappy and messed-up childhood, was putting me first even when most people in her situation would have done whatever they could to escape, including using me as a human shield.

She cared. I wasn't second best to her. The idea made my eyes sting with tears.

So what did it matter where she came from? Who—or what—her parents were? Everyone's family was messed up in some way, including my own.

And she was still the same Ariane.

"No," I said. I couldn't let her sacrifice herself. "I came here to get you out, and I'm not—"

Startled, she looked at me directly for the first time. "You did?"

"Well, I came here," I admitted. "You kind of did the getting-out part yourself."

She smiled, then, a beautiful expression that lit her up from within, reminding me of the other night in the parking lot after the activities fair. When everything had been simpler, clearer.

"Zane!" my dad shouted. "Move!"

"If we don't get off the elevator, the doors are going to close and they'll start shooting," Ariane said suddenly, all business once again. Her head was tilted to one side, her gaze slightly unfocused, and I realized she was probably "hearing" it from someone, possibly my dad.

"Okay, together, then." I held my hand out to her. She hesitated for a brief moment, and I flashed back to all the moments before she'd trusted me. But then she slipped her hand into mine, her fingers cool and light. "One, two . . ."

We stepped out, and I moved in front of her.

"Zane," she protested.

"Now is not the time to be a bleeding heart. Get out of the way," my dad said.

The elevator doors shut behind us, and I couldn't help but feel we'd just lost our only avenue of escape.

But I didn't move. I was tired of not fighting, of just accepting the way everything was. Letting other people's decisions rule my choices.

"Of the two of us, I've got a better chance of stopping bullets," Ariane pointed out.

"Yeah, but they won't shoot me," I said, though I didn't feel quite as confident about that as I sounded.

"They're not going to let you take her out of here, Zane," my dad said. "Just walk away. Don't be stupid."

That pissed me off. "I'm stupid? Because I'm too weak, too sensitive, like Mom? Yeah. I'm the one in front of the guns, Dad."

"What is this?" a new voice demanded. I looked over to see an older man, tall and imposing, at the other end of the hallway. I hadn't even realized there was anything in that direction, but clearly this guy had come from somewhere. Staring at him a moment longer, I realized it was the same man who'd been in the street last night when Ariane was captured—Ariane's father, according to what my dad had said.

Next to me, Ariane flinched, her hand tightening on mine.

"Stand down," he ordered the guards, to my relief.

Rachel peeked out from Dr. Jacobs's office to see what was going on. "Stay in there," Mr. Tucker said in a tone that brooked no argument, even from Rachel. She disappeared from the doorway, closing the doors after herself.

After the briefest hesitation, Mountain Joey and the other dude holstered their guns. "The chief said the kids were in here to cause trouble, vandalizing, maybe," Joey said.

And since Joey hadn't been happy about letting us in in the first place, it probably hadn't taken much convincing to get him to go along with the idea. And, of course, my dad knew he would have sounded crazy if he'd tried to explain what was really going on, not that he even had the whole truth.

"Then we lost contact with Dr. Jacobs, and we couldn't reach you on the radio. . . ." Joey trailed off.

"So you're going to start shooting people based on what, a hunch?" Ariane's dad raised his eyebrows.

"It's more than a hunch, Mark," my dad blustered, but he returned his gun to its holster. "And you know it. Just because it's your kid—"

"You have no jurisdiction here, Chief Bradshaw," Tucker said smoothly. "The police haven't been called. This is a private matter."

"She's holding my son hostage!"

"I'm here willingly," I spoke up quickly, and my dad glared at me.

"You need to leave, Chief. Now," Tucker said. He looked to his guards. "Joey, Xavier, take the chief out and make sure he stays out. Then return to your posts."

He gestured for Ariane and me to step away from the elevator. I tugged Ariane to the side, making room for Joey and the other guard, Xavier, to move forward and press the button.

The doors rolled open immediately. Xavier stepped in while Joey positioned himself at the threshold, gesturing for my dad to go.

But my dad stayed put. "I'm not leaving my kid here, Mark," he protested. I cringed at his repeated use of Mr. Tucker's first name. What, like that would make people think they were equals or friends or something? "If he stays, I stay."

I rolled my eyes. My dad was not one to give up easily on his GTX dreams.

Tucker turned to me, his gaze flickering over my position in front of Ariane and her hand locked in mine. "Do you want to go?" he asked.

"No," I said.

"It doesn't matter, Mark," my dad snapped. "Zane isn't eighteen."

Mr. Tucker tilted his head, as though considering his words. "But he's an invited guest of Dr. Jacobs's granddaughter. You, on the other hand, are trespassing."

I winced, waiting.

My dad sucked in a breath, his face turning red, as if he was going to argue with Mr. Tucker, but then he just looked at me with disgust. "I should have let your mother take you."

I froze. "Wait, what? She . . . she wanted me to go with her?" It felt as if the world was tilting without me.

"Of course she wanted you. You're just like her, despite my best efforts," he spat.

"Where is she?" I demanded.

He narrowed his eyes at me and then deliberately turned away.

Son of a bitch. "Dad!" I shouted. He couldn't drop that bomb on me and walk away. "Where?"

Next to me, Ariane squeezed my hand. "Illinois. Chicago suburbs." She tipped her head to one side, her expression distant, her forehead crinkled with concentration. "Gurnee, I think." She gave me an apologetic look. "It's kind of noisy in his head at the moment."

My father halted immediately and turned back, a horrified expression on his face. "How did you . . . You can't . . ."

Joey grabbed his arm and tugged him into the elevator, and my dad, in shock, offered little resistance.

I grinned, relief almost making me giddy. My mom had wanted to take me with her. She hadn't willingly left me behind. I didn't have the whole story yet, but I'd find her and get it.

Tucker watched the doors close on them, then he turned to us.

"That way." He directed us toward the opposite end of the hall, where I'd first seen him. "We don't have much time."

I started to follow him, but stopped when Ariane's fingers slipped from mine.

I turned to find her standing still, her feet planted.

"I'm not sure we can trust him," she said.

I swallowed a groan. *So. Freaking. Close.*

CHAPTER 35

Ariane

"ARIANE, IF HE'S WILLING TO GET US OUT OF HERE—lesser of two evils, right?" Zane pleaded.

"He wanted me to cooperate with Dr. Jacobs," I said. "Do you have a truck waiting?" I asked the man who used to be my father. "Or are you just going to trick me into walking into a trap?"

"I told you to cooperate because I wanted you to survive," he snapped.

Maybe. Maybe not. He couldn't seriously expect me to trust him again. He was a stranger with a familiar face. That was all.

"We don't have time for this," Mark said impatiently. "Listen to my thoughts. You'll hear what you need to."

"Yeah, it's not like you've had plenty of practice hiding what you don't want me to hear," I responded.

He let out a slow breath as if summoning patience or strength. "Jacobs picked me because I had the training and because my daughter was dying. I didn't care what happened to me," he said. "And in the beginning I didn't care about you, either."

I stiffened. I'd been expecting it, but that didn't make it hurt less.

"Jacobs told me to use Ariane's name for you, that it would be an easier backstory, fewer fraudulent papers." He hesitated. "But I don't think he thought about the consequences. The power of a name."

He met my gaze straight on. "You are not my daughter. She was a sweet and loving child who did not deserve what happened to her."

"I know that," I said tightly, breathing through my tears. "Believe me, I know." I would never have wished that fate on her.

"But you are a strong girl in your own right, and smart. Ten years in your company and I'd prefer to see you survive, one way or another. Is that wrong of me?"

I hesitated, wanting to believe him.

His voice took on a gentler tone. "You are an Ariane, just not mine."

I blinked, and tears splashed down my cheeks.

"Is that enough?" he asked.

I nodded woodenly, and Zane moved closer, taking my hand. "It's okay," he whispered, and I wasn't sure if it was my blurry vision or if he looked like this might have made him close to tears, too.

"Then let's move," my father said.

He led us down the hall, which was far more luxurious than any part of GTX I'd ever seen before, to the opposite end, where another set of elevator doors waited.

My father ran a key card through a small black card reader. "For service," he explained. "The cleaning crew. Jacobs doesn't want them soiling his personal elevator." He smirked.

I tensed when the doors opened, revealing a wide industrial metal lift. But no one was inside.

He pushed the button for the third floor, and I found myself holding my breath as the elevator descended.

But the doors opened onto a darkened office floor. No one waiting to jump out at us.

He led us through darkened cubicles to an emergency exit, glowing white and red, the most welcome beacon I could imagine.

"When the door opens, the alarm will sound," he said. "I'll call it in as a glitch, but that won't hold them off for too long, especially if Jacobs makes his way up here again." He hesitated. "What did you—"

"Knocked him out," I said.

He nodded with a tired but knowing smile. "I figured."

And if I was reading him correctly, he was *proud* that I hadn't killed him. The corresponding rush of relief made me feel wobbly and weak.

"Take the stairs down and to the left. The forest preserve is that way." He pointed out the window to an area that looked darker than the surrounding grounds. "Stick to the shadows and away from the edge of the building. The cameras don't have much range on this side. Too many deer setting off the motion sensors." He hesitated. "You remember where to go to get what you need?"

I nodded. Maybe there really was a bag duct-taped to the bottom of the Dumpster.

"Good. I've been adding to it. You'll have enough for a while, if you're careful." He reached for the push bar on the door, and suddenly it all felt too real. I would not wake up in my bed tomorrow. I would not eat breakfast with my father again (Sunday equals pancakes with bacon *and* sausage). I would, in all likelihood, never see him again. I couldn't imagine that his betrayal—helping me escape could only be seen as such—would be taken lightly.

"Wait!" I said quickly, and then I didn't know what else to say. *Thank you? I'm sorry?*

But my father seemed to know. He nodded. "Me too, kid. Me too." He shrugged out of his jacket and draped it over my shoulders.

And that made me cry.

He shoved open the door, which set off an alarm and flashing lights, and pushed me out. "Go!"

Zane slipped out after me onto the darkened landing, and my father pulled the door closed after us, dulling the alarm only slightly.

We scrambled down the stairs in the dim light, but I stopped when we reached the bottom. "The main road is that way," I said, pulling my hand free and pointing in the opposite direction of the woods.

"What are you talking about?" he asked. "Come on, we need to move." He grabbed for my hand again.

I stepped back, shaking my head. "This doesn't involve you, and it's dangerous. I don't want you to get hurt." I steeled myself against the hurt of pushing him—the only person I had left—away. "Go home."

"No," he said after a moment, fixing me with a defiant look. "I'm not going home. I'm going to find my mom."

"You can't," I protested. "That's the first place GTX will look for you." And Dr. Jacobs would not hesitate to use him to get to me, especially now.

"As opposed to my house here in Wingate?" Zane asked dryly.

I gritted my teeth. Was he really going to be this stubborn? "Your dad offers you some protection, Zane. He—"

"—will be the first one to let GTX in, if he thinks it'll get him what he wants," he said in disgust. "I'm not going back there. Not right now. He lied to me. He knew where my mom was this whole time. I need to see her, make sure she's okay."

I started to argue.

He touched my mouth lightly with his fingertips, and I tried hard not to revel in the feeling. "And if you don't want GTX to find me while I'm there," he said, "then maybe you should just come with me."

"So they can catch both of us? No thanks."

"Where else are you going to go?" he asked quietly.

That was a good—and very painful—point.

He leaned closer, and I closed my eyes, feeling my resistance weakening. "Come on. After what I've seen tonight, I'm thinking you might have some ideas about how to keep GTX off our backs," he said.

I half laughed, half choked. "I bet."

"And you'll like my mom," he continued. "I'm pretty sure she thinks foosball is an exercise in futility too."

I opened my eyes, startled. He remembered our silly conversation about eternal questions.

He held his hand out to me with an encouraging nod, and my vision went blurry with tears.

He'd come to GTX for me. If I left him unprotected now, he would pay for it. But if I went with him, I didn't know what would happen. I had no idea what I was doing. Everything I'd ever known lay in pieces behind me, including the Rules I'd devoted my life to following.

But beneath the fear I could feel the start of something new and thrilling growing, pressing for attention. I'd be running, yes. At least, at first. But with that came a chance to start over. Freedom. Choices. And maybe someday a life without GTX looming in the distance.

I just had to reach for it. And wasn't that the point of living outside of my GTX cage? So I could make those choices?

"Okay," I said, taking Zane's hand and lacing my fingers through his. Palm to palm. "Let's go."

Turn the page for the first chapter of

PROJECT PAPER DOLL

by STACEY KADE

CHAPTER 1

Ariane Tucker

UNTIL I CRAWLED BENEATH THE DESIGNATED DUMPSTER behind the abandoned Linens-N-Things and felt the brush of rough canvas against my fingertips, I really wasn't sure that the emergency bag would be there, as my father had promised.

My first Christmas, I'd been six. It had also been the first time Outside matched the color and sparkle of what I'd seen on television and in my "cultural training" videos in the lab at GTX. The houses in our neighborhood had been decked out with flashing Santas, red-nosed reindeer, and molded plastic Nativity scenes. And through cracks in the blinds, I'd watched people carry in plastic bags full of presents, brightly colored wrapping paper tubes poking through the top.

This strange but wonderful event—so much preparation and fuss over it—called to me in the worst way. I longed to be a part of it. But our living room remained dark and undecorated, the carpeting empty of pine needles and shiny wrapped packages alike, even on Christmas Day. In our house, it was just another day. Worse, even, as my father retreated to his room and didn't come out until the following morning. I was alone. And confused. According to lore, only "naughty" children were punished by an absence of gifts. But

I'd done everything I knew to do, followed precisely the Rules my father had given me.

Much later, I understood that it was because my father's true daughter, the original Ariane, had died, and the traditions of the holiday reminded him too much of her. My presence only further highlighted her absence, inflaming a wound that would never quite heal.

Still, it had been the first of many occasions that taught me to understand that my expectations, my hopes, were better kept in check. My father had done his best to be a parent for me (or so I'd believed until recently), but there'd been limits, ones I was usually unaware of until I bumped into them.

This time, though, unlike all those years of dark Christmases, my father had come through. This gift, an emergency bag of supplies, cash, and who knew what else, was exactly where he'd said it would be.

Feeling some measure of tension leave my body, I let out a breath I hadn't realized I'd been holding and promptly choked on the cloud of dirt that rose up in response.

"You okay?" Zane asked quietly. He was pacing nearby, waiting for me. I couldn't see him, but I could hear the scrape of his shoes on the concrete as he moved back and forth, watching for anyone approaching.

It had taken us a little more than two hours to make our way here from GTX. We'd cut through backyards and taken side streets, doubling back when necessary and keeping to the shadows. But before any of that, we'd had to fight through the overgrown forest preserve that surrounded the GTX campus. Nothing like taking a branch to the face when running full-speed. I'd ended up keeping an arm up to shield myself, and consequently the skin between my wrist and elbow felt shredded, burning as if it were on fire. Zane hadn't fared much better, new cuts and bruises on his face and arms joining those he'd already acquired in the last few days.

I'd expected him to protest or even quit, turning around to head home. Which was, quite frankly, probably the safest place for him. But he'd soldiered on in determined silence. Well, he hadn't said much. He had, however, crashed through the woods like a herd of drunken deer. Stealth training was not something taught in your average school system. But lucky, lucky me, I'd been enrolled in some "special" extracurriculars during my time with my father.

Other parents taught their children how to ride bikes, fish, or bake cookies from the family recipe, but my father had spent countless hours passing along much of the training he'd acquired during his years in Special Forces. It had been, I guess, our thing, our shared interest. Maybe he would have taught his biological daughter, the first Ariane, the same stuff. Maybe not. All I knew was that the day I'd managed to sneak up behind him in the patch of woods near our house where we practiced, I'd never seen him more proud of me.

Until last night.

I shoved that thought away. I wouldn't, couldn't think about that now. "Yeah, I'm fine," I said to Zane. "One second." I bit my lip, tasting sweat and unpleasant grit, and contemplated my next move. Unfortunately, just because the bag was there didn't mean I could actually get to it. I was already halfway under the Dumpster, trapped between the bottom of the trash receptacle and the concrete beneath it, which meant I had about zero leverage. And I was about ten seconds away from a major freak-out. Dark, confined spaces and I are not friends.

Sweating and keenly aware of the metal ceiling above my head, I strained at the shoulder and managed to grasp a corner of the fabric. But it slipped away before I could get a good-enough grip.

"Damn it," I panted. Though the logical part of my brain knew there was plenty of air, my emotional side was panicking and sucking in oxygen at a far too rapid rate. I could feel dizziness beginning to build.

This would have been so much easier if we could have just moved the stupid Dumpster to reach the bag from the other side. But that meant the shrill squeak of wheels and the rumbling thunder of the empty receptacle moving over the pockmarked and uneven concrete. Not an option on an otherwise quiet night when GTX security was out in force looking for us.

I squirmed closer, a hiss of pain escaping against my will when a particularly sharp bit of rock from the degraded parking lot dug into the abrasions on my forearm.

Zane knelt next to me and tugged at the hem of my lab-issued tunic. "I can get it," he whispered. "Let me."

"What?" I asked, distracted. If I could just release whatever was securing the bag, I wouldn't even have to be under here. I had the ability to move objects without touching them—one of the few perks of my extraterrestrial heritage. The scientists at GTX had played God with a scrap of preserved DNA from the alien entity found at the site of the Roswell incident in 1947, isolating the stem cells and splicing them into a fertilized human egg from a (presumably) willing human donor/surrogate.

I was the result. But it wasn't exactly ideal.

Theoretically, I could lift the whole Dumpster into the air simply by concentrating on it, but my telekinetic abilities were a little unpredictable lately, due to lack of use. So stepping under a heavy metal object that might fall on your head at any second probably wasn't a great idea.

But if I couldn't see what was holding the bag, I couldn't undo it. And just yanking at it would only pull the Dumpster along.

"I can get it," Zane repeated patiently. "My arms are longer than yours."

"No, I can—"

He bent down, his knees suddenly visible at the edge of my vision. "You know, it's okay to accept help every once in a while."

Easy for him to say. I swallowed a frustrated noise. He didn't understand. I'd spent years relying only on myself, trusting only my father (and look at how well that had turned out). I couldn't just stop doing that. I didn't know how. And with Zane, much as I wanted to trust him, much as he'd done nothing to make me doubt him, I could feel the other shoe—an ass-kicking combat boot with a steel toe and a thick tread—hanging above my head, waiting to stomp on me.

Still, retrieving the bag was taking far longer than I wanted. And if Zane thought he could do it faster, all the better.

"Fine," I said, wiggling out. "Be my guest."

I stood up and folded my arms across my chest, watching in the moonlight as Zane stretched his six-foot-four frame out on the concrete and reached under the Dumpster.

It was an ugly but appropriate bit of symmetry that the fate of my future life was tied so closely to an oversize trash can. That's what the last ten years of my life had been—a big load of garbage. Lies told to keep me quiet and compliant.

"Got it," Zane said after an annoyingly short amount of time. That eighteen inches of additional height made a difference, I guess. He'd barely had to stick his head beneath.

He dragged a small but full black duffel out from under the Dumpster until it lay next to him. Shiny metallic strips of duct tape, now twisted and tangled from Zane's efforts, hung off the edges of the bag, like legs of an upside-down spider. From space.

Zane inched out and pushed himself to his feet easily, biceps temporarily straining the sleeves of his green Ashe High lacrosse team T-shirt.

"Thanks," I said grudgingly.

"I told you. Long arms," he said with a shrug, and dusted off his hands. "My superpower." He gave me a tentative smile.

He was . . . joking. Almost like normal.

I blinked, surprised. Well, it was what had passed for normal between us before everything went to hell and he learned I wasn't who—or what—he thought I was. A few hours ago, I wouldn't have thought that anything resembling that state would be possible again.

Relief crashed into me, a heady sensation. "I guess they were out of Sasquatch DNA the day they made me," I shot back. If he could joke, I could joke, right? Humor was a human coping mechanism. I'd used it before, but never about myself to someone else. It was a strange feeling, like stripping naked and waiting to see if people would notice.

But in this case, laughing was a good thing, and I was rewarded by the bright flash of his grin. "Ouch." He rocked back on his heels, clutching at his chest, pretending to be wounded.

Then he stopped abruptly, his hands dropping to his sides.

He was remembering what I'd done to Rachel Jacobs, one of his friends, the other night. I could see the images in quick flashes:

Rachel coughing and choking at the pool party, grabbing at her chest as her heart fought against my control.

I hadn't killed her, but I'd come awfully close. And the shock and fear he'd felt at what I'd done was still close to the surface. And tied to his thoughts of me.

I stiffened.

"Sorry," he murmured, looking away.

I shook my head. "It's not your fault," I made myself say over the sudden lump in my throat. And it wasn't. He hadn't invented that scenario. I'd done it. For the right reasons, maybe, but it had gotten swiftly out of hand. Never mind that I hadn't killed her or permanently injured her, even when her own grandfather, Dr. Jacobs, had later pushed me to do so.

I couldn't—wouldn't—hold Zane's reactions against him. How could anyone be expected to respond to this messed-up situation with equanimity?

So, yeah. I guess we had a ways to go yet before "normal."

I knelt next to the bag and tugged at the zipper with shaking hands. But it was stuck.

Without a word, Zane bent down and held the canvas sides steady. And this time when I tried, the zipper slid along the track smoothly.

Before I could thank him, a tight roll of cash, bound with a rubber band, slipped out of the opening and bounced to a stop near Zane's shoe.

A quick glimpse in the bag showed there were a half-dozen identical bundles, right at the top.

Whoa.

Zane gave a low whistle. "I've got to start checking under more trash bins." He picked up the bundle that had rolled free, looking at it more closely. "These are hundreds, Ariane. That means—"

"Thousands," I managed through my shock. When my adoptive father had told me he'd been adding to the emergency cash, I'd never dreamed he'd meant this much. "It's probably his life savings," I said, fighting the rise of conflicting emotions: a bitter sadness and fury.

Mark Tucker had raised me as his daughter for the last decade. But he'd been working for GTX, the corporation that had created me, the whole time. I thought I'd escaped years ago. In reality, they'd just given me a bigger cage, so to speak, and put Mark in charge of monitoring my reactions to the world Outside. It had all been part of a larger plan, wrapped up in lies and deceit.

Beneath the cash, a flash of white caught my eye. I shifted the money carefully to one side, revealing a thin, square envelope.

My father's bold but neat print was on the front: IF I AM NOT WITH YOU.

My stomach gave an uncomfortable lurch as I plucked the envelope out, pinching it between my fingertips. A letter from Mark? I didn't want to read it. He'd first told me about the emergency bag a few years ago. That meant the contents of this letter would likely be an excruciating rehash of everything I'd learned in the last twenty-four hours, a detailed play-by-play of the worst betrayal I could have possibly imagined. No, thank you.

"Hey, Ariane? There are U.S. and Canadian passports in here. And one of those reloadable credit cards." Zane held them up and squinted. "For a Talia Torv."

He flipped to the photo page in the U.S. passport. "She looks an awful lot like you," he said, holding it up so I could see.

It was, in fact, a picture of me. Last year's school photo.

"Except," he said, frowning, "Talia's eighteen, almost nineteen."

Of course she was. I laughed in a moment of near giddiness.

"No one will believe that," Zane said, his handsome face troubled. "You barely look your age."

He was right. My less-than-average height and preternatural thinness made me look younger than sixteen. My A-cup chest wasn't doing me any favors either.

I shook my head. "It won't matter. If the documents are good"—and knowing my father's relentless attention to detail, they were—"no one will question them." Which meant, I could live on my own. Eighteen was the magic number. And with all that cash . . .

For the first time, I felt a rush of hope, lifting the weight of despair and panic I'd been carrying around. Maybe, just maybe, this would work. Maybe I could leave Wingate and start a life, a real life somewhere.

I glanced at Zane on the other side of the bag, where he was busily cataloging the rest of its contents. And maybe I wouldn't have to be alone. We were supposed to be heading to his mother's house in the Chicago suburbs, assuming we could get out of town. I couldn't stay there with him, obviously; it would be the first place GTX would look. But maybe I wouldn't have to go too far. The idea brought an unfamiliar fluttering warmth to my chest. I could make a home for myself, a life. And he could perhaps be a part of it. After all, he was still with me, a miracle if I'd ever seen one. He'd come for me at GTX and stuck by my side, even after everything I'd done.

"There are, uh, clothes in here," Zane said, restacking the items with a haste that suggested he'd discovered something personal.

Great. My face heated. Bra? Underwear? New ones or, oh God, tattered ones I hadn't even noticed were missing from the laundry? I didn't even want to think about it. It was silly to be embarrassed about something like that, I guess, considering. But I was still human. At least partially.

Zane cleared his throat. "And keys. This one looks like an old car key." He held it up, a bright orange plastic tag attached.

"Let me see." I took the key ring for a closer inspection. The plastic tag advertised U-Store-It. The first key was just a plain silver, but it was clearly too big to be for a house or a building. A smaller gold key hung below it on the ring. "Yeah, I think you're right." My father really had prepared for every contingency. Getting out of Wingate undetected would be impossible without a clean vehicle—one unassociated with me or my father.

"So, then, where's the car?" Zane asked.

That was an excellent question. The parking lot in front of the building was completely empty. I'd checked it before sliding under the Dumpster. And there certainly weren't any vehicles back here. An anemic patch of forest with massively overgrown weeds ran up to—and now over—the edge of the concrete behind the abandoned building. "I don't know." I took a closer look at the key ring. "Possibly in a storage locker."

But at which facility? There were probably a half dozen in and around Wingate, and at least a couple of them had to be U-Store-Its.

At least from what I could recall. Not that I'd ever paid that much attention. Who pays attention to storage lockers?

The trouble was, we didn't have time to waste checking them out, especially without a car to get us there.

"Maybe there's something in there?" He nodded at the envelope that I was clutching.

I glanced down at the letter, having almost forgotten it was in my hand. "Maybe." But I still didn't want to open it.

He hesitated, then asked, "Do you want me to—"

I shook my head. "No, I'll do it." He was right. If there was something in here about the car, we needed to know. With GTX nipping at our heels, getting a vehicle had to be our top priority. Besides, avoiding the letter was foolish, emotional—my human side holding sway over the rest of me. Because the fact was, even if the letter was years old, it might yet contain useful information mixed in among all the eviscerating details I'd learned in the last day.

I handed Zane the keys and then, steeling myself, I slipped my finger beneath the flap on the envelope and tore it open, the ripping noise sounding absurdly loud in the postmidnight air.

"Your dad is kind of a badass. You know that, right?" Zane said, repacking the bag carefully.

I didn't respond, my attention caught by my name in my father's painfully familiar handwriting.

Ariane—

I have to assume that, if you're reading this, our situation has been compromised and I'm either dead or unable to help you. I don't know how much I had a chance to tell you, and I'm sorry for the abruptness of what you're about to read.

I was surprised to find tears stinging my eyes. His weariness and regret permeated the page.

First, you are not free. You never were. GTX and Dr. Jacobs have known where you were the entire time. You'll never know how sorry I am for my role in this deception. Please know that I did it for reasons that seemed honorable at the time.

His daughter. The original Ariane. Jacobs had promised the latest experimental treatment for her cancer in exchange for my father taking on the job of looking after me. She'd died anyway, but Mark had stayed on, hoping the research they were doing with my "amazing" immune system would save other children from the same fate.

I wanted to hate my father for it. He'd loved his daughter more than he'd loved me. But then again, he wasn't supposed to care about me at all. I was a job. And yet, this bag was full of proof that I was more than that to him. I was caught between gratitude and the bitter pinch of self-pity. It's hard to know you'll never be enough just because you're not someone else.

"You okay?" Zane asked.

"Yeah." I wiped under my eyes. "I just—" I stopped, my attention caught by a chilling phrase that leapt out from the next paragraph.

Second, there's a tracking chip embedded on the right side of your T4 vertebrae.

My head whirled, trying to rearrange the squiggles into other words with a different meaning. But the sentence remained.

It's an older model, with very short range. But don't take the risk; disable it. According to my research, demagnetizing it should work. You'll find what you need in the bag.

"Ariane?" Zane sounded alarmed. "What's wrong? You look—"

"Is there a magnet in there?" I asked in a strangled voice. A tracking chip. It made a sort of sick and horrible sense—if my father had lost control over me during my years of "freedom" and I'd bolted, GTX and Dr. Jacobs would have needed a way to find me and bring me in. I hadn't even attempted to run, though. I'd believed their ruse.

"A what?" Zane frowned up at me.

I swallowed hard, trying to keep my panic under control. "A magnet, probably a big one." My father had never mentioned, never even hinted at such a thing, not even during our good-bye, which would have seemed like an opportune time to mention something like GTX spyware in my spine. Had it been active this whole time? Or was it something they could turn on and off at will? Were they on their way here right now?

I felt ill.

Zane rummaged deeper in the bag, beneath the clothes. "This?" He produced a flat metal circle about the size my palm.

I nodded, feeling my neck creak with tension.

"What's going on?" Zane asked warily.

"I have . . . there's a tracking device," I said.

He dropped the magnet and yanked his hands away from the bag.

"No." I gave a harsh, humorless laugh. "Not in the bag. In me."

His eyes widened, but he nodded. "What do we do?"

We. What had I done to deserve him? He should have been home right now, reviewing lacrosse plays and studying for chemistry.

"I can do it myself," I said, though I wasn't quite sure how without some significant contortions or lying on the ground, neither of which seemed like a good idea when time was of the essence.

But Zane rallied, standing up with a determined expression and the magnet in hand.

I turned away so he wouldn't see the deeply pathetic amount of gratitude I was feeling.

"Here." I shed my father's jacket and reached up to the back of my neck to point to where the last cervical vertebrae jutted out slightly. "Start here and count down about four. T4 should be between my shoulder blades."

The air shifted slightly as Zane moved closer, and I shivered.

"How do you know that?" he asked. "About T4. I wouldn't have the faintest clue."

I smiled tightly. "Years of studying human anatomy, remember?" He was already getting a front-row seat to my freak show, why not remind him once again that I was created to be a killer?

His fingertip lightly touched my neck at the point I'd showed him and moved down my spine, tripping over the fabric of my tunic.

"Ariane," he began. "I'm not sure which—"

I understood his hesitation and—well, at this point, was it really a good idea to let modesty stand in my way?—grabbed the back of my shirt and yanked it up past my shoulders, exposing my skin to the night air. That would make counting vertebrae a lot easier.

Zane sucked in a breath.

"What, can you see it?" I twisted around, trying to look, cursing my years of naiveté. I should have known GTX—Jacobs, specifically—would do something like this. If I'd searched myself, maybe I would have seen the chip before. A little bubble under the skin near my spine, like a malignant tumor just waiting to cause chaos later.

"They did this to you." It was a statement, but I could hear the question in it.

I thought he was talking about the tracker, until his finger touched my shoulder blade, tracing the letters and numbers emblazoned on my skin. The GTX logo and my project designation: GTX-F-107.

I flinched, humiliation setting my face afire. This was getting better and better by the second. In my panic about the chip, I'd forgotten about the tattoo. Normally it was covered by a bandage, but I'd taken that off before the party a couple nights ago and never had a chance to put another one on.

Now Zane knew I was marked like cattle. I was a possession. A thing.

"Yeah. They did." I bit the words off and waited, my shoulders tense. Any second now, I'd hear his uncomfortable laugh, echoing against the building, and the sound of his retreating footsteps. This would be the final straw, the piece that pushed him over the edge into seeing me for what I was instead of who.

But, somehow, miraculously, it wasn't. "This is probably going to be cold," he warned a second before applying the magnet to my back between my shoulder blades.

He was right. The sudden shock of metal against my skin made me gasp.

I started to shiver for real, then, and Zane stepped closer, looping his free arm around my shoulders in the front, a backward sort of hug, while his other hand kept the magnet pressed in place between us.

"Better?" he asked.

I could feel the rise and fall of his chest against me, the softness of his shirt on my skin, and, faintly, the solid and reassuring beat of his heart.

I wanted to cry, to turn around and bury my head against him. To cling to him, to crawl inside. Instead, I cleared my throat and said, "Yes."

"Is it supposed to beep or something?" Zane asked a moment later.

"I don't know." I looked again to the letter, now crumpled in my hand. There were only a couple paragraphs remaining.

Third, and this is the most important part: you know about Arthur Jacobs, but he is the least of your concerns. He wants you alive so you can win the trials for him. But David Laughlin (Laughlin Integrated Enterprises, Chicago, IL) and Emerson St. John (Emerson Technology, Incorporated, Rochester, NY) would rather you were dead. One less competitor for the trials they have planned.

The trials. That's what they were calling a fight to the death between the various "products" created by the three companies vying for a lucrative government contract to make supersoldiers/assassins/spies. ("Products" was the sanitized word for beings like me, lab-created hybrids of human and alien DNA.)

So now, as if the possibility of death in a formal competitive setting weren't enough, I apparently had to worry about plain old murder. That was new.

A full body shudder ran through me, and Zane pulled me closer against him.

They've had informants keeping tabs on one another's progress for years. Your escape won't go unnoticed for long. And once you leave the state—GTX's "territory" as designated by the rules they established to prevent sabotage—you'll have all of them after you. Laughlin, in particular, will not hesitate at the thought of collateral damage if it means eliminating a threat to his success.

Dizzy suddenly, I felt myself swaying. I knew where this was going even before I read my father's final words.

Cut ties to Wingate and anyone you care about, immediately. You'll want to protect those who've been kind to you, but you're a danger to anyone in your presence. Find somewhere isolated, preferably outside the country (the U.S. government is complicit in all of this, remember). Stay there.

Be good; follow the Rules I gave you. Take care of yourself. Again, I am sorry for my role in all of this.

Mark

"Are we good?" Zane whispered near my ear, his breath tickling my cheek. "Is it off?"

It took me a second to process what he was asking about. The chip. Was the chip deactivated?

I nodded numbly, even though I had no way of knowing if that was the case. Surely my father had not intended for me to walk around with a magnet permanently affixed to my back. And even if he had, there were now larger concerns.

With a quick exhale of relief, Zane removed the magnet and bent to tuck it inside the bag.

I tugged my tunic into place and put my jacket on, my head spinning with too many thoughts.

Cut ties to Wingate and anyone you care about, immediately. When my father had written that, he'd probably been thinking of my former friend Jenna or maybe even himself. But Zane . . . Oh God, he was most definitely included in that category, which meant I knew what my father would have wanted me to do.

My stomach ached. Here, at last, was the boot I'd been expecting, dropping to clobber me from a totally unanticipated angle.

The selfish part of me was shrieking "No!" at the top of her lungs. I couldn't just abandon Zane, especially not here. GTX would snap him up in a second. Not to mention, I didn't *want* to leave him at all.

I blinked back tears. But logically, reasonably, his safety had to come first. If I cared so much about him, I couldn't be a party to his death or endangerment. Which left me with what?

Take him with you, my emotional side pleaded. He's come this far. He'll go.

Maybe. Maybe not. Going to his mother's was one thing; going on the run for the rest of his life? I shook my head. I couldn't ask that of him.

Walk away now, the cooler, calmer voice in my head advised. It's the best choice for both of you. Jacobs will find him, but Jacobs is the lesser evil compared to the others. He will want to keep Zane alive to use as incentive.

I rocked back and forth on my heels, caught on twin prongs of misery and indecision. It was impossible to know what parts of my personality came from which side. What was human? What was *other*? All I knew was that when it came to big choices like this one, I was torn between emotions that raged inside and the logic that tried to snuff them out—to the point where it felt like the fight between them might spill out into the physical world. Me arguing with myself, with no peace in sight. It felt like more proof that maybe someone like me wasn't meant to exist.

"Are you all right?" Zane asked, startling me.

I turned to see him frowning at me. Then he grimaced. "I mean, I know you're not, not after everything . . . but was the letter . . ." He trailed off awkwardly.

The absolute end of everything I was hoping for? "It's fine." I forced the lie out, hearing it thud in the space between us.

Zane squinted at me, reading something on my face that I didn't want him to see. "Ariane—"

Tires crunched over loose pebbles on concrete on the other side of the building.

We froze.

Zane stood, lifting the bag with him. "Is that GTX?" he asked, barely audible.

At this point, I had to hope so. The alternative, that Laughlin or St. John had found me already, was even worse. It was laughable—a crazy person's hysterical cackle—that GTX had become the best of all possible options.

"Probably," I said, adrenaline kicking into overdrive, bringing details into hyperfocus. "Only one car, though, so far, by the sound of it. A scout, checking out the situation." Like someone who'd caught the blip of my tracking chip's signal before we'd disabled it. Or maybe it was simply someone making a U-turn in a convenient parking lot, but I couldn't take that chance. My luck was just not that good.

"Then I guess we better run like hell, 'Talia,'" Zane said. He tipped his head toward the trees and held out his free hand with a grin that hurt my heart.

I faltered, unable to move. How was I supposed to do this? How was I supposed to say good-bye to the one person in the world who knew the real me and had stuck around anyway?

"Ariane?" he asked, his smile slipping a little.

I couldn't. Not yet.

So I did the only thing I could do—selfish and human as it was.

I took his hand, and we ran like hell.